THE IRON KNIGHT

JULIE KAGAWA

HARLEQUIN®TEEN

Recycling programs
for this product may
not exist in your area.

ISBN-13: 978-0-373-21036-7

The Iron Knight

Copyright © 2011 by Julie Kagawa

Printed in U.S.A.

I'd expected to die that day. I was ready. Being ordered by my True Name to walk away, leaving Meghan to die alone in the Iron Kingdom, nearly shattered me a second time. If it wasn't for my oath to be with her again, I might've done something suicidal, like challenge Oberon to a battle before the entire Summer Court. But now that I've made my promise, there is no turning back. Abandoning my vow will unravel me, bit by bit, until there is nothing left. Even if I wasn't determined to find a way to survive in the Iron Realm, I'd have no choice but to continue.

I will be with her again, or I will die. There aren't any other options.

Praise for Julie Kagawa and The Iron Fey

"Meghan is a likable heroine and her quest is fraught with danger and adventure... Expect it to be popular with teens who liked Melissa Marr's *Wicked Lovely*."
—*School Library Journal* on *The Iron King*

"*The Iron King* surpasses the greater majority of dark fantasies, leaving a lot for readers to look forward to... The romance is well done and adds to the mood of fantasy."
—teenreads.com

"*The Iron King* has it all, a lot of action and a little romance."
—MonsterLibrarian.com

"A full five stars to Julie Kagawa's *The Iron Daughter*. If you love action, romance and watching how characters mature through heart-wrenching trials, you will love this story."
—*Mundie Moms* blog

"I picked it up and just could not put it down."
—*The Story Siren* on *The Iron Daughter*

"This third installment in the series is just as compelling and complex as its predecessors, and wholly satisfying."
—*Realms of Fantasy* on *The Iron Queen*

"The characters of the series are really what have driven this book from fantasy to fantastical."
—nyjournalofbooks.com on *The Iron Queen*

Books by Julie Kagawa available from Harlequin TEEN

The Talon Saga

Talon

Blood of Eden series

(in reading order)

The Immortal Rules
The Eternity Cure
The Forever Song

The Iron Fey series

(in reading order)

The Iron King*
"Winter's Passage"** (ebook novella)
The Iron Daughter*
The Iron Queen
"Summer's Crossing"** (ebook novella)
The Iron Knight
"Iron's Prophecy"** (ebook novella)
The Lost Prince
The Iron Traitor

*Also available in *The Iron Fey Volume One* anthology
**Also available in print in *The Iron Legends* anthology,
along with the exclusive *Guide to the Iron Fey*

Team Ash, this one is for you.

PART ONE

CHAPTER ONE

THE HOUSE OF THE BONE WITCH

"Oy, ice-boy! You sure you know where you're going?"

I ignored Robin Goodfellow as we wove through the gray murk of the wyldwood, pushing farther into the soggy swamp known as the Bone Marsh. Mud sucked at my footsteps, and water dripped from twisted green trees so covered in moss they appeared sheathed in slime. Mist coiled around the exposed roots or pooled in sunken areas, hiding what lay beneath, and every so often there was a splash in the still waters farther out, reminding us that we were not alone. As its name suggested, bones were scattered throughout the marsh, jutting out of the mud, half-hidden in tangles of weeds or shimmering beneath the surface of the water, bleached and white. This was a dangerous part of the wyldwood, more so than most— not because of the catoblepas and the jabberwocks and other monsters that called the dark swamp their home, but because of the resident who lived somewhere deep within the marsh.

The one we were going to see.

Something flew past my head from behind, barely missing me, and spattered against a trunk a few feet away. Stopping beneath the tree, I turned and glared at my companion, silently daring him to do that again.

"Oh, hey, it lives!" Robin Goodfellow threw up his muddy hands in mock celebration. "I was afraid it had become a zombie or something." He crossed his arms and smirked at me, mud streaking his red hair and speckling his pointed face. "Did you hear me, ice-boy? I've been yelling at you for some time now."

"Yes," I said, repressing a sigh. "I heard you. I think the jabberwocks on the other side of the swamp heard you."

"Oh, good! Maybe if we fight a couple you'll start paying attention to me!" Puck matched my glare before gesturing around at the swamp. "This is crazy," he exclaimed. "How do we even know he's here? The Bone Marsh isn't exactly on my list of favorite vacation getaways, prince. You sure your contact knew what he was talking about? If this turns out to be another false lead I might turn that phouka into a pair of gloves."

"I thought you wanted an adventure," I said, just to annoy him. Puck snorted.

"Oh sure, don't get me wrong. I'm all for tromping to all five corners of the Nevernever, getting chased by angry Summer Queens, sneaking into an ogre's basement, fighting giant spiders, playing hide-and-seek with a cranky dragon—good times." He shook his head, and his eyes gleamed, reliving fond memories. "But this is like the sixth place we've come to look for that wretched cat, and if he isn't here I'm almost afraid of where we're going next."

"You don't have to be here," I told him. "Leave if you want. I'm not stopping you."

"Nice try, prince." Puck crossed his arms and smiled. "But you're not getting rid of me that easily."

"Then let's keep moving." It was getting dark, and his constant chattering was getting on my nerves. Joking aside, I did not want to attract the attention of a hungry jabberwock and have to fight it in the middle of the swamp.

"Oh, fine," Puck sighed, tromping along behind me. "But if he's not here, I refuse to go to the Spider Queen's palace with you, ice-boy. That's where I draw the line."

My name, my full, True Name, is Ashallayn'darkmyr Tallyn, and I am the last son of the Unseelie Court.

There were three of us at one time, all princes of Winter, myself and my brothers, Sage and Rowan. I never knew my sire, never cared to know him, nor did my siblings ever speak of him. I wasn't even positive we shared the same sire, but it didn't matter. In the Unseelie Court, Mab was the sole ruler, the one and only queen. Handsome fey and even wayward mortals she might take to her bed, but Mab shared her throne with no one.

We were never close, my brothers and I. As princes of Winter, we grew up in a world of violence and dark politics. Our queen encouraged this, favoring the son who earned her good graces while punishing the others. We used each other, played vicious games against one another, but we were all loyal to our court and our queen. Or so I'd thought.

There is a reason the Winter Court freezes out their emotions, why feelings are considered a weakness and a folly among the Unseelie fey. Emotion corrupts the senses, makes them weak, makes them disloyal to kith and court. Jealousy was a dark, dangerous passion that ate at my brother Rowan until he did the unthinkable and turned on his court, betraying us to our enemies. Sage, my eldest sibling, fell to Rowan's treachery, and he was only the first. In a bid for power, Rowan sided with our greatest enemies, the Iron fey, helping their king nearly destroy the Nevernever. I killed

Rowan in the end, avenging Sage and the rest of my kin, but retribution cannot bring either of them back. It's only me now. I am the last, the only remaining son of Mab, Queen of the Unseelie Court.

And I'm already dead to her.

Rowan was not the only one to succumb to emotion and passion. My fall began, as many stories do, with a girl. A girl named Meghan Chase, the half-human daughter of our ancient rival, the Summer King. Fate brought us together, and despite everything I did to shield my emotions, despite the laws of our people and the war with the Iron fey and the threat of eternal banishment from my home, I still found myself falling for her. Our paths were woven together, our fates intertwined, and before the last battle I swore I would follow her to the end of the world, to protect her from all threats, including my own kin, and to die for her if called to do so. I became her knight, and would have gladly served this girl, this mortal who had captured my heart, until the last breath left my body.

But Fate is a cruel mistress, and in the end, our paths were forced apart, as I'd feared they would be. Meghan became the Iron Queen, as was her destiny, and took the throne in the kingdom of the Iron fey. A place I could not follow, not as I am—a faery creature whose essence weakens and burns at the touch of iron. Meghan herself exiled me from the lands of the Iron fey, knowing that staying would kill me, knowing I would try anyway. But before I left, I swore an oath that I would find a way to return, that someday we would be together, and nothing would separate us again. Mab tried to convince me to return to the Winter Court—I was her only prince now, and it was my duty to come home—but I bluntly stated that I was no longer part of the Unseelie Court, that my service to her and Winter was at an end.

There is nothing more terrible than a spurned faery queen, particularly if you defy her a second time. I escaped the Winter Court with my life intact, but just barely, and I won't be returning anytime soon. Regardless, I feel little regret at turning my back on my queen, my kith and my home. That part of my life is done. My loyalty—and my heart—belongs to another queen now.

I promised I'd find a way for us to be together. I intend to keep that promise. Even if it means trekking through a sprawling, deadly marsh in search of a rumor. Even if it means putting up with my fiercest and most annoying rival, Robin Goodfellow, who—despite all his attempts to hide it—is in love with my queen as well. I don't know why I haven't killed him yet. Maybe because Puck is Meghan's closest friend, and she would mourn him terribly if he were gone (though I can't understand why). Or, maybe, deep down, I'm tired of being alone.

In any case, it matters little. With every ruin we search, every dragon we slay, or every rumor we unearth, I'm one step closer to my goal. Even if it takes a hundred years, I will be with her in the end. Another piece of the puzzle lurks somewhere in this dreary swampland. The only difficulty lies in finding it.

THANKFULLY, DESPITE PUCK'S constant griping and complaining, the jabberwocks decided *not* to see what the racket was about and come stalking through the marsh to find us. That was just as well, because it took nearly the whole night to find what we were looking for.

At the edge of a scummy pond stood a house, faded and gray like everything else. A picket fence made of bleached white bones surrounded it, naked skulls topping the posts, and a few scraggly chickens milled about in what passed as a yard. The hut was old and wooden, creaking faintly though there was no wind. The most unusual thing, however, wasn't the house itself, but what held it up. It stood on a pair of massive bird legs, gnarled and yellow, blunt talons digging into the mud. The legs were crouched low, as if sleeping, but every so often they shifted restlessly, causing the whole house to shudder and groan.

"We're heeeeere," Puck sang softly. "And can I say that the old gal hasn't gotten any less creepy than when I saw her last."

I narrowed my eyes at him. "Just shut up and let me do the talking this time. It was bad enough when you insulted the centaur chief."

"All I suggested was that we could've used a ride out of the meadow. I didn't mean from *him.*"

Sighing, I opened the bone gate and crossed the weed-choked yard, scattering chickens in front of me. Before we reached the steps, however, the door creaked open and an old woman emerged from the darkened interior. Tangled white hair framed a lined, wrinkled face, and sharp black eyes peered out at us, bright and gleaming. In one gnarled hand she held a basket, in the other a butcher knife, stained with the blood of many victims.

I stopped at the foot of the stairs, wary and alert. Old as she appeared, the witch of this house was powerful and unpredictable. If Puck said something stupid or accidentally insulted her, it would be vastly annoying if we had to fight our way out.

"Well," the witch said, curling bloodless lips to smile at us. Crooked yellow teeth flashed in the light like jagged bits of bone. "What do we have here? Two handsome faery boys, come to visit a poor old woman. And if my eyes don't deceive me, that's Robin Goodfellow I see before me. The last I saw of you, you stole my broom and tied my house's legs so it fell over when we tried to catch you!"

I repressed another sigh. This wasn't starting well. I should've known Puck had already done something to earn her wrath. But at the same time, I had to fight the urge to smile, to laugh at such a ridiculous thought, the house falling on its face in the mud because the Great Prankster had tied its feet together.

I kept my expression neutral, as it was obvious the witch was not amused in the slightest. "What do you have to say for yourself, villain?" she continued, shaking her butcher knife at Puck, who ducked behind me in a pathetic attempt to hide, though I could hear him trying to muffle his laughter. "Do you know how long it took me to repair my home? And then you have the gall, the absolute gall, to leave my broom at the edge of the forest, just to prove you could take it. I've half a mind to stick you in the pot and feed you to my chickens!"

"I apologize for him," I said quickly, and those sharp black eyes suddenly turned on me. I held myself tall, unafraid but still polite, lest she lump me together with the buffoon at my back. "Excuse this intrusion, old mother," I continued formally. "I am Ash of the Unseelie Court. And I need your help, if you would hear me."

The witch blinked. "Such manners. You were not raised in a barn like that one, I see." She stabbed her knife in Puck's direction, wrinkling her long nose. "And I know who you are, son of Mab. What would you have of me? Be quick about it."

"We're looking for someone," I said. "He was rumored to be traveling through here, through the Bone Marsh. We thought you might know where he is."

"Oh?" The witch cocked her head, giving me a scrutinizing look. "And what makes you think I know where this person is?"

"Not a person," I corrected. "A cat. A cait sith. In some tales he's known as Grimalkin. And in some tales he's been rumored to keep company with a powerful witch out in the swamps, whose house stands on chicken legs in a fence made of bones."

"I see," said the witch, though her face and voice remained expressionless. "Well, I admire your tenacity, young prince. Grimalkin is not easy to find in the best of times. You must have come very far to seek him out." She peered closely at me, narrowing her eyes. "And this is not the first place you have searched. I can see it on your face. Why, I wonder? Why does he come so far? What is it that he desires so badly, to risk the ire of the Bone Witch? What is it you want, Ash of the Winter Court?"

"Would you believe the cat owes him money?" Puck's voice came from behind my shoulder, making me wince. The witch scowled at him.

"I did not ask you, Robin Goodfellow," she snapped, jabbing a clawlike finger at him. "And you had best watch your tongue, lest you find yourself neck-deep in a pot of boiling snake venom. Right now your friend's civility is the only thing keeping me from skinning you alive, and you will be silent on my land or you will leave. My question was for the prince."

"I am a prince no longer," I said softly, interrupting her rant. "My service to the Winter Queen is done, and Mab has cast me from her circle. I am dead to her."

"Regardless," the witch said, turning back to me with her piercing black eyes, "that does not answer my question. Why are you here, Ash-who-is-no-longer-a-prince? And do not attempt to mislead me with faery riddles and half truths, for I will know, and I will not be happy about it. If you wish to see this Grimalkin, you must answer my question first. What is it you seek?"

"I…" For a moment, I hesitated, and not because Puck nudged me sharply in the ribs. He knew the reason we were here, why I wanted to find Grimalkin, but I'd never voiced my intentions out loud. Maybe the witch knew this, maybe she was just curious, but saying it aloud suddenly made it all the more real. "I want to become…mortal," I said in a low voice. My stomach recoiled, hearing those words for the first time. "I promised someone… I swore I would find a way to survive the Iron Realm, and I can't go there as I am." The witch raised an eyebrow, and I drew myself up, fixing her with a cold stare. "I want to become human. And I need Grimalkin to help me find a way."

"Well," said a familiar voice behind us, "that *is* an interesting request."

We whirled around. Grimalkin sat on an overturned bucket, a bushy gray cat with his tail curled around himself, watching us lazily.

"Oh, of course!" Puck exclaimed. "There you are. Do you *know* what we've been through to find you, cat? Have you been there the whole time?"

"Do not make me state the obvious, Goodfellow." Grimalkin twitched his whiskers at him, then turned to me. "Greetings, prince. I have heard that you were looking for me."

"If you knew, why didn't you come to us?"

The cait sith yawned, curling a pink tongue over sharp white teeth. "I have grown rather bored of court politics," he continued, blinking gold eyes. "Nothing ever changes between Summer and Winter, and I did not want to become embroiled in the endless bickering of the courts. Or the games of certain Dark Muses."

Puck winced. "You heard about that, huh? Word travels fast." He shook his head at me and grinned. "I wonder if Titania has calmed down yet, after that trick we played in the Summer Court."

Grimalkin ignored him. "I wanted to know why you were looking for me, to see if I wished to make myself known. Or not." He sniffed, cocking his head at me. "But *this* request was definitely not what I was expecting of you, prince. How very...interesting."

"Foolish, if you ask me," the witch stated, waggling her knife in my direction. "Does a crow become a salmon simply because it wishes to? You do not know the first thing about mortality, prince-who-is-not. Why would you want to become like them?"

"Because," Grimalkin answered before I could say anything, "he is in love."

"Ahhh." The witch looked at me and shook her head. "I see. Poor creature. Then you will not hear a word I have to say." I gazed at her coolly, but she only smiled. "Fare ye well, then, prince-who-is-not. And Goodfellow, if I see you again, it will be to hang your skin over my door. Now, excuse me." She gathered herself up and tromped down the steps, taking a swipe at Puck as she passed, which he deftly avoided.

I didn't like the way Grimalkin continued to stare at me, a hint of laughter in his slitted eyes, and I crossed my arms. "Do you know a way for a faery to become mortal, or not?"

"I do not," Grimalkin said simply, and for a moment my heart sank. "But, there are...rumors. Legends of those who wanted to become mortal." He lifted a front paw and began washing it, scrubbing it over his ears. "There is...one...who might know the way to becoming human," he continued, much too nonchalantly. "A seer, in the wildest regions of the Nevernever. But the way to the seer is twisted and tangled, and once you step off the path, you will never find it again."

"Right, and you just happen to know the way, don't you?" Puck interjected, but Grimalkin ignored him. "Come on, cat, we all know where this is going. Name your price, so we can agree and get on the road already."

"Price?" Grimalkin looked up, and his eyes gleamed. "How well you seem to know me," he mused in a voice I didn't like at all. "You think this is some simple request, that I guide you to the seer and that will be all. You have no idea what you are asking, what lies ahead, for all of us." The cat stood, waving his tail, regarding me with a solemn gold gaze. "I will name no price, not today. But the time will come, prince, when I arrive to collect this debt. And when that day comes, you will pay it in full."

The words hung in the air between us, shimmering with power. A contract, and a particularly nasty one at that. Grimalkin, for whatever reason, was playing for keeps. A part of me recoiled, hating being bound in such a way. If I agreed to this, the cat could ask anything of me, take anything, and I would be forced to comply.

But, if it meant being human, being with her in the end...

"You sure about this, ice-boy?" Puck caught my gaze, worried as well. "This is your quest, but there's no backing out if you agree to do this. You can't just promise him a nice squeaky mouse and be done with it?"

I sighed and faced the cait sith, who waited calmly for my answer. "I will not deliberately harm anyone," I told him firmly. "You will not use me as a weapon, nor will I work evil against those I consider allies or friends. This contract will involve no one else. Just me."

"As you wish," Grimalkin purred.

"Then you have a deal." I felt a tingle in the air as the bargain was sealed, and clenched my fists. There was no backing out of it now, not that I had any intention to do so, but it seemed that I'd made more deals, accepted more contracts, in a single year than I had in my entire life as a prince of Winter.

I had the feeling I'd sacrifice more before the trip was over, but there was nothing for it now. I'd made my promise, and I would see it through.

"Then it is done." Grimalkin nodded and leaped off the bucket, landing in a patch of weeds surrounded by mud. "Let us go. We waste time dallying here."

Puck blinked. "What, just like that? You're not going to tell the old chicken plucker you're leaving?"

"She already knows," Grimalkin said, picking his way across the yard. "And incidentally, 'the old chicken plucker' can hear every word you say, so I suggest we hurry. After she is done with the fowl, she intends to come after you as well." He reached the fence and leaped up on it, somehow balancing himself on a crooked skull, peering back with glowing yellow eyes. "You did not think she would let you go so easily, did you?" he asked. "We have until nightfall to be clear of the marsh, before she comes riding after us with all of hell close behind her. So let us pick up the pace, hmm?"

Puck shot me a sideways look, grinning feebly. "Er. Never a dull moment, huh, ice-boy?"

"I'm going to kill you one day," I told him as we hurried after Grimalkin, back into the swampy marshland. It was not an idle threat.

Puck just laughed. "Yeah. You and everyone else, prince. Join the club."

CHAPTER TWO

OLD NIGHTMARES

Our exit from the Bone Marsh was far more harrowing than our journey to find the witch. True to Grimalkin's prediction, as the sun sank beneath the western horizon, a mad howl arose, seeming to echo from the swamp itself. A shudder passed through the land, and a sudden wind stole the late afternoon warmth.

"Perhaps we should move faster," Grimalkin said, and bounded into the undergrowth, but I stopped and turned to face the howling wind, drawing my sword. The breeze, smelling of rot, stagnant water and blood, whipped at my face, but I held my blade loosely at my side and waited.

"Oy, prince." Puck circled back, frowning. "What are you doing? If you didn't know already, the old chicken plucker is on her way, and she's gunning for Winter and Summer stew."

"Let her come." I was Ashallayn'darkmyr Tallyn, son of Mab, former prince of the Unseelie Court, and I was not afraid of a witch on a broom.

"I would advise against that," Grimalkin said, somewhere in the bushes. "These are her lands, after all, and she will be a formidable opponent should you insist on fighting her here. The wiser course of action is to flee to the edge of the swamp. She will not follow us there. That is where I will be, should you decide to come to your senses. I will not waste time watching you fight a completely useless battle based on ridiculous pride."

"Come on, Ash," Puck said, edging away. "We can play with extremely powerful witches some other time. Furball might disappear, and I do not want to tromp all over the Nevernever looking for him *again*."

I glared at Puck, who shot me an arrogant grin and hurried after the cat. Sheathing my weapon, I sprinted after them, and soon the Bone Marsh was a blur of malachite moss and bleached bone. A cackling scream rang out somewhere behind us, and I leaned forward, adding speed and cursing all Summer fey under my breath.

We ran for an hour or more, the cackle of our pursuer never seeming to gain, but never falling behind. Then the ground began to firm under my feet, the trees slowly gaining breadth and height. The air changed as well, losing the acrid odor of the bog and turning to something sweeter, though mixed with the faintest hint of decay.

I caught sight of a gray stillness in one of the trees and skidded to a halt, so suddenly that Puck slammed into me. I turned with the impact and gave a little push. "Oy!" Puck yelped as he careened off and landed in an ungraceful sprawl. I smirked and stepped around him, dodging easily as he tried to trip me.

"Now is not the time for playing," Grimalkin said from his perch, watching us disdainfully. "The witch will not follow us here. Now is the time for resting." Turning his back on us, he leaped higher into the branches and disappeared from sight.

Settling against a trunk, I pulled my sword and laid it across my knees, leaning back with a sigh. Step one, complete. We'd found Grimalkin, a task harder than I'd thought it could be. The next task would be to find this seer, and then...

I sighed. Then everything became fuzzy. There was no clear path after finding the seer. I didn't know what would be required of me, what I would have to do to become mortal. Perhaps it would be painful. Perhaps I would have to offer something, sacrifice something, though I didn't know what I could offer anymore, beyond my own existence.

Narrowing my eyes, I shut those thoughts away. It didn't matter. I would do whatever it took.

Memory trickled in, seeking to slip beneath my defenses, the icy wall I showed the world. I had once thought my armor invincible, that nothing could touch me...until Meghan Chase had entered my life and turned it upside down. Reckless, loyal, possessing the unyielding stubbornness of a granite cliff, she'd smashed through all the barriers I'd erected to keep her out, refusing to give up on me, until I finally had to admit defeat. It was official.

I was in love. With a human.

I smiled bitterly at the thought. The old Ash, if faced with such a suggestion, would've either laughed scornfully or removed the offender's head from his neck. I'd known love before, and it had brought me so much pain that I had retreated behind an impenetrable wall of indifference, freezing out everything, everyone. So it had been shocking and unexpected and a little terrifying to discover I could still feel anything, and I'd been reluctant to accept it. If I dropped my guard, I was vulnerable, and such weakness was deadly in the Unseelie Court. But more important, I hadn't wanted to go through the same hurt a second time, lowering my defenses only to have my heart torn away once more.

Deep down, I'd known the odds were stacked against us.

I knew a Winter prince and the half-human daughter of the Summer King didn't have much of a chance to be together in the end. But I had been willing to try. I'd given it my all, and I didn't regret any of it, even when Meghan had severed our bond and exiled me from the Iron Realm.

I'd expected to die that day. I had been ready. Being ordered by my True Name to walk away, leaving Meghan to die alone in the Iron Kingdom, had nearly shattered me a second time. If it hadn't been for my oath to be with her again, I might've done something suicidal, like challenge Oberon to battle before the entire Summer Court. But now that I've made my promise, there is no turning back. Abandoning my vow will unravel me, bit by bit, until there is nothing left. Even if I wasn't determined to find a way to survive in the Iron Realm, I'd have no choice but to continue.

I will be with her again, or I will die. There aren't any other options.

"Hey, ice-boy, you okay? You've got your brooding face on again."

"I'm fine."

"You're so full of crap." Puck lounged in the cradle of a tree, hands behind his head, one foot dangling in the air. "Lighten up already. We finally found the cat—which we should get a freaking medal for, the search for the Golden Fleece wasn't this hard—and you look like you're going to engage Mab in single combat first thing in the morning."

"I'm thinking. You should try it sometime."

"Ooh, witty." Puck snorted, pulled an apple out of his pocket, and bit into it. "Suit yourself, ice-boy. But you really should *try* to smile sometimes, or your face will freeze like that forever. Or so I've been told." He grinned and crunched his apple. "So, whose turn is it for first watch, yours or mine?"

"Yours."

"Really? I thought it was your turn. Didn't I take first watch at the edge of the Bone Marsh?"

"Yes." I glared at him. "And it was interrupted when you followed that nymph away from the camp, and that goblin tried to steal my sword."

"Oh, yeah." Puck snickered, though I didn't think it was very amusing. This sword was made for me by the Ice Archons of Dragons' Peak; my blood, glamour and a tiny piece of my essence had gone into its creation, and no one touches it but me.

"In my defense," Puck said, still grinning faintly, "she *did* try to rob me as well. I've never heard of a nymph being in league with a goblin. Too bad for them that you're a light sleeper, huh, ice-boy?"

I rolled my eyes, tuned out his incessant chattering, and let myself drift.

I ALMOST NEVER DREAM. Dreams are for mortals, humans whose emotions are so strong, so consuming, they spill over into their subconscious minds. The fey do not usually dream; our sleep is untroubled by thoughts of the past or future, or anything except the now. While humans can be tormented by feelings of guilt, longing, worry and regret, most fey do not experience these things. We are, in many ways, emptier than mortals, lacking the deeper emotions that make them so...human. Perhaps that is why they are so fascinating to us.

In the past, the only time I had dreamed was right after Ariella's death, horrific, gut-wrenching nightmares about that day I let her die, the day I couldn't save her. It was always the same: I, Puck and Ariella chasing the golden fox, the shadows closing around us, the monstrous wyvern rearing up out of nowhere. Each time, I knew Ariella would be hit. Each time, I tried to get to her before the wyvern's deadly stinger found its mark. I failed every single time, and she would look at me with those clear blue eyes and whisper my name, right before she went limp in my arms and I jerked myself awake.

I learned to freeze out my emotions then, to destroy everything that made me weak, to become as cold inside as I was outside. The nightmares stopped, and I never dreamed again.

Until now.

I knew I stood at the center of Tir Na Nog, the seat of the Unseelie Queen, my old home. These were my lands, once. I recognized distinct landmarks, as familiar to me as my own face, and yet all was not well. The jagged mountains, rising up until they vanished into the clouds, were the same. The snow and ice that covered every square inch of the land and never really melted, that was the same.

Everything else was destroyed. The great sweeping forests of Tir Na Nog were gone, now barren, wasted fields. A few trees stood here and there, but they were corrupt, twisted versions of themselves, metallic and gleaming. Barbed-wire fences slashed the landscape, and hulks of rusted metal vehicles lay half-buried in the snow. Where an icy city once stood, its pristine crystal towers glittering in the sun, now black smoke-stacks pumped billowing darkness into the overcast sky. Sky-scrapers of twisted metal towered over everything; glittering, skeletal silhouettes that vanished into the clouds.

Faeries roamed across the darkened landscape, swarms of them, but they were not my Unseelie brethren. They were of the poisoned realm, the Iron fey; gremlins and bugs, wiremen and Iron knights, the faeries of mankind's technology. I gazed around at my homeland and shuddered. No normal fey could live here. We would all die, the very air we breathed burning us from the inside out, from the Iron corruption that hung thick on the air like a fog. I could feel it searing my throat, spreading like fire to my lungs. Coughing, I put my sleeve to my nose and mouth and staggered away, but where could I go if all of Tir Na Nog was like this?

"Do you see?" whispered a voice behind me, and I whirled around. No one stood there, but from the corner of my eye I caught a shimmer, a presence, though it slid away whenever I tried to focus on it. "Look around you. This is what would have happened had Meghan not become the Iron Queen. Everything, everyone you knew, destroyed. The Iron fey would have corrupted the entire Nevernever, were it not for Meghan Chase. And *she* could not have succeeded had you not been there."

"Who are you?" I searched for the owner of the voice, but the presence slipped away, keeping to the very edge of my vision. "Why are you showing me this?" This was nothing new. I was fully aware of what would've happened had the Iron fey been victorious. Though, even in my worst imaginings, I had not pictured quite *this* much destruction.

"Because, you need to see, *really* see, the second outcome for yourself." I felt the presence move closer, though it still kept infuriatingly out of sight. "And your judgment was impaired, Ash of the Winter Court. You loved the girl. You would have done anything for her, regardless of the circumstances." It slid away, behind me, though I'd given up trying to search for it. "I want you to look around carefully, son of Mab, and understand the significance of your decision. Had Meghan Chase not survived to become the Iron Queen, this would be your world today."

The burning inside was growing unbearable. Each breath stabbed like a knife, and my skin was starting to blister as well. It reminded me of the time I'd been captured by Virus, one of the Iron King's lieutenants, and had a sentient metal bug implanted in me. The bug had taken over my body, turning me into Virus's slave, making me fight for her. And though I'd been fully aware of everything I did, I was powerless to stop it. I had felt the metal invader, like a hot coal in my mind, burning and searing, making me nearly blind with pain, though I couldn't show it. This was worse.

I sank to my knees, fighting to stay upright, as my skin blackened and peeled from my bones. The pain was excruciating, and I wondered, through my delirium, why I hadn't woken yet. This was a dream; I realized that much. Why couldn't I shake myself free?

I knew with a sudden, grim clarity. Because the voice wasn't letting me. It was keeping me here, tied to this nightmare world, despite my efforts to wake. I wondered if it was possible to die in a dream.

"I'm sorry," the voice murmured, seeming to come from far away now. "I know it's painful, but I want you to remember this when we meet again. I want you to understand the sacrifice that had to be made. I know you don't understand now, but you will. Soon."

And, just like that, it was gone, and the ties holding me to the vision were released. With a silent gasp, I wrenched myself out of the dream, back into the waking world.

It was very dark now, though the skeletal trees glowed with a soft white luminance that left them hazy and ethereal. Several yards away, Puck still sat in the branches, hands behind his head, chewing the ends of a grass stalk. One foot swung idly in the air and he wasn't looking at me; I'd learned long ago how to mask my pain and remain silent, even in sleep. You don't show weakness in the Unseelie Court. Puck didn't know I was awake, but Grimalkin crouched in the branches of a nearby tree, and his glowing yellow eyes were fixed in my direction.

"Bad dreams?"

The tone of his voice wasn't exactly a question. I shrugged. "A nightmare. Nothing I can't handle."

"I would not be so sure of that, were I you."

I glanced up sharply, narrowing my eyes. "You know something," I accused, and Grimalkin yawned. "What aren't you telling me?"

"More than you want to know, prince." Grimalkin sat up, curling his tail around himself. "And I am not a fool. You know better than to ask such questions." The cat sniffed, regarding me with that unblinking gold gaze. "I told you before, this is no simple task. You will have to discover the answers for yourself."

I already knew that, but the way Grimalkin said it sounded ominous, and it irritated me that the cait sith knew more than he was letting on. Ignoring the cat, I turned away, staring into the trees. A stray sod emerged from the darkness, a tiny green faery with a clump of weeds growing from its back. It blinked at me, bobbed its mushroom hat, and quickly slipped back into the undergrowth.

"This seer," I asked Grimalkin, carefully marking the place the sod had vanished so as to not tread on it when we left. "Where is it located?"

But Grimalkin had disappeared.

TIME HAS NO MEANING in the wyldwood. Day and night don't really exist here, just light and darkness, and they can be just as fickle and moody as everything else. A "night" can pass in the space of a blink, or go on forever. Light and darkness will chase each other through the sky, play hide-and-seek or tag or catch-me-if-you-can. Sometimes, one or the other will become offended over an imagined slight and refuse to come out for an indefinite amount of time. Once, light became so angry, a hundred years passed in the mortal realm before it deigned to come out again. And though the sun continued to rise and set in the human world, it was a rather turbulent period for the world of men, as all the creatures who lurked in darkness and shadow got to roam freely under the lightless Nevernever skies.

So it was still full dark when Puck and I started out again, following the cait sith into the endless tangle of the wyldwood. Grimalkin slipped through the trees like mist flowing over the ground, gray and nearly invisible in the colorless landscape around him. He moved swiftly and silently, not looking back, and it took all my hunter's skills to keep up with him, to not lose him in the tangled undergrowth. I suspected he was testing us, or perhaps playing some annoying feline game, subtly trying to lose us without completely going invisible. But, with Puck hurrying after me, I kept pace with the elusive cait sith and didn't lose him once as we ventured deeper into the wyldwood.

The light had finally decided to make an appearance when, without warning, Grimalkin stopped. Leaping onto an overhanging branch, he stood motionless for a moment, ears pricked to the wind and whiskers trembling. Around us, huge gnarled trees blocked out the sky, gray trunks and branches seeming to hem us in, like an enormous net or cage. I realized I didn't recognize this part of the wyldwood, though that wasn't unusual. The wyldwood was huge, eternal and constantly changing. There were many places I'd never seen, never set foot in, even in the long years of hunting beneath its canopy.

"Hey, we're stopping," Puck said, coming up behind me. Peering over my shoulder, he snorted under his breath. "What's the matter, cat? Did you finally get lost?"

"Be quiet, Goodfellow." Grimalkin flattened his ears but didn't look back. "Something is out there," he stated, twitching his tail. "The trees are angry. Something does not belong." His eyes narrowed, and he crouched to leap off the branch.

Right before he vanished.

I glanced at Puck and frowned. "I guess we'd better find out what's going on."

Goodfellow snickered. "Wouldn't be any fun if we didn't run into *some* sort of catastrophe." Pulling his dagger, he waved me on. "After you, your highness."

We proceeded cautiously through the trees, scanning the undergrowth for anything suspicious. At my silent gesture, Puck stepped away and slid into the trees to the right of me. If something was lying in ambush, it would be better if we weren't together when it pounced.

It wasn't long before we started seeing evidence that something was decidedly out of place here. Plants were brown and dying, trees had spots where they had been burned, and the air began to smell of rust and copper, tickling my throat and making me want to gag. I was suddenly reminded of my dream, the nightmare world of the Iron fey, and gripped my sword hilt even tighter.

"You think there's an Iron faery here?" Puck muttered, poking a burned, dead leaf with the point of his knife. It disintegrated at his touch.

"If there is," I muttered, "it won't be here much longer."

Puck shot me a glance, looking faintly unsure. "I don't know, ice-boy. We're supposed to be at peace now. What would Meghan say if we killed one of her subjects?"

"Meghan is a queen." I stepped beneath a rotting branch, pushing it away with my sword. "She understands the rules, just like everyone else. By law, no Iron fey can set foot in the wyldwood without permission from Summer or Winter. It would be a breach of the treaty if the courts found out, and at worst it would be seen as an act of war." I raised my sword and hacked through a cluster of yellowed, dying vines that smelled of rot. "If there is an Iron faery here, better we find it than scouts of Summer or Winter."

"Yeah? And what happens then? We politely ask it to go home? What if it doesn't listen to us?"

I gave him a blank stare.

He winced. "Right." He sighed. "Forgot who I was talking to. Well then, lead on, ice-boy."

We pushed deeper into the forest, following the trail of dying plants, until the trees thinned and the ground abruptly dropped away into a rocky gorge. The trees in this area were blackened and dead, and the air smelled poisonous and foul. After a moment, I realized why.

Sitting against a tree, his armor glinting in the sun, was an Iron knight.

I paused, my fingers tightening around the hilt of my sword. I had to remind myself that the knights were not our enemies anymore, that they served the Iron Queen and followed the same peace treaty as the rest of the courts. Besides, this one was clearly no threat to us. His breastplate had been staved in, and dark, oily blood pooled beneath him. His chin rested limply on his chest, but as we got closer, he opened his eyes and looked up. Blood trickled from one corner of his mouth.

"Prince...Ash?" He blinked several times, as if doubting his own eyes. "What...what are you doing here?"

"I could ask you the same." I didn't approach the fallen warrior, standing several feet away with my sword at my side. "It's forbidden for your kind to be here. Why aren't you in the Iron Realm protecting the queen?"

"The queen." The knight's eyes widened, and he held a hand out. "You...you have to warn the queen—"

I took two long steps forward and faced the knight, loom-

ing over him. "What's happened to Meghan?" I demanded.
"Warn her of what?"

"There was…an attempt on her life," the knight whispered,
and my heart went cold in fear and rage. "Assassins…snuck
into the castle…tried to get to the queen. We managed to
drive them off and followed them here, but there were more
than…we first thought. Killed the rest of my squad…" He
paused for breath, gasping. It was clear he wouldn't last much
longer, and I knelt to hear him better, ignoring the nausea
that came from being this close to an Iron faery. "You have
to…warn her…" he pleaded again.

"Where are they now?" I asked in a low voice.

The knight made a gesture over the rise, back into the
forest. "Their camp…on the edge of a lake," he whispered.
"Near a tower…"

"I know that spot," Puck said, standing several feet back
from the Iron knight. "A woman with crazy long hair used
to live on the top floor, but it's empty now."

"Please…" The knight raised dying eyes to me, fighting
to get his last words out. "Go to our queen. Tell her…we…
failed…." Then his eyes rolled up in his skull, and he slumped
forward.

I stood, taking a step back from the dead Iron knight. Puck
sheathed his dagger as he stepped up beside me, giving the
Iron faery a dubious look. "What now, prince? Should we
head to the Iron Court?"

"I can't." Frustration battled cold rage, and I gripped my
sword hard enough to feel the edges bite into my palm. "I'm
forbidden to set foot in the Iron Realm. That's why we're
here, remember? Or did you forget?"

"Don't freak out, ice-boy." Puck crossed his arms with a
smirk. "All is not lost. I can turn into a raven and fly back to
warn—"

"Do not be foolish, Goodfellow," Grimalkin interrupted, coming out of nowhere, hopping onto a stone. "You have no amulet and no protection from the corruption of the realm. You would perish long before you reached the Iron Queen."

Puck snorted. "Give me some credit, Furball. It's me. Did you forget who you were talking to?"

"If only I could."

"Enough!" I stared coldly at both of them. Grimalkin yawned, but at least Puck looked faintly guilty. Frustration and anger boiled; I hated that I couldn't be with Meghan, that I was forced to keep my distance. But I would not sit back and do nothing. "Meghan is still in danger," I continued, gazing up the hill. "And the assassins are close. If I can't go back to warn her, then I'll take care of the threat right here."

Puck blinked, but he didn't seem terribly surprised. "Yeah, I thought you might say that." He sighed. "And I can't let you have all the fun, of course. But, uh, you do know they took out a whole squad of Iron knights, right, ice-boy?" He glanced at the dead faery and wrinkled his nose. "I'm not saying we shouldn't do it, of course, but what if we're charging into an army?"

I gave him a brittle smile. "Then there will be a lot of fallen soldiers before the day is done," I said quietly, and walked out of the gorge.

ON THE BANKS OF A LAKE, the slim, crooked tower with its mossy gargoyles and faded blue roof stood tall and proud, easily visible through the trees. At the base, sheltered among broken rocks and crumbling stones, several sidhe knights milled around a smoldering campfire, unaware of Puck and me, crouched in the shadows at the edge of the trees. The knights wore suits of familiar black armor, long spines bristling from the shoulders like giant thorns. Though once sharp and proud, the faces beneath the helmets were now ravaged as though diseased; charred, melted flesh, open sores and naked bone gleamed in the flickering campfire. Some of their noses had fallen off, others had only one good eye. The breeze shifted, and the stench of burned, rotting flesh assaulted our senses, washing over us. Puck stifled a cough.

"Thornguards," he muttered, putting a hand to his nose. "What the heck are they doing here? I thought they were all killed in the last war."

"Apparently, we missed a few." I gazed over the camp dispassionately. The Thornguards once belonged to my brother Rowan, his elite personal guard. When Rowan joined the Iron fey, the Thornguards followed him, believing his claims that they could become immune to iron. They thought the Iron fey would destroy the Nevernever, and the only way to survive was to become like them. To prove their loyalty, they wore a ring of iron beneath their gauntlets, enduring the agony and the destruction it wreaked on their bodies, believing if they could survive the pain, they would be reborn.

The Thornguards had been misled, deceived, but they had still chosen to side with the Iron fey and Rowan in the recent war, which made them traitors to the courts of Faery. These few had gone even further, threatening Meghan and attempting to end her life. That made them my personal enemies, a very dangerous position, indeed.

"So," Puck continued, watching the camp, "I'm counting at least a half dozen bad boys near the fire, maybe a few more guarding the perimeter. How do you want to do this, prince? I could lure them away, one at a time. Or we could sneak around and go at them from different positions—"

"There are only seven of them." Drawing my sword, I stepped out of the trees and started toward the camp. Puck sighed.

"Or we could do the old kick-in-the-door approach," he muttered, falling into step beside me. "Silly me, thinking there was another way."

Shouts of surprise and alarm echoed through the camp, but I wasn't trying to be stealthy. Together, Puck and I walked down the bank to the tower, wrapped in a grim, killing silence. One sentry came at us, howling, but I blocked his sword, plunged my blade through his armor and stepped around him, leaving the guard to crumple in the dirt.

By the time we reached the center of camp, six Thornguards were waiting for us, standing in formation with their weapons drawn. Puck and I approached calmly and stopped at the edge of the firelight. For a moment, nobody moved.

"Prince Ash." The lead Thornguard smiled faintly— difficult to see because he had no lips, just a thin, ragged slash where his mouth would be—and stepped forward. His eyes, a glazed, glassy blue, flicked back and forth between us. "And Robin Goodfellow. What a surprise to find you here. We're honored, aren't we, boys?" Though his voice turned mocking, it was still hopeful, as he gestured toward the forest behind us. "News of our deeds must have spread far and wide, for the mighty Winter prince and the Summer Court jester to track us down."

"Not really." Puck smirked at him. "We were just in the area."

His smile faltered, but I stepped forward before he could say anything more. "You attacked the Iron Kingdom," I said as his attention snapped to me. "You led an assault on the Iron Queen, attempting to end her life. Before I kill you, I want to know why. The war is over. The Iron Realm is no longer a threat, and the courts are at peace. Why would you jeopardize that?"

For a moment, the Thornguard stared at me, his eyes and

face completely blank. Then, the thin mouth twisted into a sneer. "Why not?" He shrugged, and motioned to the surrounding camp. "Look at us, prince," he spat bitterly. "We have nothing to live for. Rowan is dead. The Iron King is dead. We can't return to Winter, and we can't survive in the Iron Realm. Where do we go now? There's nowhere that would take us back."

His tale sounded eerily familiar, much like my own; banished from my own court, yet unable to set foot in the Iron Realm.

"The only thing left was revenge," the Thornguard went on, gesturing angrily to his own face. "Kill every Iron bastard that did this to us, starting with their half-breed queen. We gave it our best shot, even made it as far as the throne room, but the little bitch was stronger than we realized. We were driven back at the last minute." His chin rose in a defiant gesture. "Though we did manage to kill several of her knights, even the ones that came after us."

"You missed one," I said quietly, and his eyebrows rose. "The one you left alive told us where you were and what you had done. You should've made sure all your opponents were dead before moving on. A beginner's mistake, I'm afraid."

"Oh? Well, I'll be sure to remember that, next time." He smirked at me then, twisted and bitter. "So, tell me, Ash," he went on, "did you two have a nice little heart-to-heart before he died? Since you're both so smitten with the new Iron Queen, so very eager to be with her. Did he tell you the secret of becoming like them?"

I regarded the Thornguard coldly. His sneer widened. "Don't pretend you don't know what I'm talking about, Ash. We've all heard the story, haven't we, boys? The mighty Winter prince, pining for his lost queen, promises he'll find a way to be with her in Iron Realm. How very touching." He snorted and leaned forward so that the firelight washed over his burned, ruined face. In the dim light, it was like gazing at a corpse.

"Take a good look, your highness," he hissed, baring rotten, yellow teeth. His stench washed over me, and I fought the urge to step back. "Take a good look around, at all of us. This is what happens to our people in the Iron Realm. We thought we could be like them. We thought we'd found a way to live with iron, to not fade away when humans stopped believing. Now look at us." His dead, ravaged face twisted in a snarl. "We're monsters, just like them. The Iron fey are a blight and a plague on the Nevernever, and we're going to kill as many as we can in the time we have left. Including their queen, and any sympathizers to the Iron Realm. If we can start another war with the Iron fey, and their kingdom is destroyed for good, everything we endured will be worth it."

I narrowed my gaze, imagining another war with the Iron fey, another season of killing and blood and death, with Meghan caught in the center. "You're sadly mistaken if you think I'm going to let that happen."

The Thornguard shook his head, moving back a pace and drawing his sword. "You should've joined us, Ash," he said regretfully, as the others shifted and raised their weapons. "You could've fought your way to the throne room and put your blade through the Iron Queen's heart. Destroyed your weakness, as a Winter prince should have done. But you had to fall in love with her, didn't you? And now you're lost to the Iron Realm, same as us." He gave me an appraising look. "We're not really that different, after all."

Puck sighed very loudly. "So, are you guys going to talk us to death?" he wondered, and the Thornguard glared at him. "Or are we actually going to get on with this?"

The leader flourished his weapon, the black, serrated blade

glinting in the flames. Around him, the rest of the Thorn-guards did the same. "Expect no mercy from us, your high-ness," he warned as the squad began to close in. "You're no longer our prince, and we're no longer part of the Winter Court. Everything we believed in is dead."

Puck grinned viciously and turned so that we stood back-to-back against the approaching guards. I raised my sword and drew glamour from the air, letting the cold power of Winter swirl within. And I smiled.

"Mercy is for the weak," I told the Thornguards, seeing them for what they really were: abominations to be cut down, destroyed. "Let me show you how much of an Unseelie I still am."

The Thornguards attacked with howling battle cries, coming from all directions. I parried one slash and swiped at another, leaping back to avoid a third. Behind me, Puck whooped in unrestrained glee, the clash of his daggers ringing in my ears as he danced around his opponents. They followed, savage and unrelenting. Rowan's elite guards were dangerous and well trained, but I had been part of the Winter Court for a very long time, observing their strengths and weaknesses, and knew their fatal flaws.

The Thornguards were formidable as a unit, using group tactics to threaten and harry, much like a pack of wolves. But that was their greatest failing as well. Single them out, and they fell apart. Surrounded by a trio of Thornguards, I leaped back and flung a hail of stinging ice shards into their midst, catching two guards in the deadly arc. They flinched for a brief second, and the third leaped forward, alone, meeting my sword as it cut across his neck. The warrior frayed apart, black armor splitting open as dark brambles erupted from the spot where he died. As with all fey, death returned him to the Nevernever, and he simply ceased to exist.

"Duck, ice-boy!" Puck yelped behind me, and I did, feeling a Thornguard blade hiss overhead. I turned and stabbed the warrior through the chest as Puck hurled a dagger into another rushing me from behind. More brambles spread across the stones.

Now there were only three Thornguards left. Puck and I still stood back-to-back, guarding each other's flanks, moving in perfect unison. "You know," Puck said, panting slightly, "this reminds me of the time we were underground and stumbled into that Duergar city. Remember that, ice-boy?"

I parried a blow to my ribs and returned with a swipe to my opponent's head, forcing him back a step. "Stop talking and keep fighting, Goodfellow."

"Yeah, I think you said that to me then, too."

I blocked a stab, lunged forward and ripped my blade across the guard's throat, just as Puck danced within reach of his opponent and jabbed his knife between his ribs. Both warriors split apart, their weapons clanging against the rocks as they died. As they fell, the last Thornguard, the leader who'd taunted me before the battle, turned to flee.

I raised my arm, glamour swirling around me, and flung a trio of ice daggers at the warrior's retreating back. They struck with muffled *thunks,* and the Thornguard gasped, pitching forward. Staggering to his knees, he looked up as I stepped around to face him, his glassy blue eyes filled with pain and hate.

"Guess I was wrong," he panted, his ruined mouth twisted in a last defiant sneer. "You *are* still Unseelie, through and through." He laughed, but it came out as a choked cough. "Well, what are you waiting for, your highness? Get on with it."

"You know I won't spare you." I let the emptiness of the Winter Court spread through me, freezing any emotion, stifling any thoughts of kindness or mercy. "You tried to kill Meghan, and if I let you go, you will continue to bring harm to her realm. I can't allow that. Unless you swear to me, on this spot, that you will abandon your quest to harm the Iron Queen, her subjects and her kingdom. Give me that vow, and I'll let you live."

The Thornguard gazed at me a moment, then choked another laugh. "And where would I go?" He sneered, as Puck walked up behind him, watching solemnly. "Who would take me back, looking like this? Mab? Oberon? Your little half-breed queen?" He coughed and spat on the stones between us, the spittle a dark red. "No, your highness. If you let me go, I will find my way back to the Iron Queen, and I will put a sword in her heart and laugh as they cut me down for it. And if I somehow survive, I will destroy every Iron faery I come across, tear them limb from limb, until the land is stained with their tainted blood, and I won't stop until every one of them lies de—"

He got no further, as my blade slashed across his neck and severed his head from his body.

Puck sighed as brambles erupted from the dead Thornguard, crooked fingers clawing at the sky. "Yeah, that went about as well as I expected." He wiped his daggers on his pants and looked back at the tower, at the new brambles growing around the base. "You think any more are hanging around?"

"No." I sheathed my sword and turned from my former Unseelie brethren. "They knew they were dying. They had no reason to hide."

"Can't reason with madmen, I guess." Wrinkling his nose, Puck sheathed his weapons, shaking his head. "Nice to know they were just as delusional as before, just with a different flavor of crazy."

Delusional? I blinked as the leader's words came back to

me, mocking and ominous. *You're lost to the Iron Realm, same as us. We're not really that different, after all.*

Were the Thornguards that delusional? They had only wanted what I did: a way to overcome the effects of iron. They'd bargained their lives away, endured torment no normal faery could withstand, hoping to conquer our eternal weakness. Hoping to live in the Iron Realm.

Wasn't I doing the same now, wishing for the impossible?

"You've got your brooding face on again, ice-boy." Puck squinted at me. "And I can see your brain going a mile a minute. What are you thinking of?"

I shook my head. "Nothing important." Spinning on a heel, I turned and walked away, back toward the edge of the trees. Puck started to protest, but I hurried on, unwilling to think about it any longer. "We've wasted enough time here, and this isn't getting us any closer to the seer. Let's go."

He jogged after me. I hoped he would be quiet, leave me in peace, but of course I had only a few moments of silence before he opened his mouth. "Hey, you never answered my question, prince," he said, kicking a pebble over the stones, watching it bounce toward the forest. "What were we looking for in that underground city, anyway? A necklace? A mirror?"

"A dagger," I muttered.

"Aha! So you *do* remember, after all!"

I glared at him. He grinned cheekily. "Just checking, ice-boy. Wouldn't want you to forget all the good times we had. Hey, whatever happened to that thing, anyway? I seem to recall it was a really nice piece of work."

A numbness spread through my chest, and my voice went very, very soft. "I gave it to Ariella."

"...oh," Puck murmured.

And said nothing after that.

Grimalkin was waiting for us atop a broken limb at the edge of the tree line, washing his paw with exaggerated nonchalance. "That took longer than I expected." He yawned as we came up. "I was wondering if I should take a nap, waiting for you." Giving his paw a final lick, he looked down at us, narrowing his golden eyes. "Anyway, if you two are quite finished, we can move on."

"Did you know about the Thornguards?" I asked. "And their attack on the Iron Kingdom?"

Grimalkin snorted. Flicking his tail, the cat rose and sauntered along the splintered branch with no explanation. Hopping lightly to an overhead limb, he vanished into the leaves without looking back, leaving Puck and me hurrying to catch up.

CHAPTER THREE
ARIELLA TULARYN

The wyldwood stretched on, dark, tangled and endless. I didn't count the times the light rose and fell, because the farther we went into the untamed wilderness, the wilder and more unpredictable it became. Grimalkin took us through a glen where the trees slowly followed us until we looked back, freezing them in place, only to have them creep forward again when our backs were turned. We hiked up an enormous, moss-covered hill, only to discover that the "hill" was actually the body of a sleeping giant as it raised a massive hand to scratch the itch on its cheek. We crossed a rolling, windy plain where herds of wild horses stared at us with cold intelligence, their furtive conversations blown away in the wind.

During this time, Puck and I didn't talk, or if we did, it was just useless banter, threats, insults and the like. Fighting with Robin Goodfellow, side by side against the Thornguards, had brought up memories I did not wish to deal with now, ones that were frozen deep inside, memories I couldn't thaw out for fear of the pain. I didn't want to remember the hunts, the challenges, the times we got ourselves neck-deep in trouble and had to fight our way out. I didn't want to remember the laughter, the easy camaraderie, between myself and my once-closest friend. Because remembering Puck as something more than a rival only reminded me of my vow, the one spoken in a flash of despair and rage, the one that had turned us into bitter enemies for years to come.

And, of course, I couldn't think of Puck that way without remembering…her.

ARIELLA. THE ONLY DAUGHTER of the Ice Baron of Glassbarrow, Ariella first came to the Unseelie Court during winter equinox, when Mab was hosting that year's Elysium. As tradition dictated, twice a mortal year, the courts of Summer and Winter would meet to discuss politics, sign new treaties, and basically agree to play nice for another season. Or at least to refrain from declaring all-out war on the other court. It bored me to tears, but as a Winter prince and the son of Queen Mab, my presence was required, and I had learned to dance the dance and be a good little court monkey.

It was not yet twilight, and as such the Summer Court had not yet arrived. As Mab disapproved of my locking myself in my room until Elysium began, I was in a dark corner of the courtyard, rereading a book from my collection of mortal authors and poets. If anyone asked, I was overseeing the arrival of the last of the guests, but mostly I was avoiding Rowan and the current flock of nobles who would surround me with coy, flattering, razor-sharp smiles. Their voices would be the softest purr, the sweetest song, as they offered me favors covered in honey and nectar but with a core of vilest poison. I was a prince, after all, the youngest and most favored of Mab, at least according to some. I suppose the common belief was that I was more naive, easier to trap, perhaps. I didn't know the dance as well as Rowan or Sage, who were at court far more frequently. But I was a true son of Winter, and knew the twisted steps of court better than most. And those who sought to entrap me in a web of honey and favors soon found themselves tangled in their own dark promises.

I knew the dance. I just didn't revel in it.

Which was why I was leaning against an ice-covered wall with Musashi's *The Five Rings,* only half-aware of the bustle of carriages pulling up to the gates and the Winter gentry stepping out into the snow. Most of them I knew, or had seen before. The Lady Snowfire, dressed in a gown of sparkling icicles that chimed musically as she walked. The new duke of Frostfell—having disposed of the old duke by getting him exiled to the mortal realm—glided through the snow trailed by his goblin slaves. The Baroness of the Icebound Heart gave me a chilly nod as she strode past, her two snow leopards hissing and snarling at the ends of their silver chains.

And then, *she* walked in.

I didn't know her, and that in itself piqued my curiosity. None could argue her beauty: long silver hair, pale skin, a willowy body that was delicate and strong at the same time. But, all of our kind are, if not very attractive, at least striking in some way. Being surrounded by beauty tends to dull your appreciation of it, especially if the beauty only hides the cruelty beneath. It wasn't her looks that caught my eye that day, but the way she gazed at the Winter palace, awe written plainly on her lovely features. It was an emotion that didn't belong; most would see it as a weakness, something to be exploited. The nobles could sense emotion like a shark smelled blood; they would devour her before the day was out.

A part of me told me not to care, that it was everyone for themselves in the Winter Court, and that was how it always had been. That this girl, new and untried, would take the attention off me for once. Despite that voice, I found myself intrigued.

Snapping shut the book, I started toward her.

She was turning in slow circles when I walked up, and jumped when we came face-to-face. "Oh, pardon me!" Her voice was clear and light, like tiny bells. "I didn't see you standing there."

"Are you lost?" It wasn't so much a question, rather I was testing her, probing her defenses. Admitting you were lost was a grave mistake in the Winter Court; you never wanted to be caught unaware by anyone. It annoyed me a bit that the first thing I fell back on was checking for weakness, poking at chinks in her armor. But in the Unseelie Court, you could never be too careful.

She blinked at the question and took a step back, seeming to see me for the first time. Clear, blue-green eyes rose to meet my gaze, and I made the mistake of looking right at her.

Her gaze captured mine, drawing me in, and I was suddenly drowning. Flecks of silver dotted her irises like tiny stars, as if I was staring at a whole universe in her eyes. Brilliant emotion gazed out at me, pure and clean and untainted by the darkness of the Unseelie Court.

For a moment, we just stared at each other, neither willing to look away.

Until I realized what I was doing and turned, pretending to watch another carriage pull up to the gates, furious with myself for dropping my guard. For a brief moment, I wondered if that had been her ploy all along—pretend to be naive and innocent, and lure unsuspecting princes right into her clutches. Unorthodox, but effective.

Fortunately, it seemed the girl was just as shaken as I was. "No, I'm not lost," she said a little breathlessly. Another mistake, but I wasn't keeping track anymore. "It's just…I mean…I've never been here, is all." She cleared her throat and straightened, seeming to regain her composure. "I am

Ariella Tularyn of Glassbarrow," she announced regally, "and I am here on behalf of my father, the Duke of Glassbarrow. He is indisposed at the moment and sends his apologies for not being able to attend."

I'd heard about that. Apparently, the duke had run into some trouble while hunting ice wyrms in the mountains of his territory. The court had been abuzz with who would come to represent him, as he was rumored to have only one daughter, who never left the estate.

So, this was she.

Ariella smiled again, nervously brushing her hair back, and instantly lost her regal bearing. "I said that correctly, didn't I?" she asked without a trace of guile. "That was the proper greeting, wasn't it? I'm so new at this. I've never been to court before, and I don't want to upset the queen."

Right then, I decided. This girl needed an escort, someone to show her the ways of Winter, otherwise the nobles were going to chew her up and spit her out. The thought of this girl, broken and bitter, her eyes frozen in wary contempt, filled me with a strange protectiveness I couldn't explain. If anyone wanted to toy with Ariella Tularyn, they would have to go through me first. And I was no wide-eyed newcomer when it came to the Unseelie Court.

"Come on, then," I said, offering her my arm, which seemed to surprise her, but she took it nonetheless. "I'll introduce you."

Her brilliant smile was all the thanks I needed.

FROM THAT MOMENT ON, I continued to find excuses to be around the Duke of Glassbarrow's daughter. I took secret hunting trips to the Glassbarrow Mountains, enticing her away. I made sure Mab requested both the duke *and* Ariella's presence at Elysium. I stole every spare moment I could to be with her, until the day came when I finally convinced her to leave the duke's estate completely and live at the palace. Duke Glassbarrow was livid, but I was the Winter prince, and he eventually buckled under the threat of banishment or death.

Rumors flew, of course. As part of the royal family, my life was under constant scrutiny, even when there was nothing interesting about it. When it came to my spending so much time with a young duchess-to-be…well, you'd think Mab and Oberon had decided to marry, there was so much speculation. Prince Ash was obsessed, Prince Ash had found a new plaything and, worst of all, Prince Ash was in love. I didn't care. When I was with Ariella, I could forget the court, my responsibilities, everything. When I was with her, I didn't have to worry about keeping my guard up, constantly watching my back or my words. Ariella didn't care about the games of the Winter Court, something that fascinated me. *Was* I in love? I didn't know. Love was such an unknown concept, something that everyone cautioned against. Love was for mortals and weak Summer fey, it had no place in the life of an Unseelie prince. None of this swayed me. All I knew was, when we were together, I could leave behind the intrigues and pitfalls of court and just *be*.

It was high summer when the last person I wanted to find out about us did so anyway.

Ariella and I hunted often. It was a chance to get away from the court and be alone together, without the whispers and the stares and the snide, pitying looks. She was an excellent huntress, and our outings usually turned into friendly competitions, seeing whose arrow could drop our quarry first. I lost as often as I won, which filled me with an odd sort of pride. I knew my skill was considerable; that Ariella could match it brought some excitement back into the hunt and forced me to concentrate.

We were in the wyldwood that day, resting after a success-
ful hunt and just enjoying each other's company. We stood
on the banks of a clear green pond, my arms around her waist
and her head leaning against my chest, watching two piskies
tease an enormous carp by darting close to the surface, then
zipping away as the fish lunged for them. It was getting late,
but we were loath to go back to court; Winter fey tended to
be restless and irritable during the summer months, which led
to a great amount of squabbling and backbiting. Here in the
wyldwood, it was still and quiet, and only the most desperate
or savage of wild fey would consider taking on two powerful
Unseelie.

Abruptly, the peaceful silence was interrupted.

"There you are! Jeez, ice-boy, I've been looking for you
forever. If I didn't know better, I'd think you were *avoiding*
me."

I winced. Or him, of course. Nothing was sacred to him.

Ariella jerked in surprise. "Who—" She tried looking back,
only to find I wasn't moving or letting go. Groaning, I buried
my face in her hair. "Don't turn around," I muttered. "Don't
answer him, and maybe he'll go away."

"Hah, as if that ever works." The speaker moved closer, until I could see him from the corner of my eye, arms crossed
over a bare chest, perpetual smirk stretching his face. "You
know, if you keep ignoring me, ice-boy, I'm just going to push
you into the pond."

I released Ariella and stepped back from the edge, glaring
at Puck as he retreated with a cheerful grin. "What do you
want, Goodfellow?"

"So nice to see you as well, prince." Puck stuck his tongue
out, unfazed by my glare. "Guess the next time I find a juicy
rumor, I'll just keep it to myself. I thought you might want

to check out these coatl sightings in Mexico City, but I see you're otherwise occupied."

"Goodfellow?" Ariella repeated, staring at Puck with unabashed curiosity. "Robin Goodfellow? It *is* you, isn't it? The Puck?"

Puck grinned widely and bowed. "The one and only," he stated grandly as I felt the situation sliding further from my control. "And who might you be, lady who has stolen all of ice-boy's attention?" Before Ariella could answer, he sniffed and turned to me, pouting. "Prince, I'm hurt. After all we've been through, you could at least introduce me to your new lady friend."

"This is Ariella Tularyn," I introduced, refusing to rise to Puck's goading. "Ariella, this is Robin Goodfellow, who despite my best efforts, insists on hanging around when he isn't wanted."

"You wound me, prince." Puck looked anything but hurt, and I crossed my arms. "Um, I guess you're still mad about that whole harpy fiasco. I swear, I thought those caves were empty."

"How did you overlook a hundred harpies nesting in that cave? Did the giant carpet of bones not tip you off?"

"Oh, sure, complain now. But we found the trod to Athens, didn't we?"

Ariella blinked, looking back and forth between us. "Wait, wait," she said, holding up her hands. "You two know each other? Traveled together?" She frowned and looked at us both. "Are you friends?"

I snorted. "I wouldn't go that far."

"Oh, best friends, lady," Puck said at the same time, giving her a wink. "Ice-boy will deny it until the mountains crumble, but you know how hard it is for him to admit his feelings, right?"

"But, you're Summer." Ariella glanced back at me, confused. "Robin Goodfellow is part of the Seelie Court, right? Isn't it against the law to conspire with Summer fey?"

"Conspire?" Puck grinned, looking at me. "That's a nasty word. We don't conspire, do we, prince?"

"Puck." I sighed. "Shut up." Turning away from him, I drew Ariella close, ignoring the way Puck's eyes lit up gleefully. "The answer to your question is yes," I told her quietly. "It is against the law. And within the borders of Arcadia and Tir Na Nog, Robin Goodfellow and I are enemies. We will both readily admit that." I shot Puck a look, and he nodded, still grinning.

"But," I continued, "here in the wyldwood, the laws, though they're not completely flexible, don't extend quite as far. Puck and I have been known to…bend the rules a little. Not always, and not often. But, he's the only one that can keep up with me, and the only one who doesn't care that I'm part of the Winter Court."

Ariella pulled back and looked at me, her sea-green eyes intense. "So, you're telling me that you, a prince of the Unseelie Court, are admitting to breaking the law and conspiring with the Winter Court's sworn enemy on a regular basis?"

I held my breath. Though I'd known this day would come, I'd been hoping to bring up my…association…with Puck on my own terms. That the Summer Court prankster had forced the issue wasn't surprising, but what I feared most was being forced to choose where my loyalties lay. Ariella was still Unseelie, brought up to hate Summer and everything in it. If she decided Puck was the enemy and that we had no business involving him in anything that wasn't a fight to the death… what would I do then?

I sighed inwardly. I was a prince of the Unseelie Court. I would always side with my court and kith, there was no question in my mind. If it came down to that choice, I would turn my back on Puck, turn my back on our years of camaraderie, and choose Winter. But that's not to say it wouldn't be hard.

Ariella stared at us, and I waited to see what she would do, how she would react. Finally she broke into a teasing smile.

"Well, as I've seen how Ash treats his 'associates' at the Winter Court, I'd have to say you must be an exception to the rule, Robin Goodfellow. I'm very pleased to make your acquaintance." She glanced at me and winked. "And here I was afraid that Ash didn't have any friends."

Puck roared with laughter. "I like her," he announced as I crossed my arms and tried to look bored and annoyed. They both giggled at my expense, but I didn't care. Ariella had accepted my "association" without reservation or judgment. I didn't have to choose. I could keep the best of both worlds without sacrificing either.

I should've known it would never last.

"Prince," said Puck's voice, drawing me out of my dark thoughts, back to the present. "Prince. Oy, ice-boy!"

I blinked and glared at him. "What?"

He smirked and nodded to the sky, where a massive wall of black clouds loomed overhead. "There's a nasty storm coming. Furball suggests we look for shelter, since this area has a reputation for flash floods. According to him, we should reach the seer sometime tomorrow."

"Fine."

"Wow, aren't we chatty today." Puck shook his head as I strode past him, sliding down a washed-out gully to where Grimalkin waited at the bottom. Puck followed easily, continuing to talk. "That's the most you've said to me in two days. What's going on, ice-boy? You've been very broody lately, even for you."

"Leave it alone, Puck."

"And here I thought we were doing so well." Puck sighed dramatically as he matched my pace down the slope. "Might as well tell me, prince. You should know by now that I can't leave anything alone. I'll pry it out of you somehow."

Deep within, something dark stirred. A sleeping giant sensing change in the air, like a forgotten heartbeat, faint but still alive, beginning to resurface. It was something I hadn't felt, hadn't allowed myself to feel, in years. The part of me that was pure Unseelie, pure hate and darkness and bloodlust. I lost myself to it once, the day Ariella died. I became something consumed by rage, filled with a black hatred that turned me against my closest friend. I thought I'd buried it when I froze out my emotions, training myself to become numb, to feel nothing.

I could feel it in me now, an old madness, an ancient darkness rising to the surface, filling me with anger. And hate. Wounds that had never really closed, tearing open again, seeping poison into my heart. It disturbed me, and I shoved it down, back into the blackness it had come from. But I could still feel it, pulsing and bubbling just below the surface.

Directed solely at Puck, who was, of course, still talking.

"You know, it's not healthy to keep things bottled up, prince. The whole brooding thing is really overrated. So, come on, out with it. What's bothering—"

"I said—" Whirling abruptly, I came face-to-face with Puck, close enough to see my reflection in his startled green eyes. "Leave it alone, Puck."

For all his buffoonery, Robin Goodfellow was no fool. We'd known each other a long time, both as friends and rivals, and he knew me better than anyone, sometimes better than I knew myself. The irreverent smirk vanished, and his eyes became hard as stone. We stared at each other, inches apart, while the wind picked up and howled around us, stirring up a cyclone of leaves and dust.

"Having second thoughts?" Puck's voice was soft and dangerous, a far cry from his normal flippancy. "I thought we'd put this behind us for now."

"Never," I said, matching his stare. "I can't ever take it back, Goodfellow. I'm still going to kill you. I swore to her I would." Lightning flickered and thunder rumbled in the distance as we faced each other with narrowed eyes. "One day," I said softly. "One day you'll look up, and I'll be there. That's the only ending for us. Don't ever forget."

Puck slowly cocked his head, regarding me intently. "Is this Ash talking? Or the oath?"

"It doesn't matter." I stepped back, holding his gaze, unwilling to turn my back on him. "It can never be the same, Puck. Don't fool yourself into thinking that it is."

"I've never forgotten, prince." Puck watched me with solemn eyes glowing green in the sudden darkness. Lightning flashed through the trees again, and thunder growled an answer. Puck's next words were nearly lost in the wind. "You're not the only one with regrets."

I turned and walked away from him, feeling cold and empty, the darkness coiling around my heart. At the bottom of the slope, Grimalkin sat on a stump, tail curled over his feet, watching us with unblinking golden eyes.

WE FOUND A CAVE, or rather, an annoyed, impatient Grimalkin led us to a cave, seconds before the sky opened up and the rain poured down. As the light rapidly disappeared, I left Puck poking the fire and retreated to a dark corner. Sitting with my back against the wall, I pulled one knee to my chest and glowered into the distant flames.

"And so it begins."

Grimalkin appeared beside me, seated on a rock, watching Puck tend the campfire. The flames cast a burning orange halo around the cat. I gave him a sideways glance, but he didn't return it. "What do you mean?"

"I warned you this was no simple quest. I told you before, you and Goodfellow have no idea what lies ahead." He twitched an ear and shifted on the rock, still watching the fire. "You feel it, do you not? The anger. The darkness." I blinked in surprise, but Grimalkin paid no heed. "It will only get worse the farther we go."

"Where are we going?" I asked softly. A sudden hiss from the campfire showed Puck hanging a skinned rabbit over the flames. Where he'd gotten it, I didn't even want to guess, and I turned back to Grimalkin. "I know we're going to the seer, but you still haven't told us where."

The cait sith pretended not to hear. Yawning, he stretched languidly, raking his claws over the stones, and trotted off to oversee dinner preparations.

Outside, the storm howled and raged, bending trees and blowing rain at a sharp angle across the mouth of the cave. The fire crackled cheerfully, licking at the rabbit carcass, and the smell of roasted meat began to fill the chamber.

And yet, something wasn't right.

I rose and wandered to the cave mouth, gazing out at the storm. Wind tugged at me, spattering my face with raindrops. Beyond the lip of the cavern, rain skittered over the ground in waves, like silver curtains tossed by the wind.

Something was out there. Watching us.

"Hey, ice-boy." Puck appeared at my side, peering into the rain with me. He acted perfectly normal, as if the words between us earlier that day had never happened. "Whatcha looking at?"

"I don't know." I searched the trees, the shadows, my gaze

cutting through the storm, peeling back the darkness, but could see nothing unusual. "It feels like we're being watched."

"Huh." Puck scratched the side of his face. "I don't feel anything like that. And Furball is still here, so that's something. You know if there was anything dangerous coming he'd be gone faster than you could say *poof.* Sure you're not being paranoid?"

The rain continued to fall, and nothing moved beyond in the darkness and shadow. "I don't know," I said again. "Maybe."

"Well, you can stand here and worry. *I'm* going to eat. If you see something big and hungry coming at us, just ye—"

"Goodfellow."

My voice made him pause, then turn back, wary and guarded. We stared at each other by the mouth of the cave, the storm whipping at us and making the campfire flicker.

"Why are you here?"

He blinked, made a halfhearted attempt at humor. "Uh… because I don't want to get wet?"

I just waited. Puck sighed, leaning against the wall and crossing his arms. "Do we really have to go through this, ice-boy?" he said, and though the words were light, his tone was almost pleading. "I think we both know the reason I'm here."

"What if I asked you to leave?"

"Why would you want to do that?" Puck grinned, but it quickly faded. "This is about what happened earlier, isn't it?" he said. "What's going on, Ash? Two days ago, you were fine. We were fine."

I glanced over to where Grimalkin sat watching the spitted rabbit with something a bit stronger than curiosity. I could feel the darkness in me rising again, despite my attempts to freeze it out. "I'm going to kill you," I said softly, and Puck's eyebrows rose. "Not tonight. Maybe not tomorrow. But soon.

Our past is catching up to us, Goodfellow, and this feud has gone on long enough." I looked back at him, meeting his solemn gaze. "I'm giving you this chance now to leave. Run. Find Meghan, tell her what I'm trying to do. If I don't come back, take care of her for me." I felt my chest squeeze tight at the thought of Meghan, of never seeing her again. But at least Puck would be there for her if I failed. "Get out of here, Puck. It would be better for both of us if you were gone."

"Huh. Well, you sure know how to make a guy feel wanted, prince." Puck glared at me, not quite able to mask his anger. Pushing himself off the wall, he took a step forward, never looking away. "Here's a heads-up, though—I'm not going anywhere, no matter how much you threaten, bribe, coerce, or beg. Don't get me wrong, I'm mostly here for *her,* not you, but I'm betting this isn't something you can do alone. So you're going to have to suck it up and get used to me, prince, 'cause unless you want that duel right here, right now, I'm not leaving. And I can be just as stubborn as you."

Outside, lightning flickered, turning everything white, and the gale tossed the branches of the trees. Puck and I glared at each other until we were interrupted by a loud pop from the campfire. Breaking eye contact at last, Puck glanced over his shoulder and let out a yelp.

"Hey!" Whirling around, he stalked back toward the fire, and its now-empty spit, waving his arms. "My rabbit! Grimalkin, you sneaky, gray...pig! I hope you enjoy that, 'cause the next thing over the fire might be you!"

As expected, there was no answer. I smiled to myself and turned back to the rain. The violence of the storm had not abated, nor had my feeling of being watched, though continued searches of the trees and shadows yielded nothing.

"Where are you?" I mused under my breath. "I know you can see me. Why can't I find you?"

The storm seemed to mock me. I stood, looking out, until the wind finally died down and the rain slowed to a drizzle. All through the night, I stood there, waiting. But whatever was watching me from its mysterious location never made itself known.

CHAPTER FOUR
THE HUNTED

The next day dawned dim and ominous, with a persistent fog that clung to the ground and wrapped everything in opaque silence. Sounds were absorbed into the surrounding white, and it was impossible to see more than ten feet ahead.

We left the cave, following a smug Grimalkin into the wall of mist. The world looked different from the night before, hidden and lurking, the trees dark, crooked skeletons in the mist. No birds sang, no insects buzzed, no small creatures scurried through the undergrowth. Nothing moved or seemed to breathe. Even Puck was affected by the somber mood and offered little conversation as we glided through this still, muffled world.

The feeling of being watched had not dissipated even now, and was making me increasingly uncomfortable. Even more disturbing, I had the sense that something was following us, tracking us through the silent forest. I scanned the surrounding trees, the shadows and the undergrowth, watching, listening for something that seemed out of place. But I could see nothing.

The fog stubbornly refused to lift, and the farther we

pushed into the quiet wood, the stronger the feeling became. Finally, I stopped, turning to gaze behind us. Mist crept over the ground and spilled onto the tiny forest path we were following, and through the blanket of white, I could sense something drawing closer.

"There's something out there," I muttered as Puck came to stand beside me, also peering into the fog.

"Of course there is," Grimalkin replied matter-of-factly, leaping onto a fallen tree. "It has been following us since last night. The storm slowed it down a bit, but it is coming fast now. I suggest we hurry if we do not wish to meet it. And we do not, trust me."

"Is it the witch?" Puck asked, frowning as he stared into the bushes and the trees. "Geez, tie a house's feet together and you're marked for life. The old gal can sure hold a grudge, can't she?"

"It is not the witch," Grimalkin said with a hint of annoyance. "It is something far worse, I am afraid. Now come, we are wasting time." He leaped off the branch, vanishing into the mist, as Puck and I shared a glance.

"Worse than the old chicken plucker?" Puck made a face. "That's hard to believe. Can you think of anyone you'd rather not meet in a spooky old forest, prince?"

"Actually, I can," I said, and walked away, following Grimalkin through the trees.

"Hey!" Puck scrambled after us. "What's *that* supposed to mean, ice-boy?"

The forest stretched on, and Grimalkin never slowed, weaving through trees and under gnarled roots without looking back. I resisted the urge to glance continuously over my shoulder, half expecting the mist to part as whatever was following us lunged onto the path. I hated being hunted, being tracked by some unseen, unknown monster, but Grimalkin seemed determined to outpace it, and if I paused I could lose the cat in the fog. Somewhere behind us, a flock of crows took to the air with frantic cries, piercingly loud in the silence.

"It's close," I muttered, my hand dropping to my sword. Grimalkin didn't look back.

"Yes," he stated calmly. "But we are almost there."

"Almost *where?*" Puck chimed in, but at that moment the mist thinned and we found ourselves on the edge of a gray-green lake. Skeletal trees loomed out of the water, their expanding web of roots looking like pale snakes in the murk. Small, mossy islands rose from beneath the lake, and rope bridges spanned the gulf between them, some sagging low enough to nearly touch the surface.

"There is a colony of ballybogs living on the other side," Grimalkin explained, hopping lightly to the first rope bridge. He paused to glance back at us, waving his tail. "They owe me a favor. Hurry up."

Something went crashing through the bushes behind us—a pair of terrified deer, fleeing into the undergrowth. Grimalkin flattened his ears and started across the bridge. Puck and I followed.

The lake wasn't large, and we reached the other side a few minutes later, facing Grimalkin's annoyed glare as we stepped onto the muddy bank. Puck and I had systematically cut through each of the bridge ropes after every crossing, so whatever was following us would have to swim. Hopefully, that would slow it down a bit, but it also meant that we had burned our bridges, so to speak, if we wanted to return the same way.

"Uh-oh," Puck murmured, and I turned around.

A tiny village lay in the mud at the edge of the river, thatch and peat roofs covering primitive huts built into an embankment, peeking out between the roots of enormous trees.

Spears lay in the mud, some broken, and the roofs of several huts had been torn off. Silence hung thick over the village, the mist creeping up from the lake to smother what was left of the hamlet.

"Looks like something got here before us," Puck observed, picking a shattered spear out of the mud. "Did a number on the village, too. No one's here to welcome us, Grim. We'll have to try something else."

Grimalkin sniffed and jumped atop the bank, shaking mud from his paws. "How inconvenient." He sighed, looking around in distaste. "Now I will never receive my favor."

In the distance, somewhere beyond the mist coming off the water, there was a splash. Puck looked back and grimaced. "It's still coming, persistent bastard."

I drew my sword. "Then we make our stand here."

Puck nodded, pulling his daggers. "Thought you might say that. I'll find us some higher ground. Wrestling in the mud just isn't my cup of tea, unless it involves scantily clad—" He stopped as I shot him a look. "Right," he muttered. "That hill over there looks promising. I'll check it out."

Grimalkin followed my stare, blinking as Puck sloshed his way toward a lumpy mound of green moss and ferns. "That was not there the last time I was here," he mused softly, narrowing his gaze. "In fact..." His eyes widened.

And he disappeared.

I whirled back, lunging forward as Puck hopped onto the hill, pulling himself up by a twisted root. "Puck!" I shouted, and he glanced back at me, frowning. "Get out of there now!"

The hill moved. With a yelp, Puck stumbled, flailing wildly as the grassy mound shifted and lurched and started to rise out of the mud. Puck dove forward, landing with a splat in the mud, and the hill stood up, unfolding long, claw-tipped arms and thick, stumpy legs. It turned, twenty feet of muddy green swamp troll, moss and vegetation growing from its broad back, blending perfectly with the landscape. Dank green hair hung from its scalp, and its beady red eyes scanned the ground in confusion.

"Oh," Puck mused, gazing up at the enormous creature from the mud. "Well, that explains a few things."

The swamp troll roared, spittle flying from its open jaws, and took a step toward Puck, who bounced to his feet. It swiped a talon at him and he ducked, running under its enormous bulk, darting between the tree-stump legs. The troll roared and started to turn, and I flung a hail of ice daggers at it, sticking it in the shoulder and face. It bellowed and lurched toward me, making the ground shake as it charged. I dodged, rolling out of the way as the troll hit the embankment and ripped a huge gash through the huts, tearing them open.

As the troll pulled back, I lunged at it, swiping at its thick arms, cutting a deep gash through the barklike skin. It howled, more in anger than pain, and whirled on me.

There was movement on its broad shoulders, and Puck appeared, clinging to its back, a huge grin splitting his face. "All right," he announced grandly, as the troll jerked and spun around, trying in vain to reach him, "I claim this land for Spain." And he planted his dagger in the base of the troll's thick neck.

The creature roared, a shrill, painful wail, and clawed desperately at its back. Puck scooted away, avoiding the troll's raking talons, and stuck his dagger on the other side of its neck. It screeched again, slapping and tearing, and Puck scrambled away. With all its attention on Puck, I leaped forward, vaulted off a stumpy leg, and plunged my sword into the troll's chest.

It staggered, falling to its knees and with a deep groan, toppled into the mud as I ducked out of the way. Puck sprang off its shoulders as it collapsed, rolled as he hit the ground and came to his feet, grinning, though he looked like some kind of mud monster himself.

"Yes!" he exclaimed, shaking his head and flinging mud everywhere. "Man, that was fun. Better than playing Stay on the Wild Pegasus. Can we do it again?"

"Idiot." I wiped a splash of mud from my cheek with the back of my hand. "We're not done yet. Whatever is following us is still out there."

"Also, may I remind you," Grimalkin said, peering imperiously from the branches of a tall tree, "that swamp trolls, in particular, have two hearts and accelerated healing capabilities? You will have to do more than stick a sword in its chest if you wish to kill it for good."

Puck blinked. "So, you're saying that our mossy friend isn't really—"

There was a wet, sloshing sound behind us, and Grimalkin vanished again. Puck winced.

"Right, then," he muttered as we spun around. The swamp troll lumbered to its feet, its red eyes blazing and angry, fastened on us. "Round two." Puck sighed and swept his hand down in a chopping motion. "Fight!"

The troll roared. Effortlessly, it reached out and wrapped one claw around the trunk of a pine tree, pulling it from the mud as easily as picking a dandelion. With blinding speed, it smashed the weapon toward us.

Puck and I leaped aside in opposite directions, and the tree struck the space between with an explosion of mud and water. Almost immediately, the troll swept the tree across the ground, as if it was whisking away dust with a broom, and this time Puck wasn't quite able to dodge quickly enough. The trunk hit him and sent his body tumbling through the air, striking his head on another tree and slumping into the mud several yards away. Red-eyed, the troll turned back to me, stepping forward threateningly. I retreated until my back hit the wall of the embankment, and I tensed as the huge troll loomed over me, raising its club over its head and smashing it down like a battering ram.

Something big and dark lunged between us with a booming snarl, and a monstrous shaggy *thing* slammed into the troll, teeth flashing. The troll screeched and stumbled back, its arm clamped in the jaws of an enormous black wolf the size of a grizzly bear, who growled and shook his head, digging his fangs in farther. Howling, the troll flailed and yanked back, trying desperately to dislodge the monster clinging to its arm, but the wolf wasn't letting go. I caught my breath, recognizing the creature, knowing who it was, but there was no time to wonder why he was here.

Dodging the wolf, I ducked beneath the troll's legs and turned, slashing the thick tendons behind its knees. With a shriek, the troll's legs buckled, and I leaped onto its back, much as Puck had done, as it went down. But this time, I raised my sword and drove it, point first, into the troll's head, right between the horns, burying the weapon to the hilt.

A shudder wracked the troll's body. It began to stiffen, its skin turning gray and hard. I yanked my sword free and vaulted off its back as the troll curled up on itself, much like a giant insect or spider, and turned to stone. In a few seconds, only a troll-shaped boulder sat in the mud at the edge of the village.

There was a deep chuckle beside me. "Not bad, little prince. Not bad."

Slowly, I turned, gripping my weapon, ready to unleash my glamour in one violent, chaotic burst. A few yards away, the enormous wolf of legend stared at me, eyes glowing yellow-green in the gloom, fangs bared in a vicious smile.

"Hello, prince," rumbled the Big Bad Wolf. "I told you before. The next time we meet, you won't ever see me coming."

I STARED AT THE WOLF, keeping him in my sights as he circled me, fangs bared in a savage grin, huge paws sinking into the mud. Around and inside me, glamour flared, cold and lethal, ready to be unleashed. I couldn't hold anything back, not with him. This was possibly the most dangerous, ancient creature to ever walk the wilds of the Nevernever. His stories outnumbered all the myths and legends ever told, and his power grew with every telling, every dire warning and fable that whispered his name. His legends were all born of fear; he was the consummate villain, the creature that old wives warned their children about, a monster that consumed little girls and butchered entire herds for no reason. His brethren in the mortal world had suffered terribly for the fears that birthed him—they had been gunned down, trapped, and slaughtered wholesale—but each death reinforced those fears and made him more powerful than before.

The immortal Big Bad Wolf. Meghan and I had met him once before, and he'd almost succeeded in killing me.

That wouldn't happen again.

"Put that stick away." The Wolf's voice, guttural and deep, held traces of amusement. "If I wanted you dead, I wouldn't have bothered saving your sorry carcass from the swamp troll. That's not to say I won't kill you later, but your silly little toy won't stop me then, either, so you might as well be civil about it."

I kept my sword out, which I could see annoyed the Wolf, but I was certainly not going down without a fight. "What do you want?" I asked, keeping my voice cautiously civil, but letting the Wolf know I would defend myself if needed.

I was going to walk away from this. It didn't matter that the Wolf was immortal. It didn't matter that he'd almost killed me last time we'd met. If it came down to a fight, I was determined to win this time, by any means necessary. I would not die here, on the banks of a gloomy lake, torn apart by the Big Bad Wolf. I would survive this encounter and keep going. Meghan was waiting for me.

The Wolf smiled. "Mab sent me for you," he said in a voice that was almost a purr.

I kept my expression neutral, though an icy fist grabbed my stomach and twisted. Not in surprise, or even fear, just the knowledge that, as she did with all her subjects, the Winter Queen had finally grown tired of me. Perhaps she was insulted by my refusal to return to court. Perhaps she'd decided that a former Winter prince running around free was too volatile, a threat to her throne. The *whys* didn't matter. Mab had sent the most feared hunter and assassin in the entire Nevernever to kill me.

I sighed, suddenly feeling very tired. "I suppose I should be honored," I told him, and he cocked his enormous shaggy head, still grinning. Taking a furtive breath, I calmed my mind, the glamour settling into a low, throbbing pulse. "We won't get anywhere standing around looking at each other," I told him, raising my sword. "Let's get on with it, then."

The Wolf chuckled. "As much as I'd enjoy ripping your head off, little prince," he said, and his eyes gleamed, "I am not here to end your life. Quite the opposite, in fact. Mab sent me here to help you."

I stared at him, hardly able to believe what I'd just heard. "Why?"

The Wolf shrugged, his huge shoulders rippling with the movement. "I do not know," he said, and yawned, flashing lethal fangs. "Nor do I care. The Winter Queen knows of your quest; she knows you will probably have to journey far to complete it. I am here to make sure you reach your destination with your guts on the inside. In return, she will owe me a favor." He sniffed the air and sat down, watching me with half-lidded eyes. "Beyond that, I have no interest in you. Or the Summer prankster. Who, if he wants his head to remain on his shoulders, will think long and hard about jumping me from behind. Next time, try standing downwind, Goodfellow."

"Damn." Puck appeared from a clump of reeds, a chagrined smile on his face, glaring at the Wolf. "I knew I was forgetting something." Blood caked one side of his face, but other than that, he seemed fine. Brandishing his daggers, he sauntered up beside me, facing the huge predator. "Working for Mab now, are you, Wolfman?" he smirked. "Like a good little attack dog? Will you also roll over and beg if she asks?"

The Wolf rose, looming over both of us, the hair on his spine bristling. I resisted the urge to hit Goodfellow, even though I knew what he was doing; taunting an opponent for more information. "I am not a *dog*," the Wolf growled, his deep voice making the puddles ripple. "And I work for no one." He curled his lips in a sneer. "The favor of the Winter Queen is a substantial reward, but do not think you can order me around like the weak creatures of men. I will see you to the end of your quest alive." He growled again and bared his teeth. "The request said nothing about whole."

"You're not here for a favor," I said, and he blinked, eyeing me suspiciously. "You don't need one," I continued, "not from Mab, not from anyone. You enjoy the hunt, and the challenge, but to agree to such a request without a kill at the end? That's not like you." The Wolf continued to stare at us, his face betraying nothing. "Why are you really here?" I asked. "What do you want?"

"The only thing he really cares about—" A disembodied voice came from overhead, and Grimalkin appeared in the branches of a tree, nearly twenty feet off the ground. "Power."

The hair on the Wolf's back and shoulders bristled, though he gazed at Grimalkin with a faint, evil smile on his long muzzle. "Hello, cat," he said conversationally. "I thought I caught your stench creeping through the air. Why not come down here and talk about me?"

"Do not demean yourself by stating the ridiculous," Grimalkin replied smoothly. "Just because my species is vastly superior does not mean you should flaunt your idiocy so freely. I know why you are here, dog."

"Really," Puck called, craning his head to look up at the cat. "Well then, would you like to share your theory, Furball?"

Grimalkin sniffed. "Do you people not know anything?" Standing up, he walked along the branch, the Wolf's gaze following him hungrily. "He is here because he wishes to add his name to your tale. His power, his entire existence, comes from stories, from myths and legends and all the dark, frightening and amusing tales about him that humans have invented over the years. It is how the Big Bad Wolf has survived for so long. It is how *you* have survived for centuries, Goodfellow. Surely you know this."

"Well, yeah, of course I knew *that*," Puck scoffed, crossing his arms. "But that still doesn't tell me why Wolfman is being so helpful all of a sudden."

"You are on a quest," the Wolf went on, finally tearing his gaze away from the cat to look at me. "The queen told me of this. That you, a soulless and immortal being, wish to become human for the mortal you love." He paused and shook his head in grudging admiration, or perhaps pity. "*That* is a story. That is a tale that will endure for generations, if you can survive the trials, of course. But even if you don't, even if this tale becomes a tragedy, my name will still be in it, adding to my strength." He narrowed his eyes, staring me down. "Of course, it would be a better tale if you manage to reach your destination. I can help you in that respect. It will make the story longer anyway."

"What makes you think we need, or want, your help?" Grimalkin asked loftily.

The Wolf gave me an eerie smile, all fangs, and his eyes glinted in the shadows. "I will be in this tale one way or another, little prince," he warned. "Either as the great wolf that protects and guides you to your destination, or as the tireless evil that tracks you through the night, haunting your steps and your dreams. I have been both, and such roles are easy for me to slip into. I leave the choice to you."

We stared at each other for a long moment, two hunters sizing each other up, checking strengths and weaknesses. Finally, I nodded and carefully sheathed my blade.

"All right," I said as Puck blinked and Grimalkin snorted in disgust. "I'll accept your help for now. But I make no promises about our continued alliance."

"Neither do I, boy." The Wolf regarded me the way a cat would observe a mouse. "So, now that we have an understanding, what should we do first?"

Overhead, Grimalkin sighed, very loudly. "Unbelievable," he said, and the Wolf grinned at him and ran a pink tongue over his jaws. Grimalkin was not impressed. "May I remind you," he continued in that same bored, annoyed tone, "that out of this entire party, only *I* know the way to the seer. And if a certain dog forgets its manners, you will all be up the river without a paddle, so to speak. Remember that, prince."

"You heard him," I told the Wolf, who curled a lip at me.

"No chasing or attacking our guide. We still need him to reach the seer."

"Please." Grimalkin sniffed, and leaped to another branch. "As if I would ever allow that to happen. This way, and do try to keep up."

CHAPTER FIVE
THE HOLLOW

After leaving the lake and the dead ballybog village, we followed Grimalkin through another tangled forest and across a rocky plateau, the great black Wolf trailing noiselessly behind us. The two animals didn't speak to each other, but the Wolf kept his distance from the cat, even when traveling across the open plains, so it seemed that they had worked out some sort of truce. A basilisk stirred on a rocky shelf, eyeing us hungrily as we passed beneath, but the Wolf silently curled his lip, baring his fangs, and the monster appeared to lose interest.

After we crossed the plateau, the ground turned sharply downhill and thick, thorny brambles started appearing, choking out the trees. When we reached the bottom of the slope, the briars rose around us like a spiny maze, ragged wisps of fog caught between their branches. The ground was wet and spongy, saturated with water, mud and something else. Something dark had seeped into the earth, turning the ground black and poisoned. The air was still, silent as a grave; nothing moved in the shadows or between the thorns, not even insects.

"This is as far as I go."

Startled, we both turned to Grimalkin, sitting tightly on a patch of dry ground, watching us. "From here," he said, regarding each of us in turn, "you are on your own."

"What?" Puck exclaimed. "You mean you're not going to venture into the hollow of death with us? Shocking. What kind of monster do you think lives here, ice-boy? It has to be pretty nasty for Furball to flake out on us. Oh, wait…"

Grimalkin flattened his ears but otherwise ignored the Summer faery. The Wolf sniffed the air, growled low in his chest, and the hackles rose along his spine. "This place," he muttered, curling a lip, "is not right." He shook himself and took a step forward. "I'll scout ahead, see if it's—"

"No," Grimalkin said, and the Wolf turned on him with a growl. The cait sith faced him seriously, his yellow eyes intense. "You must remain here. The valley will not tolerate intruders. This part of the journey is for them, and them alone."

The Wolf and the cat locked eyes, staring each other down. Grimalkin did not blink, and something in the cat's steady gaze must have convinced the much larger wolf. Reluctantly, he nodded and took a step back. "Very well," he growled. "I will scout along the perimeter, then." He shot a glare at me and Puck. "If you two need my help, just scream."

He turned swiftly and trotted away, melting into the shadows and the trees. Grimalkin watched him go and turned to us.

"I have brought you as far as I can," he said, rising gracefully to his feet, plumed tail waving. "The final few steps are up to you." His gaze narrowed, watching us grimly. "Both of you."

A coil of mist curled across the place where Grimalkin sat, and he was gone.

Puck crossed his arms, gazing past the edge of the valley

into the darkness and thorns. "Yep." He sighed. "A really, really nasty monster, indeed."

I gazed into the hollow, watching the mist writhe through the thorns, creating shadows and dragons where there was nothing. Silence hung thick on the air; not a peaceful, serene silence, but the silence of a tomb, or the aftermath of a battle, where death and darkness thrived and the living had no place. I could hear the whispers of hate and fear that hissed through the brambles, ghosts on the wind. I could hear them call my name.

Something in me recoiled, reluctant to set foot in that dark valley. It was waiting for me, somewhere beyond the mist. Still watching.

Filled with a foreboding I couldn't explain, I drew back, then stopped, angry with myself. Why this sudden fear? Fear meant nothing to me. Fear was the knowledge of pain, the awareness that you could be hurt, that you could die. That was all it came down to. I knew pain. Intimately. I'd welcomed it at times, because it meant I could still feel, that I wasn't completely frozen. What more could anything do to my body that I hadn't already lived through?

Nodding to Puck, I drew my sword and stepped into the hollow, feeling the mist coil around me as we slipped into the fog.

A gray shroud enveloped us instantly, lit by a flat, even glow that somehow managed to darken everything. Nothing moved in the hollow; all life had been swallowed by the thick black briars that sprang up everywhere, choking everything out. The ground beneath us was wet and spongy, though the writhing layer of mist made it impossible to see what we were stepping on.

As I moved through the brambles, my sword held up and ready, I began to sense the wrongness of the valley, right below my feet. The ground pulsed with hate and blood and despair; I could feel it clawing at me, the darkness of this place. I could feel my Unseelie nature rise up in response, cold, ruthless and angry.

"This place is cursed," Puck muttered as I struggled to control myself, to stifle the darkness rising within. "We need to find this seer and get out of here, soon."

"Ash," something whispered through the brambles, raising the hair on my neck. I whirled, but no one was there.

"Ice-boy?" Puck stepped forward, eyes narrowed in concern. "Ash. You all right?"

And, for just a moment, I wanted to kill him. I wanted to take my sword and plunge it deep into his chest, to watch the light fade from his eyes right before he crumpled at my feet. Turning away, I struggled to compose myself, to stifle the cold rage ebbing through me. The demon inside was stirring, unwilling to hold back any longer, and the core of the rage was directed, like a spearhead, at Puck.

"Ash," the voice whispered again, and I looked up.

Several yards away, barely visible through the mist, a ghostly, glowing figure walked through a space between the briars, catching my eye and then vanishing from sight. My breath caught in my throat.

Forgetting Puck, forgetting everything that had brought us here, I followed the figure into the mist. Voices hissed at me through the brambles, faint and incomprehensible, though every so often I heard them whisper my name. I caught glimpses of the lone figure through the branches, always walking away from me, just out of reach. Somewhere in the mist, I heard Puck call my name as he tried to follow, but I ignored him. Ahead of me, the thorns finally thinned, and the ghostly figure strode purposefully forward, never glancing back. It turned a corner, and I hurried to catch up....

The brambles fell away, and I found myself in a small clearing, thick briars hemming me in on either side. Before me, rising out of the mist, a bleached-white skeleton lay sprawled in the mud and stagnant water of the clearing. The skeleton was huge, an enormous reptilian creature with thick hind legs and a long, powerful tail. Wingbones lay folded beneath it, snapped and broken, and the huge jaws were open in a last, silent roar.

I started to shake. Not with fear, but with complete, all-consuming fury, and despair burned my throat like bile. I knew this place. I recognized where we were at last. It was here, on this spot, that Puck, Ariella and I had fought and killed a monstrous wyvern, slaying it but losing one of our own in the process. This was the hollow where Ariella died. This was the place where I'd vowed to kill Puck. It had all started right here.

It would end here, as well.

"Ash!" Footsteps splashed behind me, as Puck came into the clearing and stumbled to a halt, panting. "Dammit, ice-boy, what's gotten into you? Next time, give me a heads-up that you're taking off. Don't leave a guy standing in a creepy, mist-filled hollow of death all by himself."

"Do you know where we are?" I asked softly, not turning around. I felt his puzzlement, then heard his sudden intake of breath as he realized. I gripped my sword and spun slowly to face him, feeling darkness spread through me like a rush of ink. The Unseelie demon was fully awake now, the icy barrier that held it at bay shattered. Memories rose up, fresh and painful: the hunt, the chase into the hollow at Puck's insistence, the roar of the monster as it charged with lethal speed. Rage and despair swirled around me; whether mine or the memories of this dark place, I didn't know. Nor did I care. Meeting Puck's eyes, I started forward.

"Ash," Puck said, backing away, his eyes wary and hooded, "wait. What are you doing?"

"I told you." I advanced steadily, calmly, the sword heavy in my hand. "I warned you that it would be soon. It's time, Puck. Today."

"Not now." He paled, and drew his daggers. I didn't stop, and he circled with me, his weapons held up and ready. "Ash, get a hold of yourself," he said, almost pleading. "We can't do this now. You're not here for *her*."

"Look at where we are!" I roared, sweeping my blade toward the bleached skeleton in the mud. "If not now, when? This is the place, Puck! This is the place she died. I lost Ariella right here. Because of *you!*" My voice broke, and I sucked in a breath as Puck stared at me with wide eyes. I'd never said those words to him; it was always an unspoken feud that drove us to fight each other. We both knew the reason, but I'd never accused Puck out loud, until now.

"You know I didn't mean for that to happen." Puck's voice shook as we continued to circle each other, blades bare and glittering in the faint light. "I loved her, too, prince."

"Not like me." I couldn't stop myself now. The rage was a cold, all-consuming fire, fed from the darkness of the earth, from the grief and hate and painful memories that had seeped into this spot. "And that doesn't change the fact that her death is on your head. If I'd killed you when we first met, like I was supposed to, she would still be alive!"

"You don't think I know that?" Puck was shouting now, green eyes feverish. "You don't think I regret what I did, every single day? You lost Ariella, but I lost you both! Believe it or not, I was kind of a mess, too, Ash. It got to a point where I actually looked forward to our random duels, because that was the only time I could talk to you. When you were freaking trying to kill me!"

"Don't compare your loss to mine," I snarled. "You have no idea what I went through, what you caused."

"You think I don't know pain?" Puck shook his head at me. "Or loss? I've been around a lot longer than you, prince! I know what love is, and I've lost my fair share, too. Just because we have a different way of handling it, doesn't mean I don't have scars of my own."

"Name one," I scoffed. "Give me one instance where you haven't—"

"Meghan Chase!" Puck roared, startling me into silence. I blinked, and he sneered at me. "Yeah, your highness. I know what loss is. I've loved that girl since before she knew me. But I waited. I waited because I didn't want to lie about who I was. I wanted her to know the truth before anything else. So I waited, and I did my job. For years, I protected her, biding my time, until the day she went into the Nevernever after her brother. And then you came along. And I saw how she looked at you. And for the first time, I wanted to kill you as much as you wanted to kill me.

"So, here, prince!" he said, and without warning, flipped his daggers at me. They struck the ground at my feet, hilts up, glinting in the dim light. "I'm tired of fighting. You want your revenge?" He straightened and flung his arms wide, glaring at me. "Come and take it! This is the place where she died, where it all started. Here I am, Ash—strike me down already. I won't even fight you. Let's end this, once and for all!"

The rage in me boiled. Raising my sword, I went for him, sweeping the blade down at his neck, a blow that would slice through his collarbone and out the other side. I *would* end this, right here. Puck didn't move, nor did his gaze stray from mine as I lunged forward. He didn't flinch as the weapon sliced down in a blur of icy blue—

—and stopped.

My hands shook, and the sword trembled against Puck's collarbone, the edge drawing the faintest line of red against his skin. I was panting, breathing hard, but he still watched me, his face blank, and I could see my tortured reflection in his eyes. *Do it,* the rage whispered as I struggled to make my arms move, to finish what I'd started. *Strike him down. This is what you've always wanted. End the feud, and keep your promise.*

Puck took a deep, careful breath and spoke softly, almost a whisper. "If you're going to do it, prince, do it now. The anticipation is killing me."

I straightened, bracing myself for the deed. Robin Goodfellow would die today. It had to end like this. It didn't matter that Puck had lost just as much as I had, that his pain was just as great, that he loved Meghan enough to step aside, to bow out gracefully. Never mind that he loved her so much he would join his sworn enemy on a search for the impossible, just to ensure her happiness. He was here, not because of me, but because of her. None of that mattered. I had sworn an oath, here, on this very spot, and I had to see it through.

I gripped the sword handle, steeling myself. Puck stood rock-still, waiting. I raised the sword again…and whirled away with a roar of frustration, flinging my weapon into the nearest bramble patch.

Puck couldn't quite conceal his sigh of relief as I stalked away, retreating into the mist and out of sight before I fell apart. Dropping to my knees, I slammed my fist into the mud and bowed my head, wishing the earth would open up and swallow me whole. I shook with anger, with grief and self-loathing and regret. Regret of what transpired here. That I had failed. That I had ever made that vow to kill my closest friend.

I'm sorry, Ariella. Forgive me. I'm weak. I wasn't able to keep my promise.

How long I knelt there, I didn't know. Perhaps only minutes, but before I could really compose myself, I had the sudden knowledge that I wasn't alone. Wondering if Puck was really foolish enough to bother me now, I raised my head.

It wasn't Puck.

A robed figure stood at the edge of the mist, pale and indistinct, blending into the surrounding fog. Its cowl was raised, showing nothing but darkness beneath the hood, but I could feel its eyes on me, watching.

I rose slowly, muscles tensed to leap away should the stranger make any move to attack. I wished I had my sword, but there was no time to regret that now.

Watching the stranger, I felt a glimmer of recognition. We'd met before, recently in fact. This was the same presence I had felt in my nightmare of the Iron Realm, the one keeping just out of sight, holding me to the dreamworld. And as my memory returned with the shattered pieces of my composure, I finally recalled why we were here, who we had come to find.

"You are...the seer?" I asked softly. My voice came out shaky and was swallowed by the coiling fog, but the robed figure nodded. "Then...you know why I've come."

Another nod. "Yes," the seer whispered, its voice softer than the mist around us. "I know why you are here, Ash of the Winter Court. The real question is...do you?"

I took a breath to answer, but the seer stepped forward and pushed back its hood.

The world fell out from under me. I stared, staggered and frozen in a way that had nothing to do with winter.

"Hello, Ash," Ariella whispered. "It's been a long time."

PART TWO

CHAPTER SIX
THE SEER

I stared at the figure before me, hardly able to wrap my mind around it. It looked like Ariella, sounded like her. Even after all these years, I knew the exact lilt of her voice, the subtlest tilt of her head. But…it wasn't her. It couldn't be. This was a trick, or perhaps a memory, brought to life by the depth of emotion around us. Ariella was dead. She had been for a long time.

"No," I whispered, shaking my head, trying desperately to regain my scattered wits. "This…this isn't real. You're not real. Ariella is…gone." My voice broke, and I shook my head angrily. "This isn't real," I repeated, willing my heart to believe it. "Whatever you are, leave this place. Don't torment me further."

The robed figure glided forward, coils of mist parting for her as she came toward me. I wanted to move, to draw back, but my body wasn't working right anymore. I might as well have been frozen, helpless, as the thing that looked like Ariella drew very close, so close I could see the flecks of silver in her eyes, smell the faint scent of cloves that had always surrounded her.

Ariella gazed at me a moment, then raised one pale, slender hand and laid it—cool and solid—against my cheek.

"Does this feel like a memory, Ash?" she whispered as my breath hitched and my knees nearly buckled. I closed my eyes, unwilling to hope, to have it ripped from me once more. Taking my limp hand, Ariella guided it to her chest and trapped it there, so I could feel the heartbeat under my fingers. "Does this?"

Disbelief crumbled. "You're alive," I choked out, and she smiled at me, a sad, painful smile that held all the years of loss and despair I knew so well. Her grief had been just as fierce, just as consuming, as mine. "You're alive," I whispered again, and pulled her to me.

Her arms slid around my waist, drawing us even closer, and she breathed my name. I held her fiercely, half-afraid she would dissolve into mist in my arms. I felt her heartbeat, thudding against mine, listened to her breath on my cheek, and felt the centuries-old grief dissolving, melting like frost in the sunlight. I could barely believe it; I didn't know how it could be, but Ariella was alive. She was alive. The nightmare was finally over.

It seemed like an eternity before we finally pulled back, but my shock was no less severe. And when she looked at me with those star-flecked eyes, my mind still had trouble accepting what was right in front of me. "How?" I asked, unwilling to let her go just yet. Wanting—needing—to feel her, solid and real and alive, pressed against me. "I watched you die."

Ariella nodded. "Yes, it wasn't a very pleasant experience," she said, and smiled at my bewildered expression. "There are…a lot of things that need explaining," she continued, and a shadow darkened her face. "I have so much to tell you, Ash. But not here." She slid back, out of my arms. "I have a place not far from here. Go collect Robin Goodfellow, and then I can tell you both."

A strangled noise interrupted us. I turned to see Puck standing several yards away, staring at Ariella with an open mouth. His green eyes were wider than I'd ever seen them.

"I'm...seeing things," he stammered, and his gaze flickered to me. For just a moment, I saw hope flare in their depths. "Ash? Tell me you see her, too."

Incredibly, Ariella smiled at him. "Hello, Puck. It's good to see you again. And, no...you're not seeing things. It's really me." She held up her hand as Puck took a breath. "I know you both have many, many questions, but this is not the place to ask them. Follow me, and then I will try to explain everything."

NUMBLY, I COLLECTED MY SWORD from where I'd flung it discourteously into the briars, and we followed Ariella through the mist and brambles, her spectral form gliding through the fog like a ghost. Each time the mist coiled around her pale figure, my heart twisted in fear, certain that when the tendrils pulled away she would be gone. Behind me, Puck was silent; I knew he was just as dazed, trying to come to terms with what we had just seen and heard. I was still reeling from the shock, from questions that swirled maddeningly in my head, and Puck was the last person I wanted to talk to.

We trailed Ariella through a thick hedge, where the mist cleared away and the briars formed a protective wall around a snowy glen. Glamour filled the tiny space, creating the illusion of gently falling snow, of icicles that hung on branches and a chill in the air, but not everything was fantasy. A clear pool glimmered in the center of the clearing, and a lone elder tree stood beside it, its branches heavy with purple berries. Shelves full of jars, dried plants and simple bone tools had been worked into the bramble, and a narrow bed stood beneath an overhang of woven thatch and ice.

Ariella walked over to a shelf and brushed imaginary dust from between two jars, seeming to collect her thoughts. I gazed around the clearing in wonder. "Is...is this where you live?" I asked. "All this time, you've been here?"

"Yes." Ariella took a deep breath and turned around, smoothing back her hair. She'd always done that when she was nervous. "Sit, if you want." She gestured to an old log, rubbed smooth and shiny with use, but I couldn't bring myself to sit. Neither could Puck, apparently.

"So, how long have you been here, Ari?" he asked, and I instantly bristled at the casual use of his old nickname for her. He had no right to speak to her as if nothing had happened. As if everything was all right now. "Have you been here since...that day? All alone?"

She nodded, smiling tiredly. "It's not the Winter palace by any means, but I make do."

Irritation boiled over into real anger now. I tried to stifle it, but it rose up anyway as the blackest years of my existence seemed to descend on me all at once. She had been here all along, and never thought to see me, to let us know she was still alive. All those years of fighting, killing, all for nothing. "Why didn't you tell me?" I demanded, and she winced as though she'd been expecting that question.

"Ash, believe me, I wanted to—"

"But you didn't." I stalked over to the elder tree, because I couldn't remain motionless any longer. Her gaze followed me as I whirled back, gesturing to the glade. "You've been here for years, Ari, and you never came back, never made any attempt to see me again. You let me think you were dead! *Why?*" I was near shouting now, my composure shattered, but I couldn't help it. "You could've sent word, let me know you were all right! All those years of thinking you were gone, that you were dead. Did you know what I was going through? What we both were going through?"

Puck blinked, startled that I would include him as well. I ignored him, however, still facing Ariella, who watched me sadly but offered no argument. I let my arms drop, and my anger vanished as quickly as it had come. "Why didn't you tell me?" I whispered.

"Because, had I returned, you would have never met Meghan Chase."

I froze at the sound of her name.

Ariella sighed, a gesture that seemed to age her a hundred years, and smoothed back her hair once more. "I'm not explaining it well at all," she mused, almost to herself. "Let me start again, from the beginning. The day…I died."

"I'VE ALWAYS BEEN A LITTLE BIT of a seer," Ariella began, gazing not at me, but at the pool in the center of the glade, as if she could glimpse the future within. "Even before the… accident…I could sometimes predict things. Small things, never important. Never enough to threaten or compete with the factions at court. My father tried to use my gift to rise to power, but he soon gave up when he realized my visions never showed me anything useful.

"That day in the hollow," she continued, her voice growing even softer, "when the wyvern struck me, something happened. I felt myself die, my essence fade, becoming part of the Nevernever. There was darkness, and then I had a dream… a vision…of the Iron fey, the chaos that would come. And then…I don't know. I found myself waking up, alone, in the place where I died. And I knew what was coming. The Iron fey. They would destroy us, except for her.

"One girl. The half daughter of Oberon, Meghan Chase.

When the time came, when the Iron King set his plans into motion at last, she would save us—if she could survive to face the challenges ahead."

Ariella paused, smoothing back her hair, her eyes on something I could not see. "I had many visions of Meghan Chase," she went on in a distant voice. "I saw her struggles as clearly as if they were happening to me. The future is always changing—never is there a clear path to the end, and some of the visions were terrible. I saw her die many, many times. And each time she perished, the Iron fey would overcome Faery. The Iron King triumphed in the end, darkness overtook the Nevernever, and everything we knew was destroyed."

"But she didn't fail," Puck broke in. "She won. She led an army of Iron fey to the false king's fortress, kicked down the door, turned the old geezer into a tree, and became the new queen. Because of her, the Iron fey aren't poisoning the Nevernever anymore, as long as they stay within their territory. Definitely not the Armageddon you predicted, Ari."

Ariella nodded. "Yes, and I saw those futures as well, Robin Goodfellow. But she was never alone. You were always there with her, you and Ash both. You kept her safe, helped her succeed. In the end, she defeated the final evil and claimed her destiny, but you were the ones who enabled her to do it. She would have died without your help."

Ariella sighed, fiddling with the branches of the tree, her gaze distant again. "I had my own part to play, of course," she continued hesitantly, as if the things she'd done were somehow distasteful. "I was the puppet master, pulling the strings, making sure all the pieces were in place before her arrival. I watched for the signs of her coming. I began the whispers that Leanansidhe was planning to overthrow the courts, leading to her exile. I suggested the girl have a guardian to watch over her in the mortal world. And I made sure that a certain cat would be on the lookout for the half-human daughter of the Summer King, should she happen to fall into his tree one day."

I felt breathless, stunned. All the while I'd been venting my anger and grief against Puck, the cause of my suffering had been preparing for something far greater. And she hadn't even been able to tell me about it.

Ariella paused then, closing her eyes, her mouth tightening. "I knew you would fall in love with her, Ash," she whispered. "The visions showed me, years before you would see her for the first time. I wanted to go to you, to let you know that I was alive. I knew what you were going through, I heard of your oath against Puck. I wanted to tell you so badly." Her voice wavered, making my gut twist. "But I couldn't. I had to let you meet her, fall in love with her, become her knight. Because she needed you. And because we all needed her to succeed. I believe Faery itself brought me back to ensure the success of Meghan Chase. I couldn't let my feelings for you stand in the way. I...I had to let you go." She took a deep breath, and her voice hardened. "I *chose* to let you go.

"I knew you would come here." Ariella faced me, the stars glittering in her turquoise eyes. "Eventually, I knew you would come. I know your quest, Ash. And I know why you're here. You want to become human, to be mortal, so you can go back to her. But things aren't so black-and-white now, are they? And so I will ask a question of you. I know what you must do to become mortal. But the road will be hard, and some of us might not survive it. So, this is my question. Do you still want to become human? Do you still want to be with Meghan Chase?"

I took a slow breath to calm my churning mind. I couldn't answer, not when the love decades dead was standing not five yards away staring at me. Without a word, I turned and left the glade, back into the mist-shrouded hollow and the silence of my own thoughts. I felt Ariella's eyes on me as I left, but she did not follow.

Alone, I stood in the place where Ariella died, the great wyvern skeleton curled around the edge, and tried to process all that had happened. She was alive. All this time, she had been alive, knowing I was out there, watching, yet unable to contact me. She had been alone for so long. It must have been horrible for her. If the situation had been reversed, and I was the one watching, knowing she would fall for another, it would have driven me insane. I wondered if she had waited for this day, the day I finally returned to this spot, hoping that we could be together again.

But there was someone else now. Someone who waited for me, who knew my True Name and commanded my loyalty. Someone I'd made a promise to.

I felt Puck's presence at my back but didn't turn around. "This is crazy, isn't it?" he muttered, coming to stand beside me. "Who would've thought she was here all this time? If I had known..." He sighed, crossing his arms to his chest, letting his voice trail off. "Things sure would've turned out differently, wouldn't they?"

"How did you know?" I asked without turning around, and felt his confused frown at my back. "How did you know I wouldn't kill you?"

"I didn't," Puck said with forced cheerfulness. "I was really, really hoping you wouldn't. That would've sucked a lot, I think." He stepped closer, joining me in staring at the dead wyvern. His next words, when they came, were very soft. "So, is this thing between us finally over?"

I didn't look at him. "Ariella's alive," I murmured. "I think that dissolves the oath—I no longer have to avenge her death. So, if that's true, then...yes." I paused, waiting to see if the words felt right, if I could say what I'd wanted to say for decades. If the words were a lie, I would not be able to speak them. "It's over."

It's over.

Puck let out a sigh and let his head fall back, running his hands through his hair, a relieved grin crossing his face. I shot him a sideways glance. "That doesn't mean we're all right," I warned, mostly out of habit. "Just because I'm not sworn to kill you anymore doesn't mean I won't."

But it was an empty threat, and we both knew it. The relief of not *having* to kill Puck, being free from an oath I never wanted, was too great. I wasn't failing anyone by letting him live. For now, the Unseelie demon inside me had been sated.

Though I'd spoken the truth when I'd said we weren't all right. There was still too much fighting, too much anger and hate and bad blood between us. We both had years of words and actions we regretted, old wounds that went too deep. "Puck," I said without moving, "this changes nothing between us. Don't get too comfortable, thinking I won't put a sword through your heart. We're still enemies. It can't ever be the way it was."

"If you say so, prince." Puck smirked, then surprised me by turning completely serious. "But right now, I think you have larger issues to deal with." He glanced back at the glade, frowning. "Meghan and Ariella—that's a choice I'd *never* want to make. What are you going to do?"

Meghan and Ariella. Both alive. Both waiting for me. The whole situation was completely surreal. Meghan was the Iron Queen, far beyond my reach. Ariella—alive, unchanged and whole—waited just a few yards away. Possibilities and what-ifs swam through my head. For just a moment, I wondered what would happen if I just stayed here, with Ariella, forever.

The pain was swift and immediate. It wasn't stabbing, or

fiery, or unbearable. More like a fraying of my inner self, a few threads tearing away, vanishing into the ether. I winced and stifled a gasp, instantly abandoning that train of thought. My vow, my promise to Meghan, was woven into my very essence, and breaking it would unravel me, as well.

"My promise still stands," I said quietly, and the glimmering threads of pain vanished as swiftly as they'd come. "It doesn't matter what I want, I can't give up now. I have to keep going."

"Promises aside, then." Puck's voice was harder now, disapproving. "If there was no promise, Ash, no oath that bound you, would you keep going? What would you do right now, if you were free?"

"I..." I hesitated, thinking about the paths that had brought me here, the impossible choices, and the two lives that meant everything to me. "I...don't know. I can't answer that right now."

"Well, you'd better figure it out quick, prince." Puck narrowed his eyes, his voice firm. "We've screwed both their lives up pretty bad. At least you can make it right for one of them. But you can't have it both ways, you know. Pretty soon, you're gonna have to make a choice."

"I know." I sighed, glancing back at the glade, knowing she watched me, even now. "I know."

ARIELLA WAS WAITING FOR US when we returned, standing under the elder tree, talking to the empty branches. At least, it was empty until two golden eyes appeared through the leaves, blinking lazily as we came in. Grimalkin yawned as he sat up, curling his tail around his feet, and regarded us solemnly.

"Made your decision, have you?" he purred, digging his claws into the branch holding him up. "Good. All this agonizing was getting rather trite. Why does it take *so long* for humans and gentry to choose one path or the other?"

Puck blinked at him. "Oh, let me guess. You knew Ariella was here all along."

"Your kind does have a flair for stating the obvious."

Ariella was watching me, her expression unreadable. "What is your decision, Ash of the Winter Court?"

I drew close enough to see her face, realizing it hadn't changed in all the years she'd been gone. She was still beautiful, her face lovely and perfect, though there were shadows in her gaze that hadn't been before. "You told me you knew the way to becoming mortal," I said softly, watching for her reaction. Her eyes tightened a bit, but her expression remained neutral otherwise. "I made a promise," I said softly. "I swore to Meghan that I'd find a way to return. I can't walk away from that, even if I want to. I need to know how to become mortal."

"Then it is decided." Ariella closed her eyes for a long moment. When she spoke, her voice was low and distant, and it raised the hair on the back of my neck. "There is a place," she murmured, "that resides at the end of the Nevernever. Beyond the Briars that surround Faery, beyond the very edge of our world, the ancient Testing Grounds have stood since the beginning of time. Here, the Guardian awaits those who would escape Faery forever, who wish to leave the world of dreams and enter the human realm. But to do so, they must endure the gauntlet. None who accepted this challenge returned sane, if they returned at all. But legend states that if you can survive the trials, the Guardian will offer the key to becoming mortal. The gauntlet will be your test, and the prize will be…your soul."

"My…soul?"

Ariella regarded me solemnly. "Yes. A soul is the essence of humanity. It is what we lack to become mortal, and as such, we cannot truly understand humans. We were born from their dreams, their fears and imaginations. We are the product of their hearts and minds. Without a soul we are immortal, yet empty. Remembered, we exist. Forgotten, we die. And when we die, we simply fade away, as if we never existed at all. To become human is to have a soul. It is that simple."

I glanced at Puck and saw him nodding, as if this all made sense. "All right," I said, turning back to Ariella. "Then, I need to get to the Testing Grounds. Where are they?"

She smiled sadly. "It is not a place you can just walk to, Ash. No one who has gone to the Testing Grounds has ever survived. However..." Her eyes glazed over, becoming as distant as the stars. "I have seen it, in my visions. I can show you the way."

"Can you?" I gave her a long, searching look. "And what would you ask in return? What would you have me swear?" I stepped closer, dropping my voice so only she could hear. "I can't give you back the past, Ariella. I can't promise it will be the same. There's...someone else now." A face rippled across my memory, different from Ariella's; pale-haired and blue-eyed, smiling at me. "This quest, my earning a soul, is all for her."

"I know," Ariella replied. "I saw you together, Ash. I know what you feel for her. You always loved...so completely." Her voice trembled, and she took a deep breath, meeting my gaze. "All I ask is that you let me help you. That's all I want." When I still hesitated, she bit her lip and her eyes filled with tears. "I haven't seen you in years, Ash. I waited for this day for so long—please don't walk out and leave me behind. Not again."

Guilt stabbed at me, and I closed my eyes. "All right." I sighed. "I guess I do owe you that. But, it won't change anything, Ari. I have to keep my promise to Meghan. I won't stop until I've earned a soul."

She nodded, almost distracted. "It's a long way to the End of the World." Turning from me, she walked over to the shelves, her next words almost inaudible. "Anything can happen."

CHAPTER SEVEN
THE RIVER OF DREAMS

Leaving the hollow with Ariella, Puck, and Grimalkin, I was eerily reminded of another journey, one that was disturbingly similar to this. I believe the human saying was *déjà vu,* and it did seem strange, traveling with very nearly the same companions as before. Myself, Grimalkin, Robin Goodfellow…and a girl. It was strange; not very long ago, I'd thought Meghan reminded me of Ariella, but now, watching my old love glide through the mist as she led us out of the hollow, my only reflection was how similar—and how different—Ariella was to Meghan.

I pushed those thoughts away, focusing only on the task at hand. I could not let myself be distracted from my goal. I could not start comparing the two, the love from the past and the girl I would do anything for, because if I did I would go mad.

The Wolf joined us almost as soon as we left the hollow, materializing from the darkness without a sound. He sniffed Ariella curiously and wrinkled his muzzle at her, but she gazed at him calmly, as if she had expected him. No introductions were made, and the pair seemed to accept each other without reservation.

Leaving the hollow behind, we made our way through a forest of thorn trees, bristling and unfriendly, with bits of bone, fur and feathers impaled between them. Not only were the trees covered in thorns, the flowers, the ferns, even the rocks were all pointed and barbed, making it important to watch where we put our feet. Some of the trees had taken offense to our presence, or were simply bloodthirsty, for every so often they would take a swipe at us with a gleaming, bristling branch. I noticed, with a certain annoyance, that they left the Wolf completely alone, even moving aside for him to pass before taking a swat at me if I followed. After dodging several of these assaults, I finally grew tired of the game and drew my sword. When I sliced through the next thorny limb that whipped out at my face, the trees finally left us alone. For the most part.

"What is she like?" Ariella asked suddenly, surprising me. She had been quiet up until now, wordlessly leading the way until the closeness of the thorns forced her to ease back, to let me go first with my weapon. A longbow of gleaming white wood lay strapped to her back—she had always been a deadly archer—but the only blade she carried was a dagger.

Caught off guard by her question, I blinked at her, confused and wary. "I thought you already knew."

"I knew of the girl, yes," Ariella replied, ducking a vine covered in thin, needlelike barbs. "But only flashes. The visions never showed me more than that."

Behind us, Puck's gleeful whoop rang out as he dodged an attack, followed by the rustle of several trees that continued to swipe at him as he danced around. He was obviously enjoying himself, and probably stirring the forest's ire to even greater heights, but at least his attention was elsewhere. Grimalkin had long disappeared into the thorny undergrowth, stating he would meet us on the other side, and the Wolf's dark form was padding ahead, so it was just me and Ariella.

Uncomfortable with her scrutiny, I turned away, hacking through a suspicious-looking branch before it could lunge at me. "She's...a lot like you," I admitted, as the tree rattled in outrage. "Quiet, naive, a little reckless at times. Stubborn as a—" I stopped, suddenly self-conscious, feeling Ariella's gaze on the back of my neck. "Why are you asking me this?"

She chuckled. "I just wanted to see if you would answer. Remember how difficult it was getting any real answers out of you before? Like pulling teeth." I grunted and continued clearing the way, and she followed close behind. "Well, don't stop there, Ash. Tell me more about this human."

"Ari." I paused, as memories rose up, both blissful and painful. Dancing with Meghan. Teaching her to fight. Being forced to walk away as she lay dying beneath the limbs of a great iron oak. A root took advantage of my moment of distraction and tried to trip me, but I sidestepped and moved us both away. "I can't...talk about it right now," I told Ariella, whose sympathetic gaze read far too much. "Ask me again some other time."

As we left the forest of thorns, darkness fell very suddenly, as if we'd crossed some invisible barrier into Night. One moment, we were in the perpetual gray twilight of the wyldwood and the next, it was pitch-black except for the stars. And a new sound began to filter through the silence of the forest, faint at first but growing ever stronger. A constant murmur that slowly progressed to a dull roar, until we finally emerged from the trees to stand on the banks of a great black river.

"Wow," Puck mused, standing beside me. "The River of Dreams. I've only seen it a few times before, but it never ceases to amaze me."

I agreed with him, albeit silently. The surface of the river was black as night, reflecting the star-filled sky above and stretching on and on, until you couldn't tell where the water ended and the sky began. Moons, comets and constellations rippled on the surface, and other, stranger things floated upon the misty black waters. Petals and book pages, butterfly wings and silver medals. The hilt of a sword stuck out of the water at an odd angle, the silver blade tangled with ribbons and spiderwebs. A coffin bobbed to the surface, covered in dead lilies, before sinking into the depths once more. The debris of human imagination, floating through the dark waters of dream and nightmare. Swarms of fireflies and will-o'-the-wisps floated and bobbed above the waves like moving stars, adding to the confusion. This was the last familiar border of the wyldwood. Beyond the river was the Deep Wyld, the vast, uncharted territory of the Nevernever, where legends and primeval myths roamed or slept, where the darkest and most ancient creatures lurked in obscurity.

The Wolf gazed across the water, calm, unruffled, almost bored. I had the feeling he had seen the River of Dreams many times before, and wondered how far downstream he had been, if he made his home in the Deep Wyld himself.

I looked at Ariella. "Where to now, Ari?"

The lights of the river reflected in her eyes, and will-o'-the-wisps darted around her, burrowing into her hair. Standing there on the riverbank, glowing and wraithlike, she looked as insubstantial as mist. Raising a pale, delicate hand, she pointed downstream.

"We follow the river. It will take us where we need to go."

"Into the Deep Wyld."

"Yes."

"How far?" The River of Dreams supposedly ran forever; no one had ever been to the end of it, at least, no one who had survived to tell the tale.

Her eyes were as distant as the stars overhead. "Until we reach the edge of the world."

I nodded. Whatever it took, I was ready, even if it was impossible. "Let's get going, then."

A familiar gray cat sat on a barrel half-submerged in the mud at the river's edge, lazily swatting at fireflies that bobbed overhead. As we approached, a large wooden raft, covered in algae and trailing ribbons of weed, broke from a cluster of branches and floated toward us, unmanned. The planks were wide and sturdy, the logs holding it up thick and enormous, and it was large enough for even an enormous wolf to sit comfortably. A long wooden pole rested at the back, half-underwater.

"Oh, hey—look at that," Puck said cheerfully, rubbing his hands together. "Seems like the river knew we were coming. I'll drive."

I put my arm out as he started forward. "Not a chance."

"*Psh*. You never let me do anything."

The Wolf curled his lip in distaste, eyeing the raft as if it might lunge at him. "You expect to reach the End of the World on *that*? Do you know the things that live in the River of Dreams? And we're not even at the nightmare stretch yet."

"Aw, is the Big Bad Wolfie afraid of a few nasty fish?"

The Wolf gave him a baleful stare. "You wouldn't say that if you'd seen some of the fish in the Deep Wyld, Goodfellow. But more important, how will you ever reach the End of the World if I bite your head off?"

"It's all right," Ariella said quietly before we could respond. "I've seen us…following the river to the end. This is the way we need to go."

The Wolf snorted. "Foolish," he growled, but hopped lightly onto the wooden planks. The raft rocked under his weight, splashing water over the edge, but held. "Well?" He turned, glaring back at us. "Are we going to get this absurdity under way, or not?"

I helped Ariella into the boat, then stepped onto the platform near the back, grabbing the long wooden pole. As Puck entered, looking pensive, I nodded at Grimalkin, still sitting on the barrel. "You coming or not, cait sith?"

He gave the raft a dubious glance, curling his whiskers. "I suppose I must if I wish to see you to the End of the World." Standing, he tensed his muscles to leap off the barrel, but hesitated, narrowing his eyes. "Although, I will issue this one warning. If I end up in the river because some idiot decides to rock the boat—" he flattened his ears at Puck, who gave him a wide-eyed look of innocence "—I know several witches who would be happy to bring down a particularly potent curse on said idiot's head."

"Wow, if I had a favor for every time someone said that to me..."

Grimalkin did not look amused. Shooting Puck one last feline glare, he leaped to the edge of the raft, walked gracefully along the edge, and sat at the bow, facing out like a haughty figurehead. I gave the pole a push, and the raft moved smoothly into the River of Dreams, gliding toward the End of the World.

FOR A WHILE, THE RIVER was smooth. Except for the occasional bump of dream debris colliding with the raft, we slid through the water with hardly a ripple. More strange objects floated by us: love letters and wristwatches, stuffed animals and limp balloons. Once, Puck reached down and snatched up a faded copy of *A Midsummer Night's Dream,* grinned like an idiot and tossed it back into the river.

How long we floated down the river, I didn't know. The night sky, both above and around us, never lightened. The Wolf lay down, put his head on his enormous paws and dozed. Puck and Ariella spoke quietly in the center of the raft, catching up on many years of separation. They sounded at ease with each other, comfortable and content, and Ariella's laughter floated up occasionally, something I hadn't heard in a long, long time. It made me smile, but I didn't join them in reminiscing. Things were still shaky between Puck and me; I knew the dark, lingering memories of the hollow had pushed both of us to the edge that night, and we had, temporarily, put it behind us again, but I didn't trust myself just yet. Besides, I was lost in my own thoughts. Ariella's previous question had reminded me of the girl I was doing this for. I wondered where she was, what she was doing at that very moment. I wondered if she thought of me, too.

"Prince." Grimalkin's voice suddenly drifted up from near my feet. I looked down at the cait sith, standing beside me. "I suggest we stop for a bit," he said, waving his tail to keep his balance as the raft bobbed up and down in the current. "I am weary of sitting in one place, and I am not the only one." He nodded to where Ariella and Puck sat together on the planks. Ariella was slumped against Puck's shoulder, dozing quietly. I felt a tiny twinge of anger, seeing them like that, but Puck glanced back at me, offered a tiny, rueful shrug, and I squashed it down. It was ridiculous to be jealous, to feel anything. That part of my life was gone. I might regret it, I might wish it were different, but I could not bring it back. I'd known that for a long time.

I steered the raft to the bank, toward a sandy bar beneath ancient, moss-covered trees. As Puck and I pulled it to shore, Ariella woke, gazing around blearily.

"Where—"

"Relax, Ari. We're just stopping for a bit." Puck released the boat and stretched, raising long limbs over his head. "You know, it's always rafts and skinny little pole boats that you have to suffer through on these types of trips. Why can't we travel to the End of the World in a yacht?"

The Wolf leaped off the raft and stretched, baring his fangs in an enormous yawn. Shaking water from his fur, he looked around at the enormous trees and panted a grin. "I'm off to hunt," he stated simply. "It shouldn't take long." He glanced back at me, wrinkling his long muzzle. "I'd advise you not to venture into the forest, little prince. You're in the Deep Wyld now, and I'd hate to come back to find you all eaten. Well, except for the cat. He can get himself eaten anytime he wants." With that, he turned and bounded off, his black form merging with the shadows.

A few seconds later, we realized Grimalkin had also vanished. He'd probably slipped away into the forest as soon as the boat had touched ground, with no explanation and no hint to when he'd return. That left the three of us, alone.

"You know, we could just leave them," Puck suggested, grinning to show he wasn't completely serious. "What? Don't give me that look, Ari. Wolfman is probably right at home, and we couldn't get rid of Furball even if we wanted to. We'd be halfway to the End of the World and find him sleeping at the bottom of the boat."

Ariella continued to frown disapprovingly, and Puck threw up his hands. "Fine. Guess we're stuck here until their furry highnesses deign to show up again." He eyed each of us in turn, then sighed. "Right, then. Camp. Food. Fire. I'll get right on that."

NOT LONG AFTER, a cheerful fire crackled in a shallow pit, trying valiantly to throw back the darkness, failing to do so. The shadows seemed thicker near the River of Dreams, as if Night itself had taken offense to the flickering campfire and was crowding the edges of the light, seeking to swallow it whole. Light was an intruder here, much as we were.

Ariella sat cross-legged in the sand, idly poking the fire with a stick, while Puck and I attended to the business of finding food. Puck had somehow fashioned a pole from glamour, a stick, and a tangle of string from his pocket, but fishing in the River of Dreams was proving to be a strange and frustrating affair. He managed to pull a couple fish out of the river early, but they were odd, unnatural things: long and black like eels, with oversize teeth that snapped at us when we tried to handle them and bit through the sticks we tried to spear them with. We finally decided it wasn't worth the hassle of a lost finger and let them flop back into the river. His other catches included a yellow boot, a giant turtle that asked us for a pocket watch, and what looked like a large, normal catfish. That is, until it started sobbing enormous tears, begging us to return it to its family. I might've ignored the wailing fish and stuck it over the fire anyway, but the softhearted Goodfellow let it go.

"You realize you've just been duped by a fish," I said, watching the catfish grin at me before slipping into the dark waters, lost from view. Puck shrugged.

"Hey, it was going to name one of its grandfish after me," he said, tossing the line into the water again. "That's one of my rules, you know. I refuse to eat anything that names its kid after me."

"Fish don't have children," I deadpanned. "Fish have fry."

"Even so."

"Fine." I rolled my eyes and stepped back from the edge. "I'm done with this. Let me know if you manage to catch anything useful."

I wandered back to the fire, where Ariella looked up and smiled faintly, as if she knew exactly how the fishing had gone.

"Here," she said, and tossed me a round, pinkish globe. I caught it automatically, blinking as I realized what it was. A peach, fuzzy and soft and nearly the size of my fist. I glanced beside her and saw she had a whole basket of them.

"Where did you find these?" I asked in amazement. She chuckled.

"The river," she replied, nodding to the dark, glittering

water. "You can find almost anything a human would dream of, provided you know what to look for. While you and Puck have been wrestling with nightmares, I just keep an eye on the surface and let the dream debris come."

"Sounds like you've done this before," I said, taking a seat beside her.

"Not really," she admitted. "I've never been to the river in person. But as a seer I can sometimes see into dreams, whether they be faery or mortal. Dreamwalking, I believe it's called. And sometimes, I can even shape those dreams, make a person see what I want them to."

"Like you did with mine."

She was silent a moment, gazing back into the fire. "Yes," she murmured finally. "I'm sorry, Ash. But I wanted you to see what would've happened if Meghan had lost. I wanted you to understand why I chose what I did, even though I knew it would hurt."

"Did you…" I paused, gathering my thoughts. "Did you see my dreams…before?" Before I found Meghan, before I learned to freeze out my emotions—the nightmares that kept me awake at night, because I knew closing my eyes would force me to live that day over and over again.

Ariella shivered, drawing her knees to her chest, and nodded. "I wished I could have helped you." She sighed, resting her chin on a knee. "Between you and Puck, it was all I could do not to let you know I was still alive."

I frowned. Puck had had nightmares, too? I pushed that thought away, unwilling to dwell on it. If he had been suffering like me, good. He deserved it. "So," I asked, changing the subject, "what comes next?"

Ariella sighed. "I don't know," she murmured, almost to herself. "Everything is so hazy now. I've never been this far into the wyldwood."

"I haven't, either."

"But that doesn't worry you, does it?" She hugged herself and gazed out over the river. "You'll do whatever it takes, won't you? You've always been that way. Completely fearless." She shivered again and closed her eyes, seeming to sink into herself. "I wish I could be like that."

"I'm not fearless," I told her. "There are a lot of things that scare me." Failure. My own savage, Unseelie nature. Being unable to save those I had sworn to protect. Having my heart ripped from me once more. "I'm not fearless," I said again. "Not by a long shot."

Ariella gave me a sideways glance, as if she knew what I was thinking. "Yes, but you aren't afraid of the things the rest of us are afraid of," she said wryly. "The things that *should* terrify you don't."

"Like what?" I challenged, mostly to get her talking, to argue with me as she had before. This new Ariella, quiet and sad, bowed under the weight of terrible knowledge and countless secrets, was more than I could take. I wanted her to laugh again, to smile like she used to. Grinning, I bit into the peach, adopting a careless, defiant posture. "Name something you think I should be afraid of."

"Dragons," Ariella said immediately, making me snort. "Giants, hydras, manticores. Take your pick. Not only do you lack a healthy respect for them, you go charging into their lairs to challenge them to a fight."

"I have a healthy respect for manticores," I argued. "And I avoid picking fights with dragons. You're lumping me together with Goodfellow."

"Regardless—" Ariella mock-glared at me "—it's not the same. I have a healthy respect for kelpies, but that doesn't mean I'd ever go swimming with one." She wrinkled her nose at me. "Not like you and Puck, seeing how long you could stay on that kelpie's back without drowning or getting eaten."

I shrugged. "I know my abilities. Why should I fear some-thing that probably can't kill me?"

Ariella sighed. "You're missing the point. Or, perhaps you're making it for me, I'm not sure." She shook her head, giving me a lopsided smile, and for a moment, it was like old times again. Me, Puck, and Ariella, braving unknown terri-tory, not knowing what was to come.

I was suddenly aware of how close Ariella was, our shoul-ders barely touching. She seemed to realize it as well, for we gazed at each other, hardly breathing. The river flowed by us, and farther downstream Puck was shouting something, but for a quiet heartbeat it was just me and Ariella and nothing else.

A yell interrupted us. Puck was on the banks of the river, pulling and yanking at his line, his face intense. From the looks of it, whatever was on the other end was enormous, making the string lurch up and down as it fought. In the cen-ter of the river, the water boiled up like a geyser, and Puck yanked harder on the string. Then, with an explosion of debris and mist, a huge serpentine form rose fifteen feet into the air, towering over Puck, holding the line in a curved talon. Blue, green and silver scales glinted in the moonlight as a dragon lowered its massive horned head—mane and moustache rip-pling behind it—to glare at Puck with somber gold eyes.

"Oh," Puck said in a breathless voice, staring at it from where he sat in the mud and sand. "Um. Hey."

The eyes blinked. The solemn gaze shifted to Puck's left hand, narrowing. Puck looked down. "Oh, the hook." He grinned sheepishly. "Yeah. Sorry 'bout that. No harm done, right?"

The dragon snorted, filling the breeze with the scent of fish and cherry blossoms. Rippling like sea waves, it turned and coiled through the air, skimming the surface of the River of Dreams, before it sank beneath the depths once more.

Puck stood, dusted himself off, and sauntered toward us.

"Well, that was…interesting." He grinned. "Guess I've been officially slapped on the wrist for fishing in the River of Dreams without a license. Hey, is that a peach?"

THE WOLF APPEARED sometime later, gliding from the dark with no warning whatsoever, pacing up to the fire. Puck and Ariella were both asleep, peach pits scattered about, and I had taken first watch, sitting on a log with my sword in my lap. Grimalkin had not yet returned, but no one was really worried. It was an unspoken knowledge about the cait sith: he would reappear when it was time to leave.

The Wolf padded into the flickering light and flopped down across from me with a huff. A few feet away, Puck stirred, muttering something about peaches and dragons, but didn't wake.

The Wolf and I watched each other over the dying campfire for several minutes. "So," the Wolf began with a flash of bright fangs, "this quest of yours. You never told me much about it, little prince. It would be nice to know the reason behind this insane journey down the River of Dreams. I know you want to reach the End of the World, but I don't know why. What lies at the End of the World that is so important?"

"The Testing Grounds," I said quietly, seeing no reason to hide the fact. The Wolf pricked his ears.

"The Testing Grounds," he repeated, unsurprised, and nodded. "I suspected as much. Then, if you wish to go to the Testing Grounds, you must be looking for something." He paused, eyeing me over the flames, eyes glowing in the darkness. "Something you lack. Something very important. Your Name? No." He shook his head, talking more to himself than to me. "I have a feeling you already know your True Name. What, then? You have power. You have immortality, in a sense…" He paused, and his yellow-green eyes turned gleeful. "Ahhh, yes, I know why. There is only one thing left."

He looked up, smiling wickedly. "You're here because of the girl, aren't you? You're hoping to earn a soul."

I gave him a cold stare. "What do you know about that?"

The Wolf barked a laugh, and Ariella stirred. "I know you are a fool, boy," he said, lowering his voice to a low rumble. "Souls are not meant for us. They tie you to the world, make you mortal, make you like *them*. Being human…it will drive you mad, little prince. Especially one like you."

"What do you mean?"

The Wolf blinked slowly. "I could tell you," he said quietly, "but it would not sway you. I can smell your determination. I know you will see this through to the end. So why waste the breath?" He yawned and sat up, testing the breeze. "The cat is close. Pity he didn't get lost."

I turned just as Grimalkin emerged from the bushes nearby, giving me a bored look. "If you are waiting for sunrise, prince, you are wasting your time," he announced without preamble, and strode past me with his tail in the air. "The light will not penetrate this far into the Deep Wyld, and we have attracted too much attention sitting around here." He did not look back as he trotted in the direction of the raft. "Wake the others," he commanded, his voice drifting back to us. "It is time for us to go."

The Wolf and I shared a look over the flames.

"I could eat him now," he offered seriously. I bit down a smirk.

"Maybe later," I said, and got up to rouse the others.

PUCK WOKE EASILY when I kicked him in the ribs, rolling upright with a wounded yelp, making the Wolf grin with appreciation. "Ow!" he snarled. "Dammit, ice-boy, why don't you just stick a knife in my ribs and be done with it?"

"I've thought about it," I replied, and knelt to wake Ariella, curled up on her cloak by the fire. Her knees were drawn up to her chest, and she reminded me, always, of a sleeping cat. She stirred as I touched her shoulder, opening turquoise eyes to blink up at me sleepily.

"Time to go?" she murmured.

And, very suddenly, my breath caught. She looked vulnerable, lying there in the sand, her hair a silver curtain around her head. She looked slight and delicate and breakable, and I wanted to protect her. I wanted to pull her close and shield her from all the dangers in the world, and the realization made my stomach churn.

"Come on," I said, offering a hand to help her up. Her fingers were soft as I drew her to her feet. "The all-knowing cait sith has returned, and we've been ordered to move out."

That made her smile, as I'd hoped it would, and for half a heartbeat we stood there, gazing at each other in the sand, our faces a breath apart. Her fingers tightened on mine, and for a moment, it was like nothing had changed, that Ariella had never died, that we'd returned to a time when we were both happy, where there were no blood oaths between friends and no vow that stood between us.

But, yearning for the impossible didn't make it so.

Guiltily, I pulled away, breaking eye contact, and Ariella dropped her hands, a shadow darkening her face. Without speaking, we followed Puck toward the raft, where Grimalkin already sat on the edge, thumping his tail with impatience. Behind us, the Wolf trailed silently, but I could feel his ancient, knowing gaze on my back.

Under Grimalkin's impatient glare, we climbed aboard the raft, shoved off, and the current moved us out into the river once more. No one spoke, though I didn't miss the cold, angry looks I was receiving from Puck, nor the subtle glances Ariella was shooting my way. I ignored them both, keeping my gaze straight ahead and my eyes trained on the river.

Not long after that, the River of Dreams picked up speed.

No longer sleepy and tranquil, it rushed along as if it were fleeing something, a dark and faceless terror that chased it through the night. The debris that floated in the water and knocked against the raft had taken on a macabre feel. Coffins bobbed to the surface, knives and plastic doll heads went spinning by, hockey masks and clown shoes thumped against the front of the boat.

"I don't like the looks of this," Puck mused, as I barely avoided a collision with a broken tombstone that lurched out of the water. It was the first thing he'd said for several miles, which I thought might be some sort of a record. "What happened to the flowers and butterflies and all the shiny, pretty dream stuff?"

"We're nearing the nightmare stretch," the Wolf rumbled ominously. "I told you. You're not going to like what you see."

"Freaking fantastic." Puck shot him a look. "And, uh, does anyone else hear drums?"

"That isn't funny, Puck," Ariella chided, but at that moment an arrow thunked into one of the logs, causing everyone to jerk upright.

I looked to the riverbank. Small, pale things scurried through the bushes and undergrowth, keeping pace with the raft. I caught glimpses of round, red eyes, short, bulbous tails and dark cloaks, but it was difficult to see anything through the trees and shadows.

"Okay, natives definitely *not* friendly," Puck mused, ducking as another arrow shot overhead. "Hey, cat, any idea what kind of nasties we've pissed off so royally?"

Grimalkin, of course, had vanished. More darts filled the air, lodging into the planks or flying past us into the water, some barely missing us. "Dammit," Puck snarled, "we're sitting ducks out here."

With a snarl, the Wolf rose and launched himself, making

the raft spin wildly as he landed like a boulder in the river. Fighting the current, he struck powerfully for the shore, ignoring the debris that slammed into him, the water rushing over his body, failing to drag him down.

I smacked another arrow down with my sword and pulled glamour from the air, feeling it swirl around me. With a sharp gesture, I sent a flurry of ice darts into the bushes lining the riverbank. The shards ripped through the leaves, shredding them as they passed, and painful shrieks rose into the air.

Ariella stood, her bow in hand, pulling back the string. She didn't have a quiver, but glamour shimmered around her, and a gleaming ice arrow formed between her fingers just as she released the string. It flew into the bushes with a thump, and a small, pale body tumbled out of the ferns into the river.

"Nice shot, Ari," Puck crowed as the Wolf drew close to shore. The hail of arrows thinned, and the marauders shrieked as the Wolf dragged his dripping black form out of the water and shook vigorously. Yelping, they fled, scattering into the bushes, and the Wolf lunged after them with a roar. "Go get 'em, Wolfman!" Puck cheered, as the attackers vanished into the trees. "Looks like he scared them off, whatever they were."

I saw movement on the banks ahead and narrowed my eyes. "Don't be too sure about that."

Something small and pale like the other forms scrambled onto a rock jutting out over the water. Seen clearly, it looked like a squat, bipedal newt with slimy white skin and a frog-like mouth full of teeth. Its beady eyes were filmy and blue, unlike the bright crimson of the others, and it wore a strange headdress on its naked skull.

Raising a staff in both claws, it started chanting.

"That can't be good," Puck muttered.

"Ari," I called, ducking as another hail of darts flew at us from the bush. The natives were definitely protecting their shaman. "Take him down now!"

Ari pulled back and released an arrow, a perfect shot that would've gone right through the shaman's chest had another creature not leaped in front of him, taking the lethal blow itself. I flung a hail of shards at him, but several newt creatures sprang up and huddled around him, shrieking as the darts tore into them, but not moving. The chanting continued as the raft drifted by, taking us out of reach.

Around us, the water started to boil.

I drew my sword as a monstrous coil broke the surface of the river, black and shiny and thicker than my waist. Puck yelped, and Ariella cringed back. A huge head reared out of the water with a screech and an explosion of nightmare debris. Not a snake or a dragon; this monster had a round, lipless mouth lined with sharp teeth, built for sucking instead of biting. A giant lamprey, and where there was one, there were usually more.

"Puck!" I yelled, as the raft spun wildly and two more giant eels rose out of the water. "If we end up in the water, we're dead! Don't let them crush the boat!"

The first lamprey lunged at me, snaking in for an attack. I stood my ground and slashed upward with my blade, cutting through its fleshy maw. The lamprey screamed and reared back, mouth split in two, thrashing wildly. From the corner of my eye, I saw Ariella shoot an arrow right into the mouth of another eel, which convulsed fiercely and sank back into the depths. The third lunged for Puck, mouth gaping, but at the last moment Puck leaped aside, and the lamprey struck the boat instead, razor teeth sinking into the wood. It started to pull back, but not before Puck's dagger flashed down, stabbing the top of its head.

Shrieking, the eel coiled its entire body around the raft, squeezing hard. The planks creaked and started to snap in places as the mortally wounded lamprey clung to it with the strength of death. I spun and sliced through a coil, cutting it in two, but with a final snap, the raft splintered, flying outward in an explosion of wood and dumping me into the river.

The current caught me instantly, dragging me down. Still clutching my sword, I fought to the surface, calling out for Ariella and Puck. I could see the lamprey as it sank below the surface, coiled around the remains of the raft, but my companions were nowhere to be seen.

Something struck me in the back of the head. My vision went dark for a moment, and I fought to keep my head above water, knowing that if I lost consciousness now, I would die. Briefly, I hoped Puck, Ariella and Grimalkin were all right; that they would survive, even if I did not.

Then the current pulled me under again, and the River of Dreams took me away.

CHAPTER EIGHT
THE HOBYAHS

I awoke on my stomach, my cheek pressed into something hard, river water soaking my clothes. There was a dull roar in my ears, which I quickly discovered was the river behind me. I listened for other things, for familiar voices and the rustle of movement, for a snide feline voice asking if I was finally awake, but there was nothing. It seemed I was alone.

Slowly, I pushed myself up, testing for sharp pain and broken bones, anything that seemed out of place. Though there was a gash across my forehead and a throbbing ache in my skull, nothing seemed seriously injured. I was lucky this time. I hoped the others were as fortunate.

My sword lay in the mud a few feet away. As I reached for it, I became aware that I was not alone after all.

"Good," rumbled the Wolf, somewhere above me. "You're still alive. It would be extremely annoying if I had to tell Mab I let her son drown while on this ridiculous quest. Dragging your carcass out of the river isn't something I'd want to do again, prince. I hope it doesn't become a habit."

He was lying on the bank a few yards away, watching me with intense yellow-green eyes. As I pulled myself up, he nodded approval and rose, his pelt still spiky and damp from his plunge into the water.

"Where are the others?" I asked, gazing around for their bodies. The Wolf snorted.

"Gone," he said simply. "The river took them."

I stared at him, letting the words sink in. Loss was nothing new to me. I'd shielded myself from the worst of the pain; not caring for anything ensured I wouldn't miss it when it was gone. Attachments, as I'd learned, had no place in the Unseelie Court. But I could not believe that Puck and Ariella were gone.

"You didn't try to help them?"

Shaking himself, the Wolf sneezed and looked back at me, unconcerned. "I had no interest in saving the others," he said easily. "Even if I could have gotten to them in time, my only interest is keeping you alive. I warned them floating downstream was a bad idea. I suppose we'll have to find another way to the End of the World."

"No," I said quietly, looking across the foaming river. "They're not dead."

The Wolf curled a lip. "You don't know that, prince. You can't be sure."

"I'd know," I insisted. Because if they were gone, I'd have no way to reach the Testing Grounds myself, no way to honor my vow to Meghan. If Puck was dead, my world would become as cold and lifeless as the darkest night in the Winter Court. And if I had let Ariella die a second time, it would've been better if the Wolf had left me to drown, because the pain would do more than crush me this time—it would kill me.

I let out a breath, raking a hand through my wet hair. "We're going to find them," I said, looking back down the river. The water roared and foamed, clawing angrily at the rocks, rushing by at a breakneck speed. The Wolf was right—

it was difficult to imagine anyone surviving that, once the
raft had smashed apart, but Robin Goodfellow was an expert
at survival, and I had to believe Ariella was safe with him.
Grimalkin I wasn't even worried about. "Believe what you
will," I continued, glancing at the Wolf, "but Goodfellow is
still alive. He's harder to kill than you might think…perhaps
even harder to kill than you."

"I very much doubt that." But his voice was flat with res-
ignation, and he huffed noisily, shaking his head. "Come on,
then." With a last show of teeth, the Wolf turned and started
padding down the riverbank. "We waste time standing about
here. If they survived, they will likely be farther downstream.
However…" He paused and glanced back. "If we reach the
Falls of Oblivion, you might as well give up. Nothing can
survive that plunge. Not even me."

He turned and continued loping along the riverbank, head
lifted to the wind to pick up the scent of his prey. With one
last look at the foaming River of Dreams, I followed.

FOR AN INDEFINITE AMOUNT of time, we walked along the
riverbank, searching for any sign, any hint of Puck or Ariella. The Wolf loped tirelessly along with his muzzle pointed
sometimes at the ground and sometimes at the sky, tasting the
wind, while I searched the bank for footprints, broken twigs,
overturned rocks, any sign of life.

Something near the edge of the water caught my eye, and I
hurried over. A splintered length of wood lay trapped between
two rocks at the water's edge. It was part of the raft, bobbing
limply in the waves, smashed almost beyond recognition. I
stared at it for a moment, refusing to acknowledge what that
could mean, and turned away to continue the search.

Farther downstream, the Wolf suddenly came to a stop.

Lowering his head, he sniffed around the rocks and mud, then straightened with a growl, baring his teeth.

I hurried over. "Did you find them?"

"No. But a great many creatures were here recently. Small things, very unpleasant smell. Slimy. Faintly reptilian."

I remembered the pale, newtlike creatures, shooting at us down the riverbank. And their shaman, calling up river nightmares to crush the boat. "What are they?"

The Wolf shook his bushy head. "Hobyahs."

"Hobyahs," I repeated, recalling the tale of the small, unpleasant fey. "Hobyahs are extinct. At least, that's what the stories claim." Much like goblins or redcaps, the hobyahs were fierce, frightening creatures that lived in dark forests and menaced humans. Though apparently, there had been only one tribe of hobyahs, and they had met a grisly end. According to legend, the hobyahs had tried to kidnap a farmer and his wife and were eaten by the family dog in the end, so there were no more hobyahs in the world anymore.

But the Wolf snorted. "You're in the Deep Wyld now, boy," he growled. "This is the place of old legends and forgotten myths. The hobyahs are alive and well here, and there are a lot of them, if you can't guess by looking at the tracks."

Glancing down, I saw he was right. Three-toed prints were scattered haphazardly in the mud between rocks—small, light tracks with claws on the end of the toes. Here and there a blade of grass was crushed or trampled, and a strong musky odor lingered in the air.

The Wolf sneezed and shook his head, curling his lips in disgust. "Let's keep moving. I can't track anything past this abominable smell."

"Wait," I ordered, and dropped to a knee in the grass at the water's edge, brushing the trampled vegetation. Hobyah prints were everywhere, but there was a shallow indentation in the grass that faintly resembled...

"A body," I muttered, as the Wolf peered over my shoulder. "There was a body lying here, on its stomach. Not a hobyah, either. My size."

"Are you sure?" the Wolf growled. Lowering his muzzle, he sniffed the spot I pointed to and sneezed again, shaking his head. "*Pah,* I can't smell anything but hobyah stink."

"They had it surrounded," I mused, seeing the scene in my mind. "It must have come out of the water, pulled itself onto the bank, then collapsed here. No, not just one." I ran my fingers over the grass. "There was another one here. Two of them. The hobyahs probably found them when they were passed out."

"Hobyahs aren't anyone's friends," the Wolf said gravely. "And they eat almost everything. There might not be anything left once we catch up."

I ignored the Wolf, though a cold rage burned deep in my stomach, making me want to put my sword through some creature's head. As I followed the tracks farther up the bank, more of the scene played out before me. "They dragged them away," I continued, pointing at a spot where the grass was flattened and bent in one direction, "into the forest."

"Impressive," the Wolf growled, coming to stand beside me. "And unfortunate, considering those two are now at the mercy of bloodthirsty cannibals." He sniffed and gazed into the dark tangle of trees. "I suppose this means we are going after them."

Relief, swift and sudden, bloomed through me. They were still alive. Captured perhaps, in danger of being tortured or killed, but for now, they were alive. I shot the Wolf a cold stare.

"What do you think?"

He bared his fangs at me. "Be careful, boy. In some tales, the hero gets eaten by the monster after all."

TRACKING THE HOBYAHS through the dark, eerie forest proved easier than following the river. They didn't bother to cover their tracks, and their greasy odor clung to every leaf and twig and blade of grass they stepped on or brushed by.

The trail led us deep into the woods, until at last, the ground sloped away and we were staring down into a shallow basin filled with swampy water. Thatch huts stood on wooden stilts over the murk, and long spears standing point up in the mud held an assortment of rib cages, rotting carcasses and severed heads.

Small, pale creatures like those from the riverbank swarmed the village like ants whose nest had been invaded. They barely came up to my knee. Along with their dark cloaks and hoods, many of them wore thin spears that looked to be made of bone.

The Wolf growled and shifted beside me. "Disgusting things, hobyahs. And they taste even worse than they look." He turned to me. "What are you going to do now, little prince?"

"I have to find Puck and Ariella, if they're down there."

"Hmm. Perhaps they are in that pot."

An enormous kettle hung on stilts in the middle of the camp, with a crackling fire underneath. Noxious black fumes came from whatever was in the pot, and I shook my head. "No," I mused, dismissing that notion immediately. "Both of them are too smart to end up like that."

"If you say so," the Wolf mused as we circled the camp. "I hope your faith in those two does not get you killed."

"There you are!" hissed an impatient voice above my head.

"Where have you been? I was beginning to think the dog had eaten you after all."

The Wolf snarled and spun around, craning his neck at the tree, where Grimalkin peered at us from a branch safely out of reach. "I've grown tired of your insults, cait sith," he challenged, eyes blazing with pure hatred. "Come down here and say that. I'll rip that arrogant tongue right out of your head. I'll crush your skull in my teeth, tear the hide off your useless feline skeleton and eat your heart."

His voice was getting louder with each threat. I put a hand on his huge shoulder and shoved, hard. "Quiet!" I warned as he turned with a snarl. "You'll alert the camp. There's no time for this now."

"A wise statement," Grimalkin replied, giving the Wolf a lazy, half-lidded stare. "And the prince is correct, much as I would enjoy watching you chase your tail and bark at the moon." The Wolf growled again, but the cat ignored him, looking at me. "Goodfellow and the seer are being held in one of the inner huts, still unconscious, I believe. The hobyah shaman is keeping them in a drugged sleep—so much easier to put them in the kettle when the time comes. They have been waiting for it to get hot enough, but I believe it is very nearly ready."

"Then we need to move fast." Crouching, I looked over the camp again but spoke to the Wolf. "I'm going to sneak around the back. Do you think you can create a big enough diversion for me to find the others and get out of there?"

The Wolf bared his teeth in a savage grin. "I think I can come up with something."

"Wait for my signal, then. Grimalkin—" I looked to the cait sith, who blinked calmly "—show me where they are."

We crept around the outskirts of the camp, moving soundlessly through the trees and marshy undergrowth, until Gri-malkin stopped at the edge of the basin and sat down.

"There," he said, nodding to the left side of the camp. "The shaman's hut is the second one from the rotting tree. The one with the torches and the chicken feet strung across the entrance."

"All right," I murmured, staring at the hut. "I'll take it from here. You should hide—" But Grimalkin was already gone.

I closed my eyes and drew my glamour to me, creating a cloak of shadows that the light would shy away from. As long as I didn't make any noise or draw attention to myself, glances would slide past me and torchlight would not penetrate my fabricated darkness.

With the glamour cloak in place, I walked down the slope into the swampy basin.

The smells here were foul and potent; rancid water, pu-trid carcasses, rotting fish and the oily, reptilian stench of the hobyahs themselves. They hissed and snarled at each other in their garbled, burbled language, punctuated by one recognizable word: *hobyah*. Probably how they got their name. Moving from shadow to shadow, being careful not to slosh the warm swamp water that soaked my legs, I made my way to the shaman's hut. Chanting sounds and a thick, pungent smoke drifted past the veil of chicken feet at the doorway. Silently drawing my sword, I eased inside.

The interior of the tiny shack reeked of a foul incense, stinging my eyes and scratching the back of my throat. A squat, potbellied hobyah sat beside one wall on a pile of ani-mal skins, chanting and waving a burning stick over a pair of limp figures. Puck and Ariella, sprawled out on the dirty hut floor, their faces pale and slack, hands and feet bound with yellow vines. The shaman jerked his head up as I came in, and hissed in alarm.

Quick as lightning, he lunged for his staff, standing in the corner, but I was faster. Just as his claw closed on the gnarled wood, an icicle shard hit him from behind. It should have killed him, but he turned and shrieked something at me, rattling the bones atop his staff. I felt a ripple of some dark glamour go through the air, and lunged forward, slashing with my blade. The shaman's mouth opened, and he spit something at me, an acidic yellow substance that burned my skin where it hit, right before the blade struck home. He screamed a death cry and dissolved into a pile of squirming snakes and frogs. One down, but the other hobyahs would not be far behind.

My skin tingled and was starting to go numb where the shaman's spittle had landed, but I couldn't focus on that now. Kneeling beside Ariella, I cut her bonds and drew her into my arms.

"Ari," I whispered urgently, tapping her cheek. Her skin was cold to the touch, and even though that was normal for Winter fey, my stomach twisted. "Ari, wake up. Come on, look at me."

I pressed two fingers to the pulse at her throat, but at that moment she stirred and her eyelids fluttered. Relief shot through me like an arrow, and I resisted the urge to hug her close. Opening her eyes, she jerked when she saw me, and I pressed my finger to her lips. "Just me," I whispered, as her eyes widened. "We have to get out of here. Quietly."

A shriek came from the entrance of the hut. A hobyah stood there, red eyes wide as he stared at us. I hurled an ice dagger at him, but he darted away, hissing, and fled into the camp. Cries of alarm and rage echoed beyond the door, and then came the sound of many bodies rushing toward us through the water.

I cursed and lunged upright, grabbing my sword. "Get Puck on his feet," I called to Ariella, crossing the floor to the

entrance. "We're leaving now!" The first hobyah rushed into
the shack, saw me, and lunged with a howl, stabbing his spear
at my knee. My sword flashed down and sent the hobyah's
head rolling toward the corner, before both parts dissolved
into a pile of writhing salamanders. Another darted through
and hurled its spear at my face. I ducked the projectile and
sent one of my own at the hobyah. The ice shard hit it square
between the eyes and it slithered away in a tangle of snakes
and lampreys.

Stepping outside, deliberately blocking the entrance to the
hut, I raised my sword and met the horde of hobyahs swarming me from every direction. "Hobyah!" they screeched as
they rushed me. "Hobyah hobyah hobyah!" Spears flew at
me, though I managed to dodge or block most of them, lashing out at any hobyah that got too close. The pile of newts,
frogs and snakes grew at my feet, but there were always more
attackers, more hobyahs dropping from the trees, erupting
from the water, or climbing over the roof to leap at my back.

A huge black bird suddenly exploded from the hut behind
me in a flurry of wings and feathers. With an enraged *caw,*
it plunged down, sank its talons into a hobyah and carried it
high into the trees, the hobyah struggling and howling in its
grip. The others hissed and snarled, craning their necks to follow it as Ariella stepped out beside me.

"I assume there's a plan?" she asked, pale but calm as a mass
of frogs and snakes suddenly rained down from the trees. Puck
dropped onto the roof of the hut with a crash, daggers already
in hand. I smiled at Ariella.

"Always." As the swarm of hobyahs began edging forward
again, I put two fingers in my mouth and blew out a piercing
whistle.

A sudden, haunting howl echoed it. The hobyahs cringed,
spinning around, their eyes going wide with fear.

The Wolf hurled himself into the midst of the hobyahs with a roar that shook the ground, and the creatures screamed in panic. "Dog!" they shrieked, throwing up their hands and running about in terror. "Dog! Dog!"

The Wolf bared his teeth. "I. Am not. *A dog!*" he roared, and lunged for the nearest hobyah, grabbing it by the head and shaking it viciously.

I took Ariella's hand and pulled her away, Puck close behind and muttering curses. The hobyahs didn't try to stop us. Together, we fled the camp, hearing the Wolf's roars and the hobyah's squeals of panic echo behind us.

"Ash," Ariella said, grabbing my arm, "wait! We're not being followed. Stop for a moment, please."

I staggered to a halt, ignoring the urge to put my hand against the nearest tree to stop the ground from spinning. The chaos in the hobyah village had long faded behind us, but I'd wanted to get as far from the creatures as possible, in case they decided to come after us once more. If the Wolf left any alive.

My chest and shoulder still burned where the hobyah shaman had spat on me. Ignoring the pain crawling down my back, I leaned against a cool, mossy trunk and gazed around, trying to get my bearings. The trees here were giant, ancient things, and you could almost feel their eyes on you, cold and unamused by the intruders in their midst.

"Well, that was all kinds of fun." Puck blew out a breath and raked a hand through his hair. "Just like old times. Except for the whole getting drugged and having to be rescued thing. That's gonna sting later, I just know it." Groaning, he sat on a nearby rock, rubbing a bruise on his shoulder. "Nice of you to come after us, ice-boy," he drawled. "If I didn't know better by now, I'd almost think you cared."

I forced a smirk in his direction. "It wouldn't be nearly as satisfying if I didn't get to kill you myself," I replied, and Puck grinned.

A cool hand touched my cheek. I looked up into Ariella's concerned gaze. "Are you all right?" she asked, placing the other palm on my forehead. I closed my eyes against the softness. "You're burning up. What happened?"

"You smell sick, prince," the Wolf growled, coming out of nowhere. "Like weakness. You won't make it to the End of the World like that."

"The shaman," I replied. "He…spit on me. Did something to me, I think." The burning in my chest and shoulder had gone numb and was now spreading throughout my body. I realized I could no longer feel my arm.

"Hobyah venom is hallucinogenic," the Wolf continued, curling his lip. "You're in for an interesting night, little prince, if you wake up at all."

The trees were beginning to move strangely, centuries-old giants swaying like willows. I squeezed my eyes shut to clear the visions, and when I opened them again, I was lying on my back while tiny lights danced and swirled over my head.

Someone's face bent over me, starlight eyes filled with worry. She was beautiful, a vision come to life. But she was fading, growing dimmer and dimmer, until only her eyes were left, staring at me. Then they blinked, and the world cut out altogether.

CHAPTER NINE

IN DREAMS

Where am I?

Mist surrounded me, coiling along the ground in ragged patches, blanketing everything in white. The air was cool and damp, holding the quiet stillness of early morning. I smelled pine and cedar and heard the soft splash of water, somewhere up ahead in the fog. I didn't recognize my surroundings, but for some reason it all seemed vaguely familiar.

With nothing else to do, I started walking.

The mist slowly cleared away, revealing a small green pond encircled by pine trees. The faint babble of ducks echoed over the stillness, and several of the green-and-brown birds glided through the water toward a pale figure standing on the bank. I stopped and drew in a quiet breath, and for a moment I couldn't move, afraid that the scene before me would dissolve and I'd be left chasing shadows.

She wore jeans and a white shirt, and her long, pale hair was tied in a ponytail, falling softly down her back. Her body was slender, more energetic than graceful, her fingers quick as she tore bread crusts and tossed them into the water. There was a glow about her now, a flickering halo of light, swirling with glamour and power. Against the darkness of the pond and trees, she looked bright and vivid and alive, a light burning against the shadows.

For a moment, I just watched her, tossing crumbs into the water, smiling as the ducks swarmed over them. I knew this wasn't real; the real Meghan was back in the Iron Realm as the powerful Iron Queen. I knew this was a dream; or perhaps I had died and faded away and didn't know it yet. But seeing her still made my heart beat crazily, made me long to pull her close and let that light consume me. If it burned until there was nothing left, would that be such a terrible fate?

She must have heard me, or sensed my presence, for she turned and her blue eyes widened. "Ash?" she whispered, and the smile that crept over her face warmed me like the sun. "What are you doing here?"

I couldn't help but smile back. "I don't know," I told her, taking the hand she offered and letting her pull me close. "I think…this is a dream." Her arms slipped around my waist, and I held her to me, closing my eyes. No burning fire, no searing light that turned me to dust, just the feel of Meghan in my arms. "Though I'd be happy if I never woke up."

I felt her puzzled frown, and she pulled back to look at me, cocking her head. "Strange. I thought this was *my* dream."

"Maybe it is." I was having trouble thinking. The subtle shift of her body against mine, her hands tracing circles against my back, was driving me to distraction. "Maybe I'm not really here, and this will all disappear when you wake up, including me." She held me tighter, and I smiled. "I wouldn't care either way."

Something nagged at the back of my mind, something important that I had forgotten, beating against my subconscious like birds fluttering against a windowsill. Impatiently, I shoved it back, burying it in a dark corner of my mind. Whatever it was, I didn't want to remember. Not now. I didn't want to see, feel or think of anything except the girl in front of me.

As I bent to kiss her, she slipped her hand beneath my shirt, tracing soft fingers over my bare skin, and from there it was easy to forget everything.

LATER, WE LAY IN THE COOL grass at the edge of the pond, Meghan leaning against a tree with my head in her lap, gazing up at the clouds. Her fingers twirled idle patterns in my hair, and I dozed contentedly, feeling no urge to move. If I had died and this was nonexistence, then so be it. If I was sleeping still, then I had no intention of waking up.

"Ash?"

"Mmm?"

"Where have you been all these months? I mean…" She hesitated, twirling a strand of my hair around her finger. "I know you can't come into the Iron Realm, but no one has seen any sign of you, anywhere. Or Puck, for that matter. What have you two been doing?"

"I was…looking for something, I think." I reached up and trapped her hand in mine, bringing it to my lips. "I can't remember now."

She freed her fingers, stroking my cheek with them. I closed my eyes and let myself drift. "You don't think it could be important?"

"Maybe." Truth was, I didn't want to think about it. I was content here. Whatever lay beyond this glen, this small pocket of dreams or reality or whatever it was, I didn't want to know about. I couldn't remember much, but I knew, beyond a shadow of a doubt, that it involved pain. And I was tired of it. So much of my existence had been pain, or emptiness, or loss. Meghan was here. I was happy. That was all I needed to know.

Meghan tapped my forehead in a playful manner. "You do know that one of us has to wake up, don't you?" she asked, and I grunted, not opening my eyes. "I don't know if I'm a figment of your imagination or you're a figment of mine, but eventually this is going to fade away."

I rolled to my knees to face her, and she blinked as I leaned in close. "You can go if you have to," I said, smoothing her hair behind one ear. "I'm not leaving. I'll still be here when you come back."

"No, Ash," came a new voice, shattering the peaceful moment. "You cannot stay."

Meghan and I both jerked up, spinning to face the intruder in our private world. Ariella stood a few yards away, shrouded in the mist, her face grim as she watched us.

"You were very difficult to find, Ash," she said in a weary voice. "I almost gave up when I couldn't find you in nightmare. I didn't think to look for you in the dreams of another, but it makes sense that you should come here."

"What do you want here?" Meghan rose with the regal grace of a queen, calm and unruffled. I noticed she subtly moved in front of me when facing Ariella, a familiar gesture that caught me off guard. The Iron Queen was protecting *me*. "Who are you?"

"You know me, Meghan Chase." Ariella stepped forward, the mist parting for her, to stand before us clearly. "I am the one who was left behind, the one Ash knew before you ever came into the picture."

Meghan didn't move, but I saw her draw in a slow breath as the realization hit. "Ariella," she breathed, and I winced at the churning emotions in that one quiet word. Meghan shook her head, glanced back at me. "Is this another dream, Ash? Did you bring her here?"

"No," Ariella said before I could reply. "I am not a dream.

Not a memory. I am as real as you are, Iron Queen. Death could not quite hold me, all those years ago."

"Enough," I rasped, finally shaking the fog from my mind. Memory returned in a rush: the journey to find the seer, the fateful trip down the River of Dreams, the quest to earn a soul. Stepping between them, I felt the heat of both their gazes piercing me like a thousand knives. "Ari," I said, facing her, "what are you doing here? What do you want?"

Ariella narrowed her eyes. "I'm here to bring you out of this dream," she replied with a brief glance at Meghan. "Your body is very sick, Ash, and the curse the hobyah shaman laid on you was keeping you trapped in sleep. I don't know how you found your way here, but it is time for you to return to us."

Behind me, I could feel Meghan's stare burning into my shoulder blades. "You're…with her now?" she asked softly, not quite accusing—not yet. "How…how long have you known she was alive?"

"Not long," Ariella answered for me. "We haven't had much time together yet."

"Ari!" I turned to glare at her. She gazed back, unrepentant, her silver-flecked eyes watching me sadly. In that moment, I saw the jealousy she'd never shown before, the hurt that I had chosen someone else, though she knew it had to be that way. It was perhaps the first truly ugly emotion I'd ever seen from her, and my anger dissipated completely. I had done this to her. She'd given me everything, and I had turned my back on her.

"I see," Meghan whispered in a voice that trembled only slightly. I could feel her fading, her presence leaving the dream surrounding us. "Then…I'll leave you two alone."

"That is not necessary, Iron Queen." Ariella shook her head. "There is no need. I came here to bring Ash out of his nightmares, but this is your dream, not his. When you wake, the dream will fade, and he will return to us. I'm sorry to have intruded here." With a slight nod to us both, she backed up a few steps into the mist, and disappeared.

Alone with the Iron Queen again, I held my breath, waiting for the explosion, for the storm of questions. But Meghan took a deep breath and closed her eyes. "Was that really her?" she asked, still not looking up. "Ariella? Is she really alive?"

I crossed the space separating us, reaching for her hand. She blinked as I took her fingers, gazing up at me in surprise. "It's not what you think," I told her. "Please, hear me out."

Meghan gave me a sad smile. "No, Ash," she whispered. "Maybe...maybe this is for the best." And though she didn't move, I could sense she was pulling back, letting me go.

"Meghan..."

"I'm the Iron Queen," she said firmly. "No matter what I want, that will never change. And you're still part of the Winter Court. Even if you could come into the Iron Realm, you would die. We can't be together, and there's no use in wishing for the impossible. It's selfish of me to keep hoping." Her voice shook on the last sentence, but she took a deep, steadying breath and looked up at me. "Perhaps...it's time to move on, to find happiness with someone else."

I wanted to tell her, to explain what I was trying to do. That I was trying to earn my soul. I was going to the End of the World for her; that I would become mortal if it meant we could be together. I wanted to tell her so badly, but at the same time, I feared getting her hopes up only to have them dashed if I failed. I didn't want her waiting for me, worrying and constantly looking to the horizon for someone who would never appear.

"You have a chance to be happy now," Meghan went on, and her blue eyes shone with unshed tears, though she never

looked away. "Ash, this is *Ariella,* the love you've been missing for decades. If she's really back, then fate has given you
both another chance, and I...I'm not going to stand in your
way." A tear spilled over, running down her cheek, but she
still smiled as she held my gaze. "What we had was a dream,
and it was beautiful, but it was just a dream. It's time for us
to wake up." I took a breath to argue, but she laid her fingers
against my lips, silencing me. "Close your eyes."

I didn't want to. I wanted to stay in this dream almost as
much as I wanted to find a soul, even though I knew this
wasn't real. But, almost against my will, I felt my eyes slip
shut, and a moment later her lips brushed against mine, a
featherlight touch that pulled my stomach inside out. "Goodbye, Ash," she whispered. "Be happy."

And I awoke.

I was lying on my back, staring up at a roof of branches,
tiny pinpricks of light filtering through the leaves. A fire
crackled somewhere to my left, and the scent of smoke drifted
on the breeze, tickling the back of my throat.

"Welcome back, sleeping beauty."

Puck's voice filtered through the haze in my mind. Groaning, I struggled into a sitting position, rubbing my eyes. My
skin felt cold and clammy, my body drained. Mostly, I felt hollow, empty, though the dull ache in my chest reminded me
why I had closed off my emotions, freezing everyone out. It
hurt, the knowledge that the girl I loved had let me go once
more.

Ariella and the Wolf were nowhere to be seen, but Puck
sat on a log in front of a small campfire, holding a fat, speared
mushroom over the flames, turning it slowly. Grimalkin lay
opposite him on a flat rock, his feet tucked beneath him, purring in contentment.

"'Bout time you woke up, ice-boy," Puck said without turning around. "I was hoping for some groaning and thrashing, but you just lay there like the dead. And you didn't even talk in your sleep so I could torment you about it later. What fun is that?"

I struggled to my feet, pausing a moment to let the ground stop swaying. "How long was I out?" I asked, moving toward the fire.

"Hard to say." Puck tossed me a mushroom kebab as I walked up. "I haven't seen the sun in forever. We must be far into the Deep Wyld."

"Where's everyone else?"

"Wolfman is out hunting." Puck stuffed an entire mushroom into his mouth and swallowed without seeming to chew. "I guess my humble white-truffle kebabs weren't good enough for him. Do you know how hard it is to find these things? Furball turned up his nose as well—picky, ungrateful animals."

Grimalkin sniffed without opening his eyes. "I do not eat fungi, Goodfellow," he said in a lofty voice. "And if you are so enamored by these spores, feel free to chew on those spotted toadstools in that pile of elk dung."

"Oh, well, that's just gross."

I swallowed the mushrooms without tasting them, my body recognizing the need for food even though my mind was far away. "Where's Ariella?" I asked, tossing the stick back into the fire.

Puck nodded to the edge of the circle of firelight, where Ariella sat hunched on a rock, her back to us. "She walked away a few minutes before you came to," Puck said softly, watching me with narrowed eyes. "I tried following her, but she said she wanted to be alone for a while." I felt his gaze sharpen, cutting into me. "What did you say to her, Ash?"

I was such a mess, pulled in so many directions I felt like I would snap. I was still reeling from Meghan's last words, from the flash of jealousy in Ariella's eyes, from the strain of walking the line between the girl I had lost and the girl I wanted but could not have. But even though Ari had clearly been goading Meghan back in the dreamworld, I could not ignore her pain.

Disregarding Puck, I walked to where Ariella sat, her head bowed, silver hair covering her face like a shimmering curtain. As I stepped closer, she raised her head but didn't look back at me.

"So, that was her."

I paused. Her voice was flat, no emotion at all, no indication of what she was feeling. Unsure how to proceed, I answered simply. "Yes."

A few heartbeats of silence. When she spoke again, I could hear her smile, but it was as bitter as the fading autumn leaves. "I can see why you love her so much."

I closed my eyes. "Ari—"

She stood quickly before I could say more, though she didn't turn around. "I know. I'm sorry, Ash. I…" Her voice caught, and she pushed back her hair, speaking more to herself than to me. "I didn't think it would be this hard."

I watched her, in the flickering shadows. I watched the firelight rippling off her silver hair, the way her body moved, graceful and sure. And, I was suddenly reminded why I'd fallen in love with her, all those years ago. She was as beautiful as those days when I was that young, arrogant prince, and time had not dulled her perfection. I thought about what Meghan had told me: that fate had given us another chance; Ariella was back in my life, and I could be happy now.

Could I be happy with Ariella?

I shook my head, veering from those thoughts before they

got too tempting, feeling another thread of my essence unravel. It didn't matter, I realized through gritted teeth. I could not abandon my quest, regardless of my feelings. I swore that I would find a way to return to Meghan, and I was bound to that promise. I couldn't go back on my word, even if what I searched for was impossible. Even if Meghan was no longer waiting for me, that she had said her goodbyes, that she had let me go. I could not give up, even now.

Even if I died, and took everyone with me.

"Finally awake, are you?" The Wolf melted from the shadows, a piece of the night becoming real. "I was tempted to rip out your throat while you slept and put you out of your misery, little prince. Watching you sleep was becoming tiring." He licked his jaws, where a dull coating of red spattered his fur, and bared his teeth. "We've wasted enough time here, and I am getting bored. Do you wish to reach the Testing Grounds or not?"

"Yes," I said as Puck joined us, carrying several mushroom kebabs. "It's time to head out. Where do we go from here?"

Ariella closed her eyes. "We follow the River of Dreams," she murmured, "past the Briars, until we reach the final barrier, and then the End of the World. Beyond that, the Testing Grounds await."

"You make it sound so easy." Puck sighed, stuffing another truffle in his mouth. "Past the Briars you say? And then beyond the End of the World? How long is *that* going to take us?"

"As long as it takes," I said firmly. "As long as I have the breath to keep going, I will. But that doesn't mean the rest of you should do the same." I gazed around the group, meeting the stares of my companions. "From here on out," I began, "it's going to be even more dangerous. I won't ask you to stay with me. None of us know what lies beyond the Briars, at the

End of the World. If you want to go back, do so now. I won't hold it against you." My gaze caught Ariella's as I said this. "I can go on alone, if I must, if being around me is too dangerous or hard or painful to go on."

I would save you my fate, if I could. I will not watch you die again.

"Hmm. Hey, ice-boy, hold these for a second, will ya?" Puck asked, holding out the mushroom kebabs. Frowning, I took them, and he struck me upside the head, not hard, but solid enough to rock me forward a step. "Stop being so damned fatalistic," he said as I turned on him with a snarl. "If I didn't want to be here, I wouldn't be. And you know you can't do it all by your lonesome, ice-boy. Sooner or later, you're going to have to start trusting us."

I laughed at him then, bitter and self-mocking. "Trust," I said flatly. "Trust requires the faith of both parties, Goodfellow."

"Enough," the Wolf growled, baring his fangs at us all. "We're wasting time. Those who wish to leave, leave. But I believe the consensus is that everyone is staying, is that right?" No one disagreed with him, and he snorted. "Then let us go. I have no idea why two-legs wish to stand around and talk so much."

"For once, I agree with the dog." Grimalkin's voice came from an overhead branch. Golden eyes peered down at us, and the Wolf growled, raising his hackles. The cat ignored him. "If we are to reach the Briars by the River of Dreams, we must find the river first," he said, sharpening his claws on the branch. "As the dog knows this territory best, perhaps it should do something useful and lead us there. Otherwise I see no reason to have it along at all."

The Wolf snarled, tensing his muscles, as if he wished he could climb the tree after the feline. "One day I will catch you on the ground, cat," he said through bared teeth. "And you won't even know I'm there until I tear your head off."

"You have been saying that since before humans had fire, dog," Grimalkin replied, completely undisturbed. "You will have to forgive me if I do not hold my breath." And he disappeared into the leaves.

CHAPTER TEN
THE FORGOTTEN

"So, I'm curious," Puck announced, falling into step beside me. We were following the Wolf through a forest that was larger than any I'd ever seen: massive trees so tall you couldn't see the tops of the branches, with trunks so wide a dozen people couldn't encircle the base. Luminescent flowers and fungi populated this part of the forest, pulsing softly in all the colors of the spectrum. The earth was covered with a thick, spongy moss that glowed bright blue-and-green whenever you stepped on it, leaving footprints that attracted ghostly dragon-flies to hover over the indentions. The Wolf loped tirelessly through this glowing wood, pausing occasionally to glance back, often with an annoyed look that we were taking so long. Puck and I trailed doggedly after him, with Ariella bringing up the rear, moving as quietly as a shadow.

Despite assurances that she was fine, my worry for her gnawed at my insides. After the whole dream encounter and our stammering, awkward conversation, she seemed distant and withdrawn, more so than usual. With every step, she grew more shadowlike, more insubstantial, until I feared she would fade away like the mist in the hollow. I tried talking to her, but though she smiled and answered my questions and told me she was fine, her eyes seemed to stare right through me.

I couldn't get Meghan out of my head, either. I wished I had told her what I was doing. I wished I had said more, argued more. Maybe then I wouldn't have this hollow ache in my chest whenever I thought of our parting words. Had she already moved on, forgotten me? In her position, what she said made sense, but the thought of her with someone else made me wish I had something to fight, to kill, just so I could forget. Between Meghan and Ariella, I felt like I was being torn in two.

So I really wasn't in the mood to talk when Puck ambushed me, coming out of nowhere with that faint smirk on his face, looking for trouble. I knew I wasn't going to like his next question, but he still surprised me when he asked, "So, what did Meghan say when she saw Ariella?"

I glanced at him sharply, and he grinned. "Come on, ice-boy. I'm not stupid. I can put the pieces together well enough to figure out what happened. What did she say?" When I didn't answer, he suddenly reached out and grabbed my shoulder, spinning me around. "Hey, I'm serious, prince!"

I drew my sword in an instant, cutting for his head as I turned. Puck was already bringing up his dagger to block, and the two blades met in a screech of sparks.

Puck glared at me over the crossed blades, eyes gone hard and cold, reflecting my own expression. Dragonflies buzzed around us, and the forest threw odd patches of light over his forehead, almost like war paint. "You're wavering, Ash," Puck said quietly, his eyes glowing like the woods around him. "I've seen how you look at Ariella of late. You don't know what you want, and that indecision is going to destroy you, and the rest of us along with it."

"I gave you the choice to leave," I said, deliberately ignoring the accusation. "No one is keeping you here. You could've gone back to Arcadia, Puck. You could have left if you wanted—"

"No." Puck's eyes narrowed to green slits, and he spoke through clenched teeth. "I'm not going back to explain to Meghan that I left you here alone, to tell her I don't know what happened to you. If I go back, it will be to tell her that you're gone for good, or I won't go back at all."

"I see." I smiled without humor. "You want me to fail. If I die, then you'll be there for Meghan. You're hoping I never come back."

"Ash! Puck!" Ariella's voice broke our standoff as she rushed up, white-faced and frightened. "Stop it! What are you doing?"

"It's fine, Ari," Puck said, not taking his eyes from me. "Ice-boy and I are just having a conversation, isn't that right, prince?"

I held the stance a moment longer, then stepped back, sheathing my blade. Puck grinned, but the look in his eyes told me this wasn't over yet.

"If you two are quite finished," the Wolf growled, circling back, his voice tight with irritation, "we're almost there."

THIS FAR INTO THE DEEP WYLD, the River of Dreams had widened into a wide, sleepy canal of pitch-black water reflecting the darkened sky.

"I wouldn't stand so close to the edge if I were you," the Wolf warned Puck, who was about to skip a pebble along the glassy surface. "We're still very close to the nightmare stretch of the river, and we wouldn't want you pulled in by something nasty. I'd hate to go in after you again."

Puck grinned and flung the rock over the mirrorlike surface. I counted five jumps before something huge and scaly erupted from the water, snapping up the pebble in a fine spray before sinking into the depths once more.

We moved back from the edge.

"How far is it to the Briars?" I asked Ariella, who was sitting on a rock several feet from the bank, looking exhausted. Grimalkin sat beside her, washing a front paw. The Wolf wrinkled his muzzle at the cat but didn't lunge at him, so hopefully they had gone back to pretending the other didn't exist.

"I'm not sure," she said, staring down the river as if in a daze. "A long way, I think. But at least we won't get lost. We just have to follow the river...to the end."

"Wish we had a boat," Puck muttered, tossing another rock into the current. Another splash and a flash of scales erupted from the surface, making him wince. "Then again, maybe not. Our last little trip didn't work out so well, what with the giant eels and arrows and bloodthirsty newts. Guess we're walking to the End of the World after all, unless anyone has a better idea."

The Wolf sat down, his dark form outlined by moonlight, and gazed out toward the water. "There is another boat," he said in a solemn voice. "I've seen it sometimes. A ferry, always unmanned, always going in the same direction. It never appears to stop, and the river nightmares seem unaware of its existence."

"Mmm, you are speaking of the ghost ferry," Grimalkin said, pausing in his grooming to look up. "One of the more common legends, I believe. There is a similar ship that haunts the Broken Glass Sea, a pirate vessel made of the bones of men. Or something like that." He sniffed and shook his head. "According to certain legends, the ghost ferry always appears when there is need."

"Well, there's need here," Puck said, gazing up and down

the dark river. "We need it, because I don't want to go tromping down the river for who knows how long until we reach
the Briars or the End of the World or whatever." He cupped
his hands to his mouth and bellowed, "Do you hear me, ferry?
Need! Here! We need you now!"

Grimalkin flattened his ears, and the Wolf's hackles went
up as he looked at me. "How did he ever survive so long without something tearing his throat out?" he growled.

"Believe me, I've wondered the same."

"The ferry will come to us," Ariella said, causing everyone
to turn and stare at her. She gazed down the river, her eyes
glazed, distant and a million miles away. "I've seen it. In my
visions. It will appear, when it is time."

"When will that be?" I asked.

"I don't know. But it will not be here. I've seen the boat,
and a long, long pier. That is all I know."

"Well…" Puck sighed, grabbing another pebble. "I guess
we're looking for some kind of dock. Anyone know where
we can find one?"

There was no answer to that, and he sighed again. "Guess
we're hoofing it, then."

THE FOREST ON OUR SIDE of the river soon changed, almost
as abruptly as a door slamming. The lights faded, and the
trees became twisted, warped versions of themselves, branches
creaking and groaning though there was no wind. The stars
disappeared, and the river turned even blacker, reflecting
nothing but a sickly red moon, peering through the clouds
like a lone bloodshot eye. I figured we were still in the nightmare stretch of the river, and hoped nothing would come
lurching up from those dark waters or out of the trees, both
much too close for comfort.

"Don't stare into the forest too long, prince," the Wolf

growled, as something rustled in the bushes to the side. "Direct eye contact will draw attention to yourself from the things that live there. And they aren't pretty, trust me."

"You mean they're even scarier than you?" Puck joked, and the Wolf gave him an eerie smile that was all teeth.

"I was born from human fear and suspicion," the Wolf growled, sounding proud of the fact. "Their stories, their legends, gave me power. But these are creatures of human nightmares, pure, mindless, screaming terror. They come crawling out of that river and escape into the forest, and the forest twists and warps into a landscape of what humans fear the most. If you want to meet some of these creatures, feel free to draw their gaze. Just try not to go insane when you finally see one."

Puck snorted. "Please. Who do you think you're talking to? I *caused* some of those human nightmares. I've seen it all, Wolfman. There's nothing that can freak me out any—*whoa!*"

Puck leaped backward, almost tripping over himself. Grimalkin hissed and vanished, and I drew my sword. On the banks of the river, holding a fishing pole in two white, long-fingered hands, an enormous, wild-haired creature turned to stare at us.

I stared at it. It was fey, it had to be, but I'd never seen anything like it. It didn't have a body, just a huge, bulbous head covered in shaggy white hair that hung down to its knees. No, not knees...*knee*. The giant had one thick stump of a leg ending in a massive clubbed foot, dirty yellow toenails gripping the ground like a giant claw. Two long arms sprouted where its ears should've been, and a pair of huge, uneven eyes gazed down at us with detached curiosity.

I tensed, ready to attack should the giant lunge at us. That single leg, once taken out, would make it easy to bring this huge creature down. But the giant only blinked at us sleepily, then turned to gaze at the river again, where the string of his fishing pole met the water.

The Wolf panted, grinning at Puck, who had leaped to his feet, furiously brushing mud from his pants. Ariella stepped up beside me, her apathy forgotten as we gazed up at the strange creature, continuing to fish as if nothing had happened. "What is that?" she whispered, clutching my arm. "I've never seen a creature like this before. Is this some kind of human nightmare?"

"It's not a nightmare," the Wolf said, sitting down to watch us. "It's fey, just like you, but it doesn't have a name. At least, none that anyone can remember."

"I did not think any still existed," Grimalkin said, reappearing on a piece of driftwood, his tail still fluffed out to twice its size. He peered up at the oblivious giant and sniffed. "This may be the very last one."

"Well, endangered or not, maybe it can help us," Puck said, edging up to the giant's treelike leg. "Oy, stumpy! Yeah, you!" he called as the giant's massive head swiveled around to stare at him. "Can you understand me?"

The Wolf blinked at Puck, astonished, and Ariella pressed a little bit closer to me. I could feel her soft fingers gripping my arm, and casually reached for my sword hilt. "I'm not about to scrape you off the bottom of its foot, Goodfellow," I warned.

"Touched that you care, prince," Puck called back, retreating a few steps to meet the giant's gaze, craning his head up. "Hey there," he greeted, waving cheerfully. "We don't mean to intrude, but would you be able to answer a couple questions?" He blinked as the giant continued to stare. "Uh, bob once for yes, twice for no."

The faery shifted, and I tensed, ready to attack if it tried to stomp Puck like an irritating cockroach. But the giant only pulled his line out of the river and turned to face Puck square on.

"What...do...you...want?" it asked, very slowly, as if it was just remembering how to talk. Puck's eyebrows shot up.

"Oh, hey, you can speak, after all. Excellent." He turned to grin at me, and I stared back, unamused. "We were just wondering," Puck continued, giving the giant his best charming smile, "how much farther to the End of the World? Just as a curiosity. Do you know? You look like a local, you've been here awhile, right? What do you think?"

"I...do not remember," the giant said, frowning as if such a thought pained him. "I am sorry. I do not remember."

"You won't get anything useful out of him, Goodfellow," the Wolf growled, standing up. "He doesn't even remember why he's here."

"I was...looking for something," the giant mused, his large eyes going glassy. "In...the river, I think. I forgot what it was, but...I'll know it when I see it."

"Oh." Puck looked disappointed, but only for a moment. "Well, how about a boat, then?" he went on, undaunted. "If you've been here awhile, you must've seen a boat floating down the river once or twice."

The Wolf shook his head and turned to stalk down the riverbank, obviously fed up with the conversation. But the giant frowned, his huge brows knitting together, and nodded thoughtfully.

"A boat. Yes...I remember a boat. Always going in the same direction." He pointed with a pale white finger in the direction we were headed. "That way. It makes one stop, just one, at the dock on the river's edge."

I looked up sharply. "Where?"

The giant's furrows deepened. "A town? A settlement? I think I remember...houses. Others...like me. Lots of mist..."

He blinked and shrugged, which looked strange because he had no shoulders. "I don't remember."

With a final blink, he turned away, as if forgetting we were there, and none of Puck's continued prodding seemed to reach him.

"Do you know anything about this town?" I asked Grimalkin as we continued down the riverbank. Farther ahead, the Wolf had stopped again and was looking back in annoyance. I would've asked him, but he looked ready to snap someone's head off.

"I only know legends, prince." Grimalkin picked his way over the ground, avoiding puddles and mincing his way through the mud. "I have never been to this so-called town myself, but there are very, very old stories about a place in the Deepest Wyld where the fey go to die."

I stared at the cat. "What do you mean?"

Grimalkin sighed. "Among other things, the town is known as Phaed. Do not bother telling me you have never heard of it. I already know you have not. It is a place for those whom no one remembers anymore. Just as stories, belief and imagination make us stronger, the lack of them slowly kills, even those in the Nevernever, until there is nothing left. That giant we saw? He is one of them, the Forgotten, clinging to existence by the thread of those who still remember him. It is only a matter of time before he is simply not there anymore."

I shivered, and even Puck looked grave. Deep down, that was something we all feared, being forgotten, fading away into nothingness because no one remembered our stories or our names.

"Do not look so serious," Grimalkin said, hopping over a puddle, perching on a rock to stare at us. "It is the inevitable end for all of Faery. We all must fade eventually. Even

you, Goodfellow. Even the great and mighty Wolf. Why do
you think he wished to accompany you, prince?" Grimalkin
wrinkled his nose, curling his whiskers at me. "So that his
story would go on. So that it would spread to the hearts and
minds of those who will remember him. But everything he
does is only a delay. Sooner or later, everyone winds up in
Phaed. Except cats, of course." With a sniff, he leaped down
and trotted along the riverbank with his tail held high.

A ragged mist began to curl along the ground, coming
off the water and creeping through the trees. Soon it was so
thick it was difficult to see more than a few feet, the river, the
woods, the distant horizon completely obscured by the blanket of white.

The Wolf suddenly appeared, coming out of the fog like
a silent and deadly shadow. "There are lights ahead," he
growled, the fur along his shoulders and neck bristling like
a bed of spikes. "It looks like a town, but there's something strange about it. It has no scent, no smell. There
are things moving around up ahead, and I heard voices
through the fog, but I can't smell anything. It's like it's
not even there."

"That is the problem with dogs." Grimalkin sighed, nearly
invisible in the coiling mist. "Always trusting what their nose
tells them. Perhaps you should pay attention to your other
senses, as well."

The Wolf bared his teeth in a snarl. "I've been up and down
these banks more times than I can remember. There was never
a town here. Only fog. Why would there be one now?"

"Perhaps it appears as the ferry does," Grimalkin said
calmly, peering into the mist. "Perhaps it only appears when
there is need. Or perhaps—" he glanced at me and Ariella
"—only those who have died or are about to die can find
their way to Phaed."

THE RIVERBANK TURNED into a muddy path, which we followed until dark shapes began to appear through the mist, the silhouettes of houses and trees. As we got closer, the town of Phaed appeared before us, the path cutting straight through the center. Wooden shanties stood on stilts above the marshy ground, leaning dangerously to the side as if they were drunk. Tired gray hovels slumped or were stacked atop each other like cardboard boxes on the verge of falling down or collapsing with a good kick. Everything sagged, drooped, creaked or was so faded it was impossible to tell its original color.

The street was full of clutter, odds and ends that appeared as if they had been dropped and never picked up again. A fishing pole, with the skeleton of a fish on the end of the line, lay in the middle of the road, causing the Wolf to curl his lip and skirt around it. An easel with a half-finished painting rotted in a pool of stagnant water, paint dripping into the pool like blood. And books were scattered everywhere, from children's nursery rhymes to huge tomes that looked completely ancient.

The fog here was thicker, too, muffling all sound. Nothing seemed to move, or even breathe.

"Nice place," Puck muttered as we passed an old rocking chair, creaking in the wind. "Real homey. I wonder where everyone is."

"They come and go," said the rocking chair behind us. We all jumped and spun around, drawing our weapons. A strange creature with blank white eyes stared at us where nothing had been before.

As with the giant, I didn't recognize this creature. It had the body of a shriveled old woman, but her hands were gnarled bird claws and her feet ended in hooves. Feathers stuck out of her gray hair and ran down her skinny arms, but I also saw tiny horns curling from her brow. She regarded me with a dull, tired expression, and a forked tongue flicked out to touch her lips.

"Oh," she said as I took a deep, slow breath and sheathed my weapon, "newcomers. I haven't seen a new face in town for...come to think of it, I've never seen a new face." She paused a moment, peering at us, then brightened. "If you're new, then perhaps you've seen it. Have you seen it, by chance?"

I frowned. "It?"

"Yes. *It*."

I felt something odd in the air around her, a faint pulling sensation, like water being sucked through a straw. "It... what?" I asked cautiously, facing the old faery again. "What are you looking for?"

"I don't know." She sighed heavily, seeming to shrink in on herself. "I don't remember. I just know I lost it. You haven't seen it, have you?"

"No," I told her firmly. "I haven't seen it."

"Oh." The old creature sighed again, shrinking down a little more. "Are you sure? I thought you might have seen it."

"So, anyway," Puck broke in, before the conversation could go in another circle. "We'd love to stay and chat, but we're sort of in a hurry. Can you point us toward the docks?"

The creature's tongue flicked out, as if tasting the air around Puck. "You're so bright," she whispered. "All of you are so bright. Like little suns, you are." Puck and I shared a glance, and started to back away. "Oh, don't leave," the faery pleaded, holding out a withered claw. "Stay. Stay and chat a bit. It's so cold sometimes. So...cold..." She shivered and, like mist dissolving in the sunlight, faded away. An empty rocking chair, still creaking back and forth, was the only thing left behind.

Puck gave an exaggerated shiver and rubbed his arms. "Okay, that was probably the creepiest thing I've seen in a while," he said with forced cheerfulness. "Who else is for finding this boat and getting the hell outta Dodge?"

"Come on," the Wolf growled, eager to leave as well. "I can smell the river. This way." Without waiting for a reply, he turned and padded down the street.

I looked for Grimalkin, not surprised to find he had vanished as well. I hoped that didn't mean there would be trouble soon. "What do you think she was searching for?" I asked Ariella as we continued through the silent town, following the Wolf's huge silhouette through the fog. "The creature on the riverbank was looking for something, too. I wonder what they lost that's so important?"

Ariella shivered, her expression haunted. "Their names," she said quietly. "I think...they were searching for their names." She drifted off for a moment, her eyes distant and sad. I felt a twinge of alarm at how much she suddenly resembled the faery in the rocking chair. "I could feel the emptiness inside," Ariella continued in a near whisper, "the hollow places that consume them. They're like a hole, an empty spot where you'd expect something to be. That creature in the rocking chair...she was almost gone. I think it was just your and Puck's glamour that brought her back, if only for a little while."

Figures were starting to appear through the mist now, strange, unfamiliar creatures with the same dead eyes and empty faces. They stumbled through the town in a daze, as if sleepwalking, barely conscious of their surroundings. Sometimes they would turn to stare at us with blank eyes and detached curiosity, but none made an effort to approach.

A booming roar broke through the muffled silence, and a scuffle ahead in the mist made me draw my sword and hurry over. The Wolf stood, teeth bared and hackles raised, over a figure with tiny hands growing everywhere from its body. The creature's arms, as well as its dozens of hands, were thrown up to protect it, and it cringed back as the Wolf bared his teeth and went for its throat.

I lunged forward, slamming my shoulder into the Wolf's head, knocking him aside with a furious yelp. He turned on me with a snarl, and suddenly Puck was there, daggers drawn, standing beside me. Together, we formed a wall between the Wolf and his intended victim, who scurried away on multiple hands and vanished under a building.

The Wolf glared at us, eyes blazing, the hair on his spine standing up. "Move," he growled, narrowing his eyes. "I'm going to find that thing and rip its head off. Get out of my way."

"Calm down," I ordered, keeping my blade between myself and the angry Wolf. "Attack one of them and the whole place might come after us. It's gone now, so you can't do anything about it."

"I'll kill them all," the Wolf growled, his voice gone dangerously soft. "I'll rip every single one of them to bloody shreds. This place isn't natural. Can't you feel it? It's like a starving animal, clawing at us. We should kill every one of them now."

"I would advise against that," Grimalkin said, appearing from nowhere. He narrowed his eyes at the Wolf, who stared back murderously. "You would be surprised how many Forgotten exist in this world," the cat went on. "More than you can imagine, I assure you. And strong emotions like anger and fear will only attract them like ants to honey. So do try to keep your teeth in your jaws without ripping someone's head off. We might actually make it out of here."

The Wolf's baleful glare shifted between me and Grimalkin before he turned away with a snarl, snapping at the air. As he did, I saw the fur on his back and shoulders, normally pitch-black, was streaked with gray, but then he shook himself and the color faded from sight.

"Geez, this place is making even Wolfman twitchy," Puck said to me in a low voice, watching the Wolf pace back and forth, growling. Beyond him, a crowd was slowly gathering, curious faces emerging from the mist, blank eyes fixed on us. "Let's find that boat and get out of here before he starts tearing down the walls."

We followed the muddy street until, at last, it reached the banks of the River of Dreams, still shrouded in white, dark waters lapping softly against the mud. A single wooden dock stretched away until it vanished into the fog, but nothing moved out on the river or through the mists. Everything was overly quiet and still.

"Well, here's the dock," Puck said, squinting as he peered through the fog. "But I don't see a boat. Maybe we have to buy a ticket?"

"You won't find what you're looking for standing there," said a soft voice behind us.

I turned, slower this time, refusing to jump at every creature that popped up out of nowhere. But I still drew my weapon, and I still put a hand on the Wolf's shoulder to keep him from spinning and biting the speaker's head off.

At first, I didn't see anyone behind us. The voice appeared to have come from no one, though there was a long, lean shadow on the ground that seemed attached to nothing.

"Show yourself," the Wolf growled, curling back his lips. "Before I lose my temper and start tearing out your guts, invisible or not. I can smell you well enough, so you can stop hiding right now."

"Oh, apologies," said the voice again, right in front of us. "I keep forgetting…." And, a tall, impossibly thin figure *turned* out of nowhere, standing in profile so we could see him. He was nearly paper-thin, like the edge of a blade, only visible when viewed from the side. Even in profile he was still impossibly lean and sharp, with gray skin and a striped gray business suit. His fingers, long and spiderlike, waved a greeting, making sure we could see him.

"Better?" he asked, smiling to show thin pointed teeth in a lipless mouth. A name flickered through my mind, keeping just out of reach, before it was gone. "I am the caretaker of this town, the mayor, if you will," the thin man continued, watching us from the corner of his eyes. "Normally, I am here to greet newcomers and wish them a long and peaceful stay while they wait for the end. But you..." His eyes narrowed, and he tapped the ends of his fingers together. "You are not like the rest of us. Your names have not been forgotten. I am unsure how you even found this place, but it matters not. You do not belong here. You need to leave."

"We will," I said as the Wolf's growls grew louder, more threatening. "We're just waiting for the ferry. When it comes, we'll be out of your way."

The thin man tapped his fingers. "The ferry does not stop here often. Most citizens of Phaed are not even aware of its existence. But, every once in a blue moon, someone will grow tired of searching for something that is clearly not here. They come to the decision that what they seek is beyond Phaed, beyond the river, and they embark on a journey to find what they have lost. Only then does the ferry appear at the end of that pier." He pointed a long finger toward the dock that vanished into the mist. "The ferry only goes in one direction, and when it comes back around from wherever it has been, it is always empty. No one knows what happens to the passengers that step aboard that ship, but they never come back to Phaed. It's like they vanish off the edge of the earth."

"That's fine," I told him, ignoring the mock spooky looks

Puck was giving me. "We don't plan to come back, either. When does the ferry appear?"

The thin man shrugged. "Usually a day or two after the decision is made to leave. If you truly wish to wait for it, I suggest you find yourself a place to stay until then. The Wayside Inn is a good choice. Just follow the bank until you see it. It really can't be missed."

And with that, he turned, becoming a straight, nearly invisible line, and disappeared.

Ariella sighed, pressing close to me. I felt her shoulder touch mine and resisted the urge to put my arms around her. "Looks like we're staying here a little while, after all."

"Only as long as the ferry takes to arrive." I could feel eyes in the mist and shadows around me, and that strange pull tugged at my insides. "Come on. Let's find that inn and get out of the street."

Like the thin man promised, it wasn't difficult to find the inn, a large, two-story structure on stilts that leaned over the water as if it might topple into the river at any moment. Not surprisingly, it was empty as we walked through the door into a dark, gloomy foyer, the ever-present mist coiling along the floor and around the scattered tables.

"Huh." Puck's voice echoed off the walls as we ventured cautiously inside. His boots creaked horribly against the wooden floor as he circled the room. "Helloooooo, room service? Bellboys? Can anyone take my luggage to my suite? Guess this inn is self-serve."

"The rooms are upstairs," whispered a voice, and an old woman slithered down from the ceiling. She was more spiderweb than anything, fraying at the edges, though the eyes in the cloudy face were sharp and black. "Five guests? Good, good. You can each choose one. Except for him—" She pointed at the Wolf, who curled a lip at her. "He can take the big room on the end."

"Good enough," I said, secretly relieved for the chance to rest. Whether I was still feeling the effects of the hobyah poison or my body was simply reacting to the strain of keeping everyone alive, I was tired, more weary than I had been in a while. I knew the others were feeling it, too. Ariella looked exhausted, and Grimalkin had somehow fallen asleep in her arms, his nose buried under his tail. Even Puck looked worn-out beneath his constant energy, and the Wolf didn't seem as alert as he normally was, though his temper was definitely wearing thin.

Upstairs, the rooms were small, each containing a table and a single bed beneath a tiny round window. Gazing out, I saw the River of Dreams stretching away beneath me, and the lonely dock in the distance, nearly swallowed up by the mist.

For just a moment, I couldn't remember why I wanted to go to the dock, though I knew it was important. Shaking my head as memory returned, I sat on the thin mattress, rubbing my eyes. Tired. I was just tired. As soon as the ferry arrived, we could leave this place, and continue toward the edge of the world. And then the Testing Grounds, where I would finally reach the end of my quest. And then my fate would be decided. I'd return to Meghan as a human with a soul, or I wouldn't return at all. That simple.

Lying back, I put an arm over my face, and everything faded away.

I WAS KNEELING IN A FIELD of bloody snow, countless bodies of Winter and Summer fey surrounding me.

I was standing before Queen Mab, my sword plunged deep in her chest, her dimming eyes filled with shock.

I was sitting on a throne of ice with my queen beside me, a beautiful faery with long silver hair and eyes of starlight.

I was standing on the field of battle once more, watching my army tear through the enemy forces, feeling a savage glee as they killed and maimed and destroyed without mercy. The darkness in me reveled in the blood, drank in the pain, and spread it as far as it could go. But no matter how much pain I felt, the emptiness swallowed it, demanding more, always more. I was a black hole of death, needing to kill, needing to fill the terrible nothingness that existed inside. I'd become a demon, soulless and without pity, and not even Ariella's presence could sate the despair that drove me to slaughter everything I had once cared for. Only one thing would stop me, and every death, every life I destroyed, brought me that much closer.

She came for me in the end, as I knew she would. I'd made certain it would be her. The terrible Iron Queen, her eyes filled with fury and sorrow, facing me across the ravaged fields of the Nevernever. The days of her pleading with me, trying to reason with me, were long gone. I didn't remember why I wanted to see her; I didn't even remember my own name. But I knew she was the reason for my emptiness. She was the reason for everything.

She'd grown stronger during the long years of the war, infinitely more powerful, a true Queen of Faery. I'd killed so many of her subjects, so many fey had died by my hands, but it was the death of a certain Summer Court jester that finally pushed her over the edge. We faced each other, Iron Queen and Unseelic King, as the cold wind howled around us, and knew that whatever feelings we'd once had for each other didn't matter now. We'd chosen our paths, and now, one way or another, this war would end. Today, one of us would die.

The Iron Queen raised her sword, the sickly light gleaming down the edges of the steel blade as Iron glamour flared around her, a maelstrom of deadly power. I saw her lips move, a name on them, perhaps mine, and felt nothing. My glamour rose up to meet hers, cold and dangerous, and our powers slammed into each other with the roar of dueling dragons.

Flashes of images, like broken mirror shards, falling to the earth. Iron and ice, clashing against each other. Rage and hate, swirling in vicious, ugly colors around us. Glamour and pain and blood.

Myself, deliberately failing to stop the blow that would kill me. The point of a saber, piercing my chest...

I blinked, and the world slowed. I lay on my back, a dull throbbing in the vicinity of my heart, cold and numb and unable to make my body move. Above me, the Iron Queen's face filled my vision, beautiful and strong, though her face was streaked with tears. She knelt, smoothing the hair from my forehead, her fingers trailing a line of heat across my skin.

I blinked again, and for just a moment, I was the one kneeling in the dirt, clutching the Iron Queen's body to my chest, screaming into the wind.

Her fingers lingered on my cheek, and I gazed up at her, my vision starting to go fuzzy and dark. A tear splashed against my skin and in that instant, the old me regretted everything; everything that had brought us here, everything I had done. I tried to speak, to beg forgiveness, to tell her not to remember me like this, but my voice failed me and I couldn't force the words out.

From the corner of my eye, I sensed another presence, watching us from the shadows. It seemed terribly invasive, until I realized it didn't belong here, that it was somehow separate from this reality.

Meghan bent down, and though I couldn't hear her, I saw her lips murmur, "Goodbye, Ash." Then those lips touched my forehead and the darkness flooded in.

CHAPTER ELEVEN
THE FERRY

"Prince."

I groaned.

"Prince." Something patted my chin. "Wake up."

Shifting on the mattress, I struggled to open my eyes. There was a solid weight sitting on my chest, but exhaustion was making my lids heavy and awkward. I was tired; I wanted to sink back into oblivion, despite the disturbing dreams that waited for me.

"Hmm. For such a well-trained, somewhat paranoid warrior, you are certainly difficult to rouse. Very well." The weight on my chest slid off, much to my relief, and I heard a thump as it dropped to the floor and walked away. "We shall have to resort to more drastic measures."

Just as I was wondering what "drastic measures" were, a patter of footsteps scampered toward the bed. There was a brief pause…and then that solid, heavy weight landed square on my stomach.

"Oof!" I bolted upright with a gasp, the breath driven from my lungs in a painful, vicious expulsion. Instantly awake, I clutched my ribs and glared at Grimalkin, sitting on the bed with a smug, pleased expression on his face.

"All right," I gritted out, breathing slowly to dispel the nausea, "you have my attention. What do you want, cat?"

"Ah," he purred, as if nothing had happened. "There you are. I was beginning to think you had died in your sleep." He stood, waving his tail. "We have trouble. The boat is here, and I cannot wake anyone up."

"Boat?"

The cat rolled his eyes. "Yes. Boat. The ferry that you are so eager to take to the End of the World? Did you accidentally hit your head before I woke you?" He peered at me, suddenly serious. "There is something strange going on, prince," he muttered. "I cannot wake any of the others, and it is not like you to forget something this important. How do you feel?"

I thought the strangest occurrence was Grimalkin asking about my health, but after a moment I frowned. "Tired," I admitted. "Almost drained."

Grimalkin nodded. "I thought as much. Something about this place is siphoning your strength, your glamour, even your memories." He blinked and shook himself. "Even I am finding it hard to keep my eyes open. Come." Turning suddenly, he leaped off the bed. "We must wake the others. If we do not make it to the ferry in time, it will leave, and you will be stuck here forever."

I stood, frowning as the room spun around me. Rubbing my eyes, I started to follow Grimalkin, but a faint noise outside the window made me pause. Bracing myself against the wall, I looked through the glass and drew in a slow breath.

The inn was surrounded by Forgotten. Hollow-eyed, faded and famished looking, they crowded the muddy road, shoulder to shoulder, staring up at me with slack, open mouths. How long had they stood there, sucking away our glamour,

our memories? How long before we became like them, empty and hollow, black holes drawing in every little bit of life?

I stumbled back from the window and into the hall, where Grimalkin waited for me, lashing his tail.

"Hurry," he hissed, and trotted into the next room. I shook the cobwebs out of my head and followed.

A girl lay on the bed, shifting and moaning as if in the throes of a nightmare, her long silver hair spread over the pillow. For one heart-stopping moment, I couldn't remember her name, though I knew she was important to me. The sudden worry and protectiveness I felt when I saw her proved it was true.

"Go to her," Grimalkin said, backing away. "Wake her up. I will attempt to rouse Goodfellow once more. Perhaps he will waken if claws are applied in a strategically important area. Then you can all tackle the dog. I will certainly not partake in that endeavor." He wrinkled his nose and padded from the room.

I knelt down beside the bed. "Ari," I muttered, grabbing the delicate shoulders and shaking them gently. "Wake up. We have to go, now."

Ariella flinched away from me, raising her hands in sleep as if to reach out for someone. "No, Ash...no," she whispered. "Don't...please, no."

"Ari!" I shook harder, jostling her thin frame, but she only whimpered and sank deeper into sleep. Finally, I gathered her to me, lifting her in my arms. She was so light, like twigs held together by wispy cloth. Clutching her to my chest, I stumbled from the room.

Grimalkin met me at the door, followed by a yawning Puck scratching the back of his head. He gave me a sleepy nod as we passed. Together, we ventured into the last room down the hall, where the huge form of the Wolf was curled in a corner, his rumbling snores vibrating the walls.

"Okay," Puck said, leaning against the doorframe, looking like he was fighting to stay on his feet, "I agree that we have to get out of here now, but...who wants to wake up the puppy?"

I nodded toward a corner. "There's a broom. I have Ariella—I think you should take care of the Wolf."

"Hmm, that's okay, ice-boy. I'm kinda partial to not having my head bitten off."

"Goodfellow!" Grimalkin spat, right before he disappeared, "Above you!"

I spun, still holding Ariella, as a Forgotten dropped from the ceiling—the innkeeper from before, only now her eyes were blank and glassy, her mouth an open hole as she lurched toward Puck.

The Wolf's eyes snapped open. Without warning, he sprang to his feet with a roar and lunged through the doorway, massive jaws clamping over the Forgotten's spindly frame. The faery wailed and dissolved like mist in the breeze, and the Wolf shook his head, turning back to glare at us.

"It's impossible to sleep with the pair of you around," he growled, baring his teeth. "Now, are we leaving, or are you two going to stand there barking at each other all night?"

Forgotten were beginning to drift up the stairs like zombies, faces slack and mouths open. Puck and the Wolf met them side by side, teeth and daggers flashing in the dim light, cutting a path to the exit. Ariella sighed and murmured in my arms, and I held her close, determined that no Forgotten would touch her.

We burst through the door of the inn and stopped, staring at the huge mob of Forgotten surrounding the building. The Forgotten stared back, silent and motionless, mouths gaping like landed fish. The Wolf snarled and lunged forward, snapping at the air, and the Forgotten drew back, offering no resistance. But they were so starved for glamour, for memory and emotion and life, that the Wolf stumbled and nearly fell, his strength siphoned away.

The ground lurched, and I nearly sank to my knees, fighting to stay upright. "Keep moving!" I called, as Puck swiped at several Forgotten that pressed closer, driving them back. "Get to the dock! We have to make it to the ferry!"

The Forgotten parted for us like waves, not resisting, forcing no confrontation, but their hunger was a constant thing, draining our life, making it harder and harder to move. I glanced over at Puck and saw him turning as gray and washed-out as the Forgotten around us, his once-bright red hair dull and colorless. I couldn't see Grimalkin, and hoped the cat wouldn't simply fade into nothingness while invisible, which we would never know.

The dock loomed before us, a lifeline in the dark, and on the River of Dreams, I saw the faint edges of a ferryboat through the mist. Puck and the Wolf, staggering and nearly leaning on each other, reached it first, and Puck yelled at me to hurry, before vanishing into the fog.

Just as I reached the dock, something latched on to my arm. I felt a stab of pain, an emptiness so strong it was physical, and went to my knees as the sharp thin man appeared before me, his long fingers grasping my arm.

"I figured it out," he whispered, as I struggled to make my body move, respond, anything. But I was numb, drained, only barely conscious, as the thin man continued to draw out my life. I felt my glamour slipping away with my strength, sucked into the black hole that was the sharp thin man. Ariella slumped against my chest as my grip failed, and his gaze followed her.

"My, you're strong," he continued in an amiable voice. "So much life. Such powerful memories and glamour and emotion. You do not belong here. Not yet. Upset the balance, you have. Even those who are nearly faded have come back, and now they will linger even more. Because of you."

"Not...yet?" I could barely get the words out. The crowd of Forgotten had gathered again, surrounding us with open mouths, their combined pull so strong I nearly collapsed. The thin man looked at me, surprised.

"You do not know?" He tilted his head, and for a moment, it vanished. "Your essence is unraveling. Bit by bit. Soon, you will be unable to remember your name, your promise, who you are, and you will be consumed with filling the emptiness inside. But it will never be enough. In time, you will find your way to Phaed, to remain here with the Forgotten, and the Promise-breakers." He nodded, a sharp gesture in the coiling fog. "But not yet."

"Then...you'll let us...go?"

"Of course you will go," the sharp thin man said, as if that was obvious. "You will go, and life will return to normal. Everyone will forget, as is their way. You do not belong. But, her—" his gaze sharpened, staring at Ariella "—she must stay. She is the reason you found this place. No essence. No life. She is empty, like we are. She remains."

I felt a flare of anger, but it was immediately drained away by the thin man. "No," I muttered, trying to find the strength to pull back, to resist. "I...need her."

"She remains," the thin man whispered again, and reached to take her from me.

No! A fierce protectiveness roared to life, drowning out everything else. She would not be taken away. Not again. I would not fail her again.

With the last of my strength, I lunged to my feet and drew my blade, pressing it to the thin man's neck.

He seemed surprised that I could still move. "She does not belong with you," he said, watching calmly as I fought to remain on my feet, keep the blade steady and hold the girl to myself with one arm. "She belongs here, with us."

"I don't care," I told him. "I'm not letting her go."

A roar shattered the stillness, and the Wolf came bounding out of the fog, scattering Forgotten like wispy birds. Shoving his huge body between myself and the thin man, he bared his fangs at the crowd and snarled. "Get going, prince," he snapped, as the sharp thin man turned to the side and disappeared. "The boat is already leaving. Go!"

Sheathing my sword, I gathered Ariella in both arms and staggered onto the dock, where Puck met me halfway. "Geez, you love to wait till the last dramatic moment, don't you, ice-boy?" he muttered as we hurried over the planks. At the end of the dock, a small, faded paddleboat covered in moss and vines was pulling away, easing back into the River of Dreams. Grimalkin sat on the railings, watching us with glowing yellow eyes.

"Hurry!" the cat urged as the boat pulled farther away. "They are coming!"

Behind us, I heard the Wolf's growls as he backed onto the dock, and felt the emptiness of the Forgotten sucking at me, even from this distance. And then they were crawling onto the dock from beneath the water, reaching for us with ghostly fingers, mouths gaping like dead fish. Puck slashed at one, cutting through it like paper, and it frayed into coils of mist, but there were always more, grasping for us, starved and relentless.

The ferry drew farther away.

Thumping footsteps shook the dock, and I turned to see the

Wolf hurl himself out of the fog, bounding toward us. Dozens of Forgotten clung to him, hanging off his back and neck as he snarled and growled and snapped, shaking himself free only to have more take their places. The Forgotten crowding around our feet drew back, slipping away toward the Wolf. I started to go after them, but the Wolf turned, meeting my gaze with his burning green eyes, lips peeled back in a snarl.

"Get going!" he roared, and we went, hurrying after the ferry. Puck reached the edge of the dock first and leaped, flailing his arms as he hit and grabbed the railing to keep from falling off. I was right behind him, flinging myself over the dark waters, Ariella featherlight in my arms. I struck the edge of the boat and rolled, curling my body around the girl to protect her, wincing as the edge of a bench hit me in the back.

I staggered upright, laid Ariella on one of the seats, and hurried to the side of the boat, looking for the Wolf. But the fog had curled around the dock, hiding it from view. I still heard the soft splashes of the Forgotten as they hit the water, and the Wolf, snarling through the mist, but I couldn't see him anymore.

"Pity," Grimalkin remarked, sounding as if he almost meant it. "I was nearly used to his smell, too."

And then the dark form of the Wolf leaped from the blanket of fog, hurtling over the river. He landed next to the ferry with a splash, spraying everyone with water, causing Grimalkin to hiss and flee under the benches. Surfacing, the Wolf lunged out of the water, hooked his huge paws over the railing and pulled himself, dripping and panting, onto the deck.

I winced as he shook himself, sending river water flying, soaking us all once more. Yawning, he ignored Puck's indignant yell and turned to me, gold-green eyes narrowing.

"That is the second time I saved your lives, prince. Be sure to remember that part of the story when you pass it along."

He yawned again, showing off enormous canines, and padded toward the aft deck, weaving lightly through the aisles of narrow benches. Curling up near the back, he laid his head on his paws, watching us all before his eyes closed and he appeared to fall asleep.

I shook water out of my clothes and took a deep breath, watching the dock slowly vanish behind us in the fog. The ferry slid noiselessly through the River of Dreams, leaving the town far behind. Already, I had forgotten its name. The people, their voices, everything I'd seen and heard, slipping from memory. I struggled to remember something a thin man had told me, something important. Something about Ariella... and myself...

The ferry abruptly broke from the mist, punching through it like a wall, revealing the vast river before us and the night sky above. I blinked and looked around. Puck was standing at the bow of the boat, gazing over the water, and Ariella was asleep on a bench.

I frowned, feeling like I was missing something. I remembered we had been looking for the ferry, walking along the riverbank searching for it, but the memory of us actually boarding was hazy. Had something been chasing us? I vaguely recalled a dock, and carrying Ariella aboard, but beyond that...nothing. I felt groggy and disoriented, as if I'd just woken up from a dream—

The dream. My stomach turned, and I clutched the railing to remain steady on my feet. I remembered the dream. Killing Mab. Ruling Winter. Waging war. Blood and death and violence, the hollow, ravenous void that threatened to drag me down and swallow me whole.

Fighting the Iron Queen. Dying by her hand.

In a daze, I walked to the bench in front of Ariella and sat down, watching her. After a few minutes, her eyelids flickered, and she opened her eyes, blinking at me looming above her.

"Ash?"

"Was it real?" I asked, my voice sounding hoarse and dry in my ears. She frowned and sat up to face me, brushing her hair from her eyes.

"What do you mean?"

"What I saw." I leaned forward, and she drew back, a wary shadow crossing her face. "That was you, wasn't it? Showing me the future. Killing Mab. Making myself the Winter King. Going to war with the other courts—" I stumbled to a halt, not wanting to remember beyond that, to see the look on the Iron Queen's face as she killed me.

Ariella went pale. "You saw...? Oh, Ash. I'm so sorry. I didn't mean for you to see..." She stopped. Took a deep breath. "It must have been the hobyah venom. It made you hypersensitive to dreams and dreamwalking. If you were asleep, you probably—"

"Ari." My voice was soft, and she blinked at me. I raked a hand through my damp hair, fighting to stay calm, to ignore the darkness clawing at my feet, trying to drag me down. "What I saw. Is this...the future? My future? Am...am I destined to become...that? The destroyer of the courts, slaughtering everything, everyone I know?" Ariella was silent, and I reached out to take her hand, squeezing as if it were a lifeline, holding me to sanity. "Tell me," I said, forcing out the words. "Tell me, is that what I become?"

"I don't know, Ash." Her voice was a whisper, on the verge of tears. "It's a future, one of several. Probably the worst, but not the most unlikely. You...you have so much darkness in you, so much anger and grief. Not even I could reach you if you gave in to despair, if you broke your promise." She took a deep breath. "Your essence...when it's gone you'll forget everything that makes you...you. Most Promise-breakers just fade away, never to be seen again. But a few, especially those who are strong, become something else entirely."

"This is what will happen," I whispered, "if I fail."

Silence for a moment. The ferry glided steadily through the night, the only sounds the splash of water against the sides and the Wolf's deep breathing.

"Not necessarily," Ariella said at last, avoiding my gaze. "Nothing is certain, and that is only one possible future. But... yes. If you fail here, there is a real possibility of losing you to the darkness, and you becoming the Winter King."

"So it wasn't just a nightmare," Puck's voice broke in. I turned to see him standing behind us, hands in his pockets, watching me with serious green eyes. "Sorry, couldn't help but overhear you guys," he continued, not sounding the least bit apologetic. "And you know, I was just thinking, that dream you were talking about. It sounds an awful lot like the one I just had." His mouth twisted into a smirk, and his gaze narrowed. "Only, in this version, I *died*. Some Winter King bastard stuck me through the chest while we were fighting. Kinda traumatic, if you know what I mean. And that was *after* he destroyed most of the Summer Court."

I held his gaze. Puck didn't shy away and continued to stare at me, half smile firmly in place. But beyond the smirk, beyond the flippancy and cheek and cocky self-assurance, I could sense the indecision, the fear he never let anyone see.

"Do you regret it?" I asked, and he raised a brow at me. "Do you regret our feud is over, not killing me when you had the chance?"

Puck shot me a painful smile. "Oh, there's a part of me that will always miss our little duels, prince," he said cheerfully. "Nothing like a little attempted murder to feel close to someone, right?" He grinned, then a shadow fell over his face, and he sobered, shaking his head. "Truth is, I'm glad it's done," he said quietly, scrubbing the back of his head. "I never wanted it, I hated that I always had to watch my back, and I knew you really didn't want to go through with it either, prince. Especially toward the end."

"But?" I prompted.

"But, if I see any signs of you becoming...*that*." Puck shivered. "If I suspect you're about to go postal on Mab and take a shot at the Winter throne, I won't need a formal duel invitation to make me show up in Tir Na Nog." He crossed his arms and stared at me with a mix of regret and determination. "If it comes to that, prince, I *will* stop you."

I stood. A breeze blew across the surface of the river, tossing hair and tugging at clothes. I gripped the railing and stared out over the water, feeling his eyes on my back. "If it comes to that," I told him quietly, "I'd want you to."

THE FERRY CONTINUED through the seemingly endless waters of the River of Dreams. The sun never rose, the night never waned; it was all eternal midnight this far into the Deep Wyld. Farther in, the river became crowded with more dream debris, larger and wilder than before. A huge cherry tree, springing from the middle of the river, shedding pink blossoms like falling snow. A glass coffin with a black-haired princess inside, pale hands folded on her stomach as she slept. A long table floated past, complete with a full tea-party set— pot, plates, teacups. Puck snatched a large basket of scones as it drifted by.

How long the ferry slid through the River of Dreams, I wasn't sure. We took turns at guard duty, ate and slept when we could, and talked among ourselves. Puck quickly grew restless, and being trapped in a small area with a bored Robin Goodfellow and a huge, volatile wolf was a scene from a

nightmare. After one hot-tempered explosion that rocked the
boat and nearly dumped everyone into the river, I suggested
Puck adopt his raven form and "scout ahead," which he was
happy to do, much to everyone's relief.

After Puck left, things quieted down. Grimalkin slept almost constantly, and the Wolf either paced the deck like a
caged tiger or lay curled up at the stern, his burning eyes distant and far away. He rarely spoke to anyone, though there
were times, when the Wolf was on guard duty and everyone
was supposed to be asleep, that I saw him and Grimalkin talking together, their voices always too low to hear. Awake, they
studiously ignored each other or shot contemptuous glances
in each other's direction, but the night I saw them at the bow
of the ferry, gazing over the water side by side, I couldn't help
but wonder if their ancient war was just another game they
liked to play.

Ariella and I talked sparingly, and when we did, it was often
of the present, of the Winter and Summer Courts, of the Iron
fey that had so recently invaded our world. We avoided talk
of the past, the old hunts and long nights in the wyldwood,
though the memories kept springing up whenever we spoke.
But ever since the dream with Meghan, Ariella seemed like a
different person. She was so quiet, drawn into herself, brooding over a future I could not see. Her smiles seemed rigid and
forced, her laughter tinged with melancholy. Once, when I
asked if the visions had shown her anything of herself, her
eyes glazed over and she stared right through me before she
shook herself and waved it off, smiling. But for a long time
after, she stared over the River of Dreams, and though I could
reach out and touch her, feel her soft skin under my finger-
tips, it seemed I was staring at a ghost, an echo of a person I
once knew.

"Here," she said one night, joining me at the bow. It was

my turn for watch, and I was leaning against the railing staring into the passing forest. When Ariella dropped an orange into my hand, I blinked and looked at her curiously. "Eat something," she ordered, pointing to the fruit. "I hardly ever see you eat, and I know even you get hungry from time to time."

"How did you get this?"

She looked embarrassed for a second. "Never mind that. Just eat it, Ash."

Her tone was full of warning, but I couldn't let it go. "Where—"

"A group of winged monkeys threw it at me." Ariella crossed her arms and glared, and I had an odd moment of déjà vu. "On my last watch, we passed an orchard on the banks, and there were at least a dozen monkeys living there, staring down at us. I threw a rock at them and they...threw things back. And not just food items, either." She blushed with embarrassment and glowered, daring me to laugh. "So you'd better eat that before I stuff something else down your throat, and it won't be a banana."

I laughed and raised my hands in surrender. "As you wish, your highness," I said without thinking, but sobered quickly. Now I knew why this felt so familiar. For just a moment, Ariella had sounded just like Meghan.

And, judging from the look on Ariella's face as she pulled back, she knew it, too.

Guilt pierced me, sharp and painful. "Hey," I said, catching her wrist as she started to turn away, "Ari, listen. When this is all over, when we come back from this crazy venture, I'll make sure you can go home if you want to." She blinked and gazed up at me, as if such a thought had never occurred to her. "Your father's estates are still standing," I went on. "No one has tried to claim them yet. Or you can return to court—I don't think Mab will try to stop you. If she does, I can talk to her. I still have *some* influence in the Winter Court, no matter what Mab thinks of me. I want you to know that you'll be taken care of. I can give you that much, at least."

She smiled faintly, though her gaze was distant and unreachable. "If I had wanted any of those things, I would already have them," she replied in a gentle voice. "I'm grateful, Ash, but it's far too late for me to return to that life."

"I want to help you," I told her quietly. "Anything in my power, anything I can give freely is yours. Let me try to make this right. Just tell me what to do."

She stepped closer, placing a soft hand on my cheek, so near I could see my reflection in her starry eyes. "Finish this quest," she whispered, and pulled away, walking to the aft of the ferry without looking back.

An indefinite time later, I woke from a dreamless sleep and gazed around, realizing it was nearly my turn for watch again. On the opposite bench, Ariella slept soundly, a purring Grimalkin curled up beside her. A strand of silver hair fell across her eyes, and I raised my hand to brush it away before I realized what I was doing.

Clenching my fist, I turned and wandered toward the bow of the ship, where the Wolf sat in the moonlight, gazing out over the river. His ears were pricked, his nose raised to the wind, the breeze ruffling his glossy black pelt.

"Change is coming," he rumbled as I stepped up beside him and leaned against the rails, carefully balancing my weight. Even when the Wolf was sitting down, the top of my head was barely level with his shoulder, and wherever he went, the boat tilted, very slightly, to the side. "I can smell it. Either something is approaching us, or we're very nearly there."

I looked down, watching a fish twice as long as the ferry

brush up against the side, regard us with one enormous silver eye, and sink back into the depths. "Do you think we'll hit anything before we reach the Briars?"

"Hard to say," the Wolf replied. "I'm surprised we made it this far without any trouble. If you believe the cat, it's because the ferry is a part of the river, and passes through dreams without drawing any attention to itself or its passengers." He snorted and curled a lip, as if just realizing he had spoken about Grimalkin in a nonviolent manner. "If you can believe anything *he* says, anyway. Besides, that will probably change once we hit the Briars."

"How far?" I asked.

"Couldn't tell you." The Wolf raised his head and sniffed again. "But it's close. The Briars has a particular smell, unlike anything else in Faery." He turned and regarded me with burning, yellow-green eyes. "I hope your girl knows the way. I've stalked the Briars countless times, and I've never seen the End of the World."

"She'll get us there," I said softly. "I trust her."

"Really?" The Wolf snorted, looking back toward the river. "I wouldn't."

I turned, narrowing my gaze. "What do you mean?"

"*Pah,* boy. Can't you smell it? I guess you wouldn't." The Wolf turned as well, lowering his head so we were face-to-face. "Your girl is hiding something, little prince," he said in a low growl. "She reeks of sadness, of indecision and guilt. And desire, of course. It's even stronger than yours. Oh, don't pretend not to know what I'm talking about. Both of you smell like rutting deer that don't know whether to flee or just get on with it." He bared his fangs in a brief smile as I glared. "But I would be careful around her, boy. There's something she hasn't told you. I don't know what it is, nor do I care, but she doesn't want this journey to end. You can see it in her eyes."

I glanced at Ariella, knowing the Wolf was right. She was hiding something, something more than her emotions or her visions or the many futures I knew she had seen. I saw the gleam of golden eyes on the bench and knew Grimalkin was watching me, but at that moment I heard the flapping of wings, and a large black bird swooped in to perch on the deck.

It changed to Puck in a swirl of feathers, making the Wolf wrinkle his nose and sneeze. "Heads-up," Puck announced, raking feathers from his hair. "We're coming up on the Briars, and it looks like the river goes right through it."

CHAPTER TWELVE
THROUGH THE BRIARS

The Briars rose before us like the black face of a cliff, an endless wall of thorns, vines and branches, clawing at the sky. From a distance, they appeared to move, swaying and writhing, never still. Of all the places in Faery, the Briars were the most mysterious, and one of the most feared. It was here long before the first faery emerged from human dreams, and was said to encircle the entire Nevernever. No one knew how it came to be. But everyone knew about it. Within the thorns, the trods to every door and gateway in the human world lay hidden and well protected, waiting to be discovered. Find the right trod, and you could go anywhere in the world. That is, if you could survive the things that lived in the thorns. And the Briars themselves were always hungry.

No one had ever traveled all the way through the thorns; there were rumors that the maze went on forever. But if what Ariella said was true, the End of the World lay beyond the Briars, and somewhere beyond that lay the Testing Grounds.

The five of us—myself, Ariella, Puck, Grimalkin, and the Wolf—stood side by side at the front of the boat, watching the Briars loom before us. The river wound sleepily toward the wall of thorns, into a tunnel of interlocking branches. As we drew closer, we could hear the Briars move, creaking and slithering, eager to welcome us into its embrace.

"Quick question." Puck's voice broke the silence. "Did anyone think to bring a can of *Off?*"

The Wolf gave him a confused look, and I raised an eyebrow. "Do we even want to know?"

"Mmm, probably not."

Ariella leaned forward, gazing up at the looming expanse of black thorns, awe written plainly on her face. For a moment, it reminded me of the first time I had seen her, that pretty young girl staring at the winter palace in amazement, still innocent of the ways of the Unseelie Court.

But she was different now, not the girl I had once known.

Ariella caught me looking at her and smiled. "I've never seen the Briars," she said, glancing back at the wall of thorns. "Not like this. They're so much bigger in person."

The Wolf snorted, wrinkling his nose. "I hope you know where you're going, girl," he said in a dubious voice. "If we get lost in there, you'll be the first one I'm going to eat to keep from starving. Well, after the cat, anyway."

I glared at the Wolf, but Ariella shook her head. "We won't have to worry about getting lost," she said in a distant voice, not even looking at us. "The river will take us where we need to go. To the End of the World."

"Great," Puck said, grinning and rubbing his hands. "Sounds easy enough. Let's just hope we don't fall off the edge."

Gripping the railing, I stared up at the moving wall. *This is it. The last barrier before the End of the World, and one step closer to keeping my promise. Meghan, I'm almost there. Wait for me just a little longer.*

As the ferry slipped beneath the Briars, what little light

there was dimmed to almost nothing, leaving us in pitch darkness. Extending my arm, I drew a tiny bit of glamour from the air, and a globe of faery fire appeared in my palm, washing everything in pale blue light. I sent the ball ahead of us, lighting the way down the channel, where it bobbed and weaved and cast weird shadows over the bristling tunnel walls.

Grimalkin sniffed. "I do hope that does not attract anything," he mused, watching the bobbing light as if it was a bird, just out of his reach. "We are not will-o'-the-wisps, trying to get creatures to follow us, after all. Perhaps you should put it out?"

"No." I shook my head. "If something comes at us in here, I want to see it."

"Hmm. I suppose not everyone can have a cat's perfect night vision, but still…"

Puck snorted. "Yeah, your perfect kitty vision does us no good if you don't warn us that something is coming once in a while. Poofing away doesn't count. This way, we can at least have a heads-up."

The cat thumped his tail. "Additionally, you can paint a neon sign over our heads that says, 'Easy meal, follow the flashing lights.'"

"Or we could use you for bait…."

"Does anyone else hear that?" Ariella asked.

We froze, falling silent.

The Briars were never still, always rustling, slithering or creaking around us, but over the thorns and the sloshing of water against the branches, I could hear something else. A faint chittering noise, like claws clicking over wood. Getting closer…

The Wolf growled low in his chest, the fur along his spine beginning to rise. "Something is coming," he rumbled right before Grimalkin vanished.

I drew my sword. "Puck, get some light back there *now*."

Faery fire exploded overhead, a flash of emerald-green, lighting the passageway behind us. In the flare, hundreds of shiny, eight-legged creatures scuttled back from the sudden light. The tunnel was full of them, pale and bulbous, with bodies the size of melons and multiple thin legs. But their faces, elven and beautiful, stared down at us coldly, and they bared mouthfuls of curved black fangs.

"Spiders," Puck groaned, and drew his knives as the Wolf's growls turned into snarls. "Why does it always have to be spiders?"

"Get ready," I muttered, drawing glamour to me in a cold cloud, feeling Puck do the same. "This could get messy."

Hissing, the swarm attacked, dropping from the ceiling with muffled thumps, legs clicking as they scuttled over the deck. They were surprisingly quick, leaping at us with bared fangs, legs uncurling as they flew through the air.

I hurled a flurry of ice shards at the attacking swarm, killing several in mid-leap, and raised my sword as the rest came on. I cut a spider out of the air, ducked as another flew at my face and speared a third rushing at my leg. Ariella stood behind me, firing arrows into the swarm, and the Wolf roared as he bounded and spun, ripping spiders from his pelt and crushing them in his jaws. Puck, covered in black ichor, dodged the spiders that sprang at him and kicked the ones that got too close, sending them flying into the waters below.

"Aggressive little buggers, aren't they?" he called, yanking a spider from his leg and hurling it over the railing. "Kinda like redcap spawn, only uglier." He ducked as a spider flew overhead, hissing, only to be snapped out of the air by the Wolf. "Hey, prince, remember that time we stumbled into a hydra nest, just as all the eggs were hatching? I didn't know hydras could lay up to sixty eggs at a time."

I sliced two spider creatures from the air at once, black ichor splattering my face and neck. "Now's really not the time to reminisce, Goodfellow."

Puck yelped and cursed, slapping away a spider on his neck, his hand coming away stained with red. "I wasn't reminiscing, ice-boy," he snapped, angrily kicking the spider away. "Remember that cool little trick we did? I think we should do that *now!*"

The spiders' numbers were increasing; I'd cut one down only to have four others come at me from all sides. They were everywhere now, crawling over the railing and skittering across the roof. Ariella and I stood back-to-back, protecting each other, and the Wolf was going berserk, bucking and rolling as spiders crawled all over him like monster ticks.

"Come on, prince! Don't tell me you've forgotten!"

I hadn't forgotten. I knew exactly what he wanted me to do. It was risky and dangerous and would take a lot out of us both, but if the spiders kept coming, we might not have a choice.

"Ash!"

"All right!" I yelled back. "Let's do it. Ari, stay close. Everyone else, take cover now!"

I stopped fighting for an instant, feeling several of the creatures land on me, their slender legs scuttling up my clothes. Ignoring them, I knelt and drove the point of my sword into the wooden floor.

There was a flash of blue, and ice spread out from my blade, covering everything. In an instant, it had coated the deck, the railings, the benches, even some of the spider things, freezing them in place. It covered the branches of the thorns around us and spread a thin sheet of ice over the water around the boat. Though the spider things continued to pour out of the brambles, dropping onto the deck, for a moment, there was absolute, frozen silence.

"Now," Puck muttered, and I pulled up my blade.

The ice shattered. With the sound of breaking glass, it fractured into thousands of razor-sharp edges, glinting in the darkness. And at that instant, Puck unleashed the whirlwind.

With a roar of Summer glamour, Puck's cyclone whipped through the thorns and surrounded the boat, shrieking and causing the small craft to lurch sideways. It picked up debris in its wake, branches, spider bodies and thousands of fractured ice shards, spinning them through the air with the force of a tornado. I grabbed Ariella and pulled her close as the Wolf hunkered down beside us, hunching his shoulders against the wind.

When the winds finally ceased, we were surrounded by twigs, branches, melting ice and spider parts, oozing over everything. Icicles stuck out of the benches and walls like crystal shrapnel, and black ichor was splattered everywhere.

"Yes!" Puck cheered as I sat down on the floor, leaning against the railing. "Home team, one—spiders, zero!"

Ariella looked at me with wide eyes. "I never saw you two do *that* before."

"It was a long time ago," I said tiredly. "Before we ever met. When Puck and I…" I trailed off, remembering the years when Robin Goodfellow and Prince Ash thought they could take on the world. Reckless and defiant, spurning the laws of the courts, they sought out new and greater challenges, always reaching for more, and got into more scrapes than anyone had a right to come out of alive. I shook my head, dissolving the memories. "It was a long time ago," I finished.

"Regardless." Grimalkin abruptly materialized, sitting on a bench with not a hair out of place, his tail curled around himself. "If the two of them have any more tricks like that, they would do well to remember them. Summer and Winter glamour, when used in conjunction instead of against each other, can be a powerful thing. Thankfully, neither of the courts has ever figured this out."

The Wolf shook himself, spraying ichor and spider parts everywhere, making Grimalkin lay back his ears. "Magic and parlor tricks," the Wolf snorted, wrinkling his muzzle, "will not get us to the End of the World."

"Well, duh," Puck shot back. "That's why we're on a *boat*."

The Wolf gave him a sinister look, then stalked to the front of the boat, not caring about the spider parts scattered about the deck. For a moment, he stood there, sniffing the air, ears pricked forward for any hints of trouble. Finding none, he curled up in a relatively clean spot and closed his eyes, ignoring us all.

Ariella looked down at me, then at Puck, who was yawning and scrubbing the back of his head. "That took a lot of power, didn't it?" she mused, and I didn't argue. Releasing an explosion like that would leave anyone drained. Ariella sighed and shook her head. "Get some rest, the both of you," she ordered. "Grim and I will take last watch."

I DIDN'T THINK I WOULD SLEEP, but I dozed fretfully as the ferry made its way through the endless tangle of brambles. Despite assurances from Ariella and the Wolf that nothing followed us, I found it impossible to relax. Often, I would be jerked awake by a splash or a snapping of twigs somewhere in the thorns, and every once in a while the scream of some unfortunate creature would echo through the branches. Eventually, everyone gave up trying to rest and spent the journey in a constant and exhausting state of high alert. Except Grimalkin, who vanished frequently and made everyone nervous while he was gone.

The Briars went on, never changing, never still. I caught glimpses of various doors through the thorns, trods to places in the mortal world, doorways out of the Nevernever. Creatures seen and unseen skittered through the branches, furry or shiny or many-limbed, peering at us through the thorns. A giant centipede, over twenty feet long, clung to the roof of the tunnel as we drifted beneath it, close enough that we could hear the slow clicking of its huge mandibles. Thankfully, it didn't seem interested in us, but Puck kept his daggers out for several miles afterward, and Grimalkin didn't reappear for a long, long time.

Hours passed. Or days—it was impossible to tell. The Wolf and I were standing at the rear of the boat, watching an enormous snake glide through the branches overhead, when Ariella's weary voice floated up from the front.

"There it is."

I turned as the tunnel opened up into an enormous cavern made of thorns, the branches shutting out the sky. Tiny lights filled the cavern, floating in the air and bobbing over the dark waters like erratic fireflies. Torches stuck out of the river, some bent or leaning at odd angles, flickering with blue-and-orange flames. They lit the way to a massive stone temple looming at the end of the cavern. It rose from the dark waters past the ceiling of the cave, extending through the branches farther than we could see. Vines, moss and thorny creepers covered the crumbling walls, winding like possessive talons around pillars and laughing gargoyles. Even in a place as ageless as the Nevernever and the Deep Wyld, where time didn't exist and *ancient* was only a word, this temple was oldest.

I took a deep, slow breath. "Did we make it?" I asked softly, unable to take my eyes from the massive wall of stone that loomed before us like the side of a mountain. "Is this the Testing Grounds?"

Beside me, Ariella shook her head. "No," she whispered, almost in a daze. "Not yet, though I've seen this in my visions. The Testing Grounds lie beyond the temple. This is the gate to the End of the World."

"Big gate," Puck muttered, craning his neck to look up at it. No one answered him.

The River of Dreams continued, past the temple, into the thorns that surrounded the cavern, but the boat drifted lazily until it bumped against the huge stone steps that led up to the doors, and stopped.

"Guess this is our stop," Puck said, and practically leaped out of the ferry onto the steps. "Whew, it's nice to be back on solid ground again," he mused, stretching as the rest of us followed, easily crowding onto the platform at the bottom. Grimalkin appeared from under one of the benches, minced to the bottom of the steps, and began rigorously washing his tail.

Gazing up the long flight of stairs to the temple, Puck shook his head and sighed. "Stairs." He grimaced. "I swear there must be like some secret code. *All mysterious ancient temples must have a minimum of at least seven thousand steps to the front door.*"

I followed his gaze, frowning as I realized we weren't alone. "Someone is up there," I said quietly. "I can sense it. It feels... like it's waiting for me."

The rest of the group exchanged glances, except for Ariella, who stood a little apart, staring back at the river. "Well, then—" Puck sighed with exaggerated cheerfulness "—I guess it would be rude to keep it waiting."

He and the Wolf and Grimalkin started up the stairs, but paused when I didn't follow. "Uh, prince, aren't you coming?" Puck said, glancing back at me. "Seeing as this is, you know, your party and all."

"Keep going," I said, waving them on. "We'll catch up. Yell if something comes at you."

"Oh, believe me, I will," Puck said, and continued up the stairs, Grim and the Wolf leading the way.

I turned to Ariella, who still gazed out over the River of Dreams, not looking at me. "Ari," I said quietly, stepping up behind her, "what is it?"

She was silent for several heartbeats, and I was beginning to wonder whether she'd heard me at all, when she took a shaky breath and closed her eyes.

"We're almost there," she whispered, and a shiver went through her. "I didn't think it would be so soon. I guess... there's no turning back now."

"Ari." I stepped closer, putting a hand on her arm. "Talk to me. I want to help you, but I can't if you won't let me in. I could—"

She turned suddenly, and before I could react, framed my face with her hands and pressed her lips to mine.

I froze, mostly in shock, but after a moment my body uncoiled and I closed my eyes, relaxing into her. I remembered this; the feel of her lips on mine, cool and soft, the touch of her fingers on my skin. I remembered her scent, those long nights when we would lie under the cold, frozen stars, dreaming in each other's arms.

For a second, my body reacted instinctively. I started to pull us closer, to wrap my arms around her and return the kiss with equal passion...but, then I stopped.

I remembered this perfectly; every shining moment with Ariella was forever etched into my mind. What we'd had, what we'd shared, everything. I'd built a shrine to her in my memories, carefully tended with grief and anger and regret. I knew every inch of our relationship, the passion, the feeling of emptiness when we weren't together, the longing and, yes, the love. I had been in love with Ariella. I remembered what she'd meant to me once, what I'd felt for her then...

...and what I didn't feel for her now.

Gently, I put my hands on her shoulders and pushed her back, breaking the kiss. "Ari—"

"I love you, Ash," she murmured before I could say anything more, and my stomach dropped. Her voice was quietly desperate, as if she was rushing to get it out before I could speak. "I never stopped. Never. Even when I knew you would fall for Meghan, when I was so angry I wished we were both dead, even then I couldn't stop loving you."

My throat closed. I swallowed hard to open it. "Why are you telling me this now?"

"Because I won't get another chance," Ariella went on, her eyes filling with tears. "And I know, after your promise to Meghan, after everything we went through to get here, I know you can't turn back, but..." She pressed close, gazing up at me. "Do you still love me? I can't...I need to know, before we go any farther. I deserve to know that much."

I closed my eyes. Emotions swirled within me, guilt and sorrow and regret, but for once, my thoughts were clear. "Ariella," I murmured, taking her hands in mine, feeling her pulse race. This would be hard to say, but I needed to get it out, and she needed to hear it. Even if she hated me in the end. "When I lost you that day, my life ended. I thought I would die. I wanted to die, but only after taking Puck down with me. The only thing I was living for was revenge, and I nearly destroyed myself, because I couldn't let you go. Even when I met Meghan, I felt I was betraying your memory.

"But it's different now." I opened my eyes, meeting her starry gaze. "I regret a lot of things. I wish I could've been there for you, and I wish that day had never happened. But the thing I don't regret, the one good thing that came out of it all, is *her*.

"Ari...I will always love you. I always have. Nothing will change that." I squeezed her hand, then gently released it. "You'll always be a part of me. But...I'm not *in* love with you...anymore. And, despite my promise, despite seeing you again, I do this because I want to be with Meghan, nothing else." Ariella's eyes glazed over, and I eased back, speaking as gently as I could. "I can't be yours, Ariella. I'm sorry."

For a moment, she stared at me with a completely unreadable expression. Then, unexpectedly, a sad smile crossed her lips.

"That's it, then," she murmured, more to herself than me. "For us, anyway." I blinked, and she glanced up at me, her starry eyes clear. "I didn't want you to have any doubts, in the end."

"Is that what you wanted?" I stared at her, aghast. "Were you just forcing me into a decision?"

"No, Ash. No." Ariella put a hand on my arm. "I meant what I said. I've always loved you, and I wanted you to know before..." She shivered, hugging herself as she stepped back. "I'm happy for you," she whispered, though her eyes were glassy once more. "You know what you want, and that's good. It will make it easier...."

"What are you talking about?"

"Oy, ice-boy!" Puck's voice came, rough with disapproval, from farther up the stairs. "I think you'd better get up here now!"

I scowled at Puck, cursing his timing, and glanced at Ariella. She gazed up the steps, her cheeks dry, her expression resolved. I sensed she was making peace with herself, coming to some important decision.

"Ari..."

"It's all right, Ash." Ariella raised a hand, not meeting my eyes. "Don't worry about me. I knew, eventually, it would come to this." She took a breath, let it out slowly. "It's time to move on, for both of us.

"So, let's go," she said, turning and giving me a brave smile. "We've finally come to the end. We can't stop now."

PUCK WAITED FOR US near the top of the staircase, the Wolf growling low in his chest beside him. But Grimalkin was also there, calmly licking a front paw in between disdainful glances at the Wolf, so I relaxed a bit. When the cat disappeared, then I would worry.

Still, Puck looked grave as we joined him, nodding to the top of the stairs. "We've got company," he muttered, and I looked up.

A figure stood at the top of the stairs, robed and hooded, and nearly eight feet tall. Its face was hidden in the darkness of the cowl, and a pale, bony hand clutched a gleaming staff of twisted black wood.

And, though I couldn't see its face, I felt it was looking right at me.

"I know why you have come, knight of the Iron Court."

The deep voice shivered into me, coming from everywhere, from the thorns and the river and the temple itself. It echoed in my head and in my bones, cold and powerful and older than the stars. It took all my willpower not to sink to one knee before the robed figure, and by Puck's lack of an irreverent smirk and the hair standing up along the Wolf's spine, I knew they felt it, too.

"Who are you?" I asked.

"I am the Guardian at the End of the World," the figure intoned. *"I am the keeper of the Testing Grounds, the one you will have to impress to earn your soul."*

"And you came out just to say hi? That's awfully considerate of you." Puck regained his grin and turned to me. "Don't you feel special, ice-boy? We didn't even have to go to the End of the World. Be polite to the nice hooded man, and maybe you'll get a soul."

"But first, to reach the End of the World, to prove that you are worthy, you must run the gauntlet."

"I knew it." Puck shook his head. "There's always a catch."

I ignored Puck, taking a step toward the hooded figure. "I'm ready," I said, searching for a face behind that dark cowl, finding nothing. "Whatever you throw at me—gauntlets, tests, anything—it won't matter. I'm ready. What do I have to do?"

The Guardian didn't seem surprised. *"This trial is not only for you, knight,"* it said, sweeping a robed arm at the group behind us. *"Anyone who wishes to see the End of the World must first make it through the gauntlet. Alone, you will fail. Together, you might have a chance to overcome the challenges. But know this—not all who enter the temple will leave. Of that, you can be certain."*

My stomach dropped. I didn't doubt his words, much as I hated to accept them. The Guardian was telling us that not everyone would survive the gauntlet. That one or more of us was going to die.

"One thing more." The Guardian raised a hand in the silence of that revelation. *"You do not have long to find me, knight. Once the doors open, at both ends of the gauntlet, they will not remain that way forever. If you are still in the temple when they close, you will be trapped there until the end of time, joining those who have already failed. Do you understand?"*

"Yes," I said numbly. The cowl nodded once.

"Then I will see you at the End of the World, knight. Where, if you make it through, your real trial will begin."

And just like that, it was gone. It didn't fade away or vanish in a puff of smoke or even disappear like Grimalkin, becoming invisible. It simply wasn't there anymore.

I stood at the top of the stairs, feeling my companions' gazes at my back, and raised my head.

"Anyone who wants to turn back, should," I said quietly without turning around. "You heard what the Guardian said. Not all of us will make it out of here. I won't hold anything against you if you want to leave."

I heard Puck's snort of disgust as he climbed the last of the stairs and stood before me, crossing his arms. "What, and let you have all the fun? You should know me better than that, ice-boy. Though, I will admit, the thought of being trapped with you forever makes my skin crawl. Guess we'll have to make sure that doesn't happen, huh?"

"I've come this far," the Wolf growled, padding forward to stand behind Puck. "No good turning back now. I said I'd see you to the End of the World, and I will. The cat can leave if it wants. That would be in tune with its cowardice. But the story must go on."

"Please." Grimalkin trotted up the steps and turned to glance back at me, twitching his tail. "As if I would allow myself to become trapped with the dog until the end of time." He sniffed and curled his whiskers. "Fear not, prince. There is no doubt that I will leave if I think that you are close to failure. But these gauntlets always have some sort of ridiculously aimless puzzle or mind game to solve, and you will likely need someone with intelligence before it is done. Besides, you still owe me a favor."

I nodded at them all and turned to Ariella, still standing a few steps down, gazing through me at the temple. "You don't have to do this," I told her gently. "You got us this far—you've done more than I could've asked for. You don't have to go any farther."

She smiled that sad little smile and took a deep breath. "Yes," she whispered, meeting my gaze. "I do." Climbing the stairs, she came to stand beside me, taking my arm. "To the end, Ash. I'll see you to the very end."

I put my hand on hers and squeezed. Puck grinned at us, and the Wolf snorted, shaking his head. With Grimalkin leading the way, the five of us approached the massive stone doors to the temple. With an earth-shaking rumble, they slowly opened, showering us with pebbles and dirt. Beyond the doors, everything was cloaked in darkness.

We didn't stop. With Ariella and Puck beside me, the Wolf loping behind us, and Grimalkin leading the way, we crossed the threshold and entered the gauntlet.

CHAPTER THIRTEEN

THE GAUNTLET

As I expected, the temple, though huge from the outside, didn't conform to normal space. The first room we came to, past the long, narrow hallway, was a large, open courtyard, surrounded by walls and covered in moss. Strange beams of light slanted down from somewhere above, and broken statues, pillars and enormous stones were scattered throughout. The chamber looked like a miniature labyrinth of crumbled walls, archways and columns, covered in vines and shattered with the weight of time.

Ahead of us, a pair of huge double doors stood atop a platform, guarded by two hulking stone creatures, one on either side. The statues looked like a cross between a lion and some sort of monstrous canine, with broad heads, curling manes and thick, clawed forepaws.

"Fu dogs," Puck mused as we approached the doors, hopping over shattered pillars and crumbling archways. "You know, I met a Fu dog once in Beijing. Persistent bastard chased me all over the temple grounds. Seemed to think I was some kind of evil spirit."

"Imagine that," Grimalkin muttered, and the Wolf snorted with laughter. Puck flicked a pebble at him.

"These aren't like the standard variety," Puck continued, making a face at the stone guardians. "They're bigger, for one. And older. Good thing they're not real Fu dogs, eh? We'd be in big trouble if—"

And of course at that point, a loud grinding sound echoed through the room, as both statues turned their heads to stare at us.

I sighed. "You should know better by now, Goodfellow."

"I know. I just can't help it."

With snarling roars, the pair of massive stone guardians leaped from their bases, landing with deafening booms on the rocky floor, shaking the ground. Their eyes burned with an emerald fire in their craggy faces, their paws crushed the stones beneath them and their bellowing voices filled the chamber. Grimalkin vanished, the Wolf added his own howling roar to the cacophony, and the Fu dogs lowered their heads and charged.

As one Fu dog barreled past, I vaulted aside, cutting at its flank as it thundered by. My blade screeched off the stony hide, leaving a trail of frost and a shallow scratch, but the monster didn't even notice. It plowed headfirst into a stone pillar, smashing it to rubble, before it whirled around, completely unharmed, and lowered its head for another charge.

An ice arrow shattered off the broad muzzle as the Fu dog galloped toward me, as Ariella tried to catch its attention, but it didn't slow the dog. I dodged as it roared by, plowing straight through a wall like a furious bull, showering itself with rocks. A quick glance showed Puck bound onto a pillar to avoid the second statue, which simply rammed its head into the stone base to knock the pillar down. Puck managed to hop onto a second column as the Wolf lunged at the Fu dog, fangs flashing for its thick neck. He bounced off the stony hide with a yelp that was more anger than pain, and the Fu dog whirled around to attack.

This wasn't working. And we didn't have time to play keep-away with a pair of murderous stone giants. "Retreat!" I called, ducking behind a headless statue to avoid being trampled by the first guardian, which grunted and spun around before hitting anything. "Puck, get to the doors, we don't have time for this!"

"Oh sure, prince! You make it sound so easy!"

The Fu dog attacking me rumbled a growl and stalked forward. Apparently it had given up blindly charging forward in the hopes of smashing me into paste. From the corner of my eye, I spotted Ariella pulling back her bow for another shot, and waved her back without taking my attention from the dog.

"Ari, don't worry about me. Just go."

"Are you sure?"

"Yes! Get to the doors—I'll be right behind you."

Ariella slipped behind a wall and out of sight. The Fu dog glanced her way, growling, but I hurled an ice dagger at its face, smashing it right between the eyes, bringing its attention back to me with a roar.

It lunged forward, teeth bared, claws raking deep gouges in the floor. As it pounced, I leaped up, vaulting off its snout and landing on its broad shoulders. For a split second, I saw a flash of gold on its bright red collar, but then I was hurtling off its back and running toward the doors, where Puck and Ariella waited for me.

The Wolf was keeping the other Fu dog busy, dancing around and snapping at its back feet as it whirled on him. As

I bounded up the stairs, the guardian turned on me with a snarl, but the Wolf lunged forward and slammed his shoulder into it, rocking it back, keeping its focus on him. I reached Puck and Ariella, who looked grave as they turned to me.

"No good." Puck frowned and punched the stone door, making a hollow thump. "The sucker won't budge. I think there's a key or something to open it. Look."

He pointed to the doors, where two indentations side by side formed perfect half circles that met where the two doors came together, making a full sphere. A key of some sort, which probably meant it was lost or hidden somewhere in the room. With the two Fu dogs. I sighed in frustration.

"The collars, you fools." Grimalkin appeared on one of the statue bases, ears back, lashing his tail. "Look at their collars. Must I do everything around here?" He vanished again, just as a Fu dog charged up the steps and lunged at us.

We dove aside, and the dog rammed into the doors with a boom that shook the ceiling. Shaking its head, it backed off, and I saw that same flash of gold around its neck, like a tag. Or a globe that had been cut in half...

I glanced at Puck. "You take one, I'll get the other?"

"You're on, ice-boy."

We scattered to different corners of the room, Ariella following me, Puck leaping down to help the Wolf. As I'd hoped, my Fu dog stalked us persistently through the labyrinthine ruins, shattering pillars and bursting through walls to give chase.

"What's the plan?' Ariella whispered as we ducked around a corner, pressing our backs against the wall. A few feet away, the Fu dog stalked past, growling, so close I could've reached around the corner and touched it. Several aisles over, somewhere in the maze, I heard a crash and saw a cloud of dust billow into the air; the second guardian was close.

"Stay here," I told Ariella. "Get out of sight. I want that thing to focus on me and nothing else. If Puck does what he's supposed to, this should be over soon." A pillar toppled over nearby, followed by a frustrated snarl. "Head toward the door and wait for us," I continued. "Find Grim and the Wolf if you can. We'll be there as soon as we can with the keys."

"How—" Ariella began, but with a crash and a shattering of stone, the Fu dog burst through a nearby wall and roared as it spotted me.

I took off, sprinting deeper into the ruins, hearing the guardian close on my heels. Rocks flew and statues shattered into marble dust as the massive stone creature hurled itself through the aisles after me.

I turned the corner of a dilapidated wall, and suddenly Puck was there, running straight at me from the opposite direction. His green eyes widened as we closed, but it was what I was looking for. We both immediately dove aside as the Fu dogs turned the corner and slammed into each other with a crack that shook the earth.

The force rocked the two stone giants back, and for a moment they stood still, completely dazed. I saw one had a broken nose, and the other had a crack running down its face like a jagged scar. Lying on his stomach on the other side of the aisle, Puck raised himself to his elbows and grinned in triumph.

"You know, no matter how often I see that, it never gets old."

I scrambled to my feet. "Grab the key," I snapped, approaching one Fu dog. Still dazed, it didn't notice me as I stepped up and snatched the golden half orb from around its neck. Puck did the same with the second one, pausing a moment to grin at the stupefied guardian.

"Bet that stung, didn't it?" he said, waving the orb in front of the dog's face. "Yeah, that'll give you a headache for weeks. That's what you get for being so bullheaded."

"Puck!" I turned to glare at him. "Stop being an idiot and let's get out of here."

Puck laughed and sauntered toward me, tossing the half orb in one hand. "Ah, the oldies are always the goodies," he muttered, joining me at the corner. "Hey, remember when we pulled that little stunt on the minotaurs? They were so out of it they—"

Two very low, very angry growls stopped him midsentence. I shot Puck a death glare, and he gave a feeble smile.

"I know, I know. You're going to kill me."

We fled through the ruins, the spheres clutched tightly in hand, the Fu dogs crashing behind us. No side trips or luring the dogs around corners this time; we went straight for the doors, taking the shortest route possible. I saw Ariella at the foot of the stairs, her bow pulled back and aimed at the dogs, her lips drawn into a thin line of frustration. She knew her arrows could do no more than make the Fu dogs blink. The last hundred yards to the stairs was the most dangerous, flat and open, with nothing to slow down our pursuers. I felt the ground shake with their galloping footsteps as they closed the distance.

Then the Wolf flew over a broken wall in a dark blur, slamming into one of the Fu dogs, causing it to career into the second. Knocked off balance, the statues went crashing into a wall, tumbling over each other with the grinding sound of a derailed train. Panting triumphantly, the Wolf bounded up the stairs with us, joining Ariella and now Grimalkin, who appeared at the door lashing his tail with impatience.

"Quickly!" he spat, as Puck and I sprinted up. "Insert the keys!"

"You know, you can't just disappear and then pop up shouting orders when the rest of us did all the work," Puck said as we reached the doors. Grimalkin hissed at him.

"There is no time to argue your stupidity, Goodfellow. The guardians are coming. The keys—"

A roar drowned him out as the Fu dogs reached the top of the stairs, shaking their heads in fury. Trapped against the doors, we couldn't move away as they lunged forward with eager howls. The Wolf snarled in return and leaped forward to meet them as Grimalkin flattened his ears and spat at us.

"The keys must be inserted at the same time! Do it, now!"

I glanced at Puck, nodded, and we slammed the orbs into the indentions, feeling them click as they slid into place.

I looked back, ready to dart aside, but the second the keys clicked in the lock, the guardians froze. As the doors swung open, tiny cracks appeared along the dog's stony hides, growing larger and spreading across their bodies until, as one, they split apart and crumbled, strewing debris and rubble along the steps.

I sighed in relief, then pushed myself off the frame. There was no time to savor this victory. "Hurry," I said, urging everyone through the doorway. "If that's just the first challenge, we don't have any time to spare." The Guardian had not said exactly how long we had to complete the gauntlet, but I had the distinct impression that every second would prove precious.

"Man, your hooded friend really doesn't believe in easing you into this," Puck commented as we ducked through the doors and jogged down a hallway. Stone dragon heads lined the wall every few feet, jaws frozen in permanent snarls. "If that first challenge was supposed to be the easiest, we could be in a lot of trouble."

"What did you think this would be, Goodfellow?" Grimalkin said, bounding along ahead of us. "A pleasant walk in the park? They do not call it *the gauntlet* for nothing."

"Hey, I've run a few gauntlets in my time," Puck shot back. "They're basically all the same—you have your physical challenges, a pointless riddle or two, and there's always a few nasty—"

A gout of flame erupted from one of the stone dragon's jaws, searing the air over Grimalkin as he passed in front of it. Fortunately, the cat was too short to be harmed, but it made the rest of us skid to a halt.

"—traps," Puck finished, and winced. "Well, I should've seen that coming."

"Do not stop!" Grimalkin called back, still sprinting ahead. "Keep going, and do not look back!"

"Easy for you to say!" Puck yelled, but then the dull roar behind us made me glance over my shoulder and curse. *All* the dragon heads we had just passed were beginning to spout flame, and those flames were coming down the hall toward us.

We ran.

The hallway seemed to go on forever, and there were a few close calls that involved jumping or diving beneath jets of flame, and of course there was the inevitable pit at the very end that we barely managed to clear, but we made it through with minimal burns. Ariella's sleeve caught fire once, and the end of the Wolf's tail was singed, but no one was seriously hurt.

Panting, we stumbled through the arch into the next room, where Grimalkin stood on a broken pillar, waiting for us.

"Ugh," Puck groaned, brushing cinders from his shirt. "Well, that was fun, though a bit on the clichéd side. Way too *Temple of Doom* for me. So, where are we now?"

I scanned the room, which was vast, circular and carpeted in fine white sand, lying in dunes and hills like a miniature desert. Columns and pillars were scattered throughout the chamber, most broken or lying on their sides, half-buried in the dust. Vines dangled from a vast domed ceiling, impossibly far away, and roots snaked through the crumbling walls. In the faint beams of light, dust motes floated in the air. I had the impression that if I dropped a pebble in this room, it would hang in the air forever, suspended in time.

In the middle of the room, an enormous stone dais rose from the sand, the remains of four thick marble pillars spaced evenly along the edge. On either side of the dais, two elegant winged statues crouched, primly facing one another, the tips of their spread wings nearly touching the ceiling. They had the bodies of huge, sleek cats, paws and flanks resting in the sand, but their faces were of cold yet beautiful women. Eyes closed, the sphinxes sat motionless, guarding a pair of stone doors beyond them. Climbing onto the dais, we stopped at the edge, gazing up at the enormous creatures. Though the doors were only a few yards beyond the sphinxes' massive paws, no one moved to step between them.

"Huh." Puck leaned back, peering up at the statues' impassive faces. "A sphinx riddle, is it? How positively charming. Do you think they'll try to eat us if we get it wrong?"

"You," Grimalkin said, lacing back his ears, "will remain silent in this, Goodfellow. Sphinxes do not take kindly to flippancy, and your ill-contrived remarks will not be well received."

"Hey," Puck shot back, crossing his arms, "I'll have you know, I've tangled with sphinxes before, cat. You're not the only one who knows his way around a riddle."

"Shut up," the Wolf growled at both of them, and pointed his muzzle skyward. "Something is happening."

We held our breath and waited. For a moment, everything was still. Then, as one, the sphinxes' eyes opened, all brilliant blue-white with no irises or pupils, staring straight ahead. Still, I could feel their ancient, calculating gaze on me as a warm breeze hissed through the room and the statues spoke, their voices quivering with ancient wisdom and power.

Time is the cog that turns the wheel.
Winter leaves scars that do not heal.
Summer is a fire that burns inside.
Spring a terrible burden to hide.
Autumn and death go hand in hand.
One answer lies within the sand.
But seek the answer all alone,
Lest the sand claim you as its own.

"Er, sorry," Puck said as the voices ceased and silence fell over the dunes again. "But could you repeat that? A little slower this time?"

The sphinxes stood silent. Their blue eyes shut, as quickly as a door slamming, and did not stir again.

But, something *was* stirring around us. The sand was shifting, moving, as if millions of snakes writhed below the surface. And then, the sand erupted, and countless scorpions, small, black and shiny, spilled from beneath the dunes and poured toward us.

Puck yelped and the Wolf snarled, the hair on his back and neck standing up. We crowded together on the platform, drawing our weapons, as the ground became a mass of wiggling bodies, crawling over one another, until we couldn't see the sand through the carpet of living, writhing black.

"You know, I think I'd rather be eaten by the sphinxes," Puck exclaimed. He had to shout to be heard over the chittering that filled the air, the clicking of millions of tiny legs skittering over each other. "If anyone has a plan, or an idea, or a can of scorpion repellant, I'd love to hear about it."

"But, look." Ariella pointed over the edge of the platform. "They're not attacking. They're not coming any closer."

I peered over the edge and saw it was true. The scorpions surged against the stone wall, flowing around it like a rock in a stream, but they weren't climbing the three feet it would take to get to us.

"They will not attack us," Grimalkin said calmly, sitting well away from the edge, I noted. "Not yet. Not unless we answer the riddle incorrectly. So, do not worry. We have a little time."

"Right." Puck didn't look reassured. "And this is the part where you tell us you know the answer, right?"

Grimalkin thumped his tail. "I am thinking," he said loftily, and closed his eyes. His tail twitched, but other than that, the cat didn't move, leaving the rest of us to gaze around nervously and wait.

Impatient and restless, I scuffed a boot over the stone floor, then stopped. In front of one of the broken pillars, half-buried in sand, I saw letters carved into the stone.

M-E-M-O-R. Kneeling down, I brushed away the dirt to reveal the entire word.

Memory.

Something stirred in my mind, an idea still too hazy to make out, like a forgotten name keeping just out of reach. I had something here, I just couldn't bring it together.

"Look for other words," I told Puck, who'd come up behind me, peering over my shoulder to see what I was doing. "There have to be others."

Memory, knowledge, strength and *regret.* Those were the words we uncovered, carved into the stone floor in front of each broken pillar. With each one we unearthed, the hazy puzzle pieces started to join, though still not enough to form the whole picture.

"Okay." Puck dragged his hands down his face, scrubbing his eyes. "Think, Goodfellow. What do memory, knowledge, strength, and regret have to do with the four seasons?"

"It's not the seasons," I said quietly, as the pieces slid into place. "It's us."

Puck frowned at me. "Care to explain that logic, prince?"

"Winter leaves scars that do not heal," I recited, recalling the second line of the riddle. "Doesn't make much sense, does it?" I pointed to a pillar. "But, replace it with that word, and see what you get."

"Memory leaves scars that do not heal," Puck said automatically. He frowned again, then his eyes widened, looking at me. "Oh."

The Wolf growled, curling a lip at the pillar as if it was a waiting demon disguised as a rock. "So, we are to believe that the answer to this riddle, this ancient puzzle that has stood here for countless centuries, is *us?*"

"Yes." In the center of the platform, Grimalkin opened his

eyes. "The prince is correct. I have reached the same conclusion." He gazed calmly around the platform, pausing at each of the four broken pillars. "Memory, knowledge, strength, regret. The seasons represent the four of us, so we must match the right word to the correct stanza."

"But, there are five of us," Ariella pointed out. "Five of us, but only four pillars. Which means one of us is missing. Or, left out."

"We shall see," Grimalkin mused, unconcerned. "First, though, we must figure out the rest of the puzzle. I believe the prince has already found his place. What about you, Goodfellow?" He looked at Puck, twitching his tail. "Summer is a fire that burns inside. What word best describes you? Knowledge has never been your strong suit. Strength...perhaps."

"Regret." Puck sighed, with a quick glance at me. "Regret is a fire that burns inside. It's regret, so shut up and get on with the others." He moved toward the pillar opposite me, crossing his arms and leaning against it.

The scorpions were getting louder, more frantic, as if they knew we were scant seconds away from solving the riddle. Their legs and carapaces scraped against the rock, an ocean of noise surging around us. Grimalkin sniffed and shared a glance with the Wolf.

"I believe the last two are fairly obvious, are they not?" he mused, sauntering toward the pillar that said Knowledge. "I do agree, knowledge is sometimes a terrible burden. The last pillar is yours, dog. I do not think we can argue your strength. Your intelligence, perhaps, but not your strength."

"What about Ariella?" I glanced at her, looking a bit lost on the edge of the platform. "She has the burden of knowledge as well, not just you, cait sith."

"Ariella is a Winter fey, and we already have a Winter,"

Grimalkin replied easily, hopping onto the broken pillar of Knowledge, peering down at us all. "And I think you would be in favor of solving this quickly, prince. In any case, I believe we have to stand on the pillars together. That is generally how these puzzles work."

The Wolf growled, leaping atop the broken stone, huge paws close together on the edge. "If this does not work, cat, I will make sure to eat you first before the scorpions get to us," he muttered, balanced precariously on the small platform. Grimalkin ignored him.

Puck and I followed suit, jumping easily onto the broken pillars, as the sea of scorpions chittered and writhed below us. For a few seconds, nothing happened. Then, the sphinxes' eyes opened, searing blue, their voices echoing through the room.

"You—" they breathed, sending a ripple of power over the sand "—have chosen…incorrectly."

"What!" Puck yelped, but it was drowned by the furious buzz of millions of scorpions, stirred into a frenzy. "No, that can't be right. Furball's never wrong! Wait—"

"You—" the sphinxes breathed again "—will die."

I drew my sword, tensing to drop down as the scorpions rushed forward, scaling the platform and spilling over the edge. Ariella gasped and stumbled backward, as the living carpet of claws and legs and stingers began covering the platform.

"Stay where you are!" Grimalkin's voice rang through the chamber, booming and steely with authority. We froze, and the cat turned wild golden eyes on Ariella, baring his teeth, all his fur standing on end. "Time!" he spat, flattening his ears. "Time is the fifth answer, the cog that turns the wheel! Stand in the center now!"

I clenched my fists as Ariella ran to the middle of the platform, the flood of scorpions closing in from all sides. They swarmed up the pillars, crawling over my clothes, legs and pinchers digging into my flesh. I lashed out and sent dozens of them flying, but of course there were always more. They were not stinging…yet. But I felt the seconds ticking away, and knew that if the creatures beat Ariella to the heart of the dais, we were finished. Puck yelled a curse, flailing wildly, and the Wolf roared in fury as Ariella finally reached the center of the dais.

As soon as she set foot in the middle, a shiver went through the air, starting from the center of the dais and spreading outward, like ripples on a pond. The flood of scorpions halted, inches from swarming Ariella, and started flowing backward, leaving the platform and crawling down from the pillars. I shook the last of the tiny predators off me and watched the carpet recede, disappearing beneath the sands once more. In seconds, they had vanished completely, and the dunes were still.

"You have chosen…correctly," the sphinxes whispered, and closed their eyes again.

Ariella was shaking. I leaped from the platform and went to her, wordlessly pulling her close. She trembled in my arms for a moment, then gently freed herself and drew away, smoothing her hair back.

"Wow," Puck muttered, dusting off the front of his shirt, "now, *that* was weird. And to think, I never thought I'd live to see the day…." He trailed off, grinning.

I eyed him wearily. "Fine, I'll bite. You don't mean the scorpions or the sphinx. We've seen much stranger than that."

"No, ice-boy. I never thought I'd see the day when Grimalkin was *wrong*."

Grimalkin, still on his broken pillar, didn't react, but I saw his whiskers bristle as he glanced our way. "Goodfellow," he said with an enormous yawn, "I feel obliged to point out that, had I been wrong, you would all be full of tiny holes right now. Anyway, we are wasting time. I suggest we move out, quickly. I certainly do not wish to be stuck here until the end of time with any of you." And before we could reply, he leaped down and trotted off in the direction of the now-open door, passing between the sphinxes with his tail held high.

I looked at Puck, smirking. "I think you offended him, Goodfellow."

He snorted. "If I ever worried about that, I'd never open my mouth."

CHAPTER FOURTEEN
REFLECTION

The door past the sphinxes opened to another narrow corridor, empty of fire-breathing dragons this time, but no less strange. It stretched away into the darkness, lit only by orange candlelight, flickering against walls. The flames seemed to float in the air, reflecting off the surfaces of hundreds of full-length mirrors lining the corridor on both sides.

Glancing at my own image, I paused, faintly surprised at the stranger in the mirror. The pale, dark-haired reflection stared back grimly, clothes tattered around the edges, eyes touched with exhaustion. I barely recognized myself, but maybe that was a good thing. After all, that was why I was here; to become something else, some*one* else. If all went as planned, Ashallayn'darkmyr Tallyn, third prince of the Unseelie Court, would no longer exist.

What will it be like as a human? I wondered at my reflection. *Will I still be myself? Will I remember everything about my life in the Winter Court, or will all those memories disappear?* I shook my head. It was useless to wonder about that now, when we were so close, but still….

"Come on, handsome." Puck put a hand on my shoulder,

and I brushed it off. "Quit preening. I think we're almost there."

As we started down the corridor, wary of traps and pits and ambushes, I thought of Meghan, back in the Iron Kingdom. It would be dreadfully ironic, I mused, if once I earned a soul, I forgot everything about being fey, including all my memories of her. That sort of ending seemed appropriately tragic; the smitten fey creature becomes human but forgets why he wanted to in the first place. Old fairy tales loved that sort of irony.

I won't let that happen, I told myself, clenching my fists. *If I have to have Puck tell me everything, even if he has to go through our entire history, I will find a way to make it back to her. I will not become human only to forget it all.*

The hallway went on. The flickering candles cast strange lights in the opposite mirrors, endless rows of flame, stretching to infinity. From the corner of my eye, I saw my own dark reflection, walking along beside me. Smirking.

Except, I wasn't.

I stopped and slowly turned toward the mirror, dropping my hand to my sword. In the glass, my reflection did the same...but it wasn't me. It was someone who looked like me, pale and tall, with dark hair and silver eyes. He wore black armor, a tattered cape and a crown of ice rested on his brow. I drew in a slow breath and I recognized him.

It was me, the me I'd seen in the dream, the Ash who gave in to the darkness. Who killed Mab, claimed the throne and cut a bloody path through the Nevernever and the other courts. Ash the Winter King.

He was smiling at me, that same cold, empty smirk that showed the madness behind it, but otherwise our movements were the same, identical.

Backing away, I looked to my companions, who had also

discovered the new reflections in the mirrors. Behind me, Ariella stared in horror at herself, pale and statuesque in an elegant court gown. Her slender hands gripped an icy scepter. But her eyes were empty and cruel, her face without emotion. A circlet glittered on her forehead, not unlike the crown of the Unseelie King. A Queen of Winter, she stared with cold, impassive eyes until Ariella turned away with a shudder.

"Prince," Puck murmured, coming up beside me, standing so that he faced my shoulder, his back to the mirror. His voice, though light, was curiously shaken. "Are you seeing what I'm seeing, or is it just me?"

I glanced at Puck in the mirror behind us and had to stifle the urge to shove him away and draw my sword. Puck's head gazed over my shoulder, lips pulled into a vicious grin that was almost animalistic, teeth gleaming in the firelight. His eyes were narrowed gleefully, but it was the kind of mad glee that sent shivers through you, the type of glee that found humor in drowned kittens and poisoned cattle. This was the prankster whose jokes had turned deadly, who put adders in pillowcases, let wolves in with the sheep and made all light go away at the edge of a cliff. He was shirtless, barefooted and wild looking, the Robin Goodfellow I'd seen glimpses of when he was truly angry and out for revenge. The Robin Goodfellow that everyone worried about, because we all knew Puck could turn into this.

"You can see it too, huh?" Puck murmured when I didn't say anything right away. I nodded, once. "Well, your reflection isn't too encouraging either, ice-boy. In fact, it's kinda weird seeing us like this, because you look like you really, really want to cut my head off."

I pushed him away, and our images did the same. "Ignore them," I said, walking toward Ariella. "They're only reflections of what could be. They don't mean anything."

"Wrong." Grimalkin appeared, trotting up and sitting down in front of a mirror, curling his tail around his legs. His golden eyes observed me lazily. "It is not what could be, prince. It is what already is. You all have that reflection inside you. You just choose to suppress it. Take the dog, for example," he continued as the Wolf came loping back, his ruff standing on end. Ariella gasped, shrinking against me, and Puck muttered a curse under his breath.

The Wolf's reflection was enormous, filling three mirrors side by side, a huge, snarling monster with blazing eyes and foaming jaws. It stared at us hungrily, red tongue lolling between huge fangs, eyes empty of rational thought.

"A beast," Grimalkin said calmly as the real Wolf curled a lip at him. "A beast in its truest, savage nature. With no intelligence, no clear thoughts, no morals, just raw animal instincts and the desire to kill. That is what your reflections show you—yourself in your purest form. Do not dismiss them as having no meaning. You only deceive yourself if you do." He stood and curled his whiskers at us. "Now, hurry. We have no time to stand around doing nothing. If the mirrors upset you, the logical answer would be not to look at them. Let us go."

He lashed his tail and trotted off, back down the hallway into the dark. As he padded away, not bothering to glance back, I noticed that the cait sith's reflection looked no different from the real Grimalkin. Somehow, I wasn't surprised.

As we hurried after Grimalkin, I glanced at my reflection once more and received another shock. It wasn't there anymore, and neither were any of the others. The candles, the flickering flames, still cast their reflections, stretching away into infinity, but our images were gone.

"Hurry!" came Grimalkin's voice, echoing out of the darkness. "Time is running out."

We broke into a sprint, footsteps echoing down the narrow corridor, passing hundreds of eerily empty mirrors. I could see the candles flickering around us, thousands of orange lights reflected in the glassy walls. But other than the lights and the opposite walls, the mirrors showed nothing else. It was like we weren't even there.

We came to a crossing, where another hallway stretched away in opposite directions, vanishing into the black. In the middle sat Grimalkin, calmly washing a front paw. He blinked as we stopped, gazing up with a bemused expression on his face.

"Yes?"

"What do you mean, yes?" Puck said. "Did your feline brain finally snap? You said to hurry, and now you're just sitting here. What's the deal?"

"The exit is farther down." Grimalkin yawned, curled his tail around his legs, and smiled at us. "But I doubt you will ever reach it. I find it amusing that you can speak so freely of intelligence, when you cannot tell the difference between what is real and what is not."

"What?" Puck looked startled, but the Wolf suddenly let out a snarl that raised the hair on the back of my neck. I drew my sword and looked up, searching for hidden attackers.

Robin Goodfellow smiled at me from the mirror's reflection, arms crossed to his chest, a demonic grin on his face. I spared a quick glance at Puck, and saw him backing away, pulling his daggers, different actions from his image on the wall. His reflection waved cheerfully...

...and stepped out of the mirror.

"Where do you think you're going?" Goodfellow smiled, drawing his own weapons as he faced the real Puck. "The party's just getting started."

Movement rippled behind me. I spun, throwing myself to

the side as the monstrous head of the other Wolf exploded from the frame and lunged at me. I felt its hot breath and heard the snap of its massive jaws inches from my head. Backing away, I drew my sword as it slid out of the mirror and into the hall, a monstrous creature with burning green eyes, drool hanging in ribbons from its teeth. It howled, making the mirrors tremble, and crouched to spring at me, and that's when the real Wolf hit it from behind.

I leaped aside as the two giant wolves careened past, ripping and tearing at each other, vanishing down the side hallway. The smell of blood filled the air, the roars and snarls adding to the din of chaos. I turned to see Puck locked in battle with his twin and a second Robin Goodfellow stepping out of the mirror behind him, raising his blade.

An arrow streaked through the air, striking the second false Puck in the chest, causing him to explode in a swirl of leaves. Ariella, grim-faced and determined, raised her bow again, but a tall, pale figure slid out of the mirror beside her. I shouted and lunged forward, but the false Ariella raised her scepter and struck her twin in the back of the head. Ariella crumpled to the floor, dazed, and the false Ariella loomed over her with a vicious smile.

Roaring, I flew at the false Ariella, but the Ice Queen raised dead, cold eyes to me and slipped back into the mirror. I swung at her retreating form, and my blade struck the surface of the glass, shattering it. Shards flew from the force of the blow, glinting in the light, and the entire surface collapsed in a ringing cacophony, scattering pieces over the floor.

"My love." The false Ariella appeared in another frame, empty gaze boring into me. I slashed at her, shattering another mirror, but she slipped into the one beside it, her eyes beseeching mine. "Why?" she murmured, fading back, appearing in a frame on the opposite wall. "Why was I not enough?

Why could I not keep you from giving in to despair?" She slid away, vanishing from sight, and I turned warily, waiting for her to appear again. "I loved you," her voice whispered, giving no indication of where she was. "I would have given everything for you. But you couldn't stop thinking of *her*. A human! You let a human replace me." She finally appeared again, her face twisted into a mask of bitter hate, her eyes blazing with jealously. "So now you can *die* for her!"

Too late, I realized where she was looking and spun, bringing up my sword. Not fast enough. The point of a blade bit my shoulder as the other Ash stepped from the mirror behind me, slamming me against the wall.

I gritted my teeth as fire bloomed through my shoulder, nearly making me drop my sword. The other Ash smiled as he pushed the blade in farther, pinning me to the wall. Focusing through the pain, I switched my weapon to my other hand and stabbed at his chest, but he yanked his sword free and parried as if he'd been expecting it.

We circled each other, movements identical, almost as if I was looking through a mirror again. Other Ash smiled and lunged, a familiar attack I'd done thousands of times. I spun away and slashed at his head, but he was ducking almost before I had moved. We surged forward and met in the center of the hall, blue sparks flying as we cut and blocked and parried, the din of swords ringing down the corridor.

Other Ash slid away, lashing out with his sword. "You can't beat me," he said as I parried. We went up and down the hall, blades clashing, Other Ash's face blank but calm. "I *am* you. I know all your secrets, all your weaknesses. And unlike you, I can keep this up forever." He thrust out a hand, and an ice spear erupted from his palm, stabbing at my chest. I twisted aside and returned with a flurry of daggers. He stepped back into a mirror, and the shards fractured the surface into a spiderweb of cracks.

I spared a moment waiting for him to appear again. When he did not, I broke away and hurried toward Ariella, slumped against one of the walls. Puck still fought with two of his doppelgängers, the Other Pucks grinning madly as they took turns darting in. Somewhere in the shadows beyond, the snarls and howls of the Wolves rang out even over the clash of blades. A screaming, high-pitched yelp suddenly echoed through the din, making my stomach clench. I'd hunted often enough to know a death cry when I heard it.

"Ari!" I called as I approached her, and she raised her head, a flicker of pain crossing her face. "Don't move, I'll be right there."

A flock of screeching ravens suddenly burst out from one of the mirrors, surrounding me and diving at my face, pecking and clawing. Wincing, I flung up one arm and slashed at them with the other, cutting them from the air. Blood and dismembered crows rained down on me, before the last one broke off, changing to a familiar grinning figure in an explosion of feathers.

"Where ya going, ice-boy?" Other Puck smiled and dodged back as I stabbed at him. "You can't leave now, it's just getting interesting."

"Get out of my way, Goodfellow," I threatened, but the other Puck only laughed.

"My other half seems a bit preoccupied at the moment, so I thought I'd come say hello. La-la-la-lee," he sang, pulling his daggers, "which one is the real me?" He gave me that demonic grin and twirled his weapons. "You only get one chance to guess right, prince."

"Oy, ice-boy," the real Puck called, still fighting his two

doppelgängers. "Quit playing around with my evil twin—
you have your own!"

Frustrated, I glanced at Ariella, beyond the Puck blocking
my way, and my blood ran cold. The Ice Queen, the other
Ariella, was kneeling over her twin's body, looking down with
her teeth bared in a wicked smile, one hand pressing Ariella's
throat to the floor. Ariella struggled weakly, but her twin
didn't relent. Slowly, she raised a thin, jagged knife over her
head, the twisted blade gleaming red in the candlelight, her
eyes filled with hate.

"No!" I shouted, and tried lunging past Other Puck. He
blocked my way, grinning, swiping at me with his dagger.
With a roar of fury, I grabbed his wrist and jerked him to
me, plunging my blade through his chest. His eyes bugged,
and he exploded in a scattering of leaves, fluttering around
me. Without sparing him a glance, I hurled myself at the Ice
Queen, knowing it was already too late.

A different roar echoed through the hall behind her, and
she turned, her eyes going wide with fear. Scrambling off Ariella, she leaped back, vanishing into a mirror, barely avoiding
the huge jaws of the Wolf as he lunged out of the darkness.
Snarling, the Wolf, *our* Wolf, met my eyes, his muzzle covered in blood and gore, and shook himself vigorously.

"Ari—" I panted, flinging myself down beside her. Taking her wrist, I eased her into a sitting position, as the Wolf
loomed over us, growling. "Are you all right? Can you stand?"

"Maybe in a minute." Ariella winced, holding her head.
"If the room would kindly stop spinning." Glancing at my
worried expression, she gave me a weak smile. "Don't worry
about me, Ash. I think I'm going to sit here and shoot at anything that comes within twenty yards of me. Go help Puck.
I'll be fine."

I nodded reluctantly and glanced at the Wolf. "What about you? Where's the other Wolf?"

Our Wolf bared his fangs.

"Pale imitations cannot hope to take *me* down," he snarled. But he favored his left forepaw, and his shaggy coat was streaked with blood. Glancing down the hall, he narrowed his eyes at the melee behind me. "Too many Goodfellows for my taste." He snorted, and curled a lip. "Should I start biting off heads?"

"No." I put a hand on his shoulder, stopping him. "You're hurt. Stay here and guard Ariella. Make sure nothing happens to her. Don't leave her side, no matter what happens to me, understand?"

The Wolf growled, but nodded. I glanced over my shoulder at Puck; he was still hanging on, surrounded by his twins. "Watch out for her reflection," I said, backing away from the Wolf. "It's still around here somewhere."

"So is yours," the Wolf replied. "In fact, I'd say it's waiting for you."

I looked up. Other Ash stood within a mirror a few yards away, gazing right at me. He gave me a mocking salute, then walked away, through the mirrors, around a corner and into the other hallway.

I rose, gripping my sword tightly. "Take care of her," I said without turning around. "I'm ending this now."

I walked steadily to the place where Other Ash waited, cutting down another Puck as he lunged out of a mirror. Two more Pucks stepped out to face me, grinning, but a pair of ice arrows struck them in the chest, one after the other, and they vanished in a swirl of leaves and twigs. Around the corner, out of reach of the deadly arrows, Ash the Winter King waited for me, the walls and mirrors around him coated in frost.

My reflection regarded me with a look that was almost pitying, his sword held at his side. "What are you doing, Ash?" he asked coldly, and gestured around the hallway. "What are *we* doing here? Becoming human? Gaining a soul?" He chuckled without humor, shaking his head. "Souls aren't meant for us. Do you think, with all the blood and death on our hands, that we could ever earn something as pure as a soul?" He narrowed his eyes, seeming to stare right into me. "She's lost to us, Ash," he whispered. "We were never meant to be together. Let it go. Let it go, and give yourself to the darkness. It's the only way we'll survive."

"Shut up," I growled, and lunged at him.

He parried my thrust easily, cutting at my face. I dodged, and we circled each other in the hall, looking for weaknesses. There weren't many I could exploit, however. This opponent knew all my moves, my fighting techniques, and though I could say the same of him, it didn't help that I was fighting an enemy who knew exactly what I was thinking before I knew myself.

"You can't beat me." Other Ash smiled, cold and vicious, reading my mind. "And your time is running out. The doors are about to close, and I have all the time in the world."

I took a half step back and bumped into Puck, retreating from his own doppelgängers.

"Hey, ice-boy," Puck greeted without looking at me. I could feel him breathing hard against my back. "I'm getting kinda bored of this. Wanna trade?"

I blocked Other Ash's jab to the face and slashed at him in return. "Can't you take anything seriously?"

"I am serious! Duck."

I ducked as a dagger flew overhead, barely missing my ear. A false Goodfellow whooped with laughter, and my anger flared. "All right," I snapped, swinging my sword in a wide arc, forcing Other Ash back a step. "On three, then. One… two…three!"

We spun, half circling to the left, taking each other's places and the reflections that came with them. The two Other Pucks blinked at me, surprised, and leaped back as I lunged at them with a snarl. One pulled something out of his pocket and threw it at me, but I'd fought Puck on countless occasions and knew all of his tricks. The furry ball erupted into a squealing badger, flying at my face, but I was already slicing at it, cutting it from the air. It shattered in a tangle of twigs and pine needles, and I lunged through the cascade, plunging my sword into Robin Goodfellow's chest.

He dissolved into a swirl of autumn leaves as the last Puck leaped through the curtain with a howl, stabbing viciously with his dagger.

"This seems familiar, ice-boy," Other Puck said, grinning savagely as we parried and sliced at each other. "Think you've got the guts to actually go through with it this time?"

I responded by slashing at his face, barely missing him as he ducked. "Oooh, that had a bit of temper behind it." He sneered, eyes gleaming as he circled back. "But don't think I'll go easy on you, just because of our history. I'm not like my other half—weak, pathetic, restrained…"

"Loud, obnoxious, immature," I added.

"Hey!" the real Puck called from farther down, dodging as Other Ash slashed at him. "I'm standing right here, you two!"

Other Puck laughed, a cruel sound that made me bristle with loathing. "That's the problem with my other half," he said, lunging forward with a series of vicious cuts that forced me back a few steps. "Somewhere in the long centuries, he managed to grow a conscience and turn completely boring. If he dies here, I'll be all that's left. As it should be."

"Interesting." Grimalkin appeared in front of a mirror.

"I do not know which is more annoying, the real Goodfellow or the reflection."

"Well, considering they are one and the same," said a second, identical Grimalkin, materializing next to the first, "we should be thankful that there will be only one left when this is all over."

"Agreed. Two Goodfellows would be more than anyone in this world could take."

"I shudder to think of the implications."

"You are so not helping, Grimalkin!" the real Puck called, ducking beneath a savage head strike. "And we're not here to have tea with our evil doppelgängers! Shouldn't you two be trying to kill each other?"

The Grimalkins sniffed. "Please," they said at the same time.

Over my opponent's shoulder, I saw Other Ash block an upward strike, then lash out with a kick that sent Puck sprawling onto his back. The reflection stepped forward, raising his sword, but Puck reached back, grabbed a handful of twigs and flung it at his assailant. They turned into a swarm of yellow jackets, buzzing around the fake prince, until a vicious burst of cold sent them plummeting to the ground, coated in frost.

"Hey!" Other Puck stabbed forward viciously, making me leap back to avoid him. "The fight's here, ice-boy. Don't worry about your boyfriend, worry about yourself."

I backed farther into the hall, and Other Puck followed, smiling demonically. "Running away?" he taunted, as I drew my glamour to me, feeling it surge beneath my skin. "Always a coward, weren't you, prince? Never had the guts to really go for the kill."

"You're right," I murmured, startling him. He frowned in wary surprise, and I smiled. "I always regretted my words against Puck. There was always a part of me that didn't want to go through with it." I lowered my blade, touching the tip to the floor. Ice spread from the point of the weapon, coating the ground and the walls, freezing the mirrors with sharp crinkling sounds.

"But, with you," I continued, narrowing my eyes, "it's different. You're the part of him that I hate. The part that revels in the chaos you cause, the lives you destroy. And I can say this with complete certainty—killing you will be a pleasure."

Robin Goodfellow's face twisted into a vicious sneer. Snarling like a beast, he lunged at me, dagger gleaming in the icy hallway. I stepped back, raised my arms and brought them forward with a shout and a burst of glamour. The frozen mirrors shattered, flying outward in an explosion of deadly, razor-sharp shrapnel, catching Puck in the very center.

There was one high-pitched yell of dismay.

And then there was nothing except the shards tinkling to the ground and a few black feathers spiraling down to the floor. Other Puck was gone.

"Very nice, Ash." My reflection's voice echoed through the hallway. "But you're still too late."

I looked up, my stomach tightening. Other Ash stood in front of Puck, one hand on the faery's throat, pinning him to the wall. Puck dangled weakly, his face covered in blood, his daggers glinting several feet away.

"You defeated Goodfellow's reflection," Other Ash mused as I started forward, already knowing I wouldn't get there in time. "Congratulations. Now it's my turn."

He raised his sword, and drove it through Puck's chest, staking him to the wall. The mirror behind Puck shattered, raining to the floor in a softer imitation of the havoc I had just caused. Puck's mouth gaped; he clutched at the sword in his chest—

—and disappeared, vanishing in a shower of leaves. Other

Ash blinked, startled for just a moment, then quickly yanked his sword out of the wall and stepped back.

There was a blur over his shoulder, and he stiffened, jerking his head up. As I reached him, his sword fell from his hand, clattering to the ground, and he turned cold, hateful eyes on me.

"You...will fail," he whispered in a choked voice, and disappeared, like mist in the sunlight.

Puck stood behind him, eyes hooded and grim. His dagger, where it had been stuck in the prince's back, floated in the air for a split second before plummeting toward the ground. Puck caught it as it fell and smoothly slid it back into its sheath, giving the broken mirror a rueful look.

"Yeah, two can play at that game, ice-boy," he muttered, and shook his head. Glancing at me, he offered a wry, slightly pained grin. "I found that oddly therapeutic, how about you?"

"Idiot," I told him, to hide the relief on my face. His grin widened as if he saw it anyway, and I scowled, embarrassed. "Come on, we're not out of here yet."

"No, you can't leave!" hissed a voice behind me. I spun, bringing up my sword, as Other Ariella lunged out of the mirror, her eyes blank and terrible.

Something streaked past my face from behind, and Other Ariella jerked, freezing in place, as the shaft of an arrow jutted from her chest. She slumped, reaching out for me, then evaporated from sight, the arrow dropping to the ground and shattering on the floor.

I turned and saw Ariella on her feet beside the Wolf, her bow raised and the string still vibrating from where it had loosed the shaft. Her gaze met mine, eyes hard, and she nodded.

"Well, that was fun," Puck stated as we hurried over, passing the two Grimalkins, watching us with identical bemused expressions. "I've always wanted to see myself die in a horrible ice explosion. You never pulled that stunt while *we* were dueling, ice-boy."

"Save it for later," I said quickly. "We have to keep moving."

"It is too late."

We turned as the Grimalkins stood, waving their tales. "You have failed," one of them stated, regarding each of us imperiously. "Your time is up. The doors are getting ready to close." And, in true Grimalkin fashion, he vanished without a trace.

"Hold on," Puck said, pointing to the one remaining cat. "Which Grimalkin disappeared...?"

"Puck, there's no time! Come on!"

We tore down the mirrored hallway, past our reflections, which were back to normal again. The corridor finally opened into a large circular room with pillars soaring up into the darkness of the ceiling. On the other side, through another long corridor, I could just see a tall, rectangular space of light.

And it was shrinking.

As we tore across the room, voices suddenly echoed around us, low moans and wailings, making the candles flicker. From the walls and the floors, pale, misty figures began emerging, clawing at us as we passed. A troll, coming up through a broken pillar, latched on to my belt, trying to drag me down. I struck out with my blade, cutting through its arm, dissolving it into mist. With a wail, the troll drew back, but its arm reformed and knitted itself back onto the elbow, coming at me again. I dodged and continued my mad rush to the door.

The chamber was rapidly filling with wraiths, grabbing for us, snatching at clothes and limbs as we passed. They didn't hurt us, only latched on and held tight until we cut ourselves free. "Staaaaaay," they whispered, reaching for us with ghostly hands, dragging us down. "You cannot leave. Stay with us, those who have failed. Your essence can remain here with us forever."

The Wolf gave a defiant growl and surged forward ahead of us all, but for the rest of us, it was too late. As we sped across the room and down the corridor, I already knew we wouldn't make it. The rectangle was just a tiny square now, the stone door slowly grinding shut. So close. We were so close, only to run out of time in the end.

The Wolf hit the door with just enough room to slide out, lowering his head to dart beneath the opening. But instead of going through, he slammed his broad shoulders into the bottom edge, splaying his feet to brace himself in the opening. Panting, he locked his legs against the frame and heaved up against the inevitable push of the door, and amazingly, the huge stone rectangle ground to a halt. Wraiths crowded around him, grabbing his legs and fur, leaping onto his back. He snarled and snapped at them, but didn't move from his position in the doorway, and the ghostly figures could not budge him.

Slashing at wraiths, I reached the doorway first and whirled around, waiting for Puck and Ariella. Wraiths followed them, clawing and grabbing. One snagged Ariella by the hair, yanking her back, but Puck's dagger sliced down, cutting through its hand and pushing Ariella on. She stumbled into me, and I caught her before she could fall.

"Puck—" She gasped, turning in my arms.

"I'm fine, Ari!" Puck howled, leaping back from the crowding wraiths. "Just go!"

I nodded and released her. "Go," I repeated, echoing Puck. "We're right behind you."

She rolled beneath the door, barely avoiding a banshee that

lurched out of the floor. I stabbed the wraith through the head and glanced at Puck.

He was backing down the corridor, stabbing at hands and dodging the fingers that grabbed for him.

"Geez, you guys. I know I'm popular and all, but seriously, you're a bit too co-dependent for me. I'm going to need you to step away from my personal bubble." A wispy vine-woman curled ivy tendrils around his arm, and he sliced through them with his dagger. "No! Bad wraith! No touchie!"

"Will you get over here?" I shouted, stabbing a redcap clinging to my leg.

Puck gave a final swipe with his dagger and lunged toward the door, scrambling through the opening. I turned to help the Wolf.

He was covered in wraiths, so many that I could barely see him through the ghostly figures. And more were floating up, rising out of the floor and coming through the walls, trying to drag us back into the room. An ogre lunged through the wall from behind, reaching for my arm, and I twisted away.

"Don't worry about me," the Wolf snarled. "Just go!"

I sliced through a ghostly sidhe knight that reminded me faintly of Rowan. He dissolved instantly but began reforming as soon as my blade passed through his body. "I'm not leaving you here to die."

"Foolish prince!" The Wolf glared back at me, baring his fangs. "This is your story. You must reach the end of it. This is why I came—to ensure the story would go on." He snapped at a goblin near his face, and the thing erupted into a misty cloud. "The wraiths cannot leave the temple, it seems, but they are not letting me through, either. Go now, while there is still time!"

"Ash!" Puck called from the other side of the door. "Come on, ice-boy, what are you waiting for?"

I gave the Wolf one last glance, then dove through the opening, rolling to my feet on the other side. The wraiths wailed, crowding beneath the door, reaching out for us, but they could not get past the threshold.

The Wolf panted, shaking from the strain of holding the door and the dozens of bodies that tugged and yanked at him. "Get going, prince," he growled, looking me in the eye. "You cannot help me now. Finish your quest, complete the story, and don't forget to mention me when you pass it on. That was our bargain."

I stared at the Wolf, my mind churning, trying to think of a way to help him. But the Wolf was right; there was nothing we could do. Raising my sword, I gave him a solemn salute. "I won't forget what you've done."

"Pah!" The Wolf, despite the strain, bared his teeth in a disdainful laugh. "You think this will kill me, boy? You should know better than that. Nothing in this pitiful gauntlet can harm me. Nothing."

I seriously doubted that. The Wolf was strong, and he was immortal, but he could be killed. He could die, same as anything else.

"Now, go," he told us, a hint of irritation creeping into his voice. "I'm getting tired of watching you gape like a herd of startled deer. I will hold the door for your return, assuming we will have to come back the same way. Nothing will move me until we are done here for good."

"How very...doglike," said Grimalkin, appearing beside Ariella, gazing at the Wolf in disdain. "Brave. Loyal. And ultimately stupid."

The Wolf panted, baring his teeth. "You wouldn't understand, cat," he growled, curling a lip in his own show of contempt. "Your kind knows nothing of loyalty."

"As if that is a bad thing." Grimalkin sniffed and turned

away, waving his tail. "And yet, who is on the correct side of the door? Come, prince." He twitched an ear at me. "We did not come all this way to be stopped at the finish line. The dog has made his choice. Let us move on."

I gave the Wolf one last glance. "I'll be back," I told him. "Try to hang on. When I'm done with this, I'm coming back for you."

He snorted. Whether it was because he didn't believe me, or because it took too much strength to talk, I didn't know. But I turned my back on him and walked the final few paces out of the temple.

Grimalkin was sitting at the end of the hall, silhouetted beneath a stone archway, his tail curled primly around himself. Beyond him, I could see a black sky littered with stars. But they were huge, glowing things, almost blinding, as if we were far closer than we had been in the Nevernever. I heard the roar of water as I approached Grimalkin, and heard Puck's slow exhale as we joined the cat at the end of the hall.

The vast emptiness of space stretched before us, endless and eternal. Stars and constellations glimmered above and below, from tiny pinpricks of light to huge pulsing giants so bright it hurt to look at them. Comets streaked through the night sky, and in the distance, I could see the gaping maw of a black hole sucking in the surrounding galaxy, billions of miles away. Huge chunks of rock and land floated, weightless, in empty space. I saw a cottage perched on a boulder, spinning endlessly through space, and a massive tree grew from a tiny plot of grass, its roots dangling through the bottom. Beyond a stream of jagged rocks, past a treacherous-looking rope bridge over nothing, an enormous castle floated among the stars.

Below our feet, the River of Dreams flowed from beneath the hall and roared over the edge into empty space, falling into the void until we couldn't see it anymore.

I drew in a deep, slow breath, feeling my companions' amazement match my own.

We had reached the End of the World.

PART THREE

CHAPTER FIFTEEN

THE TESTING GROUNDS

Ariella found the stairs. We made our way down the narrow, crumbling path to the bottom of the cliff, gazing out into the void. A rock floated past my face; I tapped it and sent it spinning away into space.

"The end of the Nevernever," Ariella mused, her silver hair floating around her like a bright cloud. She sounded sad again, and I wanted to comfort her, but restrained myself. "How many have been here, I wonder? How many have seen what we're seeing?"

"How many have dropped off the edge and are drifting through space right now?" Puck added, peering over the end of the cliff while hanging on to a sickly tree trunk growing from the rocks. "I keep expecting a skeleton to float by. Or maybe they just keep falling forever?"

"Let's not find out," I said, turning to the castle, feeling it beckon me like a distant siren call. "The Testing Grounds are our goal—we're going to reach it without anyone falling off the edge of the world or drifting through space. Watch out for each other, and be careful."

"Hey, don't worry about me, ice-boy. Gravity isn't so much

of a problem when you're a bird." Puck glanced at me and sighed in mock aggravation. "Someday, I have *got* to teach you people how to fly."

A river of floating rocks stood between us and the castle. Grimalkin strode up to one and looked back at us, twitching his tail.

"I will meet you at the castle," he stated, and hopped lightly onto one of the rocks. It spun lazily, easily holding the cat's weight. Grimalkin blinked at us as the rock drifted away. "I trust you can make it to our destination without me for once," he said, and headed for the castle, leaping from rock to rock with the inborn grace of a cat.

"You know, sometimes I just hate him," Puck grumbled.

I stepped onto one of the rocks, bracing myself as it tilted slightly, but it appeared to hold my weight well enough. "Come on," I said, holding out a hand for Ariella. She took it, and I pulled her up beside me, though she didn't meet my eyes. "We're almost there."

We picked our way over the treacherous terrain, leaping from rock to rock, trying not to look down. I glanced back once and saw the door of the temple jutting from the face of a cliff, and that cliff sprang from a wall of briars, stretching away to either side, farther than I could see. It emphasized the vast infinity of this part of the world and made me feel very small.

"I wonder if anything lives out here," Puck mused as we crossed a shattered stone bridge, twirling aimlessly through space. "I thought the End of the World was supposed to be filled with monsters and *here there be dragons* and things like that. I don't see any...oh."

I knew by the tone of his voice that I wasn't going to like what I saw next. "Don't tell me." I sighed without turning around. "There's some sort of huge monster out there, and now it's coming toward us."

"Okay, I won't tell you." Puck sounded faintly breathless. "And, uh, you probably don't want to look down, either."

I peered over the side of the bridge.

At first, I thought I was looking at a continent floating beneath us; I could see lakes and trees and even a few houses scattered about. But then the continent twisted around with a flash of scales and teeth and drifted toward us, a leviathan so huge it defied belief. It spiraled up beside the bridge, a mountain of scales and fins and flippers, rising out of the void. Its eye was like a small moon, pale and all-seeing, but we were insects beneath its gaze, dust mites, too microscopic for it to know we were there. An entire city was perched on its back, gleaming white towers standing at the edge of a glistening lake. Smaller creatures, as big as whales, swam beside it, looking like minnows compared to its bulk. As we stood gaping at it, unable to move or look away, it twisted lazily through the air and continued into the etherealness of space.

For a long moment, we could only stare after it, hardly able to process what we had seen. Finally, Ariella drew in a shaky breath and shook her head in disbelief. "That…was…" She seemed unable to find the right description.

"Incredible," I finished softly, still gazing after the creature, and no one disagreed with me. Not even Puck.

"Here there be dragons," he murmured in an awed voice.

Gathering my wits, I took a step back. "Come on," I said, glancing at the others, who seemed a little dazed. "Let's find the Testing Grounds and get this over with so we can go home."

Leaping carefully from rock to rock, wary now of the monsters at the End of the World, we finally reached the gates of the castle. Past a courtyard filled with statues and twisted trees of a kind I'd never seen before, up another flight of steps flanked by snarling gargoyles, Grimalkin waited for us at the hallway into the castle.

He was not alone. A familiar robed, hooded figure stood beside him, watching us as we walked up the stairs.

"You have come far," the Guardian intoned, nodding his head. "Few have made it to this point, and fewer still can keep their sanity intact at the End of the World. But your journey is not yet over, knight. The trials await, and they will be more harrowing than anything you have encountered thus far. No one has ever survived what you are about to face. I give you one last chance to depart, to turn around and leave this place alive and whole. But know this—if you leave, you will remember nothing of what brought you here. You will never find the End of the World again. What is your decision?"

"I've come this far," I said without hesitation. "I'm not backing out now. Bring on your tests. When I leave this place, it will be as a human with a soul, or not at all."

The Guardian nodded. "If that is your choice." It swept out an arm, and a ripple of power went through the air, freezing me in place. "Let it be known, before these witnesses, that the former Winter prince Ash has accepted the trials of the Guardian, the prize for completing the tests being a mortal soul." It lowered its arm, and I could move again. "Your first trial begins when dawn touches the outside world. Until then, the castle is yours. When the time comes, I will find you."

And it was gone.

Grimalkin yawned and looked up at me, cat eyes blinking. "I am supposed to show you your rooms," he said in a bored voice, as if the very idea wearied him. "Follow me, then. And do try to keep up. It would be vastly annoying if you became lost in here."

THE CASTLE WAS DIM and empty, with torches set into brackets, and candles flickering along the walls. Except for the flames and candlelight, nothing moved; there were no insects scuttling over the flagstones, no servants prowling the halls. It felt frozen in time, like a reflection on the other side of a mirror—perfect, but lifeless.

And it was endless, much like the void that floated just outside the windows. I got the distinct feeling, following Grimalkin down its many halls, that I could wander its chambers and corridors forever and not see the entirety of the castle.

Regardless, we found the guest rooms easily enough, on account of the open doors and the crackling fireplaces along each wall. These rooms were fairly well lit, with food, drink and a clean bed already laid out for us, though there were no servants to speak of. Puck and Ariella each vanished into their separate chambers, though each room was easily big enough for the three of us and I was wary of being separated in this huge place. But Puck, after peering into a room, whooped when he saw the food-laden table and vanished through the door with a hasty, "Later, ice-boy," slamming the door behind him. Ariella gave me a tired smile and said she was going to turn in for the night, declining my offer of staying through dinner. Grimalkin, of course, trotted down the hall without any explanation of where he was going and vanished into the shadows, leaving me alone.

Truthfully, I was relieved. There were so many thoughts swirling around my head, and I think the others recognized my need to be alone, to process all that had happened and to prepare for what was to come. Or perhaps they were weary of me, as well.

I ate a little, prowled my room, and tried to read some of the huge tomes on the bookcase in the corner to pass the time. Most were written in strange, ancient languages I didn't recognize, some oddly blank, some with runes and symbols that made my eyes burn just from looking at them. One book let out a chilling wail when I touched it, and I quickly withdrew my hand. I finally discovered, of all things, a small book of poems by the mortal author e.e. cummings, and leafed through that for a while, pausing at the poem, "All in green went my love riding," one of my favorites. I smiled wistfully as I followed the stanzas, reminded of all the hunts Ariella and I had been on and their sudden end.

Guilt gnawed at me, though it wasn't quite as sharp as before. I'd finally come to terms with what I felt, both for Ariella and Meghan. I would always love Ariella, and there was still a part of me that longed for the past, for those days when it was me and Ari and Puck before—before her death and my oath and the decades of duels and fighting and bloodshed. But those days were gone. And I was tired of living in the past. If I managed to survive here, I would actually have a chance at a future.

Still, I couldn't sleep; my mind worried at the situation like a dog with a bone and my body was too hyped up to relax. I was sitting in the window with my back against the frame, watching the stars and bits of rock drift by, almost close enough to touch, when my door creaked open and footsteps padded into the room.

"Don't you ever knock?" I asked Puck without turning around. He snorted.

"Hi, I'm Robin Goodfellow, have we met?" Walking up beside me, he leaned against the frame and crossed his arms, staring out at the End of the World. After a moment, he shook his head. "You know, out of all the places we've seen, and we've seen some weird places, this probably takes the cake for Most Crazy Landscape Ever. No one will believe the stories when we get home." He sighed and shot me a sideways glance. "Are you sure you're up for this, ice-boy?" he asked. "I know you think you can handle anything, but this is some serious stuff you're going to face. Crazy Ash just doesn't have the same ring as Don't-bother-me-or-I'll-kill-you Ash."

I smirked at him. "You're awfully concerned for an arch-nemesis."

"*Psh,* I just don't want to have to tell Meghan that you turned into a vegetable while trying to gain a soul. I don't see how *that* would turn out well for me."

Smiling, I gazed out the window again. In the far distance, something like a giant manta ray soared lazily by, fins rippling like water. "I don't know," I admitted softly, watching it vanish behind an asteroid. "I don't know if I'm ready. But it's not just Meghan that I'm doing this for now." I glanced down at my hands, resting in my lap. "I think…this is who I'm supposed to be…if that makes any sense."

"Nope, that's just screwed up." I shot him an annoyed look, and Puck grinned to soften the words. He raised his hands. "But, if that's the way you feel, then more power to you. At least you know what you want. Just thought I'd make sure." With a grunt, he shoved himself off the wall, tapping my shoulder as he passed. "Well, good luck to you, prince. There's a bottle of plum wine and a fluffy down pillow calling my name. You need me, I'll be in my room, hopefully well into a stupor."

"Puck," I called before he could leave the room.

He turned in the doorframe. "Yeah?"

"If I…don't make it back…"

I felt him nod. "I'll take care of her," he promised quietly. "Both of them." And the door clicked softly behind him.

I didn't sleep. I stayed in the window and watched the stars, thinking of Meghan, and Ariella and myself. Remembering those bright, shining moments with each of them…in case I didn't see them again.

CHAPTER SIXTEEN
THE FIRST TEST

"It is time."

The Guardian's voice cut through the silence, and I jerked my head toward the robed figure in the middle of the room. It stood expectantly, gripping its staff, watching me through the darkness of the cowl. The door behind it was still closed.

"Are you ready?" it asked without preamble. I took a deep breath and nodded.

"Then follow me."

Puck and Ariella joined us as soon as we left the room. Together, we trailed him through the vast halls of the castle until he led us outside, into an ice-covered garden. Skeletal trees stood encased in crystal, sparkling with icicles, and a fountain in the middle spouted frozen water. For a moment, it reminded me of home, of the Winter Court, before I shook that thought away. Tir Na Nog was not my home any longer.

Above us, across a stone bridge over nothing, a huge jagged mountain rose up from the depths, the peak barely visible through the haze that surrounded it. Wreathed in ice, it glittered in the cold lights of the stars, slick and sharp and treacherous.

The Guardian turned to me. "Your first trial begins now. From here on, you must do this alone. Have you prepared yourself?"

"Yes."

The cowl nodded once. "Then meet me at the top." And it was gone, leaving us to stare at the mountain for a few moments of silence.

"Well," Puck remarked, gazing up at the looming obstacle with his hands on his hips. "As tests go, climbing a mountain isn't that bad."

Ariella shook her head. "I seriously doubt that's all there is to it." She glanced at me, worried and solemn. "Be careful, Ash."

I glared up at the obstacle before me. The first thing that stood between me and a soul. I clenched my fists and smiled.

"I'll be back soon," I muttered, and sprinted across the bridge. Leaping onto the base of the mountain, I started to climb.

PULLING MYSELF ONTO a narrow ledge, I sat down with my back against the wall to catch my breath. I didn't know how long I'd been climbing, but it felt like days. And I was still a good way from the top.

Far below, the castle looked comically small, like a child's toy, even as large as it was. The mountain was proving harder and more treacherous to climb than I'd expected. The jagged obsidian rocks were as sharp as a knife's edge in places, and the ice refused to honor my Unseelie heritage. I had never slipped or stumbled on ice before, but here, it seemed all bets were off. My hands were cut open from gripping the rock, trying to balance myself, and I left smears of blood against the mountainside where I passed.

I shivered, rubbing my arms. It was also freezing up here,

which was a complete shock for me, as I *never* got cold. The sensation was so alien and unfamiliar I didn't know what it was at first. My teeth chattered, and I crossed my arms, trying, for the first time in my life, to conserve heat. So this was what it was like for mortals and Summer fey in the Unseelie realm. I'd always wondered why they looked so uncomfortable in the Winter palace. Now I knew.

I licked dry, cracked lips and pushed myself to my feet, staring up at the top. It was still so far away. I started climbing again.

The jagged cliffs went on. I lost track of time. I lost more blood as the bitter cold ate into my limbs and turned them heavy and clumsy. Eventually, I wasn't thinking anymore, my body moving on its own, just putting one limb in front of the other. Exhausted, bleeding, and shaking with cold, I finally pulled myself onto a ledge, only to find there was no mountain left. A flat expanse of rock and ice stretched out before me. I had finally reached the top.

The Guardian waited, patient and motionless, in the center of the plateau. Panting, I pushed myself to my feet and walked toward it, forcing myself not to shiver, to ignore the cold. It didn't move or say a word as I came to stand before it, the blood from my hands dripping slowly to the ground.

"I'm here," I rasped into the silence. "I passed the first of your tests."

A deep chuckle. "No," the Guardian said, making my stomach sink. It lifted its staff a few inches into the air, and a ripple of power erupted from the tip, spreading outward into space. "You have only found the location of the first testing ground. We are not done yet, knight. The real test begins... now."

It brought the staff down, striking the point on the rocks. Cracks appeared from the tip, spreading outward, as a rumbling shook the ground. I dove away as part of the earth collapsed beneath me, revealing gaping holes deep into the mountain. A hellish red glow spilled out of the craters, and a wild shrieking filled the air, along with the sound of wings.

"Survive," the Guardian told me, and disappeared.

Creatures poured from the opening in a mad rush of wings; scaly, furry, feathered and smooth. They looked like dragons, or wyverns, or monstrous birds, a chaotic mass of wings and claws and teeth, none of them the same. Except for one thing. Their chest cavities were open, and where their hearts would lie, there was only a void, a black hole filled with stars and black spaces of their own. The beings exploded from the gash, wailing in voices that seemed to echo across the emptiness of time, and dropped from the sky to attack.

I drew my sword, startled by how cold the hilt was, and slashed at the first creature, cutting through a spindly neck. It shrieked and collapsed on itself, the hole in its chest seeming to draw it in. Crying, it was sucked into its own black hole, and I leaped back as the rest of the flock descended on me all at once.

I stumbled, my limbs heavy with cold, and one of the creatures struck out with a furry talon, catching my shoulder and ripping a gash down my chest. Pain erupted through me, greater than any I'd felt before, and I clenched my teeth to keep from screaming. My body wasn't moving as it should, too clumsy and awkward, as if it belonged to someone else. Another creature slashed at me as I retreated, striking my face and leaving deep claw marks across my cheek.

Half-blinded by pain, I lurched backward, bringing up my arm to unleash a hail of ice daggers into the swarm. If anything, it would at least slow them down. But as I swept my hand out as I had done thousands of times before, nothing happened. Only a few spits of ice, instead of the deadly flurry

I was used to. Stunned, I opened myself up to my glamour, trying to draw it from the air as I'd always done.

Nothing. No glamour, no magic, no swirling emotions or colors. I felt a deep stab of terror and loss as I backed away, trying to think. Had a binding been placed on me, locking away my glamour? Was there a seal over the area, preventing magic use? I realized with horror that it was none of these. Even through a binding or a seal, I would have been able to sense my glamour. I felt only emptiness. As if I had never had magic in the first place.

In the split second my guard was down, one of the creatures pounced on me with a snarl, driving us both to the ground. I felt teeth in my shoulder before I plunged my blade through its throat and it was sucked into oblivion. But the other creatures swarmed around me, shrieking, clawing, biting and kicking. I struck out with my weapon, slashing wildly from my back, and several creatures vanished into themselves. But there were always more, tearing and ripping, almost frantic as they pressed in, their shrill voices echoing all around me. I felt jaws crush my arm, hooked talons in my stomach, gouging it open. I felt my flesh being torn away, my blood misting in the air and streaming to the ground. I tried to get up, to make one last stand, to live, but the pain suddenly drew a red-and-black curtain over my vision, and I knew nothing more.

AND THEN, IT WAS OVER. I was lying on the cold stone floor of the castle, whole and intact, the Guardian gazing down at me. From the corner of my eye, I saw Puck and Ariella peering on anxiously, but the pain streaming from every part of my body made it difficult to focus on anything.

"I failed." The words were bitter in my mouth, the weight

in my chest threatening to crush me. But the Guardian shook its cowled head.

"No. You were never meant to survive that, knight. Even had you killed the first wave, they would have kept coming. No matter what you did, or how long you stood against them, they would have torn you apart in the end."

I wanted to ask why. Why I'd been spared. Why I wasn't dead yet. But, through the pain and the confusion and the shock of still being alive, my mind was still reeling from everything that had just happened. The strangeness of my own body, suddenly weak and awkward, refusing to move as it should. The blinding pain, the agony I couldn't shut out as I used to. And the complete emptiness I felt when I tried to use glamour was worst of all.

"This is what a mortal body feels like," the Guardian continued, as if reading my thoughts. "It is physically impossible for a human to move as you do. Their bodies are clumsy and tire easily. They are susceptible to cold, weakness and pain. They cannot draw on any magic to aid them. They are, in the end, quite unremarkable. Strength is the first thing you must give up if you wish to gain a soul."

The Guardian paused, allowing time for that statement to sink in. I could only lie there, panting, as my mind recovered from the shock of being torn apart. "The first trial is over," the Guardian intoned. "Prepare yourself, knight. The second begins at dawn."

When it disappeared, Ariella hurried over and knelt beside me. "Can you stand?"

Wincing, I struggled to a sitting position. My wounds were gone, I was alive, but my body still blazed with pain. Taking her hand, I let her pull me to my feet, clenching my jaw to keep the gasp from escaping. "I didn't realize…how fragile humans really are."

"Well, duh." Puck strolled over, not quite able to mask the worry on his face. "I could've told you that. Though some are stronger than others. Or more stubborn." He crossed his arms, giving me an appraising look. "You okay, ice-boy?"

I didn't answer. Turning from Ariella, I ignored her offered arm and limped away, down the long corridors, back to my room. They followed silently, at a distance, but I didn't turn to look back. More than once, I nearly fell but forced myself to keep going, without help.

In my room I collapsed on the bed, cursing my strange, unfamiliar body and the weakness that came with it.

How am I going to protect her like this? How can I protect any-one *like this?*

Puck and Ariella hovered in the doorway. A part of me wanted to tell them to leave, hating that they saw me weak and helpless. But, my whole life, I had pushed others away, closing myself off to the world and everyone around me. It had brought me nothing but more pain, despite my attempts to freeze everything out. That was why I was here, after all; I was trying to become someone else.

I shifted to my back and put an arm over my face, closing my eyes. "I'm not going to throw icicles if you step through the door." I sighed. "So you can stop lurking and come in already."

I felt them pause, imagined them exchanging glances, but then footsteps padded into the room. Ariella perched on the edge of the mattress, laying a soft hand on my arm. "Are you in a lot of pain?" she asked.

"Some," I admitted, relaxing under her touch. "It's getting better, though." And it was, the fire beneath my skin ebbing away, as if my body finally realized it was whole and healthy, not torn apart on a desolate peak.

"What happened up there, ice-boy?"

"What do you think happened?" I lowered my arm and sat

up, scrubbing a hand over my eyes. "I lost. I can't use glamour,
I can't move like I used to. My head was telling me to move a
certain way, to go faster, and I couldn't. I got *cold*, Puck. Do
you know what that was like, when I finally realized what was
happening?" I leaned forward, raking my hands through my
hair, shoving it back. "I would've died," I said softly, reluctant to admit it. "If the Guardian had left me there, I would
have died. Those things would've torn me apart."

"But you're not dead," Puck pointed out. "And the
Guardian didn't say you failed. At least, we weren't tossed
out on our ears. So what's the problem, ice-boy?"

I didn't answer, but Ariella, who was watching my face,
drew in a quiet breath. "Meghan," she guessed, making me
wince. "You're worried about Meghan, how she'll react to
seeing you like this."

"I can't protect her like this," I said bitterly, clenching a
fist, fighting the urge to punch the mattress. "I'm useless—a
liability. I don't want her to feel she has to constantly watch
out for me, that I can't hold my own anymore." I sighed in
frustration and leaned back, thumping my head against the
wall. It was satisfyingly painful. "I guess I didn't realize what
being human really meant."

You do not know the first thing about mortality, prince-who-is-
not. The Bone Witch's voice echoed in my head, mocking me
with its smugness. *Why would you want to be like them?*

Puck snorted. "And what, you think that if you're human
you can't protect anyone?" he asked, crossing his arms and
glaring at me. "That's a load of crap. How did you think you
were going to protect her while she was in the Iron Kingdom, prince? I thought we were here to get you a soul, so
you could be with her without your skin melting off. Are you
telling me, now that you're more human, you don't want to
be with her?"

I glared at him. "You know that's not what I meant."

"Doesn't matter." Puck loomed over me as if daring me to argue. "The way I see it, there are only two options here, ice-boy. You can be a human and be with Meghan, or you can be fey and not. And you'd better figure out what you want real fast, or we've wasted our time here."

Ariella stood. "Come on," she told Puck, falling back into an old tradition. Since the three of us had known each other, she had always been the peacekeeper. "Let's let him rest. Ash, if you need us, we'll be close."

Puck looked defiant, but Ariella put a hand on his arm and gently but firmly pulled him from the room. As the door closed, I clenched my fists and stared at the wall. Throwing out my arm, I tried sending a flurry of ice darts at the door, but nothing happened. Not even a cold wind.

I had no glamour anymore. My magic was gone; centuries of feeling the pulse of the earth, seeing the swirl of emotion and dreams and passion all around me, in every living creature, all vanished in a heartbeat. Could I get used to this? Any of this? I couldn't move like I used to, I wasn't as strong, and my body was susceptible to pain and sickness and cold. I was weaker now. I was...mortal.

I punched the mattress in frustration, feeling the blow rattle the frame. The Bone Witch was right. I didn't know the first thing about mortality.

The pain had almost faded now, just a dull, ragged throbbing around the edges of my mind. Wearied by the battle and the cold and the shock of being torn apart, my head dropped to my chest, and I felt myself drifting....

"THERE YOU ARE," Ariella said, smiling at me in my dreams. "I knew you had to fall asleep sooner or later. You were exhausted."

I blinked, stepping beneath the boughs of a huge, snow-covered cypress, every leaf outlined in frost. "Is this something I should expect every time I fall asleep?" I asked the figure sitting beneath the trunk.

Ariella stood and walked forward, brushing away glittering curtains of leaves. "No," she said, taking my hand and drawing me forward. "My time as the seer is coming to an end. Soon, I won't be able to dreamwalk anymore, so bear with me for a little while. I want to show you something."

As she spoke, the scene around us changed. It blew away, like dust in a storm, until we were standing on a long gravel driveway, gazing up at an old green house.

"Do you recognize this?"

I nodded. "Meghan's old house," I said, gazing at the weathered, faded structure. "Where her family lives."

A bark interrupted me. The front door creaked open, and Meghan emerged, followed by a small child of about four or five, an enormous German shepherd trailing them both.

I drew in a breath and stepped forward, but Ariella put a hand on my arm.

"She cannot see us," she warned. "Not this time. This is more a latent memory than a true dream. Meghan's consciousness is not here—you would not be able to speak to her."

I turned back, watching Meghan and Ethan sit on the old porch swing, swaying gently back and forth. Ethan's feet dangled over the edge, kicking sporadically, as Meghan passed him a small blue box with a straw sticking out of it. Beau, the German shepherd, put his huge paws on the swing and tried scrambling up as well, causing Ethan to shriek with laughter and Meghan to yell at him to get down.

"She dreams of them often," Ariella said. "Her family. Especially him, the small one."

"Her brother," I murmured, unable to take my eyes from her. Having successfully ordered Beau off the swing, she patted her lap and scratched the big dog behind the ears, kissing his muzzle as he came up. Ariella nodded.

"Yes. The child who started it all, in a way. When he was kidnapped by the Iron King and taken into the Nevernever, she didn't hesitate to go after him. And she didn't stop there. When her magic was sealed by Mab, leaving her defenseless in the Winter Court, she somehow managed to survive, even when she thought you had turned on her. When the Scepter of the Seasons was stolen by the Iron fey, she went after it, despite having no magic and no weapon with which to defend herself. And when the courts asked her to destroy the false king, she accepted, even though the Summer and Iron glamours within her were making her sick, and she couldn't use either of them effectively. She still went into the Iron Kingdom to face a tyrant she didn't know if she could overcome.

"Now," Ariella finished, turning toward me, "do you still believe humans are weak?"

Before I could answer, the scene faded. Darkness fell, Meghan and her brother vanished before me, and everything went black. I opened my eyes to find myself alone in my room, sitting on the bed with my back to the wall.

Do you still believe humans are weak?

I smiled ruefully. The half-blood daughter of Oberon was one of the strongest human beings I'd ever encountered. Even when her magic was sealed, or when it was making her horribly sick, she'd managed to defeat everything Faery threw at her through sheer stubborn determination. She had brought an end to *two* faery wars, and when it was all over, she had become a queen.

No, I told myself. Humans weren't weak. Meghan Chase

had proven that, many times over. And it didn't matter if I had no magic, or if I wasn't as strong as before. My vow to the Iron Queen, the one I'd sworn when I became her knight, still stood.

From this day forth, I vow to protect Meghan Chase, daughter of the Summer King, with my sword, my honor and my life. Should even the world stand against her, my blade will be at her side. And should it fail to protect her, let my own existence be forfeit.

I couldn't protect her in the Iron Realm, not as Ash the Winter prince. All the glamour in the world couldn't help her if I wasn't there. I had to become human to stand beside her. For a moment, I'd lost sight of that.

That wouldn't happen again. The loss of my glamour wouldn't deter me. I was still a knight, *her* knight. And I'd return to the girl I'd sworn to protect.

I rose, prepared to find Puck and Ariella and tell them I was fine, that I was prepared to continue the trials. But before I could move, a dark shaped appeared in the corner of my eye, and the Guardian stood beside me. No warning, no ripple of power or magic to announce its arrival. It was just there.

"It is time," the hooded figure stated as I stifled the urge to step out of its cold, dark shadow. "You have made your decision, so let us continue."

"I thought I had till dawn."

"It is dawn." The Guardian's voice was cold, matter-of-fact. "Time moves differently here, knight. A single day can pass in a heartbeat, or a lifetime. It matters not. The second test is upon us. Are you ready?"

"How will I know if I've passed?"

"There is no pass or fail." That cold, informal tone never changed. "There is only endure. Survive."

Endure. Survive. I could do that. "All right, then," I said, bracing myself. "I'm ready."

"Then let us begin." Raising its staff, it tapped it once against the stone floor. There was a flash, and everything disappeared.

CHAPTER SEVENTEEN
THE SECOND TRIAL

"Nice shot, little brother. Maybe next time, we can find something that puts up more of a fight. I was about to fall asleep in the saddle."

I ignored Rowan and approached the stag where it lay, still thrashing in the grass. A white arrow jutted behind its front legs, straight through its heart, and the beast's mouth and nostrils were spattered with bloody foam. It rolled its eyes at me and tried to rise, but fell, kicking weakly, not quite realizing it was dead. I drew my hunting knife, and one quick slash to the throat ceased its struggles forever.

I sheathed the blade, gazing down at the twitching creature, somehow smaller in death than in life. "Too easy," I muttered, curling a lip in disdain. "These mortal beasts are no challenge at all. It's no fun hunting something that dies so easily."

Rowan snickered as I yanked my arrow free and walked back to my horse, leaving the pathetic creature to bleed out in the dirt. "You're just not hunting the right quarry," he said as I swung into the saddle. "You keep chasing these animals, hoping they can survive more than an afternoon. If you want a challenge, maybe you need to change tactics."

"Like what? Talk them to death? I'll leave that up to you."

"Oh, har har." Rowan rolled his eyes. "My little brother is around a few decades and thinks he knows everything. Listen to someone who's lived a few centuries. If you want a real challenge, you need to stop chasing these animals and pursue a quarry that can actually think."

"You're talking about humans," I muttered as we rode through the forest, back toward the trod that had brought us here. "I've hunted them before. They're less of a challenge than shooting dead goats."

"Oh, little brother." Rowan shook his head at me. "You have such a one-track mind. There are other ways to 'hunt' humans, other than riding them down and putting an arrow in their skulls. They're a much more interesting quarry alive than dead. You should try it sometime."

"You mean how *you* hunt them?" I snorted. "That's less hunting and more toying with your prey, like a cat."

"Don't be so smug, Ash." Rowan smirked at me, a silent challenge. "Pursuing a mortal's heart, making her fall for you, slowly entangling her to the point where she would promise you anything, takes much more skill than simply sticking an arrow through someone's chest. The human heart is the most difficult quarry of all." His smirk grew wider, turning into a leer. "In fact, I'm not sure you could do it."

"Who said I'd want to?" I ignored his baiting. "I've seen mortals 'in love' before. They're blind and foolish, and their hearts are so fragile. What would I do with such a thing if I had it?"

"Whatever you want, little brother. Whatever you want." Rowan gave me that smug, superior grin that made me bristle. "But, I understand if you're afraid. If you don't think you can do it. I just thought that you'd want a more interesting hunt, but if it's *too* challenging for you…"

"All right." I sighed. "You'll give me no peace otherwise. Point me to a mortal and I'll make it fall in love with me."

Rowan laughed. "My little brother is growing up." He sneered, as we turned our mounts toward the edge of the forest.

Once we were close to our prey, it didn't take us long to find a likely target. As we approached the crude wooden fence that separated the human's glade from the rest of the forest, faint, off-key singing suddenly reached our ears, and we pulled our mounts to a halt.

"There." Rowan pointed. I followed his finger, and my eyebrows rose in surprise.

Beyond the fence and the edge of the trees, a stream babbled its way across a rocky field, where a gathering of thatched huts stood in a loose semicircle around a large fire pit. One of the many small human settlements in the area, this one tempted fate by sitting on the very edge of the forest. They rarely ventured close to the trees, and never left their houses after dark, for good reason. Goblins still considered this their territory, and I knew of more than one phouka that roamed these woods at night. I didn't know much about these humans except that they were a small druidic tribe, attempting to live in peace with the land and the forest just outside their village walls. It was risky and foolish, as all humans tended to be, but at least they showed the proper respect.

So it was surprising to see one of them alone on the banks of the stream, humming as she picked the wildflowers that grew close to the forest. She was young as humans went, dressed in a simple shift, barefoot and barefaced. Her dark hair gleamed in the sunshine.

Rowan smiled his toothy wolf-smile and turned to me.

"All right, little brother. There's your target."

"The girl?"

"No, fool. Haven't you been listening to me?" My brother rolled his eyes. "Her heart. Her body and mind and soul. Make her love you. Ensure that she gives herself to you completely, that she can think of nothing else but you. If you can do that, *then* you'll be a hunter among hunters." He sneered and looked down his nose. "If you're up to the challenge, that is."

I looked back to the girl, still humming as she picked handfuls of forget-me-nots, and felt a smile stretching my face. I'd never pursued a mortal heart before; this could be...interesting. "Is there a time in which I have to do this?" I asked.

Rowan pondered that question. "Well, the best-laid plans are not conceived in a day," he mused, watching the girl. "But, it shouldn't be difficult for you to win a mortal's affections, especially one as young as that. Let's say, the next full moon. Get her to follow you to the stone circle and pledge her undying love. I'll be there, waiting for you both."

"I'll be there," I said quietly, reveling in a worthy challenge, "with the human. Let me show you how it's done."

Rowan gave me a mocking salute, turned his horse and vanished into the forest. Dismounting, I approached the human silently, using glamour to mask my presence until I stood at the very edge of the forest, the girl only a stone's throw away. I didn't reveal myself to her at first. Like all pursuits, I began by studying my quarry, observing its strengths and weaknesses, learning its habits and patterns. If I just appeared out of the trees, I might spook her and she might not return to the area, so caution was necessary at first.

She was slender and graceful, very deerlike in some ways, which made the hunt all the more intriguing and familiar. Her dark eyes were quite large for a human, giving her a constant startled expression, but she moved from bush to bush with a general unawareness, as if a bear could come lumbering out of the trees and she wouldn't even notice.

She swooped down abruptly, plunging her hand into the stream and emerged clutching a smooth turquoise pebble, which she turned over in obvious delight. At once I smiled, watching her drop the stone into her pocket, knowing the bait that would lure my prey to me.

So, you like shiny things, do you, little mortal? Crouching, I picked up a plain gray pebble and covered it in my fist, drawing a tiny bit of glamour from the air. When I opened my hand, the once dull stone was now a glittering sapphire, and I tossed the glamoured item into the stream.

She found it almost immediately, and pounced with a squeal of delight, holding it up so it sparkled in the sun. I smiled and drew away, walking back to my mount with a feeling of satisfaction, knowing she would be there tomorrow.

I left her a silver chain the next day, watching her coo over it with the same delight the glamoured gem had given her, and the next afternoon she admired the golden ring on her finger for a long, long time, before dropping the treasure into her pocket. I didn't have any fear of her showing it to anyone else; much like crows and magpies, she didn't want anyone to steal her treasures, or question where she got them. And the glamour on the items eventually faded, leaving rocks and leaves in their place. I knew she wondered what had become of them; perhaps she told herself that she dropped or misplaced her treasures, choosing to ignore the obvious answer. Perhaps she suspected the truth and knew she should be wary, but I also knew her greed would keep her coming back.

The following day, I didn't leave her anything, but watched her flounder about in the stream for hours, searching and growing despondent, until evening fell and she left on the verge of tears. And I smiled to myself, already planning the next stage. It was time to move in for the kill.

The next afternoon, I put a single white rose on a flat rock near the stream, faded into the woods and waited.

She wasn't long in coming, and when she saw the rose she gasped and picked it up almost reverently, holding it as if it was made of purest crystal. As she straightened and gazed around, eyes shining with hope, I dropped the glamour and stepped out of the trees.

She jumped like a startled deer but, as I had predicted, made no move to run. I let her stare at me, waiting for the shock to fade. Knowing humans found us beautiful, I'd dressed the part of the prince in black-and-silver, my cape falling over one shoulder and my sword at my waist. She gaped at me like a landed fish, her dark eyes wide with fear, but also with a little wonder and excitement.

Very carefully, I let my glamour settle over her, taking away her fear, leaving only the awe behind. Human emotions were fickle things, easy to influence. I could have enchanted her, made her fall completely in love at first sight, but that would be cheating, according to Rowan. That was fabricated love, where the mortal was no more than a fawning, glassy-eyed slave. To completely own her, body and soul, took careful manipulation and time.

Still, there was no reason I couldn't level the field a bit.

"Forgive me," I said in a cool, soothing voice as the girl continued to stare. "I didn't mean to startle you. I've been watching you for some time, and I couldn't stay away any longer. I hope you didn't find my gifts ill-mannered."

The girl opened her mouth, but no sounds escaped. I waited two heartbeats, then turned away, bowing my head.

"What am I saying?" I continued before she could respond. "Here I am, acting like an uncivilized barbarian, stalking you from the woods. Of course, you don't want to see me like this—I should go."

"No, wait!" the girl cried, just as I had planned. I turned back with a "dare I hope" expression, and she smiled at me across the water. "I don't mind," she said, suddenly bashful and coy, twisting her hands behind her back. "You can stay... if you want."

I hid my smile. *Easier than I thought.*

The girl's name, she told me, was Brynna, and she was the daughter of the druid priestess who led the village. Her grandmother was a very powerful shaman, and very strict, forbidding anyone to go into the forest or even near its borders, for fear of the Good Neighbors that lurked within the trees. But the flowers that grew along the edge of the forest were the most beautiful, and Brynna loved beautiful things, so she waited until her grandmother was napping before she slipped out of the village and down to the stream.

"And why does your grandmother hate the Good Neighbors so?" I asked, smiling at the mortals' odd name for us, which they used because, supposedly, voicing our real names might draw our attention. I smiled at the girl, feigning curiosity while tinting the air with glamour, subduing any fears she might have.

"She...she doesn't hate them," Brynna went on, nervously pushing her hair back. "She fears them. She's afraid of what they might do—kill our livestock, steal our children, make the women unfertile."

"And, are you afraid of them?" I asked in a low voice, closing the final few feet between us. Very gently, I reached for her rough, work-callused hands, holding them to my chest. "Are you afraid of me?"

She gazed up at my face, dark eyes shining with foolish trust, and shook her head.

"I'm glad." I smiled and kissed the back of her hand. "May I see you again tomorrow?"

I knew the answer even before she nodded.

IT WAS EASY after that, though I took my time with her, wanting to play the game right. Every afternoon, right before twilight, I met her at the stream. Sometimes with trinkets, sometimes with flowers, always with some sort of gift that would keep her returning to me. I showered her with compliments and tender kisses, playing the smitten fool, smiling as she melted under my touch. I never pushed too far, being sure to end each meeting before it got out of hand. When I eventually took her, at the stone circle on the night of the full moon, I wanted there to be no doubts in her mind.

As the game progressed, I even found myself enjoying these little encounters. Humans, I discovered, loved so passionately, without reservation, and the stronger the emotion the brighter their glamour became. The glamour aura of a mortal in love outshone anything I'd ever seen before, so pure and intense it was almost addictive. I could see why the Summer Court pursued these emotions with such passion; there was nothing like them in any of the courts.

Still, it was only a game. I might've mimicked the words and gestures of a man in love, but emotion, as the Winter Court taught me, was a weakness. And when the full moon rose over the trees on the last night of the game, I knew she was mine.

She approached eagerly through the grass under the pale light of the full moon, so eager in her haste to reach the stream she tripped a few times and went sprawling. She didn't spare any glances back at the village, despite the unusual time I'd requested to meet. A few days ago, she might've balked at the thought of meeting a virtual stranger alone in the woods in the dead of night. But now she hurried eagerly forward, no doubts in her mind. She trusted her prince, completely and without reservation. What love will do to a mortal.

I hung back a few minutes, observing her as she reached the stream, gazing around for my shadow. She wouldn't see me, of course, even though I was standing but a few yards across the stream. Glamoured and invisible, just another shadow in the trees, I watched her. Though her eagerness soon turned to concern at my absence, and she began walking up and down the stream, looking for me, her confidence never wavered, never turned to doubt. She was certain her prince would be there, or that something had detained him from coming. Foolish mortal.

Finally, as she hovered on the verge of tears, I shed my glamour and stepped out of the trees. She gasped and brightened instantly, love filling her eyes and making them shine, but I didn't cross the stream and go to her. Feigning sorrow, I stood on the opposite bank, with the woods at my back, and gave her a gentle smile.

"Forgive me for being so late," I said, putting the right amount of remorse in my voice. "But I wanted to see you one last time. I'm afraid this will be our last meeting. I've come to realize we are from two different worlds, and I cannot give you the kind of life you'd want. You are beautiful and kind, and I would only take that away. So, it is best that I leave. After tonight, you will not see me again."

The result was devastating, as I knew it would be. Her eyes filled with tears, and her hands flew to her face, covering her mouth in horror. "No!" She gasped, a thread of panic in her voice. "Oh, no! Please, you can't! What…will I do…if you are gone?" And she collapsed into shaking sobs.

I hid a smile and crossed the stream, gathering her into my arms. "Don't cry," I whispered, stroking her hair. "Truly, it's better this way. Your people would never accept me—they would drive me away with iron and torches and do their best to kill me. They would do it to protect you. I am only being selfish, meeting you like this."

Brynna sniffled and gazed up at me, ugly black despair swirling with fierce determination. "I don't care what anyone says! Take me away with you. I'll do anything, anything you want. Just please don't leave. I'll die if you go!"

We embraced, the girl resting against my chest, her glamour aura shimmering around us. Finally, I drew back, gazing into her eyes. "Do you love me, Brynna?"

She nodded without hesitation. "With my whole heart."

"Would you do anything for me?"

"Yes." She clutched at my shirt. "I would, my love. Ask me. Anything."

I drew back, beyond the fence, until the shadows of the trees fell over my face. "Come, then," I murmured, holding out a hand to her. "Come with me." And I waited. Waited to see if years of upbringing, of fears and cautionary tales and countless warnings about following a beautiful prince into the forest, would be forgotten in a heartbeat.

She didn't hesitate. Without even a backward glance at her village, she stepped forward and put her hand in mine, smiling up at me with childlike trust. I smiled back, and led her into the forest.

"Where are we going?" she asked a bit later, still holding my hand as we hurried through the trees. Shadows clawed at us, and branches reached out, trying to snag her clothes with twiggy talons. They knew a human in the forest didn't belong, but Brynna remained blissfully unaware, only happy to be with her prince even as he dragged her through a dark wood where the very trees took offense at her presence.

"You'll see," I replied, deftly pulling her sideways to avoid a thornbush that lurched into her path. And, because I knew she would continue to pester me until I gave in, I added, "It's a surprise."

A will-o'-the-wisp trailed behind us, bobbing through the trees, attempting to catch her attention. I glared at it and it spun away, faint laughter echoing through the branches. A goblin raised a warty head and glared at us through the bushes, running a black tongue over jagged teeth, but didn't dare approach. Brynna seemed blind to any of this, humming softly as she followed me through the woods.

The forest opened into a tiny, round clearing, where stone pillars stood in a circle around a marble altar. It was used for many things—dancing, bloodletting, sacrifices—and tonight it would be used for something else. Brynna cast one curious glance at the circle of stone before turning her attention back to me, smiling. She suspected nothing.

Rowan stood nearby, leaning against one of the pillars with his arms crossed, smirking at me. He was glamoured, invisible to mortal eyes, and the sight of him filled me with resolve. I'd come this far. It was time to finish the game.

Gently, I drew Brynna toward the altar, and she followed without hesitation, still trusting her prince to keep her safe. Lifting her up, I sat her on the altar, taking her hands in mine, gazing into her eyes.

"Do you love me?" I asked again, my voice very, very soft. She nodded breathlessly.

"Then, prove it," I murmured. "I want your body, and your soul and everything you have. I want it all. Tonight."

She hesitated for a moment, puzzled, but then understanding dawned in her eyes. Without a word, she leaned back and slipped out of her dress, baring young, naked skin to the moonlight. Reaching back, she pulled out the tie that held her hair back, letting it fall about her shoulders in a dark cascade. I let my eyes roam down her slim, pale body, so fragile and untainted and stepped up beside her.

Lying back on the cold stone, she welcomed me with open arms, and I took everything she offered, everything she could give, as Rowan stood nearby and watched with a vicious smile.

WHEN IT WAS OVER, she lay dreaming and spent in my arms. Without waking her, I stood, slipped noiselessly off the altar and into my clothes, pondering what had just happened.

"Well, congratulations, little brother." Rowan appeared beside me, still hidden from human senses, grinning like a wolf with a lamb. "You brought down your quarry. The game is almost finished."

"Almost?" I'd glamoured myself to remain unseen and unheard, as Brynna slept on. "What do you mean, almost? I have her heart. She gave it to me freely and willingly. She loves me—that was the game."

"Not quite." Rowan glanced at the sleeping girl with a sneer. "To truly finish the game, you have to break her. Body and soul. Crush her heart, and make it so she can never find true love again, because nothing will compare to what she had with you."

"Isn't that a little excessive?" I waved a hand at the mortal on the altar. "I brought her here. She gave herself to me. It's done. I'll leave her with her village and won't see her again. She'll forget, eventually."

"Don't be so naïve." Rowan shook his head. "You know they can't forget us. Not when we've gone through all the trouble of earning their love. If you leave without breaking her heart, she'll be at that stream, looking for you, until the day she dies. She might even venture into the forest in her despair and get eaten by trolls or wolves or something horrible. So, it's actually a kindness that you set her free." He crossed his arms and leaned back, giving me a mocking look. "Really, little brother. Did you think this would have a happily-ever-after? Between a mortal and a fey? How did you think this was going to end?" His grin turned faintly savage. "Finish what you started, Ash, unless you'd like me to kill her now, so you won't have to."

I glared at him. "Very well," I snapped. "But you'll stay hidden until it's done. This is my game still, even now."

He grinned. "Of course, little brother," he said, and backed away, gesturing to the altar. "She's all yours."

I turned back to Brynna, watching her sleep. I didn't care what Rowan said; breaking her was not part of the game. I could easily take her back to the village and leave her there, and she would never know what had become of her prince. Breaking a mortal's heart was Rowan's game; something he reveled in, after using humans so completely they were empty husks. I wasn't like Rowan; everything he touched, he made sure to destroy.

Still, perhaps it was better to ensure she never came after me. She was only a mortal, but I'd grown somewhat fond of her in our time together, like a favorite dog or horse. It wouldn't bother me if she got herself hurt or eaten wandering aimlessly through the forest, but it wouldn't please me, either.

I let her sleep until dawn, giving her one last night of peace, her dreams whole and intact. As the moon waned and the stars began to fade from the sky, I covered the altar with a thin sheet of frost, and the cold was enough to wake her.

Blinking, she sat up, shivering and confused, taking in her surroundings. Seeing me standing beside one of the pillars, she brightened and the sleepiness dropped from her face. Finding her shift, she quickly slipped it on and trotted up, arms open to embrace me.

I didn't smile as she came up, fixing her with a cold glare, filling the air with glamour so the air around me turned frigid. She stumbled to a halt a few feet away, a flicker of confusion crossing her face.

"My love?"

Looking down at her, I realized it would be easy. She was so fragile, her heart like a thin glass ball in my fist, filled with emotion and hopes and dreams. A few words, that was all it would take, to turn this bright, eager creature into a broken, hollow shell. What Rowan said came back to me, taunting my ignorance. *Did you think this would have a happily ever after? Between a mortal and a fey? How did you think this was going to end?*

I met her eyes, smiled coldly and shattered the illusion. "Go home, human."

She faltered, her lip trembling. "W-what?"

"I'm bored with this." Crossing my arms, I leaned back and gave her a disdainful look. "You've become boring, all that talk of love and destiny and marriage."

"But...but, you said...I thought..."

"That, what? We'd get married? Run away together? Have a brood of half-human children?" I sneered, shaking my head, and she wilted even further. "I never intended to marry you, human. This was a game, and the game is over now. Go home. Forget all of this, because I'm going to do the same."

"I thought...I thought you loved me...."

"I don't know what love is," I told her truthfully. "Only that it's a weakness, and it should never be allowed to consume you. It will break you in the end." She was shaking her head, whether in protest or disbelief, I couldn't tell. Nor did I care. "None of this was real, human. Don't try to find me, because you will not see me again. We played, you lost. Now, say goodbye."

She sank to her knees in a daze, and I turned away, striding into the trees. A few moments later, a horrid, gut-wrenching scream rent the air, sending flocks of birds flying. I didn't look back. As the screams continued, each one more terrible than the last, I continued deep into the forest, the sense of achievement overshadowed by a tiny bit of doubt.

As I approached the trod back to Winter, I suddenly realized I wasn't alone. A figure watched me through the trees; tall, dark, wearing a loose robe and cowl that covered its face. As I went for my sword, it raised a gnarled, twisted staff and pointed it at me...

...I JERKED UP ON THE STONE floor of the temple, gasping, as the present came flooding back. The Guardian loomed over me, cold and impassive. I struggled to my feet and leaned against the wall, the memory of that day flashing before me, bright and clear and painful.

Brynna. The girl whose life I'd destroyed. I remembered seeing her once after our last meeting, wandering along the stream, her eyes glazed over and blank. I never saw her after that, never thought about her, until an old druid priestess found me one day. She introduced herself as Brynna's grandmother, the high priestess of the clan, and demanded to know if I was the one who had killed her granddaughter. The girl had fallen into a deep depression, refusing to eat or sleep, until one day her body simply gave out. Brynna had died of a broken heart, and the priestess had come to exact her revenge.

I curse you, demon! Soulless one. From this day forth, let everyone you love be taken from you. May you suffer the same agony as the girl you destroyed, may your heart know pain unlike any other, for as long as you remain soulless and empty.

I'd laughed at her then, claiming that I had no capacity to love, and her pathetic curse would be wasted on me. She only bared her yellow teeth in a smile and spat in my face, right before I cut off her head.

I sank to the floor as their faces crowded my mind, dark eyes glaring at me in accusation. My breath came in short gasps. I closed my eyes, but I couldn't escape her face—the girl I had killed—because she had fallen in love.

My eyes burned. Tears ran down my face and fell to the cold floor, making my vision blurry. "What...have you done to me?" I gasped, clutching at my chest, hardly able to breathe—it felt so heavy. The Guardian regarded me without expression, an unmoving shadow in the room.

"Conscience," it intoned, "is part of being human. Regret is something no mortal can escape for long. If you cannot come to terms with the mistakes of your past, then you are not fit to have a soul."

I pulled myself into a sitting position, slumping against the bed. "Mistakes," I said bitterly, trying to compose myself. "My life has been full of mistakes."

"Yes," the Guardian agreed, raising its staff. "And we will revisit them all."

"No, please—"

Too late. There was a blinding flash of light, and I was somewhere else.

CHAPTER EIGHTEEN
VOICES OF THE PAST

I raised my head from where I knelt before Mab's throne, finding the queen smiling down at me. "Ash," Mab purred, gesturing for me to rise, "my *favorite* boy. Do you know why I called you here?"

I stood warily. I'd learned never to trust Mab when she used the word *favorite*. I'd seen her call someone her favorite right before she froze them alive, "to remember them always like this." More often, it was a ploy to make my brothers jealous, to drive us to compete with one another. This entertained her greatly but made life difficult for me. Rowan took great offense each time I was the favored son, and punished me for it whenever he could.

I could feel Rowan's glare as I stood, but I ignored him while facing the queen. "I know not, Queen Mab, but whatever your reasons, I will comply."

Her eyes glittered. "Always so formal. Would it hurt you to smile for me once in a blue moon? Rowan is not afraid to look me in the eye."

Rowan was at court a lot more than I was, being groomed as her councilor and confidant, and he shared her vicious sense of humor. But there was no way I could tell her that, so I managed a small smile, which seemed to please her. She settled back on her throne and regarded me in an almost affectionate manner, then gestured to something behind me.

A pair of Winter knights in icy-blue armor stepped forward, dragging something between them, throwing it at Mab's feet. A wood nymph, brown-skinned and delicate, with a sharp pointed face and brambles in her long green hair. One of her legs was broken, snapped like a dry twig and hanging at an odd angle. She moaned, only barely conscious, dragging herself across the floor, away from the foot of the throne.

"This creature," Mab said, gazing down at the broken, pathetic body, "and several of its friends attacked and killed one of my knights while they were patrolling the border of the wyldwood. The knights were able to subdue this one, but the rest fled into the wyldwood and escaped. Such an attack cannot go unchallenged, but it refuses to disclose the whereabouts of its home glade. I was hoping that you, with the vast amount of time you spend hunting there, would know where to find them."

I looked down at the nymph, who had dragged herself across the floor and was reaching out for me. "M-mercy," it whispered, clutching at my boots. "Mercy, my lord, we were only trying to save our sister. The knight...the knight was... assaulting her. Please...my friends...my family. The queen will kill them all."

For just a moment, I hesitated. I did not doubt her words; the knights were cold and violent, taking what they wanted, but to attack the servants of the Winter Court was a crime punishable by death. Mab would kill the nymph's entire family if she found them, just for protecting their own. I could not lie, of course, but there were other ways to bend the truth.

"Prince Ash." Mab's voice had changed. No longer inquiring and friendly, it now held a dangerous undertone of warning. "I believe I asked you a question," she continued, as the nymph grabbed at my coat hem, pleading for mercy. "Do you know the location of these creatures, or not?"

What are you doing, Ash? Clenching my fist, I shoved the nymph away with my boot, ignoring her cry of pain. Mercy was for the weak, and I was the son of the Unseelie Queen. There was no mercy in my blood. "Yes, your majesty," I said, as the nymph collapsed, sobbing, to the icy ground. "I've seen this tribe before. They have a colony on the edge of the Bramblewood."

Mab smiled. "Excellent," she rasped. "Then you will lead a force there tonight, and destroy it. Kill them all, cut down their trees, and burn their glade to the ground. I want nothing left standing, not a single blade of grass. Set an example for those who would defy the Winter Court, is that clear?"

I bowed my head as the nymph's wails and shrieks rose into the air. "As you say, my queen," I murmured, backing away. "It will be done."

THE FOREST ELF STARED AT ME, clutching his staff, fear written plainly on his wrinkled face. The small elven tribe that lived here, on the outskirts of the wyldwood and Tir Na Nog, were simple hunter-gatherers. They didn't get many visitors, especially not from the Unseelie Court. Especially not a prince of the Winter Court himself.

"Prince Ash?" He bowed stiffly, and I nodded once. "This is…a surprise. To what do we owe this honor, your highness?"

"I'm here on behalf of Queen Mab and a warrior named Hawthorn," I replied formally, and his bushy eyebrows rose. "Is this name familiar to you?"

"Hawthorn?" The elder's brow furrowed. "Yes. Hawthorn

was on a warrior quest, to become the strongest wood elf in the wyldwood. Why do you know him?"

I sighed. "Hawthorn found his way to the Unseelie Court," I went on, as the elder's brow wrinkled further. "He came before Queen Mab, begging her to allow him to be part of her guard, that he would be honored to serve as one in her court. When Mab refused, he demanded a duel, to prove himself the strongest warrior. He swore on the lives of his kin and tribe that he would be victorious, and that if he won, he would be allowed to serve her. Mab was amused, and allowed him to fight one of her warriors."

"I don't understan—"

"Hawthorn was defeated," I continued softly, as the elder's face went from deep brown to the color of toad stools. He stumbled back, falling to his knees, mouth working soundlessly. Drawing my sword, I started forward, as gasps and screams began to rise from the huts around me. "The lives of his kin and tribe are forfeit should he lose. I am here to collect on that debt."

"Mercy."

The human stared up at me from where he knelt in the snow, an arrow piercing his calf, dripping bright mortal blood onto the ground. Trembling, he clasped his hands together and raised them beseechingly at me, eyes filling with tears. Pathetic human.

"Please, lord of the forest, have mercy. I didn't mean to trespass."

I smiled at him coldly. "The forest is forbidden—your people know this. Venture within our territories, and we have leave to hunt you down. Tell me, human, why should I be merciful?"

"Please, great lord! My wife, my wife is very sick. She

is having...birthing difficulties. I needed to take a shortcut through the forest to reach the doctor in the town."

"Birthing difficulties?" I narrowed my eyes, appraising him. "Your wife will be dead before you get home. You will never reach her in time, not with that wounded leg. You've killed them both by trespassing here."

The human began to sob. His glamour aura flickered blue-and-black with despair. "Please!" he cried, pounding the snow. "Please, spare them. I care nothing for myself, but save my wife and child. I'll do anything. Please!"

He collapsed, crying softly, in the snow, murmuring "please" over and over again. I watched him for a moment, then sighed.

"Your wife is lost," I stated bluntly, making him moan and cover his face in hopeless agony. "She cannot be saved. You child, however, might still have a chance. What will you give me if I save its life?"

"Anything!" the man cried, gazing up at me in earnest. "Take anything you want, just save my child!"

"Say the words," I told him. "Speak them out loud, and let the trees witness your request."

It must have dawned on him then, what was happening, for his face went even paler and he swallowed hard. But he licked his lips and continued in a shaken but clear voice: "I, Joseph Macleary, am prepared to offer anything for the life of my child." He swallowed again and looked straight at me, almost defiant. "Take what you wish, even my own life, as long as my child lives and grows up healthy and strong."

I smiled at him as the invisible strings of magic wove around us, sealing the bargain. "I'm not going to kill you, human," I said, stepping back. "I have no interest in taking your life now."

Relief crossed his face, for just a moment, before alarm flickered in his eyes. "Then, what is it you want?"

Still smiling, I faded from sight, leaving the human to gaze around the empty woods alone. For a moment, he knelt there, confused. Then, with a gasp, he whirled and began limping back the way he came, leaving a speckled trail of blood in his wake. I laughed silently, sensing his panic as he realized what he had promised. He would never get home in time.

Glamoured and invisible, I turned my steps in the direction of a small shanty on the edge of the woods.

The Samhain festival arrived at the Winter Court, and with it the gifts and favors and goodwill blessings for the Winter Queen. Mab was extremely pleased with my gift that year; a dark-haired baby boy, and the look on Rowan's face when I presented the child to her was unforgettable. The boy grew up, healthy and strong, in the Winter Court, never questioning his past or his heritage, becoming a favorite pet of the queen. Eventually, when he got a little older and weaker and not so handsome anymore, Mab placed him in an endless sleep and encased him in ice, freezing him as he was forever. And so the bargain made in the snow the night of his birth was fulfilled.

"ENOUGH!"

Slammed back into the present, I lurched away from the Guardian, the faces of the lives I had destroyed staring at me from the shadows of the room. Hitting the wall, I squeezed my eyes shut, but I could not escape the memories, the accusing eyes, boring into me. The screams and wails, the stench of burning wood, the blood and terror and sorrow and death; I remembered it all as if it was yesterday.

"No more," I whispered, my face still turned to the wall, feeling wetness against my skin. My teeth were clenched so hard my jaw ached. "No more. I can't…remember…the things I've done. I don't want to remember."

"You will." The Guardian's voice was calm, ruthless. "Everything. Every soul you destroyed, every life you took. You will remember, knight. We have only just begun."

IT WENT ON FOREVER.

Each time, I was there, watching the scenes play before me as the heartless Unseelie prince, cold, violent and uncaring. I hunted more humans through the forest, tasting their fear as I ran them down. I slaughtered at the queen's whim, whether it was a single creature that earned her wrath, a family for her entertainment or an entire village to set an example. I competed with my brothers for Mab's favor, playing my own vicious, courtly games that often ended in betrayal and blood. I seduced even more human females and broke their hearts, leaving them empty and hollow, writhing in their loss.

Each time I lived these atrocities, I felt nothing. And each time, the Guardian would pull me out, for just a moment, and the horror of what I'd done would threaten to crush me. Crime after crime stacked upon one another, weighing me down, adding new memories and shame to the nightmares of my life. Each time, I wanted to curl up and die with my guilt, but the Guardian gave me only a moment's reflection before hurling me into the next massacre.

Finally, after what seemed like years, centuries, it was over. I lay on the floor gasping, my arms around my head, bracing myself for the next horror. Only this time, nothing happened. I heard the Guardian speaking above me, its voice distant and matter-of-fact: "The final trial begins at dawn." Then it vanished, leaving me alone.

My thoughts, now my own again, reached out tentatively, probing the silence. And in the sudden calm, every single memory, the crimes of my past, every nightmare and horror and depravity committed by the Unseelie prince, all rose up and descended on me with screams and cries and anguished howls, and I found myself screaming, too.

Puck and Ariella burst through the door, weapons drawn, scanning the room for attackers. Seeing me, kneeling on the floor, my face wet and tormented, their expressions went blank with shock. "Ash?" Ariella whispered, walking toward me. "What happened? What's wrong?"

I lurched away from her. She couldn't know—neither of them could ever know—the horrors I'd committed, the blood staining my hands. I couldn't face their shock and contempt and disgust when they found out who I really was.

"Ash?"

"Get back," I rasped at her, and her eyes widened. "Stay away from me. Both of you. Just…leave me alone."

Ariella stared at me…and for a moment, I saw Brynna's face when I'd told her everything was all a game. It was more than I could bear.

Ignoring their calls, I rushed past them, escaping into the halls of the castle.

Faces followed me down the corridors, their cold, accusing eyes boring into me, crowding my mind.

"Ash," Brynna whispered, hugging herself in an alcove, watching me pass, "you said you loved me."

"My sisters," the nymph said, appearing from around a corner, glaring at me with burning black eyes. "My family. You killed them all. Every single one."

"Demon," whispered the old farmer, his eyes glazed over with tears, pointing at me with a trembling hand. "You took my child away. All I had left, and you took him from me. Monster."

I'm sorry, I called to them, but of course they wouldn't hear.

They were long dead, their grief and hate unresolved, and nothing I said or did could make any of it right.

I could hear Puck and Ariella's voices down the hall, calling my name, searching for me. I didn't deserve their concern. I didn't deserve to know them, two bright spots in a life of darkness and blood and death. I'd destroyed everything I touched, even those I loved. I would end up destroying them, too.

"Murderer," Rowan whispered, appearing from a doorway, and I shied away from him, nearly blinded by tears and not watching where I was going. The floor suddenly gave way beneath me. I fell down a long flight of steps, the world spinning madly, until I landed with a gasp at the bottom, pain stabbing through my arm and side.

Gritting my teeth, I struggled upright, pressing a hand to my bruised shoulder, and looked around. It was dark here, shadows choking everything, the only light coming from a dying candle in the mouth of a stone gargoyle. Beside the leering creature stood a massive stone door, like the entrance to a crypt, standing partially open. Cold, dry air wafted from the crack beneath it.

I staggered forward, squeezed through the opening, and put my uninjured shoulder to the stone, pushing with all my might. The massive door closed with a rumbling groan, shutting out the feeble light and plunging me into complete darkness.

I didn't know what surrounded me, and I didn't care. Feeling my way forward, I eased into a corner, put my back to the wall and slid to the floor. I was cold, even starting to shake, but I welcomed the discomfort. The darkness smelled of dust, limestone, and death. But I couldn't escape the voices, the whispers that hissed accusations in my ears, furious, hateful, completely justified.

Monster.

Demon.

Murderer.

I shivered, with cold and with shame, and buried my face in my knees, letting the accusations swirl around me.

So, this was what we really were. What I really was.

Dawn, the Guardian had told me. My final test began at dawn. If I didn't show up for it, I would fail. And if I failed, I'd remain here forever, alone.

As it should be.

Time slipped away. I lost myself in the darkness, listening to the voices. Sometimes they sobbed, sometimes they railed at me, cruel, vicious words filled with grief and hate. Other times they would only ask questions. Why? Why had I done this? Why had I destroyed them, their lives, their families? Why?

I couldn't answer. Nothing I offered would bring them peace, no apology would suffice for what I'd done. My words were hollow, empty. How could I have been so blind as to want a soul? It was laughable now, to think that a soul could live inside me without being tainted by the centuries of blood and evil and death.

The voices agreed, laughing at me, mocking my quest. I didn't deserve a soul; I didn't deserve happiness, or peace. Why should I get my happy ending, when I'd left a swath of horror and destruction behind me wherever I went?

I had no answer for them. I was a monster. I was born in darkness, and I would die here, as well. It was better this way. Ash, the demon of the Unseelie Court, would finally perish alone, mourning the lives of those he'd destroyed.

A fitting end, I thought, giving in to the voices, letting them rail and laugh at me. I would not hurt anyone any longer. My quest ended here, in this hole of darkness and regret.

And, if I didn't die here, if I lived on forever, listening to the voices of those I'd wronged until the end of time, perhaps I would start to atone for what I had done.

"HERE YOU ARE."

I raised my head as the voice slipped out of the darkness, different from the others surrounding me that were whispering their vengeance and hate. It was nearly pitch-black in the crypt, and I could barely move more than a few feet from where I sat. But I recognized the voice, as the gleam of golden eyes, appearing out of the darkness, floated closer to me.

"Grimalkin." My voice sounded raspy in my ears, as if I hadn't used it for months, though I didn't know how much time had passed down here. Perhaps it *had* been several months. "What are you doing here?"

"I think," Grimalkin said, blinking solemnly as he came into view, "that is what I should be asking *you*. Why are you hiding out with the dead when you should be preparing for the final test?"

I hunched my shoulders, closing my eyes as the voices started again, angry and painful. "Leave me, cait sith."

"You cannot stay down here," the cat went on as if I hadn't spoken. "What good is it to sit here and do nothing? You help no one if you remain here and bemoan the past."

Anger flickered, and I raised my head to glare at him. "What would you know about it?" I whispered. "You have no conscience. You think of everything in terms of bargains and favors, caring nothing for those you have manipulated. I simply can't forget...what I've done."

"No one is asking you to forget." Grimalkin sat down and curled his tail around himself, gazing at me. "That is the whole point of a conscience, after all—that you do not forget those you have wronged. But answer me this—how do you expect to atone for the crimes of your past if you do nothing? Do you think your victims care now, whether you live or die?"

I had no answer for him. Grimalkin sniffed and stood up, waving his tail. His yellow eyes regarded me knowingly.

"They do not. And there is no point in obsessing about what cannot be. They are dead, and you live. And if you fail this test, nothing changes. The only way to ensure that you do not become that which you despise is to finish the quest you have started."

The voices hissed at me, sounding desperate, reminding me of my crimes, the blood on my hands, the lives I'd destroyed. And they were right. I could do nothing for them now. But I had been someone else then. Uncaring and soulless. A demon, like they said. But…maybe I could start again.

Grimalkin flicked an ear and began to trot away into the shadows. "Earn your soul, knight," he called, his gray form fading into the dark. "Prove that you can learn from your mistakes. Only then can you become human."

His words remained with me long after he was gone. I sat in that cold corner and thought about my past, the people I'd hurt, manipulated, destroyed.

Grim was right. If I died here, who would remember them? If I failed and returned home without a soul, I would continue to feel nothing for my past, no remorse, no guilt, no conscience.

Brynna's voice, broken and filled with hate, whispered into my head. *I loved you. I loved you so much, and you killed me. I will never forgive you.*

I know, I told her memory, and finally pulled myself to my feet. My limbs screamed in protest, but I braced myself against the wall and stayed upright. *And you shouldn't. I don't want for-*

*giveness. I don't deserve to be forgiven for my past. But I will make it
right. Somehow, I will atone for those mistakes, I swear it.*

I was tired, my body stiff and sore and exhausted; it took all
my strength to push open the stone doors and climb the long
flight of steps out of the crypt. But with every step, every jolt
of pain through my bones, I felt lighter, freer somehow, the
voices silenced and left back in the tomb. I could not forget
them, or the crimes of my past, but I no longer wanted to die.

It was waiting for me at the top of the stairs, staff in hand,
watching me behind its cowl. I felt its ancient gaze sweep
through my bruised, battered body. It nodded, as if it had
discovered within me something that pleased it. "The final
trial is upon us, knight," it said as I climbed the last step and
stood before the Guardian. "You have survived human weakness and a conscience. One last thing remains for you to earn
a soul."

"Where are Puck and Ariella?" I asked, feeling guilty that
I'd been gone for so long. They'd be worried about me by
now. I hoped they didn't think I was dead.

"They search for you," the Guardian said simply. "But this
is not their test. The trial begins now, knight. Are you ready,
or not?"

I took a breath. Puck and Ariella would have to wait. I
hoped they would understand, because the Guardian wasn't
giving me time to think about it. "Yes," I replied, feeling my
stomach knot. The last trial. The only thing between me and
a soul. And Meghan. "I'm ready. Let's get this over with."

The Guardian nodded and raised its staff once more.

CHAPTER NINETEEN

HUMAN

Rain pounded my back, and I opened my eyes.

I lay on my stomach on the hard ground, my cheek pressed against what felt like cobblestones, water soaking my hair and clothes. From my drenched state and the feel of the small, round stones pressing into my face, I must have been lying there for some time. Wincing, I pushed myself to my elbows, peering through the rain to determine where I was.

A green-and-silver garden stretched out before me, lush with vegetation and blurry through the rain. Cobblestone paths twisted around small bushes and shrubs, and larger trees hugged the edges of the high stone wall surrounding it. A few feet away, a marble fountain spilled water into a shallow basin, the sound of trickling water drowned out by the larger deluge.

Around me, the trees shimmered in the rain, thousands of leaves flashing like knives as the wind tossed their branches. At my feet, wires slithered over the ground in strange patterns and curled around tree trunks, glowing like neon signs. Lampposts, glimmering yellow in the twilight, grew right out of the ground and lined the narrow paths. I turned and saw an enormous castle of stone, glass and steel looming above me, spires and towers stabbing at the clouds.

I blinked, trying to take it all in. I was back in the Iron Kingdom. The twisted metallic trees, the wires slithering over the ground, the castle of stone and steel—they couldn't belong anywhere else. And the rain...my heart skipped a beat, and I turned my face to the sky. The water was clear and pure, not the acidic, flesh-eating rain that had swept through the Iron Realm before Meghan became queen.

But, if that was the case...if I was in the Iron Kingdom...

I took a deep breath, breathing in the cool, damp air, drawing it into myself and holding it there, waiting.

Nothing. No sickness, no pain. I stepped beneath a warped iron tree and placed my palm against the trunk, bracing myself out of habit. The metal was cold and wet beneath my fingers, not burning at all.

I couldn't help the smile stretching my face as I whirled around, taking in the garden, the estate, everything. Throwing back my head, I raised my arms and howled a victory cry into the rain, hearing it echo off the castle walls. I was in the Iron Kingdom with no amulet, no protection, and I still felt nothing. Iron had no power over me, now. I was human. I had won!

A thunderous bark behind me made me spin around, as a lean, furry creature came bounding toward me out of the rain. For a moment, I thought it was a wolf. Then I saw it was a dog, a huge German shepherd with enormous paws and a thick, shaggy pelt spiked up with rain. It skidded to a stop a few feet from me and growled, lowering its muzzle and baring sharp white fangs.

I smiled and crouched down so that we were at eye level, despite the teeth flashing in my direction. "Hello, Beau," I greeted quietly. "Nice to see you, too."

The dog blinked, swiveling its long ears at the sound of my voice. Eyeing me suspiciously, as if it was just beginning to recognize the intruder in the garden, it gave a tentative tail wag.

"Beau!" called a voice, echoing out of the rain, making my heart jump to my throat and pound wildly. I stood as the voice drifted closer. "Where are you, boy? Chasing gremlins again?"

Beau barked happily and turned, bounding in the direction of the voice, splashing noisily through the puddles. And then, *she* appeared under the gate arch, scanning the courtyard for the missing dog, and I stopped breathing.

Ruling a kingdom hadn't changed her. She still wore faded jeans and a T-shirt, her pale hair long and unbound. But power glowed around her, and even through the rain, she looked real and solid and larger than life, and completely beautiful. Beau came splashing up to her, and she dropped to her knees, scratching the dog's ears. Then Beau looked back at me, wagging his tail, and she glanced up. Our eyes met.

We both froze. I saw my name on her lips, but no sound escaped her. Beau looked back and forth between us, whined, and nudged Meghan's hand, snapping her out of the spell. She rose and walked toward me, uncaring of the rain, until we were inches apart. My heart pounded, and I looked down into the intense sapphire eyes of the Iron Queen.

"Ash." The word was hesitant, as if she wasn't quite sure whether I was real or not. "You're here. How..." She blinked, and her voice became stronger as she took a step back. "No, you can't...you shouldn't be here. I told you never to come back. The iron..."

I reached out and took her hand, silencing her. "It can't hurt me," I promised. "Not anymore." She gazed up at me, hope and uncertainty warring in her eyes, and I softly touched her cheek, her tears mingling with the rain. "I said I'd be back," I told her, "and from now on, I'll never leave your side. Nothing will keep me from you again."

"How...?" she whispered, but I bent down and kissed her, cutting off any protests. She gasped, and her arms slid around my waist, pulling us together. I hugged her close, wanting to feel her against my body, to prove that this was real. I was in the Iron Realm, and Meghan was in my arms. Beau barked and danced around us, and the rain poured down, drenching us completely, but we felt no urge to move for a long, long time.

WHEN I AWOKE NEXT, I was afraid to open my eyes, afraid even to move. Blackness pressed against my lids, and I kept them shut, fearful that when I opened my eyes, everything would have disappeared. I would be back at the Testing Grounds, the Guardian looming over me, its booming voice telling me I had failed. Or worse, that this was all a dream, and I had yet to complete the tests at all.

Very cautiously, I peeked through my lids, bracing myself, half expecting to see the stone walls of the castle, to feel a sudden stab of pain as my mind caught up to reality.

A white-walled room greeted me as I opened my eyes, hazy curtains drawn across a large glass window on the opposite wall. Sunlight slanted in through the crack, spilling across the carpeted floor, touching a pile of damp clothes lying in a heap next to the bed. The bed I was lying in. I blinked, memories of the previous night beginning to surface like wisps of smoke, foggy and unreal.

There was a sigh behind me, and something shifted against my back.

Carefully, afraid that this entire scene might shatter into reality, I turned. Meghan lay beside me under the covers, her eyes closed, her pale hair spilling over her face. I took a slow, ragged breath to calm my racing heart, taking a moment just to watch her. It was real. This was real. I gently brushed her hair from her cheek and watched her stir under my fingers, opening her eyes. Her smile brightened the whole room.

"I was afraid it was a dream," she whispered.

"You have no idea how desperately I was hoping it wasn't." Cupping the back of her neck, I drew her close and kissed her again. She trailed her fingers over my bare chest, and I shivered, almost frightened by how much I loved this girl. But then, I'd gone to the End of the World, endured trials no creature should ever face, for her. I would do it again if I had to.

And compared to that, the question on my mind should've been easy. But as Meghan pulled back to look at me, I found my mind had gone blank, and I was more nervous than I had been in all my years as a Winter prince.

The question stayed on my mind as we lingered under the covers for the rest of the morning, feeling lazy and content and reluctant to leave each other's arms. It continued to plague me when we finally got up in the middle of the afternoon, after the servants knocked meekly on the door asking if we were all right. Meghan ordered them to bring dry clothing, and I slipped into dark jeans and a T-shirt, feeling strange and slightly awkward in human clothes. I fidgeted, still pondering how I was going to ask her. It made my stomach twist every time I thought of it.

"Hey." Meghan's fingers on my arm nearly made me jump out of my skin. She smiled up at me, though her eyes were puzzled. "You seem awfully nervous this morning. Is something wrong?"

Now or never, Ash. I took a deep breath. "No," I replied, turning to her, "nothing's wrong, but I did want to ask you something. Come here a moment."

Taking both her hands, I backed away to the middle of the floor, to an open space in front of the curtains. She followed, still wearing a bemused expression, and I paused a moment to gather my thoughts.

"I don't…know how it's done in your world," I began, as she tilted her head at me. "I've seen it before…but, I'm not sure how to ask. It never really comes up in the Winter Court."

Meghan blinked, frowning slightly. "What do you mean?"

"I know my role here," I continued. "Whatever happens, I'm still your knight, and nothing will change that. You are queen of this realm, and I have no desire to rule. That said, I want to do this human thing right. I'll still be at your side, fighting your enemies, standing with you no matter what comes at us. But I'm no longer satisfied with just being your knight and protector. I want something more." I stopped and took a deep breath, then slowly released her hands, stepped back and sank to one knee. "What I'm trying to ask is… Meghan Chase, will you do me the honor of marrying me?"

Meghan's eyes got big and round, then a brilliant smile broke over her face. The rest of the day passed in a blur, faces flashing by, unimportant, excitement and disbelief thick on the air. All I remembered clearly was that one moment, that one simple word that would change my life forever.

"Yes."

THE WEDDING OF THE IRON QUEEN turned out to be much more extravagant than either of us expected. Marriage within fey society was almost unheard of—the most famous joining was Oberon and Titania's, and they were from the same court. Even I had no idea why the two Summer monarchs chose to wed, but I suspected it involved power, much like everything else. But once it was announced that the Iron Queen was getting married to the former prince of the Winter Court, the news sent the entire Nevernever into an uproar. The other courts were scrambling over one another to find out what was going on. Rumors began to surface, spreading like wildfire: Meghan and I were making a bid for power, the Iron Realm was trying to gain more territory, I was a spy sent by Mab to join Iron with the Winter Court against Summer. None of the other rulers were pleased with the marriage. Oberon even tried to stop the wedding, stating that the laws of Summer and Winter forbade a marriage between courts. Of course, when Meghan heard this, she calmly told the Summer monarch that, as Queen of the Iron Realm, she could do what she pleased within her own land. Nor was I a prince of Winter any longer, so he could take his laws and sit on them.

Regardless, the actual wedding was an enormous affair, with representatives from all three courts present. Meghan's human family would not be there, of course. I doubt any of them would've survived with their sanity intact, but I agreed to a smaller private ceremony with her family in the human world. I didn't really see the point of two weddings, but Meghan insisted her family would see her married as well, so I had no choice but to concede.

The real wedding was held in the wyldwood, as the other courts couldn't venture into the Iron Realm without poisoning themselves. And within a grove carpeted in wildflowers, where three courts of Faery gathered beneath the trunk of a truly massive tree, Meghan and I were wed before Summer, Winter, Iron and the entire Nevernever.

Human weddings have nothing on fey weddings, at least not the ones I've seen over the years. I wore the black-and-silver uniform of a Winter prince, as I had when I first saw Meghan at Elysium, so long ago. Though I was no longer part of the Unseelie Court, I wanted everyone to remember that I was still Ash, that I still belonged here, in the Nevernever.

Mab and the Winter Court stood behind me, and I could feel their chill against my back, the frost coating the flowers around me. On the opposite side, Oberon, Titania and the Summer Court loomed tall and proud, glaring at Winter over the aisle separating them. And surrounding us all, the Iron fey, the third court of Faery, looked on. Gremlins and wood nymphs scampered through the grass and the trees, snarling and hissing at each other. Iron knights, their armor polished to a blinding metallic sheen, stood at attention down the aisle, opposite the sidhe knights of the Summer and Winter courts, awaiting the procession. For a moment, I marveled at the impossibility of it all; not long ago, the Iron fey were the deadliest threat the Nevernever had seen, and no one would tolerate them to live, much less share space within the wyldwood. But gazing around at the gathered faces of Summer, Winter and Iron, I felt a flicker of hope. It had taken a determined, half-human Summer princess and an ancient prophecy to mend the rift between the three courts, but she had done it. It would be hard, and it would take a lot of work, but maybe we could live in peace with each other, after all.

Movement in the crowd caught my attention. Directly opposite me, on the Seelie side, a familiar redhead poked his head from the crowd and saluted, giving me a devilish grin. I suppressed a wince. Puck and I hadn't spoken much since the wedding announcement, and though he'd never show it, I suspected this day was going to be hard for him. I also had the sneaking suspicion that the Great Prankster had a few surprises in store for us, and that the after-party was going to get a little wild. I hoped that, whatever happened, the party wouldn't turn into a riot and then a bloodbath.

But when the music started, I forgot about all of that. I didn't think of the crowd and the courts and their endless squabbles. I didn't see Puck and Mab, Oberon and Titania, or the Iron fey. I didn't see anyone but her.

Meghan was stunning in her long white gown, bright gray embroidery scattered about like stars, catching the light. Her hair had been pinned up beneath the veil, with a few wispy, silver-blond strands hanging down to brush her bare shoulders. A satin train billowed behind her, a rippling river of white, carried over the grass by a trio of packrats. Her adoptive human father, Paul, stood beside her, his young-old face beaming with pride and a little fear. As the trumpets blared and the knights raised their swords, the faeries around us howled, raising their voices in a joyful cacophony, the tumult echoing over the trees and making the air shiver. As my bride-to-be drew closer, our eyes met through the veil, and I nearly stopped breathing. This was it. This was really happening.

I couldn't keep the smile from my face as she reached the front, taking her place at my side. Meghan smiled back, and for a moment, we just stood there, lost in each other's gaze. The howling fey, the stares of Summer, Winter and Iron, the blaring trumpets, all that faded away until it was just me and Meghan and nothing else.

Then Grimalkin leaped onto the old stump between us and sighed.

"I still do not see the point of my presiding over this ridiculous spectacle, but very well." The cait sith yawned and sat down. "Of all the favors I have granted, this is by far the most tiresome. Shall we get it over with then?" Grimalkin sat up straighter and raised his voice, somehow being heard over the crowd. "We are gathered today," he began in a lofty tone, "to witness the joining of these two in the completely useless, ostentatious ceremony of marriage. For reasons beyond me, they have decided to make their love official, and—"

"Grimalkin." Meghan sighed, though she wore a faint, exasperated smile. "Just this once, could you please not be an ass?"

The cat twitched an ear. I could sense he was secretly amused. "I make no promises, Iron Queen." He sniffed, and looked at me. "You have your own vows, then?"

We both nodded.

"Thank the heavens." Under Meghan's glare, he blinked and nodded sagely. "Very well. Let us get on with it. You may proceed when ready, prince."

I reached for Meghan's hand, exhaling slowly as I made my oath. "Meghan Chase," I began, gazing into her eyes, "from this day forth, I vow to be your husband and your knight, to stand with you when no others will, to protect you and your kingdom with everything I have for the rest of my life. I swear I will be faithful, and I will love you until the very last breath leaves my body. Because you have more than my heart and my mind—you also own my soul."

Meghan gave me a brilliant smile, her eyes going misty behind the veil. "Ash," she murmured, and even though she didn't say it out loud, I heard the echo of my True Name in her voice. "It's because of you that I can be here today. You have always been there, never wavering, protecting me with no thought for yourself. You've been my teacher, my knight and my only love. Now, it's my turn to make that promise." She squeezed my hand, her voice soft but never faltering. "Today, I vow that we will never be apart again. I promise that I will be forever by your side, and I will be ready to face everything the world has to offer us."

"Very touching," remarked Grimalkin, scratching behind an ear. We both ignored him, and he sat up with a sniff. "Well, then. Shall we end this exercise ad nauseam? If there are any here who object to this joining, let them speak now or forever hold their peace. And if you do object, please have a valid reason for the objection so I do not have to stay here while you debate the problem."

I could sense the rulers of both courts wanting to say something, arguments and objections ready to burst forth. But what could they offer? I wasn't part of the Winter Court, a mere mortal, and Meghan was a queen. There was nothing they could say that was a valid argument. Grimalkin knew it as well, for after only a moment or two of strained silence, he stood up and raised his voice.

"Then let it be known, before these witnesses and the courts, that these two are joined forever as husband and wife, and let no force in the mortal world or Faery tear them apart. I now present to you the Queen and Consort of the Iron Court." He yawned and looked at us affectionately. "I suppose now is the part where you kiss the—well, never mind, then."

I had already raised Meghan's veil and drawn her close. And beneath the great tree, in the midst of a roaring, hooting faery crowd, I kissed my new bride until everything around us faded away.

TIME PASSED, and I slowly adjusted to life in the Iron Court. I became used to the gremlins scurrying around the castle, trailing Meghan like faithful dogs yet still managing to wreck havoc where they passed. I no longer went for my sword when a squad of Iron knights approached Meghan. The curious, suspicious stares when I passed grew less and less frequent, until I became just another presence in the castle.

The Iron fey, I discovered, were a much more structured group than the faeries of Summer and Winter. Except for the ever-chaotic gremlins, they welcomed order, understood rank and hierarchy and the chain of command. I was prince consort to their queen, second only to Meghan herself: therefore, I was to be obeyed. Even Glitch, Meghan's First Lieutenant, rarely questioned me. And the Iron knights obeyed my orders without fail. It was strange, not having to constantly watch my back for fear someone might stick a knife in it. Of course, there were always squabbles and politics within the Iron Court, as there were in any court of Faery. But for the most part, the fey here were more straightforward and businesslike, not seeking to trap me in a deadly game of words just for the fun of it.

Once I figured that out, I began to appreciate the Iron Realm a lot more.

Especially when, as a mortal, I could do things I never would've dreamed of doing as a fey.

Not long after the wedding, I awoke alone in the bed, with light coming from the room adjacent to us—Meghan's office. Rising, I wandered into the room to find Meghan sitting at her desk with the small, flat screen she carried around like a tablet. It was a truly foreign device to me; with a mere touch of the screen's face, she could pull up "files" and "email," make pictures bigger or smaller, or whisk them away with a flick of her hand. I, of course, thought it was Iron glamour that allowed such magic, though when I mentioned this to Diode, a hacker elf in charge of the castle's computer systems, he laughed so hysterically he couldn't answer me, and I left in annoyance.

"Hey," I murmured, slipping my arms around her from behind. "What are you doing?"

She paused a moment, resting her head against my arm, then reached up and pulled a pair of thin white wires from her ears. "Checking the itinerary for the day. Seems the Cog Dwarves have been having trouble with disappearances in the Undercity. I'll have to get Glitch to see what's going on down there. Diode wants me to ban all gremlins from the security rooms, saying he can't think with them running around getting into everything." She sighed and leaned back in the chair, lacing an arm around my neck while the other hand still held the tablet. "And there are a ton of requests from the northern territories, saying knights from the Winter Court are causing trouble, harassing the locals on this side of the border. Looks like Mab and I need to have a talk. That's going to be a fun conversation."

She sighed and laid the tablet flat on the desk. I stared at the words flashing across the screen, a completely foreign vocabulary to me, even if I understood the language. Meghan glanced up at me, and a mischievous smile crossed her face.

"Here." Rising, she plucked the screen off the desktop and shoved it toward me. "Take it. I'll show you how it works."

I balked, taking a step backward, eyeing the tablet as if it was a venomous snake. "Why?"

"Ash, you're human now." Meghan smiled and continued to hold the screen toward me. "You don't have to be afraid of this anymore. It can't hurt you."

"I don't have Iron glamour," I told her. "It won't work for me."

She laughed. "You don't need glamour to work this. It's not magic, just technology. Anyone can use it. Now, come on." She waggled it in my direction. "Just give it a try."

I sighed. Very cautiously, I reached out and took it, still half expecting to feel a searing pain in my hands as my flesh reacted to the metal. When nothing happened, I held it gingerly in both hands and stared at the screen, not knowing what to do.

Meghan slipped beside me, watching over my shoulder. "Touch the screen here," she ordered softly, demonstrating with graceful fingers. "See? You can access files here, pull up pictures, make them bigger like this. Try it."

I did, and to my surprise, the tablet responded to my clumsy attempts, working exactly as it had for Meghan. I dragged a picture onto the screen, made it bigger, shrank it and whisked it away, feeling a foolish grin creep across my face. I discovered an entire library within the files of this strange device, more books than I had thought possible, all contained in this tiny screen. With the touch of a finger, music filled the air, one of the thousands of songs Meghan had "downloaded" from the "web." I must've played with the thing for at least twenty minutes, before Meghan laughingly took it back, saying she still had work to do.

"See, now," she told me, as I reluctantly gave it up, "being human isn't all bad, is it?"

I watched as she sat down and began working again, fingers flying across the screen, eyes half-closed in concentration. Eventually, she became aware of me staring at her and looked up, raising a quizzical eyebrow. "Yes?"

"I want one," I told her simply. She laughed and this time, I grinned back.

THAT WAS THE BEGINNING.

Humanity didn't come easily for me, or all at once. I still missed my glamour, the easy way my body used to move, the quickness and the strength of my Unseelie heritage. To keep up my skills, Glitch and I would spar daily in the training yard as the Iron knights looked on, and though I remembered how to wield a sword, I never seemed to move fast enough. The maneuvers that used to be second nature were extremely difficult to impossible now. True, I had been fighting for a very long time, and my experience was such that none of the knights could touch me in a one-on-one match. But I lost to Glitch more often than not, and it was frustrating. I had been better once.

My physical limitations weren't my only worries. I was often plagued with nightmares of my past, where I would wake in the night gasping, covered in cold sweat, ghostly faces ebbing into reality. Voices haunted my sleep, accusing, hateful voices, demanding to know why I was happy when they had died. My dreams were filled with blood and darkness, and there were many nights when I couldn't sleep, staring at the ceiling, waiting for dawn. Gradually, however, the nightmares diminished, as I began to forget that part of my life and focus on my new one. The dreams never ceased completely, but the demon at the heart of those nightmares wasn't me any longer. I was no longer Ash the Unseelie prince. I had moved on.

But, every once in a great while, I would have the surreal feeling that I was missing something. That my life with Meghan wasn't what it appeared to be. That I had forgotten something important. I would shake it off, convincing myself I was simply adjusting to being human, but it always returned, taunting me, a memory keeping just out of reach.

Regardless, time moved on in the Iron Realm. Meghan ruled without opposition, maneuvering the labyrinth of fey politics as if she had been born for it. I immersed myself in technology; laptops, cell phones, computer games, software. And gradually, I grew accustomed to being human, slowly forgetting my faery side—my glamour, speed and strength—until I couldn't remember what it felt like at all.

CHAPTER TWENTY

THE MARCH OF TIME

A frantic beeping dragged me out of a comfortable sleep. Groggily, I raised myself up, being careful not to disturb Meghan, and reached for the phone on the end table. The glowing blue numbers on the screen proclaimed it 2:12 a.m., and that Glitch was going to die for waking me up like this.

I pressed the button, put the phone to my ear and growled: "Someone better be dead."

"Sorry, highness." Glitch's voice hissed in my ear, whispering loudly. "But we have a problem. Is the queen still asleep?"

I was instantly awake. "Yes," I murmured, throwing back the covers and rising from the bed. The Iron Queen was a somewhat heavy sleeper, often exhausted by the demands of ruling a kingdom, and tended to be cranky when woken up in the middle of the night. After getting snarled at several times for a middle-of-the-night emergency, Glitch started directing all midnight problems to me. Between us, we were usually able to handle the situation before the queen knew something was wrong.

"What's going on?" I asked, shrugging into my clothes

while still pressing the phone to my ear with a shoulder. Glitch gave a half angry, half fearful sigh.

"Kierran has run off again."

"What?"

"His room was empty, and we think he managed to slip over the wall. I have four squads out looking for him, but I thought you should know your son has pulled another vanishing act."

I groaned and scrubbed a hand across my face. "Get the gliders ready. I'll be right there."

GLITCH MET ME on the highest tower, the lightning in his hair snapping angrily, his purple eyes glowing in the darkness.

"We've already searched his usual hideouts," he informed me as I came up. "He's not in any of them, and we've been looking since midnight. We think he managed to get out of the city this time."

"How did he get over the wall?" I asked, glowering at the first lieutenant, who grimaced.

"One of the gliders is missing," he said, and I growled a curse. Kierran, blue-eyed and silver-haired, was nearly eight in human years, and had just enough faery blood to make him as troublesome as a phouka. From the time he could walk, the household staff had been unable to keep up with him. Nimble as a squirrel, he scaled the walls, climbed out windows and perched on the highest towers, grinning in delight while everyone scrambled about to coax him down. His daring and curiosity only increased with age, and if you told him he *could not* do something, you pretty much ensured that he was going to try.

His mother was going to kill me.

Glitch looked faintly ashamed. "He was asking about them

this morning. I should've picked up on it then. Any idea where he might've gone?"

Thinking back, I sighed. Kierran had been obsessed with the other territories of late, asking about the Summer and Winter courts and the wyldwood. That afternoon, we had been practicing archery in the courtyard, and he'd asked what type of things I had hunted. When I told him about the dangerous creatures in the wyldwood, about giants and chimeras and wyverns that could rip you apart or swallow you whole, he'd almost glowed with excitement.

"Will you take me hunting someday, Father? In the wyldwood?"

I looked at him. He gazed back innocently, diamond-blue eyes sparkling beneath long silver bangs, gripping his bow tightly in both hands. The tips of his pointed ears peeked out of his hair, a constant reminder that he wasn't quite human. That the blood of the Iron Queen flowed through him, making him faster, stronger, more daring than a normal child. He had already demonstrated a talent for glamour, and he picked up archery and sword fighting faster than he had a right to. Still, he was only eight, still a child, and innocent to the dangers of the rest of Faery.

"When you're older," I told him. "Not yet. But when you're ready, I'll take you."

He grinned, lighting up his whole face. "Promise?"

"Yes." I knelt beside him and straightened out the bow, pointing it the right way. "Now, try to hit the target again."

He giggled, apparently satisfied, and didn't bring it up again. And I didn't give it another thought the rest of the afternoon. I should've known better.

"I have an idea." I sighed, and whistled for one of the gliders hanging from the wall. It turned its insectlike head and buzzed sleepily. "Have the knights search the wyldwood, particularly around the borders of the courts. And let's hope he's not found his way into Tir Na Nog."

"The other courts won't like it," Glitch muttered. "We're not really supposed to go into the wyldwood without their permission."

"This is my son." I fixed him with a piercing glare, and he looked away. "I don't care if we have to tear up the entire wyldwood. I want him found, is that understood?"

"Yes, sire."

I nodded curtly and stepped to the edge of the balcony, spreading my arms. The glider spiraled down from the wall and crawled up my back, unfurling its wings. I looked back at Glitch, watching us solemnly, and sighed.

"Wake the queen," I told him. "Tell her the situation. This is something she needs to know right away." He winced, and I didn't envy him the job. "Tell her I'll be back with Kierran soon."

And with that, I pushed myself off the edge and swooped into empty space. The air currents caught the glider's wings, bearing us aloft, and we soared in the direction of the wyld-wood.

I DIDN'T HAVE TO SEARCH FAR. Only a few miles after I crossed the border of the Iron Realm and entered the wyldwood, I spotted the glint of a glider's wing in the moonlight and pushed my own glider to land nearby. Leaving the two iron creatures to buzz at each other excitedly, I clicked on a flashlight and studied the ground around the landing site. Despite my human vision, centuries of hunting and tracking through the wyldwood could not be forgotten in a few short years, and I soon found a set of small footprints, leading off into the tangled undergrowth. Grimly, praying nothing would find him before I did, I followed.

A few miles in, the tracks took on an ominous cast, as something large and heavy joined the smaller prints through the forest. Stalking them. Soon after that, the stride between the prints lengthened, stretching out to a run, joined by snapped branches and twigs, and my blood ran cold. When I found his bow, broken and splintered, dread squeezed my chest until I could hardly breathe, and I started to run.

A scream shattered the stillness of the night. It turned my blood to ice, and I charged blindly in that direction, drawing my sword as I went. The icy fey weapon seared my hands with cold, but I was too far gone to notice.

"Kierran!" I shouted, bursting through the undergrowth.

A roar answered me. Something huge and terrible clung to a tree a few yards away, beating batlike wings for leverage and clawing at the branches. Its body was bony and leonine, with blood-red fur and a matted black mane. Its long tail ended in a spiky ball, bristling like a huge sea urchin and leaving spines in the adjacent trees as it thrashed in frustration.

High overhead, a small, bright figure pressed back into the limbs of the tree, trying to scramble higher, away from the vicious beast swiping at him a few feet away. His tearful blue eyes met mine, but his cry was drowned out by the bellowing of the monster below.

"Hey!" I roared, and two burning red eyes snapped to me. "Get away from him now!"

The manticore howled and leaped off the tree, landing with a booming crash on the ground. Lashing its tail, it stalked toward me, its shockingly human face pulled into an animalistic snarl, baring pointed teeth. I gripped the sword, ignoring the numbing chill that spread up my arm, and took a deep breath.

The manticore lunged, hooked talons swiping at my face, jaws gaping to tear into my throat. I dodged, lashing out with the sword, cutting a gash in the monster's shoulder. It screamed, an oddly human wail, and spun with blazing red eyes. Its tail flicked out, almost too quick to see, and I felt something thwap against my legs.

Blinding pain came seconds later, nearly dropping me to my knees. I reached down with one hand and felt the long black spines of the manticore's tail sunk deep into my leg. Knowing it would continue to pump venom into me the longer I left it, I grasped the spine and ripped it away, clenching my jaw to keep from screaming. The spine was barbed at the end, and tore a gaping hole in my leg, but manticore venom would quickly paralyze and kill its victim if left in the body.

Overhead, Kierran cried out in terror. The manticore growled and stalked closer to me, red eyes glowing in the darkness.

I could feel the poison burning its way through my leg, and fought to remain steady on my feet, watching as the monster circled me, twitching its deadly tail. Waiting for the venom to take effect. Casually, it flicked its tail again, and I felt another barb slam into my shoulder, making me gasp. I didn't have much time left. Numbness was creeping through my leg, and soon my arm would follow. But I had to save Kierran. I would at least make sure Kierran got home safe.

Feigning weakness, I staggered and fell to my knees, letting the tip of my blade strike the earth. It was what the manticore was waiting for. The monster sprang at me with a howl, going in for the kill, jaws gaping. I fell backward, bringing my sword up as the manticore lunged over me, sinking my blade deep into its shaggy chest.

The creature screamed and collapsed on top of me, pinning me to the earth. Its body smelled of blood and rotten meat. I tried shoving it off as it twitched and kicked in its death throes, but it was too heavy and I was in too much pain to move it. And so I lay there, pinned under a dead manticore, knowing I probably wouldn't walk away from this. I could feel the venom working its way through my leg, the spine still piercing my shoulder. Ash the Winter prince would have healed from such wounds, his fey body instinctively drawing in glamour to throw off the sickness, repairing itself with an unending supply of magic. But I was only mortal, and had no such power.

As I fought for consciousness, I became aware of Kierran, grunting and crying as he tried pulling the dead manticore off me. "Get up," I heard him sniffle. "Father, get up."

"Kierran," I called softly, but he didn't seem to hear me. I tried again, but a shout echoed through the trees, and Kierran jerked his head up. "Over here!" he cried, waving both arms. "Glitch, we're over here!"

Familiar voices surrounded us. Glitch's voice, frantic and angry. The clanking of the Iron knights as they pulled the manticore away. Kierran's sobs as he tried explaining what had happened. I tried answering the questions that buzzed around my head, but my voice was as numb as the rest of me, and the shapes crowding my vision were blurry and indistinct.

"That leg looks pretty bad," I heard someone murmur to Glitch as they bent over me. "We'll try to save it, but he *is* a mortal, after all."

"Do what you can," Glitch muttered back. "I'm just glad we found him alive. The queen is not going to be happy."

Their voices became garbled after that, blending into the background. Eventually, sounds, people, voices, all blurred together like ink, and turned into darkness.

I THOUGHT I WOULD DIE, but I lived.

My leg was never the same. The venom had damaged it too badly. Luckily for me, the barb in my shoulder had passed clean through and come out the other side, leaving nothing behind but a puckering scar. But forever after that fight, I walked with a limp, and if I stood on the leg too long or put too much weight on it, it would give out from under me. The sparring matches with Glitch and the knights came to a halt, and I had to lean on a cane when traveling or walking any distance.

I didn't mind…too much. I still had my son, my wife and my health, though that last fight demonstrated yet again how fragile mortality was. A fact Meghan made painfully clear once I was on my feet again. The Iron Queen had been livid, blue eyes flashing as she ripped into me, demanding to know what I'd been thinking, going into the wyldwood alone.

"You're human now, Ash," she said, finally calming down a bit. "I know you think you can take on the world, but that isn't the case anymore. Please, please, promise me you'll be more careful."

"I don't really have much of a choice now, do I?" I sighed, grabbing my cane to limp out of the room. Her gaze followed me, sad and concerned, and I paused in the doorway. "Don't worry, your majesty. I'm aware of my limitations." I tried to keep the bitterness and pain from my voice, but it slipped out anyway. "I won't be fighting anything for a long time. I can promise you that."

"That's not what concerns me," Meghan replied softly, but I was already out the door.

Time passed, and in the Iron Realm, the great clock tower in the center of the city kept track of its march. Kierran grew into a fierce warrior, deadly, light on his feet, possessing a speed unnatural in a human. And when he reached a certain point in his life, just past his seventeenth birthday, he simply… stopped aging. As if he'd decided that he was happy as he was and refused to grow up any more.

Meghan never changed; though she matured with the passing of time, becoming shrewd and wise and a truly formidable queen, her body remained as young and beautiful as the rest of Faery.

And I, as a human in the Iron Realm, where time *did* pass and seconds ticked by the years, did not.

"WHAT WERE YOU THINKING?"

I turned my head at the sound of Meghan's voice, seeing the Iron Queen paused in the doorway, her arms crossed in front of her. Though she was stunning in a long evening gown, her hair hanging in glittering curls down her back, she did not look pleased.

"Thinking?" I asked, hoping to derail her by acting bewildered and innocent. Unfortunately, that rarely worked with the Iron Queen, and tonight was no exception.

"Don't give me that, Ash." Meghan came into the bedroom, glowering at me. "You know what I'm talking about. Why did you tell Kierran he could go to Elysium this year? The last thing we need is him picking a fight with a Winter gentry, or seducing someone in my father's court. They're already leery enough of him as it is."

"He's been asking to go for years," I told her, swirling my cloak around my shoulders. "I think he's old enough to see what it's like. We can't shelter him forever. He's going to have to learn about the other courts, as prince of the Iron Realm."

Meghan glared at me a moment longer, then relented with a sigh. "Oh, fine. I know you're right," she said, giving me an exasperated smile. "It's just…he still seems so young to me, still just a kid, getting into trouble. Where does the time go?" She crossed to the window, gazing out at Tir Na Nog. The sun was setting, and the huge clock tower in the very center of the city was silhouetted black against the evening sky.

"Twenty years, Ash," she murmured. "It's hard to believe it's been more than twenty years since we beat the false king. It feels like yesterday."

For you, perhaps, I thought, glancing at the reflection in the mirror. Gray eyes in a worn, lined face stared back at me. Wrinkles crouched under my eyes and at the corners of my mouth, marring my skin, and a scar traced its way from my left cheek to under my jaw, a trophy from a cockatrice hunt in the wyldwood. Lately, my temples had become touched with gray and my shoulder—the one that had taken the manticore sting—still ached, a dull, persistent throb, whenever it rained. Twenty years had left its mark, and I was all too aware of the passing of time.

And Meghan, my beautiful, half-faery wife, was unchanged.

"The carriage is here," Meghan announced, peering over the windowsill. "And there's Kierran, waiting for us by the gate. I guess we should go." She turned to me, a flicker of worry passing through her eyes. "Do you need help getting down the stairs?"

"I'm fine," I told her quietly. "You go on ahead. I'll be right there."

"Are you sure?"

I nodded, and Meghan drew back, still worried. "All right, but I want you to call for a servant if you—"

"Meghan, I'll be fine," I interrupted, and she frowned at me. I forced a smile to soften the words. "Take Kierran on ahead. I'll ride with Glitch and the guards. Just go. Please."

Her eyes flashed, and for a moment I thought she would argue with me, slip into the firm, no-nonsense Iron Queen persona that had everyone terrified. But after a pause, she simply nodded and left the room, leaving me alone with my thoughts.

Another Elysium. Another gathering of the courts, coming together to pretend they got along, when all they wanted was to rip each other into bloody strips. As a faery prince, I hadn't liked Elysium, and as a human I despised it. Those who remembered me as Prince Ash—the cold, dangerous ice prince who, for centuries, demanded fear and awe and respect—saw only a human now. A weak, crippled human who grew older and weaker every year, relying more and more on the protection of his queen. I saw the looks of hunger and pity and contempt that went around the courtyard when Meghan walked in with me limping beside her. I also didn't miss the subtle looks of interest between the nobles of Summer and Winter; if I was the weakest link in the Iron Court, how could they use it to their advantage? Faery politics and power plays; they would never do anything that would force a head-on confrontation with the Iron Queen, and yet I hated being thought of as exploitable.

With a sigh, I reached for the cane sitting against the wall and pushed myself upright, taking a last glance in the mirror. The black cloak partially hid the cane but could not quite conceal the limp or the stiffness of my right leg. I still carried my sword, however, refusing to abandon it, even if I didn't draw it often. The day I was unable to use my weapon was the day I would finally give it up.

Glitch met me at the bottom of the stairs, keeping his expression carefully neutral as I limped painfully down the last step. "Her Majesty and Prince Kierran have already left for Elysium," he informed me with a slight bow. "She told me that you wanted them to go on ahead. Is anything wrong, sire?"

"No." I ignored his offered arm and kept walking, slowly, painfully, down the hall. My leg throbbed, but I gritted my teeth and continued lurching forward, refusing to pause or look back. Glitch fell into step beside me, ready to grab my arm if I stumbled, but said nothing through the long, agonizing journey to the waiting carriage.

We reached the Unseelie palace without speaking, and I turned to Glitch as the carriage pulled up at the entrance. "Wait here," I told him, watching his eyebrows arch in surprise. "You don't have to accompany me. I know this castle like the back of my hand. I'm going on alone."

"Sire, I really don't think—"

"That's an order, Glitch."

He looked reluctant, but the Iron fey had always bowed to rank, and finally he nodded. "All right. Just...be careful, Ash. Meghan will kill me if anything happens to you."

He meant well, but the resentment inside only grew stronger. Gripping my cane, I turned my back on the First Lieutenant and walked into the icy, frozen halls of the Winter palace alone.

I really should have known better, but pride had always been my downfall, even before I became human. Save for a few brutish ogre guards, the frigid halls of the Winter palace were mostly deserted, meaning everyone was already at the gathering in the ballroom. But as I turned a corner, a snicker crept from an open doorway, and a motley of redcaps spilled into the hall, blocking my path.

I stumbled to a halt, observing the situation. Like most redcaps, these were short, stocky and savage looking, their wool hats soaked in the blood of their victims and their eyes a vicious yellow. All of them wore jagged grins that showed off their razorlike fangs, and most had crude weapons tucked into their belts. Redcaps were stupid and violent, and their dangerous reputations stemmed from the fact that they viewed everything in terms of predator and prey. Any concept of rank, title, and hierarchy was lost on them. It didn't matter if you were a king or a prince or a noble; if you were weak, if they thought they could take you apart, they would, regardless of the consequences.

I cursed my stubbornness and faced the redcaps with a calm, blank expression. Any sign of weakness on my part would trigger an attack. Redcaps might be crass and stupid, but there was a reason they were feared throughout the Nevernever. Ash the Winter prince had nothing to fear from a redcap motley, but I hadn't been him for a long time.

"Well, well." The leader grinned, cracking his thick knuckles. "Look who it is, boys. Fancy meeting you here, *prince*. Especially without the queen's skirt to hide behind." The other redcaps snickered and eased forward, closing the circle like hungry wolves. "Did the queen finally get tired of her little human pet and turn you out into the cold?"

I took one careful step forward, meeting the leader's eyes. "If you think this will be easy," I said in a soft, low voice, "you're sadly mistaken. I might not be your prince any longer, but there's still enough of him left to turn the lot of you into a few smears on the floor."

The leader's grin faltered. The other redcaps eyed each other and shifted nervously, but didn't back down. For just a moment, I wished Ash the Winter prince *were* here; just the chill he could produce when angry or threatened was enough to send most would-be challengers running.

The redcap leader shook himself then, and his leer came creeping back. "Pretty bold words, little man." He sneered. "But your scent says otherwise. You smell completely, utterly *human*. There's nothing left of the Winter prince, not any-more." He bared his fangs, running a black tongue over sharp yellow teeth. "And I'm betting you taste exactly like humans, too."

The redcaps tensed, ready to fling themselves at me, their

eyes glowing with eager bloodshed. I reached beneath my cloak and gripped the sword hilt, ignoring the chill that burned my fingers. I might not survive this, but I'd take as many of the bloodthirsty creatures with me as I could. And hope that my son or my queen would avenge my death.

"Father!"

The shout echoed down the corridor, loud and clear, making the icicles tremble on the ceiling. The redcaps snarled and whirled around, brandishing weapons at the intruder who would ruin their fun.

Kierran stood at the end of the hallway, tall and imposing in a uniform of black-and-gray, his eyes flashing like angry stars in the shadows. His pale hair was tied behind him, making him look older, more severe than I'd seen before. Sharp cheekbones led up to his long, pointed ears, which were usually hidden by his hair, masking his true nature. But tonight, standing motionless and proud at the edge of the light, he looked inhuman, beautiful and completely fey.

The redcap leader blinked at the sudden arrival of the Iron prince. "Prince Kierran," he growled, sounding nervous. "What a surprise to see you here. We were just…ah…"

"I know what you were doing." Kierran's voice was cold, making me blink at how much he sounded like a certain Winter prince, long ago. "Threatening the consort of the Iron Queen is a crime punishable by death. Do you think, just because he is human, that I will spare any of your lives?"

His words stung. Just a human. Just a mortal, weak and unimportant. Kierran wasn't looking at me, however. His icy gaze fastened on the redcaps, who snarled and bared their fangs at him. The redcap leader drew himself up with a sneer.

"All right, boy, just look—"

A flash of metal, as Kierran's arm whipped out, faster than anyone could see. The leader blinked, going silent midsentence, mouth open as if he had just lost his train of thought. The other redcaps frowned in confusion, until the leader's head abruptly tumbled from his shoulders, striking the ground with a thump.

Howls and shrieks filled the air, and the motley turned to flee. But Kierran was already lunging into their midst, iron blade flashing in short, deadly arcs. I knew what a lethal fighter he was; I'd trained him myself, and his lessons had not gone to waste. Watching my son slaughter the redcap gang— without effort, without mercy—I felt a nasty glow of pride, as well as a bitter lump settle in my chest. That was me once.

It never would be again.

It was over in seconds. Kierran wasted no effort or time destroying the motley, striking with lightning speed and precision. I'd trained the boy well. The last redcap was still tumbling to the floor in pieces when Kierran slammed his blade home with a flourish, then turned to grin at me.

"Father." Kierran bowed, and a mischievous smile crept over his face. Amazing how he could go from a cold, icy killer to a charming young prince in no time at all. At the Iron Court, Kierran was the darling of everyone, especially the ladies, with a devilish streak a mile wide.

"Kierran." I nodded back, not really liking that gleeful look. "What are you doing here?"

My son grinned at me. "The queen was getting worried that you hadn't arrived yet. I offered to go look for you, in case you got into trouble. She said you would be all right, because Glitch would be there with you, but I said I'd make sure. So…" He made a great show of looking up and down the hall. "Where is Glitch, anyway? Did you leave him at home? I bet he's not happy about that."

"He's back in the carriage." I motioned Kierran forward, taking his arm as he helped me down the carnage-strewn hallway. Already the bodies were disappearing, disintegrating into mud and leeches and other nasty things. Redcaps left nothing pleasant behind when they died. "And you'll say nothing of this to your mother, understand?"

"Of course not," Kierran replied, but he was still grinning.

Together we entered the ballroom, packed wall to icy wall with Summer and Winter fey. Iron fey were present as well, but only a scattering here and there, keeping well back from the crowds and the hostile glares from Summer and Winter. Music played, dark and dramatic, and in the center of the floor, dozens of fey gentry spun and danced with each other.

Beside me, Kierran was scanning the room, his blue eyes clearly searching for someone. His gaze stopped on a willowy Summer girl with long chestnut hair and green eyes, standing in a corner talking to a dryad. She glanced at him, smiled shyly and quickly looked away, feigning disinterest. But her gaze kept straying back, and Kierran fidgeted at my side.

"Kierran," I warned, and he grinned sheepishly, as if he'd been caught with his hand in the cookie jar. "Don't get any ideas. You know the rules here."

He sighed, becoming sober in an instant. "I know," he murmured, turning away from the girl. "And it's not fair. Why should individuals have to bend to the prejudices between the courts?"

"It is what it is," I replied as we made our way through the room, weaving through ranks of fey gentry. They moved aside with looks of disdain and contempt. "And you won't be changing it, no matter how hard you try. It's been this way since the beginning of Faery."

"It never stopped you," Kierran said. His voice was calm and matter-of-fact, but I caught the hint of a challenge below the surface. That would have to end, here and now. I did not want my son getting ideas into his head that might kill him.

I stopped, pulling him to a halt, and leaned close. My voice was low and rough as I met his eyes. "Do you really want to be like me?"

He met my gaze for a few seconds, before lowering his eyes. "Forgive me, Father," he muttered. "I spoke out of turn." He didn't look at me, but I continued to stare at him until he bowed and took a step back. "I will comply with your wishes, and the laws of this realm. I will not engage the Summer or Winter courts in anything beyond diplomacy." He finally looked up, his blue eyes hard as he met my gaze. "Now, if you will excuse me, Father, I will return to the queen and inform her of your arrival."

I nodded. It was a victory, but a hollow one. Kierran bowed once more and slipped away, vanishing into the crowd, the chill from his passing making me shiver.

Alone in a crowded room, I found an isolated corner and leaned against the wall, watching the beautiful, dangerous and volatile creatures around me with the barest twinge of nostalgia. Not long ago, I had been one of them.

Then, the crowd parted a bit, and through the sea of bodies, I saw the dance floor.

Meghan, my beautiful, unchanged faery queen, swirled around the room, as elegant and graceful as the gentry surrounding her. Holding her in his arms, as handsome and charming as he had been twenty years ago, was Puck.

My stomach tightened, and I gripped my cane so hard my arm spasmed. I couldn't catch my breath. Puck and Meghan glided around the floor, flashes of color among the other dancers, their eyes only on each other. They were laughing and smiling, oblivious to the crowd watching and my slow death in the corner.

I pushed myself from the wall and walked forward, shouldering my way through the crush, ignoring the growls and curses thrown my way. My hand reached under my cloak and grasped the sword hilt, welcoming the searing pain. I didn't know what I would do, nor did I care. My mind had shut off, and my body was on autopilot, reacting instinctively. If it had been anyone but Puck...but it *was* Puck, and he was dancing with my queen. Rage tinted my vision red, and I started to draw my sword. I couldn't beat Robin Goodfellow in a fight, and my subconscious *knew* I couldn't, but emotion had taken over and all I could see was Puck's heart on the end of my blade.

However, as I neared the floor, Puck spun Meghan around, long silvery hair swirling about her, and she threw back her head and laughed. Her chiming voice hit me like a brick wall, and I stumbled to a halt, my gut clenching so hard I felt nauseous. How long had it been since I'd heard that laugh, seen that smile? As I watched them together, my former best friend and my faery wife, the sick feeling spread to every part of my body. They looked...natural...together; two otherworldly, elegant fey, forever young, graceful and beautiful. They looked like they belonged.

In that moment of despair, I realized I couldn't give her any of that. I couldn't dance with her, protect her, offer her eternity. I was human. Destined to age, wither and eventually die. I loved her so much, but would she feel the same when I was old and doddering and she was still as ageless as time?

My hand slipped off the hilt of my sword. Puck and Meghan were still dancing, laughing, spinning about the room. Their voices stabbed at me, a thousand needles piercing my chest. I turned and melted back into the crowd, left the ballroom and limped down the dark, icy corridors of the palace until I reached the carriage. Glitch took one look at my face and silently climbed out of the seat, leaving me in the shadows.

Slumping forward on the bench, I put my face in my hands and closed my eyes, feeling completely and utterly alone.

Even more time passed.

Dropping my hands, I raised my bleary eyes to an empty hall, squinting to see through the gloom. The light streaming in the windows behind me did little to chase back the shadows, but I was almost sure I had heard someone come in. One of the servants, perhaps, come to check on the withered, gray-haired human, to make sure he hadn't fallen from his chair. Or to help him totter back to his room, to curl up in his single bed, alone and pushed aside.

Meghan was gone. War had come to the Iron Kingdom at last, despite many years of peace, and the Iron Queen had gone to help the Summer King in the battle against Winter. Glitch was there beside her, commanding her army and Kierran had become a monster on the battlefield, carving through enemy ranks with the icy sword that had once belonged to me. Most of the castle had gone to war, following their queen into battle. Even the gremlins had gone, their constant chatter and buzzing voices missing from the walls, leaving the palace silent, cold and empty. Only I had been left behind. Waiting for everyone to return. Forgotten.

Rain plinked against the windowpanes, and I stirred. Outside, lightning blazed in the sky, and thunder rumbled in the distance. I wondered where Meghan was, what she and Kierran were doing right now.

Lightning flickered again, and in the flash, a figure appeared beside me, a dark, robed figure in a hood and cowl, standing silently at my arm. Had I been younger, I might've leaped up, drawn my sword. Now I was simply too tired.

I blinked and stared at the intruder, peering through my filmy vision. The robed figure gazed back, its face hidden in shadow, not attacking or threatening, just watching. Waiting. A memory stirred to life, rising from the cobwebs of the past, like a long forgotten dream. "I...remember you."

The Guardian nodded. "We are at the end of your trials, knight of the Iron Court," it said, and thunder rumbled outside, shaking the windows. "And you have discovered the final truth about being human. No matter how strong, no matter how brave, mortals cannot escape the march of time. As a human in the Iron Court, you will grow old, while everyone around you will remain as they are, forever. That is the price of mortality. You will die, and you will die alone."

As it said these words, a cold hand touched my shoulder, and a spasm went through one side of my body. I jerked, nausea and dizziness flooding through me, and tried to stand, groping for the door. My bad leg crumpled and I fell, striking my head on the cold floor, the breath knocked from my lungs. Gasping, I dragged myself across the room with one arm, my left side numb and dead, but the room spun violently, and darkness crawled along the edge of my vision. Fighting pain and nausea, I tried calling for help, but my voice left my throat in a hoarse rasp, and there was no one to hear.

Except the Guardian, which hadn't moved from where it stood watching me struggle. Watching me die. "Death," it droned, cold and impassive in the flickering lights, "comes for all mortals. In the end, it will come for you as well."

I made one last effort to get up, to keep living, though a part of me wondered why I would even resist. But it didn't matter. I was so tired. My head touched the cold floor, darkness covered me like a soft, cool blanket and I felt the last breath escape my lips as my heart—finally and irreversibly—stopped fighting.

CHAPTER TWENTY-ONE
THE FINAL SACRIFICE

Cold.

Everything was cold.

I was flying down a dark tunnel, watching fragments of my life flash before me, unable to stop. Riding with Meghan through the wyldwood. Watching Kierran and Glitch practice in the courtyard. The birth of my son. Dancing with Meghan in the ballroom. Our wedding...

Gasping, I bolted upright on a cold, hard floor, my heart slamming against my ribs, panicked, loud and alive. Clutching my chest, I gazed around, not knowing where I was. Stone walls surrounded me, candles flickering in the alcoves, casting everything in shadow. The tall hooded figure stood nearby, silently watching, and with a jolt, everything came flooding back.

The Testing Grounds. The trials. I had come here in the desperate need to earn a soul, to be with Meghan in the Iron Realm. I hunched forward, holding my head in my hands. I couldn't think straight. My mind felt like a tangle of old string, trying to sort out what was real and what was imagined. I could feel the cold stare of the Guardian, weighing me, watching what I would do.

"Was it real?" My voice came out hoarse and raspy, unfamiliar to me. "Was any of it real?"

The Guardian watched me, unmoving. "It could be."

"Ash!"

Footsteps pounded toward me and Puck came into view. For a moment, I felt a stab of hatred as I gazed at my old nemesis, the memory of him and Meghan dancing and laughing together raging in my mind...but then I paused. That hadn't happened. None of it had happened. My entire human life—my marriage, my wife and son—that was all an illusion.

"Dammit, ice-boy—" Puck panted as he jogged up. "We were looking everywhere for you. What happened? Did we miss the test? Is it done already?"

I gazed at him in disbelief. Seconds. Only a few seconds had passed, but to me, it had been a lifetime. Gingerly, I stood, drawing in a slow breath. My leg was straight and healthy, my eyesight clear and undimmed. When I looked at my hands, pale, smooth skin greeted my sight, when I'd become used to seeing wrinkles and age spots. I clenched my fist and felt the strength in my limbs,

"It is done," the Guardian intoned. "The trials are complete. You have passed the gauntlet, knight of the Iron Court. You have seen what it takes to become human—weakness of the flesh, conscience and mortality. Without these things, a soul would wither and die inside you. You have come far, farther than anyone before you. But there is still one final question. One last thing you must ask yourself, before you are ready for a soul.

"Do you truly *want* one?"

"What?" Puck, coming to stand beside me, glared at the Guardian. "What kind of question is that? What do you think he's been doing all this time, picking daisies? You couldn't spring that question *before* you put him through hell?"

I groped for his shoulder, putting a hand on it to stop him. Puck bristled, angry and indignant, but I knew what the Guardian was asking. Before, I didn't know what being human meant. I couldn't understand. Not as I was.

I did now.

The Guardian didn't move. "The Ensoulment Ceremony begins at dawn. Once started, it cannot be stopped. I offer you this one final choice, knight. Should you wish it, I can unmake everything that happened to you—all memories of this place, everything you have learned, as if the trials never happened. You can return to Winter with your friends, no different than you were before, an immortal, soulless fey.

"Or, you can claim your soul and keep everything that comes with it—conscience, human weakness, mortality." The Guardian finally moved, switching its staff to the other hand, preparing to disappear. "Whatever your decision," it continued, "when you leave this place, you will never return. So choose wisely. I will return when you have decided which path you want to take."

Choice.

I drew in a slow breath, feeling the promise that bound me, that oath I had made to Meghan, dissolve. I'd kept my vow: I had found a way to return to her, to be at her side without fear. I was free.

And I had a choice.

I DIDN'T GO BACK to my room, though I vaguely remembered where it was. Instead, I sought out the courtyard, found a stone bench beneath a withered tree, and watched the stars float through the End of the World.

Mortal or faery? Right now I was nothing, balanced on the

edge of humanity and soullessness, neither human nor fey. I was so close to having a soul, to finishing my quest and being with Meghan. But if the future the Guardian had shown me was true…if I was destined to die, forgotten and alone, then was it worth that pain?

I didn't *have* to go back to the Iron Realm. My vow had been fulfilled; I was free to do as I wished. There was no guarantee Meghan would be waiting for me to come back, no assurance she *wanted* me to come back. I could return to the Winter Court, with Ariella. It could be as it was before….

If that was what I really wanted.

"Hey." Ariella's soft voice broke through my musings, and she joined me on the bench, so close our shoulders were touching. "Puck told me about the last test, and the ceremony in the morning. I take it you haven't come to a decision yet." I shook my head, and her soft fingers brushed a curl from my forehead. "Why are you still agonizing, Ash?" she asked gently. "You've come so far. You know what you have to do. This is what you wanted."

"I know." I slumped forward, resting my elbows on my knees. "But, Ari, that last test…" Closing my eyes, I let the memories of another life wash over me. "I saw my future, with Meghan," I said, opening my eyes to stare at my hands. "I became human and went back to the Iron Realm to be with her, just like I wanted. And, at first we were happy…*I* was happy. But then…" I trailed off, watching a blue comet soar lazily through the sky above. "She never changed," I murmured at last. "She and my son, they never changed. And I…I couldn't keep up with them. I couldn't protect her, couldn't fight beside her. And in the end, I was alone."

Ariella was silent, watching me. I raked my hands through my hair with a sigh. "I want to be with them," I admitted softly. "More than anything, I want to see them again. But, if that's my future, if I can't avoid what lies ahead..."

"You're wrong," Ariella said, surprising me. I sat up, blinking at her, and she smiled. "That's *a* future, Ash. Only one. Trust a seer on this. Nothing is certain. The future is constantly changing, and no one can predict what will happen next. But let me ask you this. In this future, you said you had a son?"

I nodded, feeling a hollow ache in my chest at the thought of Kierran.

"Do you miss him?"

I let out a breath and nodded, slumping forward again. "It's strange," I murmured, feeling a lump rise to my throat. "He isn't even real, and yet...I feel like he's the one who died. His existence was an illusion, but I *knew* him. I remember everything about him. And Meghan." The lump grew bigger, and I felt my eyes stinging, moisture crawling down my cheeks. I could see Kierran's smile, feel Meghan's breath against me as we slept. And though my head knew those memories were illusions, my heart violently rejected that thought. I knew them. Every part of them. I remembered their joys, their sorrows, their triumphs and hurts and fears. They were real to me.

"My family." The admission was a mere whisper, and I covered my eyes with a hand. "Meghan, Kierran. I miss them... they were everything. I want them back."

Ariella put a hand on my shoulder, easing me close. "And even if that future came to pass," she murmured in my ear, "would you want to miss it? Would you change anything, knowing how it will end?"

I pulled back to look at her, realization slowly dawning on me as we gazed at each other. "No," I muttered, surprising myself. Because all the hurt, all the pain and loneliness and watching everyone leave me behind was overshadowed

by the joy and pride I felt for Kierran, the deep contentment
in Meghan's arms, and the blinding, all-encompassing love I
had for my family.

And maybe, that was what being human was all about.

Ariella smiled back, though there was a hint of sadness in
her eyes. "Then you know what you have to do."

I pulled her close and gently kissed her forehead. "Thank
you," I whispered, though it was hard for me to say, and I
could tell it surprised Ariella, as well. The fey never say thank-
you, for fear it will put them in another's debt. The old Ash
would never have let such a phrase escape his lips; perhaps this
was just a sign of how human I was becoming.

I stood, pulling her up with me. "I think I'm ready," I said,
gazing back at the castle. My heart beat faster in anticipation,
but I wasn't afraid. "I know what I have to do."

"Then," said the Guardian, appearing behind us, "let us
not waste another moment. Have you made your decision,
knight?"

I pulled away from Ariella and faced the Guardian squarely.
"Yes."

"And what have you decided?"

"My soul." I felt a great weight lifted off my shoulders as
I said this. No more doubts. No more agonizing. I knew my
path, what I had to do. "I choose humanity, and all that comes
with it. Weakness, conscience, mortality, everything."

The Guardian nodded. "Then we come to the end at last.
And you will be the first to claim what you have always
sought, knight. Follow me."

PUCK JOINED US AT THE DOOR, and together we followed the
Guardian down the shadowed hallways, up a twisting spiral
staircase, to the landing of the highest tower. Through the
door, the roof disappeared into open sky. Here, beneath the

stars and constellations, where sparkling bits of moon rock drifted by, trailing silver dust, the Guardian walked to the center of the platform and turned, beckoning me with a pale hand.

"You have endured all the trials," it said as I stepped forward. "You have accepted what it means to be human, to be mortal, and without that knowledge a soul could not live within you for long. You have passed, knight. You are ready.

"But," the Guardian continued in a solemn voice as my gut twisted nervously, "something as pure as soul cannot grow out of nothing. One final sacrifice remains, though it is not yours to make. For a soul to be born within you, a life must be given, freely and without reservation. With this unselfish act, a soul can bloom from the sacrifice of one who loves you. Without it, you will remain empty."

For a split second of blissful ignorance, the true meaning of what the Guardian said escaped me. Then the realization hit all at once, and an icy fist gripped my heart, leaving me numb. I stared at the Guardian for several heartbeats, horror slowly turning to anger. "Someone has to die for me," I whispered at last. The Guardian didn't move, and I felt a gaping hole tear open within, dropping me into blackness. "Then all this was for nothing. Everything you threw at me, all I went through, was for nothing!" Despair now joined the swirl of rage. I'd been through so much, endured so much, just to throw it away in the end. But this was something I could not allow. "Never," I gritted out, backing away. "I'll never let that happen."

"It's not your sacrifice to make, Ash."

Stunned, I turned as Ariella walked past me, coming to stand before the Guardian. Her voice trembled a bit, but she held her head high. "I'm here," she murmured. "He has me. I'm willing to make that choice."

"Ari," Puck breathed behind me.

No! I staggered toward her, panicked by what she was offering. My chest clenched in horror, in helpless desperation. It was the same feeling I'd had when I saw the wyvern strike her in the heart, when she lay dying in my arms, and I could only watch as she slipped away. This, I could stop. This, I *would* stop. "Ari, no," I rasped, stepping in front of her. "You can't do this! If you die again…"

"This is why I'm here, Ash." Tears filled her eyes as she turned to look at me, though she still tried to smile. "This is why I came. I was returned to life for this moment, my final task, before Faery takes me back."

"I won't accept that!" Desperately, I grabbed her arm, and she made no move to pull away. The Guardian watched us, silent and unmoving, as I faced her, pleading. "Don't do this," I whispered. "Don't throw your life away. Not for me. Not again."

Ariella shook her head. "I'm tired, Ash," she murmured, gazing right through me, at something I couldn't see. "It's been…long enough."

Behind me, Puck blew out a shaky breath, and I hoped he would protest as well, keep her from this insane plan. But Robin Goodfellow surprised me again, his voice subdued but calm. "I'm glad I got to see you again, Ari," he said, and from the tremor beneath the surface, I could tell he was holding back tears. "And don't worry—I'll take care of him for you."

"You were a good friend, Puck." Ariella smiled at him, though her eyes were shadowed, far away. "I'm happy I could give you two another chance."

Feeling betrayed, I gripped her shoulders, hard enough to make her wince, though she still didn't look at me. "I won't let you go," I snarled, though my voice was beginning to crack. "You can't do this. I'll keep you alive by force if I have to!"

"Prince." Grimalkin's cool, stern voice broke through my desperation. The word lanced into me, shimmering with power, compelling me to listen, to obey. I closed my eyes, fighting the compulsion, feeling my panic grow. The cait sith was calling in his favor.

"Don't, Grimalkin." My words were a hoarse rasp through gritted teeth. "I will kill you if you order me, I swear I will."

"I would not force you," Grimalkin said in that same quiet, calm voice. "But this is not your decision, prince. It is hers. All I ask is that you let her make that choice. Let her choose her own path, as you have done."

My composure broke. I fell to my knees with a sob, clutching at Ariella's dress, bowing my head. "Please," I choked, tears streaming down my face. "Ari, please. I'm begging you, don't go. I can't watch you die again."

"I was already gone, Ash." Ariella's voice shook, too, her hand resting against the back of my head. "All we had was borrowed time." I sobbed, kneeling before her, as her fingers stroked my hair. "Let me do this," Ariella murmured. Her fingers slipped under my jaw, gently turning my face to hers. "Let me go."

I couldn't speak. Shaking, nearly blinded by tears, I let my hands fall to my lap. Ariella pulled away, but her palm lingered against my cheek for a silent moment. I caught the tips of her fingers at the end, felt them slip from my grasp. "Remember me," she whispered.

Then she turned and stepped toward the Guardian, who raised a hand to guide her forward. "It will not take long," it said, and I thought I heard a note of admiration in the impassive voice. Ariella nodded, taking a shaky breath as the Guardian raised a hand to her forehead, brushing back her silver hair.

"Will it hurt?" she whispered, so faint I barely caught it. The Guardian shook its cowled head.

"No," it said gently, and a light began to form under its fingers, growing brighter with each passing second. "There will be no pain, Ariella Tularyn. Never again. Close your eyes."

She glanced at me. For a moment, she looked exactly as she had when I first met her, unbowed by sorrow, her eyes shining with joy. She smiled, a real smile of love and happiness and forgiveness, and then the light grew too bright to look at and I had to turn away.

Deep within me, something stirred. The darkness that I'd kept locked away, the part of me that was all Unseelie: hate, violence and black rage, rushed to the surface with a roar, seeking to overwhelm me. But it was met by something bright and pure and intense, a miasma of light that seared away the darkness, filling every corner and expanding outward, until there was no place left for the blackness to hide. I shivered, reeling from the flood of light and color and emotion, not knowing how empty I had been until that moment.

The brightness faded. I was kneeling on an empty platform at the End of the World, moondust and rock swirling around me. The Guardian stood a few feet away, alone, leaning on its staff as if winded.

Ariella was gone.

The Guardian straightened, gazing at me through the darkness of its cowl. "Take a few moments for your grief," it said, cold and formal once more. "When you are ready, meet me at the gates of the Testing Grounds. I have one last thing to give you before we part."

I barely noticed when the Guardian left. Numbly, I gazed at the spot where Ariella had stood seconds before. Grimalkin had also disappeared, the parapet that held him empty and bare, as if he'd cleared out the second the ceremony was finished. I tried to be angry at the cat, but it was futile. Even if he hadn't come, Ariella would still have made her decision. I knew her well enough to know she would've found a way. I couldn't muster any rage through the numbing grief weighing me down like a heavy blanket. Ariella was gone. She was gone. I had let her go, again.

A presence stepped up beside me, but it wasn't the Guardian. "It wasn't your fault, Ash," Puck said quietly. "It never was. She made her choice a long time ago."

I nodded, still not trusting myself to speak. Puck sighed, crouching next to me, gazing around the tower. "I don't know about you," he said, completely serious, "but I'm about ready to go home. Let's get Furball, check to see if the Wolf is still alive, and get out of here."

"Yeah," I muttered without getting up. "Just…give me a few minutes."

"Right," Puck said, and I expected him to leave. He didn't, but settled on the ground beside me, crossing his long legs. And we gazed at the spot where Ariella had smiled at me and disappeared in a brilliant burst of light, as fitting an end as I could think of. After a moment, Puck put a hand on my shoulder.

This time, I didn't brush it off.

CHAPTER TWENTY-TWO
THE RETURN

Puck and I didn't speak as we walked through the empty, dark corridors of the Testing Grounds together, lost in our own thoughts. I glanced over once and saw him hastily wipe his eyes before quickly turning a corner. The hallways seemed emptier now, the shadows deeper, as we navigated the halls with one less than when we had started out.

Ariella was gone. I didn't know how she'd done it, accompanying us, helping us, knowing all along that she wasn't coming back. This was twice I had lost her, twice I'd been forced to watch her die. But at least she had chosen her path this time. She had made her choice long ago, and if Faery brought her back, then surely it would not let her disappear as if she had never existed. A life as bright as hers must linger on somewhere; Ariella Tularyn was far too loved and cherished to simply fade away and be forgotten. It was a small comfort, but I clung to it with my remaining composure and hoped that, wherever she was, whatever state she existed in, she was happy.

Outside, the tall figure of the Guardian waited at the

bridge, the stars and the dark, hazy outline of the distant Briars floating behind him.

"This is where we part," it announced as we joined it at the edge. "Your quest is finished, knight, your journey complete. You will not see me, or the End of the World, ever again. Nor will you remember the path you took to get here. But, as you are the first to earn your soul and survive, I offer you one last gift for the journey home."

It extended an arm, dropping something small and glittering into my palm. It was a globe of darkened crystal, about the size of an orange, the glass fragile and warm against my skin.

"When you are ready," the Guardian said, "break the globe, and you will be transported out of Faery, back to the human world. From there, you may do as you wish."

"Back to the human world?" Puck peered over my shoulder at the glass. "That's kind of out of the way. Can't you give us something that will take us to the wyldwood or Arcadia?"

"It does not work that way, Robin Goodfellow," the Guardian said, speaking to him for perhaps the very first time. "You may choose to return to the wyldwood the way you came, but it is a long way up the River of Dreams, and you will not have the ferry to protect you."

"It's all right," I told Puck, before he could argue. "I can get to the Iron Realm through the mortal world. If...you can open a trod for me, that is."

Puck glanced at me, understanding in his eyes, and nodded. "Sure, ice-boy. Not a problem."

"But," I added, looking at the Guardian, "there's one more thing we have to check on before we leave. We left a friend behind at the temple when we came here. Is he still there? Can we save him?"

The Guardian straightened. "The Wolf," it said. "Yes, he

is still alive, though his spark has grown weak. He remains trapped beneath the door, and you will have to free him before you can take him to the mortal world with you."

"You can't open the door?" Puck asked, scowling.

"The gauntlet was never closed," the Guardian said flatly. "As long as your friend remains in the door, keeping it open, the gateway is still in effect. The door must seal completely before it can be opened once more."

"I suggest you hurry," Grimalkin said, appearing on a floating rock near the edge, watching us disdainfully. "If you insist on helping the dog, do it quickly so that we may go. I, for one, would like to get home sometime this century."

Home, I thought with a sharp longing in my chest. Yes, it was time to go home. It had been too long. Was Meghan still waiting for me? Or, as she'd suggested in the dream, had she moved on, found happiness with someone else? Would I return only to find her in the arms of another? Or, even worse, as a terrible fey queen like Mab, unmerciful in her power, ruling through fear?

I was afraid, I could admit that. I didn't know what waited for me at the end of my quest. But despite what I might find, even if Meghan had forgotten me, I would return to her, no matter what.

"Knight," the Guardian said as we started to cross the bridge. Puck looked back, and I waved him on. He made a face and left us. "Do not discount the gift you have been given," the Guardian continued in a low voice, as Puck followed Grimalkin over the bridge. "The soul of a Winter fey resides within you. You are no longer part of Faery, but neither are you completely mortal. You are...unique." The Guardian drew back, the faintest hint of amusement beneath its impassive voice. "We shall have to see where it takes you."

I bowed to the robed figure and crossed the bridge, feeling

ancient eyes on me the whole way. When I reached the other side and turned back, however, the Guardian was gone. The enormous bulk of the Testing Grounds was floating away, growing rapidly smaller and less distinct, until it vanished into the End of the World.

Following Grimalkin down the corridor back to the temple, we reached the heavy stone door of the gauntlet. For a moment, I feared we were too late. The Wolf lay in the doorway, unmoving, his huge head resting on his paws. Bloody foam spattered his mouth and nostrils, his fur was dull and flat and his ribs stood out sharply against his black pelt. Through the opening, the spirits still clawed at him, trying to drag him back into the temple, lost and trapped forever. But even collapsed and apparently lifeless, he was still as unmovable as a mountain.

"Pity," Grimalkin remarked as we drew close. "Not the end I would imagine for the Big Bad Wolf, crushed under a door, but I suppose he is not invincible after all."

The Wolf's eyes opened, blazing green. Seeing us, he gave a feeble cough and raised his head from his paws, staring at me. Blood dripped from his nose and mouth.

"So, you made it after all," he stated. "I suppose I should congratulate you, but I find I care very little at the moment." He panted, his eyes flickering between me, Puck and Grim, and pricked his ears. "Where's the girl?"

Puck looked away, and I took a breath, raking a hand through my hair. "She's gone."

The Wolf nodded, unsurprised. "Then, if you wish to leave by this route, I'm sure you can slide under the stone. These spirits are annoying, but they should not pose a problem anymore."

"What about you?"

The Wolf sighed, resting his head on his paws again.

"I have no strength left." Closing his eyes, he shifted painfully on the rocks. "Nor do you have the strength to move this door. Leave me."

I clenched my fists. The memory of Ariella's sacrifice was still a painful burning in my chest. "No," I said, making the Wolf crack open an eyelid. "I've already watched one friend die today. I will not lose another. Puck…" I stepped forward and put my shoulder against the bottom of the slab. "Come on. Help me move this."

Puck looked dubious, but he stepped up and braced himself against the rock, wincing as he tested it. "*Oof,* are you sure about this, ice-boy? I mean, you're human now.…"

He trailed off at the look on my face. "Right, then. On three? Hey, Wolfman, you're gonna help out, too, right?"

"You cannot free me," the Wolf said, eyeing each of us in turn. "You are not strong enough. Especially if the prince is a mere mortal."

"How very sad." Grimalkin strode up, stopping just shy of the Wolf's muzzle, barely out of snapping range. "That the great dog must rely on a human to save him, because he is too weak to move. I shall sit right here and watch, to remember this day always."

The Wolf growled, the hair rising along his back. Planting his feet, he braced his shoulders against the slab and tensed, baring his fangs. "Go."

We pushed. The stone resisted us, stubborn and unmovable. Even with the combined efforts of Puck and the exhausted Wolf, it was too heavy, too massive, for the three of us to move.

"This isn't working, prince," Puck said through gritted teeth, his face red from the strain. I ignored him, digging my shoulder into the rocky slab, pushing with all my might. It scraped painfully into my skin, but didn't move. On instinct,

I opened myself up to the glamour around me, forgetting I was only human.

I felt a shiver go through the air, a rush of cold and suddenly, the slab moved. Only a fraction of an inch, but we all felt it. Puck's eyes widened, and he threw himself against the rock, pushing with all his might, as the Wolf did the same. The spirits shrieked and wailed, clawing at the Wolf as if sensing he was slipping from their grasp. Closing my eyes, I kept myself open to the cold, familiar strength flowing through me and shoved the stone block as hard as I could.

With a final, stubborn groan, the slab gave way at last, rising a mere few inches, but it was enough. The Wolf gave a snarl of triumph and skittered out from beneath it, ripping himself from the grasp of the spirits still clinging to him, leaving them in the doorway. Puck and I jerked back as well, and the door slammed shut with a hollow boom, crushing a few spirits into mist.

Panting, the Wolf staggered to his feet, then gave himself a violent shake, sending fur and dust flying. Glancing at me, he gave a grudging nod.

"For a mortal," he growled, heaving in great, raspy breaths, "you are remarkably strong. Almost as strong as..." He paused, narrowing his eyes. "Are you sure you received what you came for, little prince? It would be annoying if we came all this way for nothing." Before I could answer, he sniffed the air, nose twitching. "No, your scent is different. *You* are different. You do not smell like you did before, but neither do you smell...entirely human." Flattening his ears, he growled again and stepped back. "What are you?"

"I'm...not really sure myself."

"Well." The Wolf shook himself again, seeming to grow a bit more steady on his feet. "Whatever you are, you did not leave me behind, and I will not forget that. If you are in need of a hunter or someone to crush your enemy's throat, you have only to call. Now…" He sneezed and bared his fangs, glaring around. "Where is that wretched feline?"

Grimalkin, of course, had disappeared. The Wolf snorted in disgust and began to stalk away, but with a shiver and a loud grinding noise, the stone door started to rise.

We tensed, and I dropped a hand to my sword, but the spirits on the other side of the door had disappeared. So had the entire room. Instead, a long, narrow hallway stretched out beyond the frame, empty and dark, fading into the black. The cobwebs lining the walls and the dust on the floor were thick and undisturbed, as if no one had walked this way in centuries.

The Wolf blinked slowly. "Magic and parlor tricks." He sighed, curling a lip. "I will be glad to be done with it. At least in my territory, things are honest about trying to kill you." He shook his great, shaggy head and turned to me. "This is where we part ways, prince. Do not forget my part in the story. I might have to hunt you down if you happen to forget, and I have a very long memory."

"It's a long way back to the wyldwood," I told him, pulling out the small glass orb. The swirls of magic within left faint, tingling sensations against my palm as I held it up. "Come with us. We'll return to the mortal realm, and from there you can easily find a trod to the Nevernever."

"The mortal world." The Wolf sniffed and backed up a step. "No, little prince. The human realm is not for me. It is too crowded, too fenced in. I need the vast spaces of the Deep Wyld or I shall quickly suffocate. No, this is where we say goodbye. I wish you luck, though. It was quite the adventure." The Wolf padded toward the dark, empty hallway, a lean black shadow that seemed to fade into the dark.

"You sure, Wolfman?" Puck called as the Wolf paused in

the frame, sniffing the air for any remaining foes. "Like ice-boy said, it's a long way back to the wyldwood. You sure you don't want a faster way home?"

The Wolf looked back at us and chuckled, flashing a toothy grin. "I am home," he said simply, and bounded through the door, melting into shadow. His eerie howl rose into the air, as the Big Bad Wolf vanished from our lives and returned to legend.

Grimalkin appeared almost immediately after the Wolf had gone, licking his paws as if nothing had happened. "So," he mused, regarding me with golden, half-lidded eyes, "are we returning to the mortal realm or not?"

I raised the globe but then lowered it, gazing at the cait sith, who stared back calmly. "Did you know?" I asked in a low voice, and the cat blinked. "Did you know the reason Ariella was here? Why she came along?" Grimalkin turned to groom his tail, and my voice hardened. "You knew she was going to die."

"She was already dead, prince." Grimalkin paused and looked back at me, narrowing his eyes. "She perished the day you swore your oath against Goodfellow. Faery brought her back, but she always knew how it would end."

"You could have told us," Puck chimed in, his voice flat and strangely subdued.

Grimalkin sneezed and sat up to face me, his golden eyes knowing. "If I had, would you have let her go?"

Neither of us answered, and the cat nodded at our silence. "We are wasting time," he continued, waving his tail as he stood. "Let us return to the mortal world so that we may be done with this. Grieve for your loss, but be grateful for the time that you had. She would have wanted it that way." He sniffed and lashed his tail. "Now, are you going to use that globe, or should I wish for wings to fly back to the wyld-wood?"

I sighed and raised the glass, watching the magic swirl within. Taking it in both hands, I gazed past it to the End of the World, at the brilliant void that never ceased to amaze. With a deep breath, I brought my hands together and crushed the glass between them, releasing the magic into the air. It expanded outward in a burst of light, engulfing us, and for a moment everything went completely white.

THE LIGHT FADED, and the sounds of the human world began: car engines and street traffic, honking horns and the shuffle of feet over pavement. I blinked and gazed around, trying to get my bearings. We were in a narrow alleyway between two large buildings, overflowing Dumpsters and heaps of trash lining the walls. A ragged lump in a cardboard box stirred, mumbled sleepily, and turned its back on us, frightening a large rat that went scurrying over the wall.

"Oh, of course." Puck wrinkled his nose, stepping back from a pile of rags crawling with maggots. "With all the meadows and forests and big swaths of wilderness that I *know* still exist in the human world, where do we end up? A filthy, rat-infested alleyway. That's just great."

Grimalkin leaped atop a Dumpster, looking surprisingly natural in the urban environment, like a large alley cat prowling the streets. "There is a trod not far from here," he stated calmly, picking his way across the rim. "If we hurry, we should reach it before nightfall. Follow me."

"Wait, you *already* know where you are?" Puck demanded as we edged toward the mouth of the alley, stepping over trash and piles of debris. "How does that work, cat?"

"Most cities are very much the same, Goodfellow." Grimalkin reached the edge of the sidewalk and peered back, waving his tail. "Trods are everywhere, if you know where to look. Also, I am a cat." And he trotted off down the street.

"Hold it, ice-boy," Puck said as I started to follow. "You're forgetting something." He pointed to my sword, hanging at my side. "Normal humans don't walk around city streets with big, pointy weapons. Or if they do, they tend to draw unwanted attention. Better give it to me for now. At least until we reach the wyldwood."

I hesitated, and Puck rolled his eyes. "I swear I'm not going to lose it, or drop it in the gutter, or give it to a homeless guy. Come on, Ash. This is part of being human. You have to blend in."

I handed the belt and sheath over reluctantly, and Puck looped it around one shoulder. "There, that wasn't so bad, was it?"

"If you lose that…"

"Yeah, yeah, you'll kill me. Old news, ice-boy." Puck shook his head and motioned me forward. "After you."

We emerged from the alleyway onto a sidewalk bustling with people, rushing by with barely a glance. Overhead, huge towers of glass and steel loomed against the sky, flashing in the evening sun. Cars honked and slid through the streams of traffic like giant metal fish, and the smell of asphalt, smoke, and exhaust fumes hung thick on the air.

The changes were subtle, but I could still see a difference. The world wasn't quite as sharp as it had been. Edges were dull, colors not quite so bright anymore. Sounds were muted; the murmur of voices around me had merged into a babble of human noise, and I could no longer pick out conversations just by listening to them.

I took a step forward, and someone ran into me, knocking me back a pace. "Watch where you're going, jackass," the human snapped, shooting me a glare without breaking stride. I blinked and joined the flow of street traffic, following Grimalkin as he expertly wove his way through the multitude of feet and swinging legs. No one seemed to notice him, or Puck, walking right beside me, glamoured and invisible. Even on a crowded sidewalk, they swerved around him or stepped out of his way, often at the last second, without even knowing there was a faery in their midst. But I caught several glances— curious, appreciative, or challenging—as I maneuvered my way through the crowd, jostling and bumping into me. It was a good thing Puck still had my sword; otherwise I might've been tempted to draw it to get them all out of my way.

As I swerved out of the path of yet another human, I brushed against a wrought-iron fence encircling the base of a small tree on the edge of the sidewalk and instinctively recoiled, jerking back from the metal. But the weakness and pain of being so close to iron didn't come, though I did earn a few strange looks from various passersby. Cautiously, I reached out and touched the fence, ready to yank my hand back as centuries of fey survival screamed at me to stop. But the iron, once akin, for me, to touching live coals while being violently ill, was cold and harmless beneath my fingers. I looked up the street at the long line of trees similarly encased in iron, and grinned.

"Will you stop doing that?" Puck hissed a moment later, shuddering as I trailed my fingers along every fence that we passed. "You're freaking me out. I get chills every time we pass one of those things."

I laughed but moved away from the fences and the iron, back to the center of the walk where traffic was thickest. Now that I knew they wouldn't just swerve around me, it was easier to dodge and weave through the unending masses. "Does this mean I can put a fence around my yard and you'll leave me alone?" I asked, grinning back at Puck. He snorted.

"Don't get cocky, ice-boy. I've been playing with humans since long before you ever thought of becoming one."

The crowds thinned as it got later, and Grimalkin led us farther downtown. Streetlights flickered to life, and the buildings lining the streets grew more run-down and shabby. Broken windows and graffiti were commonplace, and I could sense eyes on me from shadows and dark corridors.

"That's a fancy jacket, boy."

I stopped as four humans melted out of an alley, wearing hoodies and bandannas, sidling up to block my path. The biggest, a mean-looking thug with a shaved head covered in tattoos, sauntered forward, leering at me. I gave him and his companions a quick once-over, searching for horns or claws or sharp, pointed teeth. Nothing. Not half-breeds, then. Not exiles from the Nevernever, scraping out a living in the mortal world. They were human through and through.

"My boy Rico here. He was just thinking that he needed a fancy coat like that one." The thug leader smiled, showing off a gold tooth. "So, why don't you hand it over, boy? That, and leave your wallet on the ground, too. Wouldn't want to have to bash your pretty head in, now, would we?"

Beside me, Puck sighed, shaking his head. "Not terribly bright, are they?" he asked, gazing at the leader, who paid him no attention. Stepping away, he slipped around behind them, grinning and cracking his knuckles. "I guess we have time for one last massacre. For old time's sake."

"Hey, you deaf, punk?" The thug leader shoved me, and I took a step back. "Or are you so scared you pissed your pants?" The others snickered and drew forward, surrounding me like hungry dogs. I didn't move. There was a flash of metal, and the leader brandished a knife, holding it before my face. "I'll ask nicely one last time. Gimme that coat, or I'm gonna start feeding you your fingers."

I met his eyes. "We don't have to do this," I told him softly. Behind them, Puck smiled wickedly, tensing his muscles. "You can still walk away. In eight seconds, you're not going to be able to."

He raised an eyebrow, ran a tongue over his teeth. "Fine," he nodded. "We'll do this the hard way." And he slashed at my face.

I jerked back, letting the blade whiz by my cheek, then stepped forward and slammed a fist into the leader's nose, feeling it break under my fingers. He reeled back with a shriek, and I whirled toward the second thug, who was lunging at me from the side.

Time seemed to slow. In my peripheral vision, I saw Puck loom up behind the two remaining thugs and knock their heads together, dropping his glamour as they staggered and turned around. His mocking laughter rang out over the howls and curses of his opponents. I dodged the knife of my second foe and kicked him in the knee, hearing it snap as he crashed to the ground.

The thug leader was still bent over, holding his nose. Suddenly he circled, dropping the knife, reaching for something at the small of his back. I lunged forward as he brought up the gun, a dull black pistol, catching the inside of his wrist just as a roar of gunfire nearly deafened me. A twist, a snap, and the thug screamed, the deadly weapon clattering to the ground. Slamming him into a wall, I put my arm to his throat and shoved hard, seeing his eyes widen and his mouth gape for air. My adrenaline was up; my ears rang from the gunfire, and the sudden brush with death made my soul cry out for blood. This human had tried to kill me. He deserved no less himself. I leaned harder against his throat, intending to crush his windpipe, watching as his face turned blue and his eyes started to roll up in his head....

And then, I stopped.

I wasn't fey any longer. I was no longer Ash, prince of the Unseelie Court, ruthless and unmerciful. If I killed this human, I would only be adding his death to my long list of sins, only this time, I had a soul that could be tainted by needless killing and bloodshed.

Releasing the pressure on the thug's neck, I stepped back and let him slump, gasping, to the cement. A quick glance in Puck's direction showed the red-haired fey surrounded by two moaning humans, cradling their heads, while Puck looked on smugly. Satisfied, I turned back to the leader. "Get out of here," I said quietly. "Go home. If I see you again, I won't hesitate to kill you."

Cradling his broken wrist, the thug fled, his three companions limping after him. I watched them until they disappeared around a corner, then turned back to Puck.

He grinned, rubbing a hand over his knuckles. "Well, that was fun. Nothing like a good bare-fisted, knock-down, drag-out brawl to get the blood pumping. Though I will admit, I thought you were gonna kill the guy after he shot at you. You feeling all right, ice-boy?"

"I'm fine." I looked at my hands, still feeling the human's blood pumping under my fingers, knowing I could've ended his life, and smiled. "Never better."

"Then, if you two are quite finished starting random brawls in the middle of the street—" Grimalkin appeared on the hood of a car, staring at us reproachfully. "Perhaps we can move on."

He led us down another long alley, until we came to a faded red door in the bricks. Beside the door, a sign on a barred, grimy window read, *Rudy's Pawn Shop. Guns. Gold. Other.* A brass bell tinkled as we pushed our way inside, revealing a tiny shop crammed floor to ceiling with junk. Stereos sat on dusty shelves next to racks of televisions, car radios and speakers. One whole wall was dedicated to guns, protected by high counters and a blinking security camera. Racks of video games were displayed prominently, and a glass case near the front sparkled with a fortune's worth of gold: necklaces, rings, and belt buckles.

A lone, pudgy figure was leaning against the glass case, playing solitaire and looking bored, but he glanced up when we came in. Pale ram's horns curled back from the sides of his head, and his arms, gathering up the cards, were exceptionally shaggy. For a human, anyway, but not for a satyr. Or a half satyr, I realized as we drew closer. He wore a stained T-shirt and tan shorts, and his skinny legs, though hairy, were decidedly human.

"Be right with ya," he grunted as we approached the counter. "Just gimme a second to—" He stopped, really looking at us. Puck grinned at him, and he paled, breathing out an expletive. "Oh. Oh, sorry your…ah…your royalness? I didn't realize…I don't get many full-bloods through here. I mean…" He swallowed, going even paler as Puck continued to smile at him, obviously enjoying himself. "What can I do for you today, sir?"

"Hello, Rudy." Grimalkin leaped onto the counter, and the half satyr yelped, stumbling back. "I see you are still limping along with this fire hazard you call a store."

"Oh, wonderful." Rudy gave the cat a sour look, grabbing a cloth from below and wiping the countertop. "Look who's here. Back to plague me again, are you? You know that information you traded nearly got me killed?"

"You wanted the location of the giant ruins. I gave it to you. My end of the bargain was upheld."

"I thought they were deserted! You didn't say they were still occupied."

"You did not ask if they were."

While they were talking, I took the moment to look around the store, fascinated by all the mortal items hanging on racks and from the shelves. I knew what they were, of course, but this was the first time I could really touch them without fearing the burn of metal. Wandering behind the weapons counter, I gazed at all the different guns and firearms lining the walls. So many different types. There was so much I didn't know about the mortal world. I would have to remedy that soon.

Grimalkin sniffed, his voice drifting back from the counter. "If one is going to go traipsing around ancient giant ruins hunting for treasure, one should first make sure they are abandoned. In any case, it matters not. I believe we still have unfinished business."

"Fine." Rudy waved his arm dismissively. "Fine, let's get it over with. I assume you want something from the back, is that it? Hey!" he yelped suddenly, as I grabbed a pistol from the rack of guns, the same kind that had been fired at me before. "Careful with that! Geez, since when can faeries handle guns, anyway?"

"Ice-boy." Puck grimaced at me, looking nervous. "Come on. Let's not freak out the nice gun dealer. We're almost home."

I replaced the gun and walked back to the front, where Rudy eyed me suspiciously. "Uh, right. So, you need something from the 'special room,' is that it? I've got monkey paws and hydra poison and a pair of cockatrice eggs came in yesterday—"

"Spare us your dealings with the goblin market," Grimalkin interrupted. "We need to use the door to the wyldwood."

"Door?" Rudy swallowed, looking at each of us in turn. "I, uh, don't know of any door."

"Liar," Grimalkin stated, narrowing his eyes. "Do not seek to deceive us, half-breed. Who do you think you are speaking to?"

"It's just…" Rudy lowered his voice. "I'm not supposed to have direct access to the Nevernever," he admitted. "You know how the courts are. If they find out that a stinkin' half-breed owns a trod, they'll turn me into a goat and feed me to the redcaps."

"You owe me," Grimalkin said bluntly. "I am collecting that debt now. Either give us access to the trod, or I will turn Robin Goodfellow loose in your store and then we will see how much of it is left to protect."

"Goodfellow?" Rudy's face turned the color of old glue. He glanced at Puck, who grinned and waved cheerfully. "S-sure," he whispered, moving away from the counter in a daze. "Follow me."

He unlocked a door and led us into an even smaller, more crowded room. Here, the merchandise lining the walls and piled in corners was even stranger than the stock outside, but more familiar to me. Basilisk fangs and wyvern stingers. Glowing potions and toadstools of every color. A huge tome of puckered flesh rested beneath a headdress made of griffin feathers. Rudy maneuvered through the clutter, kicking things out of the way, until he came to the back wall and pushed back a curtain. A simple wooden door stood on the other side.

"Open it," Grimalkin ordered.

Sighing, Rudy unlocked the door and pushed it open. A cold breeze, smelling of earth and crushed leaves, fluttered into the small room, and the gray, murky expanse of the wyldwood came into view through the frame.

Puck blew out a long breath. "There she is." He sighed, sounding wistful. "Never thought I'd be so happy to see her again."

Grimalkin was already through the door, tail held straight up as he vanished into the mist. "Hey," Rudy called, frowning through the doorway. "No more favors, okay, cat? We're even now, right?" He sighed and eyed us as we started to follow. "I, uh, I'd appreciate it if this didn't get out, your highnesses. Seeing as I helped you and all...uh..." He trailed off as Puck gave him an appraising look in the door. "That is, if it's okay with you."

"I don't know." Puck frowned and crossed his arms. "Didn't you hear Oberon saying something about a certain pawnshop, ice-boy? And redcaps? Or was that something else?"

Rudy looked faint, until Puck slapped him on the shoulder with a laugh, making him jump three feet in the air. "You're a good guy." He grinned, walking backward through the frame. "I might come back to visit someday. Hurry up, prince."

"Prince?" The half satyr blinked as I stepped forward. "Robin Goodfellow and a prince, come to my shop?" He stared hard at me, then his eyebrows shot up as something clicked into place. "Then...you must be...are you Prince Ash?"

The wyldwood breeze was cool against my face. I paused in the doorway and glanced over my shoulder, giving my head a small shake.

"No," I told him, and walked through the door. "I'm not."

CHAPTER TWENTY-THREE
THE IRON KNIGHT

The wyldwood was exactly as I remembered it—gray, dark, misty, with huge trees blocking out the sky—and yet, it was vastly different. I used to be a part of this world, part of the magic and the energy that flowed through all living creatures in the Nevernever. I wasn't now. I was apart, separate. An intruder.

But now that I was back in the Nevernever, I could feel the glamour swirling within me, familiar and strange at the same time. Winter glamour, but different. As if…as if it wasn't *my* magic anymore, but I could still reach it, still use it. Perhaps it was part of this soul I had gained, the part that Ariella had given up, freely and without reservation. And, if that was true, then in some small way, she was still with me.

I found that thought very comforting.

"So." Grimalkin appeared out of the mist, jumping onto a fallen log, his plumed tail waving behind him. "Here we are at last. I trust the two of you can manage the rest of the way without me?"

"Running off again, cat?" Puck crossed his arms, but his

grin was an affectionate one. "And here I was just getting used to having you around."

"I cannot look over your shoulder every step of the way, Goodfellow," Grimalkin replied in a bored tone. "It was a good adventure, but now it is done. And, as difficult as it is to believe, I have things of my own to attend to."

"Yeah, that nap must be terribly pressing. How do you survive?"

Grimalkin ignored him this time, turning to me. "Farewell, knight," he said formally, startling me with the term he'd never used before. "I wish you luck on your journey, for I fear it will not be easy. But you have been through much, more than anyone could reasonably have hoped to survive. I suspect you will be all right in the end."

I bowed to the cat, who blinked but seemed pleased with the gesture. "Couldn't have done it without you, Grim," I said quietly, and he sniffed.

"Of course not," he replied, as if it were obvious. "Give the Iron Queen my regards, but tell her not to call on me *too* soon. I find pulling you both out of sticky situations increasingly tiresome."

Something rustled in the bushes a few yards away, drawing my attention for a split second. When I glanced back at the log, Grimalkin was gone.

Puck sighed. "Cat sure knows how to make an exit," he muttered, shaking his head. "Well, come on, ice-boy. Let's get you to the Iron Realm. You're not getting any younger."

THE JOURNEY TOOK US TWO DAYS, mostly due to the goblin border skirmish we ran into in the Gnashwood. Because, as nothing ever came easily in the wyldwood, the goblin tribes were at war again and were even more intolerant of trespassers through their territory. Puck and I had to flee from several angry war parties, eventually fighting our way through the lines to reach the outskirts of goblin lands. For a while, it was like old times again, the two of us, fighting side by side against much greater odds. My body felt like my own again, my sword fluid and natural in my hands. A poisoned goblin arrow hit me once in the thigh, and I spent an evening in pain trying to stave off the effects, but I was able to shake it off by morning and continue.

But despite the thrill of battle and the excitement of simply being alive, I was anxious to get to the Iron Realm. I could feel the seconds ticking away, like grains falling through the hourglass, each day that brought me closer to my inevitable end. Whether it was an ordinary mortal life span, or if I was still faery enough to slow the advance of time, I wanted to spend the days I had left with Meghan. With my family.

The last night before we reached the border of the Iron Realm, Puck and I camped on the edge of a small lake, having finally escaped the Gnashwood and the territory of angry, bloodthirsty goblins. We were so close—I could feel it, and it was difficult for me to relax, much to Puck's amusement. I finally dozed, leaning back against a tree, facing the water.

Sometime during the night, I dreamed. Ariella stood on the banks of the water smiling at me, her silver hair glowing in the starlight. She didn't speak, and I didn't say anything, having no voice in this dream, but I think she wanted me to know that she was happy. That her quest was fulfilled, and that I could finally let her go. I could put her memory to rest at last. I woke with blurry eyes and an ache in my chest, but for the first time since that fateful day, I felt lighter. I would never forget her, but I no longer felt guilty that I had moved on, that I could be happy with someone else. I finally knew that's what she would want.

At last, forty-eight human hours after we'd entered the

wyldwood, Puck and I stood at the edge of the Iron Realm, gazing at the metal trees stretching to either side as far as one could see. It seemed the Nevernever itself had done its best to separate from the Iron Kingdom, for a great chasm ran between the wyldwood and the Iron Queen's territory, the earth having fallen away. A wooden bridge had been hastily constructed to span the gulf, but the wyldwood was slowly attempting to destroy that as well, for vines and weeds were already wrapped about the planks, as if trying to drag it down.

Puck and I stopped at the edge of the bridge. "Well, here we are." The Summer jester sighed, scrubbing the back of his head while eyeing the forest. "Home sweet home for you, ice-boy, strange as it is to think about that. Sure you can make it to Mag Tuiredh on your own? I really don't know where it's located from here."

"It doesn't matter," I said, gazing into the glimmering forest of steel. Not long ago, the sight of it had made my stomach recoil. Now it churned with excitement. "I'll find it."

"Yeah, I've no doubt you will." Puck sighed, crossing his arms. "Anyway, you probably won't see me for a while, ice-boy. The thought of returning to Summer just isn't as appealing as it once was. Maybe it's time for a road trip." He flung out his arms dramatically. "The wind in my face, the open road stretching out before me, excitement and adventure just around the next bend."

"Huh." I eyed him shrewdly. "Oberon didn't give you permission to go tromping through the Deep Wyld with me, did he?"

"Not so much." Puck grimaced. "Anyway, I think it's time for a vacation, let Lord Pointy Ears cool down for a bit. Give Meghan a hug for me, will ya? Maybe I'll see you both in a few decades."

"Where are you going?"

Robin Goodfellow shrugged, uncertain and carefree. "Who knows? Maybe I'll try to find the End of the World again. Maybe I'll travel the mortal realm for a while. It really doesn't matter where I go, or where I end up. There's a whole huge world out there, and it's high time for us to get reacquainted." He looked at me, and his eyes gleamed. "I'm glad we had one last little adventure, ice-boy, but it's time for me to strike out on my own. Try not to have too much fun without me, okay?"

"Puck," I said, stopping him as he started to leave. Turning back, he raised an eyebrow, a faint, wary smile crossing his face.

Taking a deep breath, I stepped forward and held out a hand.

Puck blinked, then very seriously reached out and gripped my palm, squeezing hard, as I did the same. "Good luck," I said quietly, meeting his eyes. He grinned, not one of his leering, mocking smiles, but a real one.

"You, too, Ash."

"If you're ever in Tir Na Nog, say hi to Mab for me."

Puck laughed, shaking his head as he backed away. "Yeah. I'll be sure to do that." On the other side of the bridge, he raised one hand in a salute as glamour shimmered through the air. "See you around, ice-boy."

A ripple of magic, and Puck's form twisted and shrank into a huge, black raven, beating the air with powerful wings. With a raucous caw, he rose above me, shedding glamour and feathers, and spiraled away over the trees, until he became a tiny black dot on the horizon and disappeared.

I smiled, turned my back on the wyldwood and crossed the bridge, slipping into the Iron Kingdom alone.

EPILOGUE
THE IRON QUEEN

My name is Meghan Chase, monarch of Mag Tuiredh, sovereign of the Iron territories, and queen of the Iron fey, and whoever said kings and queens had it easy certainly didn't know what they were talking about.

The throne room of the Iron palace was filled to capacity again, and the murmur of voices along the walls was a constant buzz in my mind. Today was going to be another long day. As sole ruler of the Iron Realm, it was up to me to resolve disputes, manage resources, listen to complaints and somehow keep my own lands and people safe from the other fey courts that wanted them dead, all while trying to rebuild and establish my own kingdom. I wasn't complaining, but it seemed a lot to ask of a once-normal seventeen-year-old who had only recently inherited an entire realm of Iron fey. And, admittedly, some days were more trying than others.

I shifted on my throne, a great monstrosity of wood and iron, made no more comfortable by the thick cushions I was sitting on. At first, I'd jokingly suggested using a La-Z-Boy recliner for these long hearings, but that was rather fervently vetoed by both Glitch and my chief adviser, a packrat named Fix. The Iron Queen had to appear strong and imposing, they said, even while sitting down. At least in public, the Iron Queen had to seem invulnerable. I suppose, to them, *invulnerable* meant rigid and uncomfortable. At least, that's what my back thought.

This is the Iron Kingdom, I thought during a short break in the hearings. *This doesn't have to be so old-fashioned. I bet I can get Diode to set it up so that some of these petitions come in by email or something.*

Another petitioner approached, a wire nymph whose territory rested very close to Tir Na Nog and the Winter Court. I listened patiently as she poured out the latest development: groups of Winter knights terrorizing the tribes that sat closest to the border. I'd have to speak to Mab about that, make sure her court was following the treaty agreement, as well. That was going to be loads of fun. The Winter Queen already hated me for being Oberon's daughter, and now that I was a queen as well, the look in her eyes whenever she saw me was downright scary. Still, I *was* queen. I ruled a court, and by Faery law, the Winter monarch would have to hear me out, whether she liked it or not.

"Alkalia," I said, making sure to remember the nymph's name. "You were right to bring this to my attention. I'll speak to Queen Mab about it as soon as I am able."

"We are very grateful, your majesty," the wire nymph said, bowing as she was ushered away. I nodded at Fix, and he punched the request into my planner, adding it to the already lengthy list of things that needed doing.

"Let's take a break," I said, and stood up, feeling my back pop as I stretched. Fix chittered a question, the junk on his back swaying as he turned to me. "We've been here nearly four hours," I replied. "I'm hungry, I have a headache and my butt has gone numb from sitting on that torture device. Let's pick back up in an hour, yes?"

Fix warbled an agreement, but at that moment, the doors of the throne room swung open with a groan, and Glitch walked in. Scores of Iron fey scurried aside as the First Lieutenant marched down the aisle to the foot of the throne, his sharp face intense. Behind him, a robed, hooded figure matched his steps, cloak torn and dusty from travel, a dark cowl hiding its face.

"Majesty." Glitch bowed at the foot of the dais, and though his voice was solemn, I could sense my First Lieutenant was trying hard not to smile. "This traveler has come far to request an audience with you. I know you are very busy at the moment, but as he has come a great distance, perhaps you could hear him out."

Glitch bowed again and backed away, melting into the crowd. I shot him a look, but he was staring straight ahead, giving nothing away. The First Lieutenant normally didn't take it upon himself to show petitioners to the throne room, having other duties that kept him busy, like managing the army. If he made an exception for this traveler, he must've thought it was very important.

I frowned and looked at the stranger in the middle of the hall, waiting for me to acknowledge him. "Come forward," I said. He approached the foot of the throne and sank to one knee, bowing his cowled head.

"Where have you come from, traveler?"

"I have come from the End of the World," said a quiet voice that made my heart stop beating. "From the River of Dreams, through the gauntlet and the Briars and the Deep Wyld, in order to stand before you today. I have but one request—to take my place at your side. To resume my duty as your knight, and to protect you and your kingdom for as long as I draw breath." He raised his head and pushed back the hood, and a gasp went around the throne room. "I am still yours, my queen," Ash said, looking me straight in the eye. "If you'll have me."

For a moment, the shock held me immobile. He couldn't be here; it was impossible. No normal fey could set foot in the Iron Realm and live. And yet, here he was, looking tired and dusty and slightly ragged, but completely fine. "Ash," I whispered, stepping toward him in a daze. He didn't move, gazing up at me with those intense silver eyes I knew so well. Reaching down, I drew him to his feet, taking in the lean, muscular frame, the unruly black hair, covered in dust from his travels, the way he was looking at me, as if the entire court had disappeared, and we were the only two people in the world.

"You're here," I murmured, reaching out to touch him, hardly believing this was real. "You came back." Ash's breath hitched, and he put his hand over mine.

"I came home."

Our fragile composure shattered. I stepped into him, holding him tight, and he hugged me close as the room around us exploded with noise. Applause and cheers rose into the air, but I barely heard any of it. Ash was real. I could feel his breath on my neck, feel his heart pounding with mine. I didn't know how he could be here; it should've been impossible, but I didn't want to face that now. If this was a dream, I wanted to have one perfect moment of happiness, before reality intruded and I'd have to let him go.

Finally, I pulled back to look at him, running a palm over his cheek, as he gazed at me with those eyes I could lose myself in. And I finally voiced the question that I had been dreading, not sure I wanted to know the answer. "How?"

Amazingly, Ash smiled. "I told you I'd find a way, didn't I?" He chuckled at my disbelief, and I could sense the secret pride—the knowledge that he had set out to do something impossible and had succeeded. Taking my hand, he guided it to his chest, where I could feel his heartbeat thudding against my palm. "I became human. I went to the ends of the Nevernever and found my soul."

"What?" I pulled back to look at him, really look at him. He did seem a little different than before. Maybe his features were a little less sharp, and he wasn't quite as cold, but he still had those intense silver eyes, that same unruly hair. He might have been human now, but he was still Ash, still the same person I'd fallen in love with, loved still with my entire heart. And if he had really found a soul and become human…

We can be together. We can be together without fear of anything now. He really did it.

Ash blinked under my scrutiny. "Do I pass?" he almost whispered.

"Wait a minute." Frowning slightly, I reached up and brushed his hair back, revealing a graceful, pointed ear. "If you're human, how do you explain that?"

Ash grinned. His eyes sparkled, and I could suddenly see the soul shining through, bright and pure and beautiful. "Apparently, I have a *little* fey magic still left in me," he said, running his fingers through my hair, stroking my cheek with his thumb. "Enough to keep up with the rest of Faery, anyway. Maybe enough to keep from growing old." He laughed softly, as if the very idea thrilled him. "Better get used to this face, your majesty. I plan to be here a long, long time. Probably forever."

My eyes misted over, and there was a balloon in my chest, swelling with happiness, pushing away the darkness until there was no room for anything but joy. But all I could think to say was, "Aren't you already centuries old?"

Ash lowered his head, drawing us even closer. "I went to the End of the World for you, and all you have to say is how well I've aged?" But his eyes danced, and he was still smiling.

I decided I liked this Ash; this light, free creature, as if a soul had unlocked a part of him that hadn't been allowed to sur-face in the chill of the Winter Court. It made me feel I could tease him a little more.

"I didn't say anything about aging *well*—" But at that moment, amid the cheers and whistles of the Iron Court, Ashallayn'darkmyr Tallyn gently took my face in his hands and covered my mouth with his own, beginning the first day of our forever exactly as he should.

A WARM WIND HOWLED through the branches of a certain hol-low, rustling the leaves, whistling through the skeleton of an enormous reptile in the center of the glade. Sprawled in the grass in the center of the hollow, it seemed extraordinarily out of place, a token of death in the midst of so much life. Flowers carpeted the once muddy ground, birds twittered in the branches, and the sun shone full and bright through the clouds, slowly burning away the mist that still clung to small patches of bramble throughout the glen. The skeleton, with its bleached white bones and snarling maw, looked pale and insignificant among the riot of color, but nature was slowly doing its work. Moss and weeds were already creeping up the dead giant, and tiny flowers were just beginning to sprout through its rib cage, coiling delicate vines around the bones. In a few seasons, it would be unrecognizable.

A shadow melted out of the brambles, blinking as it stepped into the sun, a large gray cat with glowing yellow eyes. It padded its way across the hollow, past the slowly disappear-ing skeleton, until it reached the trunk of a great tree, white blossoms fully in bloom. Sitting down at the trunk, it curled its bushy tail around itself and closed its eyes, listening to the sound of the wind in the trees. A pair of blossoms swirled around it, teasing its long whiskers, and it appeared to smile.

"I am happy that you have finally found peace."

The branches above it rustled, sounding suspiciously like laughter. Standing, the cat raised its head, letting the breeze toss its coat, watching a petal dance on the wind. Then, with a flick of its tail, it bounded into the undergrowth, a streak of gray fur in the sun, and the light swallowed it completely.

★ ★ ★ ★ ★ ★ ★

ACKNOWLEDGMENTS

Ah, the Acknowledgments page. Once more, we come to the end of a novel, and once more, I have many, many people to thank. My parents, for without them, I wouldn't be the stubborn, idealistic daydreamer I am today. My agent, Laurie McLean, who is always there to field questions and calm authorly panic attacks, sometimes well after business hours. My wonderful editors, Natashya Wilson and Adam Wilson, and the talented, amazing staff at Harlequin TEEN. This year especially has been a wild and crazy ride, and I could not have been in better company.

To all the awesome bloggers of the YA world, and the fans of Team Ash, this book is especially for you. It is partially because of you that a certain Unseelie prince got his own story, that his journey ended as it did. Thank you.

And, of course, my deepest gratitude goes to my first editor, sounding board, proofreader, problem solver and amazing husband, Nick. You are my knight in shining armor.

SURVIVAL GUIDE TO THE NEVERNEVER

SURVIVAL GUIDE TO THE NEVERNEVER
DISCLAIMER

This guide is intended to give intrepid travelers into the realm of the fey a minimal chance at surviving the creatures and denizens that dwell within. Please note, the author of this guide is in no way responsible for lost or damaged souls, ensnarement, or accidental or intentional death. Entering the realms of fey can, and likely will, be hazardous to your health and is not recommended. You have been warned.

Preparations

One can never prepare adequately for entry into the Nevernever. There are, however, a few rules that one can follow to help increase the chances of surviving.

What Should I Wear?

Dressing for the Nevernever means blending utility with comfort. If you have questions about whether or not an item is appropriate, ask yourself the following: If running for my life, would this slow me down? And: If caught while running for my life, would this protect me? If the answer to the first question is yes, and the second question is no, then the item is inappropriate. Here are a few suggested items to wear to help you make it out of the Nevernever alive.

- A light pack (either a backpack or large satchel) can be helpful for storing necessary items. Make sure to avoid large, bulky, or heavy packs, as they will slow you down when (not *if*) you need to run for your life.

- Comfortable clothing that covers the arms and legs (the Briars have thorns, after all). Be sure to wear muted colors, as bright or flashy colors will attract the fey. Layers are also strongly recommended, as the temperature can vary quite drastically from one part of the Nevernever to the next.

- A protective charm may reduce the chances of being eaten. Cold iron blessed by the druids during a new moon works best, but if that is not available, a twist of St. John's Wort, a four-leaf clover, or a rabbit's foot might help. If you have none of the above, wearing your clothing inside out may work in a pinch.

- A high-quality pair of cross-trainers or running shoes. Remember, buying the shoes is not enough. A strong cardio program is highly recommended before crossing into the Nevernever.

What Should I Pack?

It is a common mistake to take a large amount of gadgetry (cameras, cell phones, portable computers, etc....) into the Nevernever. The second problem with these devices is that they will not work well (if at all) in Faery. The first and larger problem is that any fey you chance across will not take kindly to the presence of so much mortal technology, which, in turn, could lead to a situation where the running shoes mentioned above are needed. Better to stick with a few simple items.

- Food. Any type of small, high-caloric, portable food items will suffice. Energy bars, candy bars, trail mix, dehydrated foods, etc., will extend the amount of time you can spend in the Nevernever. (Note: Extending the amount of time spent in the Nevernever is not recommended.) It *is* recommended that you do not eat anything you find or are offered while in the Nevernever. Side effects of faery food include but are not limited to: mood swings, inebriation, memory loss, shape changing, obsession, coma, inability to leave the Nevernever, and death.

- Weapon of steel or cold iron. Modern steel (e.g., a knife, sword, or other implement of death) is serviceable in this regard, but cold iron (e.g., a spike from a wrought-iron fence, a length of pig iron, etc....) is preferable as it has a more direct impact on the fey. Before entering Faery, an intense training program with your chosen weapon is strongly encouraged. Several years of training should be enough to adequately protect yourself from the weakest fey. If you wish to protect yourself from the strongest fey, you will need several mortal lifetimes.

- Gifts for the fey. If you encounter creatures of the Nevernever, many can be won over by offering gifts, free of obligation. Suggested items include jars of honey, bags of candy, bronze weapons and young children. Please check with the laws of your home country before procuring any of these items.

- Water. While most of the water in the Nevernever is drinkable without direct side effects, it is also the home of many aquatic fey of the nastier variety, and drinking it or venturing too near it may result in numerous indirect side effects: nausea, vomiting, sudden blood loss, inexplicable need to flee and death.

Entering the Nevernever

This guide will not lay out explicit directions on how to enter the Nevernever. The publishers consulted with their legal teams and determined that the associated liability of such an act was, as one attorney put it, "Certain to lead to financial ruin for this company, reprisals from the Summer and Winter courts, and, quite possibly, the end of the world as we know it." Suffice it to say, one enters Faery through trods, paths between the mortal realm and the realm of the fey. Finding those trods is, per Legal, up to you.

The Geography of the Nevernever

The Nevernever is a diverse and wild realm populated by strange creatures and ancient powers. The land itself is said to have a consciousness and a sometimes malicious will. When traveling through the Nevernever, there are four primary realms with which one may have to contend.

- Arcadia, the Summer/Seelie Court. Thick forests, ancient hills, and flowering grasslands dominate Arcadia, home of the Summer fey. Newcomers to the land of the Summer King might falsely believe that Seelie territory is not as dangerous as the rest of the Nevernever, but do not be deceived. Arcadia is sunny and beautiful year round, but it is not safe. Satyrs, dryads and trolls roam the forests of Arcadia, and the lakes teem with mermaids and nixies. The Seelie Court rests beneath an enormous faery mound, where King Oberon and Queen Titania rule without opposition.

- Tir Na Nog, the Winter/Unseelie Court. The territory of Mab, the Winter Queen, is as hostile and icy as the fey that dwell there. Snow covers everything, and the frozen woods, fields, streams and lakes all rest beneath several inches of ice. All sorts of vicious creatures call the Winter Court home, from goblins and redcaps to bogeymen and ogres. The Winter palace lies beneath an enormous cavern, home of the terrible Winter Queen. Few mortals who set eyes on the Unseelie Court and Mab ever live to tell of it.

- The wyldwood. The dark, tangled forest called the wyldwood is the largest territory in the Nevernever, completely encircling both courts and extending into the Deep Wyld. It is neutral territory; neither Summer nor Winter hold sway here, and the wyldwood denizens owe allegiance to no one. The wood is vast and endless, and the creatures that roam there come from every corner of the imagination. Not only does this make the wyldwood one of the most dangerous places in the Nevernever, but one of the most mysterious as well.

- The Iron Court. Until recently, not much was known about the mysterious emergence of a new court within the bounds of Faery. One would think that a realm called the Iron Kingdom, born from the very substance most harmful to the fey, would be a rumor at best and quickly exterminated at worst. But such a court does exist, and is now ruled by a young faery queen called

Meghan Chase. The Iron Queen is said to be half faery and half human, and it is within her realm that you will find the strange and wondrous species known as the Iron fey. These faeries—for they are indeed true fey—are thought to have evolved from mankind's love of technology and progress. Currently, however, not much information is known about them.

Encountering Denizens of the Nevernever

If you are wise, you will do as little as possible to draw the attention of the fey. Sometimes, even if you are a quiet observer, the fey will find you. If this occurs, there are a few steps you can follow that may allow you to escape with your free will and, if you are lucky, your life.

- Always be polite. Discourtesy is a deep insult to the fey and will not be well received, no matter how cool you think it will make you look.

- Do not be deceived by the politeness of the fey. Fey are almost always polite. This does not mean they will not happily remove your head. They will, however, be grateful for the entertainment you provided. Or, if you are very unlucky, the sustenance.

- There is no such thing as a free lunch. In the Nevernever, there is no "free." Accept no gifts, no matter how sure you are that there are no strings attached. There are always enough strings attached to tie you up in a pretty bow and deliver you to someone who will be grateful for the sustenance.

- Give gifts freely. The fey will either think you are a masterful manipulator and respect you more, or be completely befuddled by the notion of a gift with no obligations.

- Never, ever, under any circumstances, enter into a contract with the fey. It always ends badly and often fatally. In the rare cases where it does not end badly, that is because it does not end. You will be bound for eternity.

- If you have to run, zig and zag. Many faeries carry bows and arrows.

- If you chance upon a big, gray cat, you probably owe him a favor. Even if you do not remember the favor, do it anyway. In the long run, you will do it, but it will be far less painful if you do it up front.

How Do I Leave Faery?

The best answer to this question is, quickly. Spending a lot of time within the realms of the Nevernever can lead to many strange effects. A few minutes in Faery may be years in the mortal realm, or the reverse may be true. If you leave by a different trod than you entered, even one only a few feet away, you may find yourself on the other side of the world, or at the bottom of the ocean. Here are a few things to remember when attempting to leave the Nevernever.

- Always keep track of how to return to the trod from which you entered.

- Never, ever ask for directions or a way out. Most fey will help you, but they will charge a steep price, most commonly your tongue, as they do not want you to share this information. Note: If they ever catch on to texting, they may start asking for thumbs, as well.

- If you cannot find your way back to your original trod, purchase a way out by using the gifts mentioned earlier in this guide. If you enter into this type of bargain, make sure to phrase things appropriately. "I'm lost and can't get home," is sure to lead to trouble. Try something different, like, "I'll pay two jars of honey to a fey who will take me to the mortal realm, alive and whole, with my mind and soul intact, neither physically nor mentally harmed, to be placed on solid ground at an altitude and in an environment that can readily sustain human life, no farther than a mile from a human settlement, at a time not more than thirty minutes from now." Even then, be careful.

Conclusion

The above procedures should afford you the barest chance at survival in the Nevernever. There are, of course, no guarantees and any and all interactions with the denizens of Faery must be handled with the greatest of care. If, however, you proceed according to the above, you will have a leg up on the other mortals who wander from time to time through the Briars and into the heart of Faery. You have been warned. Proceed at your own risk.

Q&A WITH JULIE KAGAWA,
PLUS A FEW UNEXPECTED GUESTS

Q&A WITH JULIE KAGAWA,
PLUS A FEW UNEXPECTED GUESTS

1. You've taken faery lore and created a unique spin on it—the Iron fey. How did you come up with the idea for iron faeries?

   Julie: I always loved faeries (the dark dangerous kind, not the glittery Tinkerbell kind), but when it came to writing *The Iron King,* I started thinking—what are the fey afraid of? The answer in traditional mythos is iron, so what if there was a type of fey who had evolved from the very thing faeries dread? Then I remembered we already have "monsters" living in machines: gremlins, bugs, viruses and so on. And from that thought the Iron fey were born.

   Puck: Yeah, and speaking for all of us normal fey, I want to thank you for creating another species that acts like our kryptonite, heavy sarcasm.

   Ash: For once, I agree with Goodfellow.

   Julie: Where did you two come from?

2. Who is your favorite character in the series? Or...if that's too hard, why do you like each one and who drives you crazy?

   Puck: Well, she likes me best, of course. I'm the handsome, charming one.
   Ash: Yes, that's why she gave you your own book. Oh, wait.
   Puck: No one asked you, ice-boy.
   Julie: I like them all in different ways. But I will say that Ash was the hardest character to write sometimes. It's so hard to get him to talk! I'll be pushing him to open up and say something and he just crosses his arms and acts stubborn.
   Ash: ...
   Julie: See?

3. What is your favorite part of the Nevernever? Where would you live if you were a faery?

   Julie: I was going to say the wyldwood, but on second thought, I think I'd live in the Iron Realm with Meghan and Ash.
   Ash: See? She prefers my company to yours.
   Julie: Not really. It's just hard to find a wireless signal in the wyldwood.
   Puck: *snicker*

4. Originally, the Iron Fey was meant to be a trilogy. How did *The Iron Knight* come about?

   Julie: *The Iron Knight* came about because I love Ultimate Noble Sacrifice endings, and my editor (who is fantastic, by the way) liked HEAs (Happily Ever Afters). I had a very specific character arc in mind for Meghan, and Iron Queen was supposed to be the end of her journey, her accepting responsibility even at great cost. But my editor convinced me that we couldn't leave Meg and Ash apart, and so I started work on *The Iron Knight*.

5. Do you have a writing routine? Anything you must have/not have in order to work?

Puck: Here we go.
Julie: My routine: Wake up. Get morning stuff done. Turn on laptop. Curse 'cause it's not picking up the router signal again. Wait two minutes until it does. Check email. Check Twitter. Check *other* email account. Check blogs. Chat a little on TweetDeck. Tell everyone I'm off to write. Open up document. Stare at it. Decide I need music to write to. Fiddle around with my playlist. Decide I'm hungry and need food. Forage in the kitchen. Come back, stare at document a little longer. Check email….
Ash: Why don't you just turn off the internet?
Julie: Because then I couldn't do any research.
Puck: Oh, *research.* Silly me, I thought you were just playing around on YouTube.
Julie: Shut up, Puck.

6. Tell us a little about other things that interest you, besides writing.

Julie: Well, I enjoy reading, painting and drawing, but I also love anime, manga and comics. I'm an avid gamer— I have a PS3, an Xbox 360 and a Wii. My favorite food in the whole world is sushi, and I'm taking classes in Wing Tzun kung fu.
Puck: *singing* "Everybody was kung fu fighting…"

Julie: *Agh*. Ash, stop him before that song is stuck in everyone's head.
Ash: Too late.

7. Who are some of your favorite authors? What do you read for fun?

   Julie: I have so many favorites I can't list them all, but Neil Gaiman is one author whose books I adore. I read mostly fantasy and paranormal, both in YA and adult, but I'm trying to branch out into other genres, too. And I love manga, even though I can tear through the newest edition of *Shinobi Life* in twenty minutes flat.

8. Besides being a talented writer, you are also an artist. What sort of art do you do?

   Julie: I like sketching and drawing, mostly cartoon-style art with pens and Prismacolor markers. For instance, I did a webcomic on my blog with Ash and Puck, "chibi style."
   Ash: It was mortifying.
   Puck: But you looked so cute— Ow!
   Julie: I also paint rocks. And I'll let you ponder that one for yourself, lol.

9. Any advice for aspiring writers?

   Julie: Persist. Never stop believing in yourself or your stories. Know that the road to publication may be long and hard, but the ones who made it are the ones who never gave up.

Thanks, Julie!

QUESTIONS FOR DISCUSSION

QUESTIONS FOR DISCUSSION

1.) Ash begins his journey in *The Iron Knight* to keep a promise he made to Meghan Chase. How important is it to keep promises when circumstances change? Under what, if any, circumstances would you not keep a promise?

2.) Ash and Puck have an intense relationship based on a friendship gone wrong. We might call them frenemies. Ash felt that Puck was responsible for Ariella's death in the past. Do you believe Ash was justified in making his vow to kill Puck? How would you handle having a close friend cause hurt to another friend, whether accidentally or on purpose?

3.) In *The Iron Knight,* we learn of the many terrible things Ash has done in the past, including murder. How did learning the details of Ash's past affect your opinion of him? In real life, who do you believe deserves a second chance?

4.) Through Ash's quest to gain a soul, *The Iron Knight* explores what it means to be human, to have humanity.

What are the key qualities of being human? What traits do you value in yourself and your friends and family?

5.) In the gauntlet, Ash, Puck, Ariella and Grimalkin face mirror images of themselves that represent their dark sides. Why is it important that they see what they might become? How does it help Ash to succeed in his quest? Why didn't Grimalkin's reflection fight with the others?

6.) Ariella chooses to give up her life so that Ash can have a soul. How might that sacrifice affect Ash in the future? In real life, what kinds of sacrifices are worth making, and what might constitute going too far?

7.) How does Puck change over the course of the story? Why do you think he chose to come with Ash and support him in his quest to win the woman whom Puck also loves? Who do you believe should be with Meghan, and why?

8.) One of the premises behind Julie Kagawa's faery world is that faeries exist and become more powerful when humans remember them, tell stories about them and dream of them. What kind of power do dreams and the imagination have on humankind? How are they important in our lives?

Turn the page for an exclusive excerpt from book 1 of
Julie Kagawa's dark and thrilling series
BLOOD OF EDEN.

THE IMMORTAL RULES
In a future world, vampires reign.
Humans are blood cattle.
And one girl will search for the key to save humanity.

I started to look around to get my bearings, but suddenly noticed something that turned my blood to ice. "Stick," I said softly, looking down at his leg, "what happened?"

Blood was oozing from a gash in his knee, spreading through the thin fabric of his pants. "Oh," Stick said, as if he'd just noticed it himself. "I must've cut it when I fell off the fence. It's not very deep...." He stopped when he saw my face. "Why?"

I stood slowly, carefully, my mouth going dry. "Blood," I murmured, backing away. "Rabids can smell blood for miles. We have to go n—"

It leaped atop the car with a howl, lashing out at the space I'd been a moment before, ripping through the metal with its claws. Stick yelled and dived away, skittering behind me as the thing atop the car gave a chilling wail and looked right at us.

It had been human once—that was the most horrible thing about it. It still had a vaguely human face and emaciated body, though its skin, nearly pure white and stretched tightly across its bones, looked more skeleton than human. The tattered threads of what had been clothes hung on its frame, and its hair was tangled and matted. Its eyes were white orbs with no irises or pupils, just a blank, dead white. It hopped off the car and hissed at us, baring a mouthful of pointed teeth, the two oversize fangs extending outward like a snake's.

Behind me, Stick was whimpering, soft choked noises that made no sense, and I caught the sharp ammonia smell of urine. Heart pounding, I eased away from him, and the Rabid's hollow gaze followed me for a brief second before returning to Stick. Its nostrils flared, and bloody foam dripped from its jaws as it took a lurching step forward.

Stick was frozen in terror, watching the Rabid like a cornered mouse would a snake. I had no idea why I did what I did next. But my hand reached into my pocket and grabbed the knife. Pulling open the blade, I closed my fist around the edge and, before I thought better of it, sliced it across my palm.

"Hey!" I yelled, and the Rabid snapped its horrible gaze to me, nostrils flaring. "That's right," I continued, backing away as it followed, leaping atop another car as easily as walking. "Look at me, not him. Stick," I called without taking my eyes from the Rabid, keeping a car between it and me, "get out of here. Find the drain—it'll take you back to the city. Do you hear me?"

No answer. I chanced a sideways glance and saw him still frozen in the same spot, eyes glued to the Rabid stalking me. "Stick!" I hissed furiously, but he didn't move. "Dammit, you spineless little shit! Get out of here, now!"

With a chilling shriek like nothing human, the Rabid lunged.

I ran, ducking behind a truck, hearing the Rabid's claws screech off the rusty metal as it followed. I dodged and weaved my way through the vehicle-littered street, keeping the cars between me and the pursuing Rabid, glancing back to gauge the distance between us. It snarled and hissed at me over the vehicles, hollow eyes blazing with madness and hunger, its claws leaving white gashes in the rust.

Dodging behind another car, I gazed around frantically for

a weapon—a pipe, a branch I could use as a club, anything. The Rabid's shriek rang out behind me, horrifyingly close. As I reached down and grabbed a chunk of broken pavement from the curb, I glimpsed a pale form in the corner of my eye and turned quickly, swinging with all my might.

The jagged concrete hit the Rabid square in the temple as it lunged for me, grasping claws inches from my face. I heard something crack beneath the stone as it knocked the creature aside, smashing it into the door of a car. The Rabid collapsed to the pavement, trying to get up, and I brought the stone down again, smashing the back of its skull.

The Rabid screamed and twitched, limbs jerking sporadically, before collapsing to the sidewalk. A dark puddle oozed from beneath its head and spread over the street.

Trembling, I dropped the stone and sank to the curb. My hands shook, my knees shook and my heart was doing its best to hammer its way through my ribs. Up close, the Rabid looked smaller in death than in life, all brittle limbs and protruding bones. But its face was as horrible and terrifying as ever, fangs frozen in a snarl, soulless white eyes staring up at me.

And then a hiss behind me made my heart stop a second time.

I turned slowly as another Rabid slid out from behind a car, arms and mouth smeared with wet crimson. It clutched a branch in one claw...only, the branch had five fingers, and the tattered remains of a shirt clung to it, soaked with blood. Seeing me, the Rabid dropped the arm to the pavement and crept forward.

Another Rabid followed. And another leaped to the roof of a car, hissing. I spun and faced two more, sliding from beneath a truck, pale dead eyes fastened on me. Five of them. From all directions. And me, in the center. Alone.

In the rain, everything grew very quiet. The only thing I heard was my pulse, roaring in my ears, and my ragged breathing. I gazed around at the foaming, blood-soaked Rabids, not ten yards from me in any direction, and for just a moment I felt calm. So this was the knowledge that you were about to die, that no one could help you, that it would all be over in a few short seconds.

In that brief moment between life and death, I looked between cars and saw a figure striding toward us, silhouetted black against the rain. Something bright gleamed in its hand, but then a Rabid passed through my field of vision and it was gone.

Then survival instincts kicked in, and I ran.

Something hit me from behind, hard, and warmth spread over my neck and back, though there was no pain. The blow knocked me forward and I stumbled, falling to my knees. A weight landed on me, screeching, tearing at me, and bright strips of fire began to spread across my shoulders. I screamed and flipped over, using my legs to shove it away, but another pale creature filled my vision, and all I could see was its face and teeth and blank, dead eyes, lunging forward. My hands shot out, slamming into its jaw, keeping those snapping teeth away from my face. It snarled and sank its fangs into my wrist, chewing and tearing, but I barely felt the pain. All I could think of was keeping the teeth away from my throat, though I knew its claws were ripping open my chest and stomach—I had to keep it away from my throat.

And then the others closed in, screaming, tearing. And the last thing I remembered, before the bloody red haze finally melted into blackness, was a flash of something bright, and the Rabid's body dropping onto my chest while its head continued to bite my arm.

Then, thankfully, there was nothing.

When I woke up, I knew I was in hell. My whole body was on fire. Or at least it felt that way, though I couldn't see the flames. It was dark, and a light rain was falling from the sky, which I found strange in hell. Then a dark figure loomed over me, jet-black eyes boring into mine, and I thought I knew him from...somewhere. Hadn't I met him before...?

"Can you hear me?" His voice was familiar, too, low and calm. I opened my mouth to reply, but only a choked gurgle escaped. What was wrong with me? It felt as if my mouth and throat were clogged with warm mud.

"Don't try to speak." The soothing voice broke through the agony and confusion. "Listen to me, human. You're dying. The damage the Rabids did to your body is extreme. You have only a few minutes left in this world." He leaned closer, face intense. "Do you understand what I'm telling you?"

Barely. My head felt heavy, and everything was foggy and surreal. The pain was still there, but seemed far away now, as if I was disconnected from the rest of my body. I tried raising my head to see the extent of my wounds, but the stranger put a hand on my shoulder, stopping me. "No," he said gently, easing me back. "Don't look. It's better that you do not see. Just know that, whatever you choose, you will die today. The manner of your death, however, is up to you."

"Wha—" I choked on that warm wetness, spit it out to clear my throat. "What do you mean?" I rasped, my voice sounding strange in my ears. The stranger regarded me without expression.

"I'm giving you a choice," he said. "You are intelligent enough to know what I am, what I'm offering. I watched you draw the Rabids away to save your friend. I watched your struggle to fight, to live, when most would have lain down and died. I can see...potential.

"I can end the pain," he continued, smoothing a strand of

hair from my eyes. "I can offer you release from the mortal coil, and I will promise that you will not rise again as one of them." He nodded to a pale body, crumpled against a tire a few yards away. "I can give you that much peace, at least."

"Or?" I whispered. He sighed.

"Or…I can make you one of us. I can drain you to the point of death, and give you my blood, so that when you die you will rise again…as an immortal. A vampire. It will be a different life, and perhaps not one that you would suffer through. Perhaps you would rather be dead with your soul intact than exist forever without one. But the choice, and the manner of your death, is up to you."

I lay there, trying to catch my breath, my mind reeling. I was dying. I was dying, and this stranger, this vampire, was offering me a way out.

Die as a human or become a bloodsucker. Either way, the choice was death, because the vampires were dead; they just had the audacity to keep living. I could not become like them—a soulless predator, a walking corpse that preyed on the living to survive. I hated the vampires; everything about them—their city, their pets, their domination of the human race—I despised with my entire being. They had taken everything from me, everything that was important. I would never forgive them for what I had lost.

But the other choice. The other choice…was to die for real.

★ ★ ★ ★ ★